Escape to Ecstasy

Escape to Ecstasy

JODI LYNN COPELAND

APHRODISIA

KENSINGTON PUBLISHING CORP.

http://www.kensingtonbooks.com

APHRODISIA BOOKS are published by

Kensington Publishing Corp.
850 Third Avenue
New York, NY 10022

ISBN-13: 978-0-7582-2712-6
ISBN-10: 0-7582-2712-4

First Trade Paperback Printing: February 2009

10 9 8 7 6 5 4 3 2 1

Printed in the United States of America

To Kayla, who keeps me young, and Pat, who keeps me sane.

CONTENTS

KILLING ME SOFTLY

1

"Missing my college graduation last week, I can forgive. *Just.* Missing Mom's birthday party last night, no way. Fifty years. That's *old*, Claire. One freaking step away from the grave."

Claire Vaughn lifted her face off her red silk brocade pillow and, with her open eye, glared at the phone in her hand and the chastising voice rattling from the receiver. Damn her natural reflex for answering. And damn her younger sister even more for calling so early. It was barely after seven, and Erin knew she slept till nine.

Claire would never be able to fall back asleep now. Because of Erin, Queen of the Melodramatic, over an hour and a half had been added to her day.

An extra hour and a half to do what exactly? Read the *New England Herald*, where she'd been relegated to a miniscule online-vendor review column in the last pages of the paper's entertainment section? Flipping dandy.

Facing the inevitable, Claire rolled onto her back. Hot Stud, her portly white Persian and co-recluse, stretched out next to her on the Victorian four-poster. Scratching the cat's neck in the manner that soothed them both, she brought the phone to her ear. "Fifty is not old, Er. Besides, Mom knew I couldn't attend."

"Wouldn't."

"*Couldn't.*"

"That's no one's fault but your own."

Claire groaned. It wasn't enough Erin had to call before the sun was up and royally screw with her schedule, but she was going to detour down the "I know what's best for you" road again. "This is about the quack again, right?"

"You need professional help."

"I need a sister who knows how to mind her own business!" Beneath Claire's fingertips, Hot Stud jumped at the severity of her tone. Finger-kissing the cat's pink nose, she mouthed an apology.

"I miss you." Sorrow entered Erin's voice. "It's like losing Dad all over again, only worse. I can barely remember him. You . . . you were someone to envy."

Low blow, Sis. Dredging up first their runaway father and then her once-flourishing life into the conversation . . . Once upon a time Claire's columns had substance enough to garner more than a few front-page spreads and syndication to boot. Not to mention brought in enough of a wage to buy groceries, pay bills, and support her antiquities-buying habit in the same month. "Maybe I do need help. Maybe I'm a regular nut job. Considering I can barely afford to make rent on the peanuts the *Herald*'s tossing me these days, there's no way I can swing a shrink's fee."

"What if I knew of a place with great credentials and minimal fees?"

"I'd ask to hear the catch." And why she could hear hesitation past her sister's sudden exuberance. With their mother working two jobs to make ends meet, Claire had been Erin's primary caregiver from the time her sister was seven and Claire thirteen, and it left her with those all-hearing ears generally reserved for parents.

Erin sighed. "I know you'll never believe me, but the whole world isn't out to get you, Claire. These guys are good. Their healing rate top notch. Just give them a try." After pausing—no doubt for effect—she added a pleading, "For me."

Ah, hell. The effect paid off, pummeling Claire in the belly with illogical guilt. She pulled in a heavy breath and then let it whoosh out. "All right. Fine."

Maybe she'd only imagined her sister's hesitation because of the topic under discussion. Even if she hadn't, and guilt or no, they both knew she would cave to Erin's appeal. Sooner or later, she always did.

The obvious positive to caving this time around was that therapy sessions could prove worthwhile. Some of the things Claire left behind in the wake of The Incident six months ago, she would never miss: relying on short skirts, low-cut blouses, and killer heels to earn her the same stories her male colleagues got in their standard wear, for one. But then there were things she did miss: the smell of the New England shoreline after a rainstorm. Handpicking her fruits and vegetables from the vendors at the Saturday morning farmers market instead of relying on her elderly neighbor's taste. Sex that wasn't of the autoerotic variety.

Yeah, not having that last one definitely sucked.

Not so long ago she'd been dating and doing one of the most affluent attorneys in Massachusetts. Then the side effects of The Incident set in and he'd bailed on her, saying he dealt with too many victims during the day, he didn't need one in his bed at night. Now the only male who ever saw her, naked or otherwise, was Hot Stud.

"Killer." Erin's jubilant grin sounded in her voice. "I'll call their office as soon as they open at nine."

Maybe these guys wouldn't be so bad; they were smart

enough to start their day at a respectable— "Office?" The word invaded Claire's mind and snapped past her lips. Fingers stalled on Hot Stud's neck, she sat up in bed, stomach lurching. "This is something I'd have to leave the apartment for? Because if it is, I think you're seriously forgetting the point of why I need to see a shrink."

"Trust me, there's no way I could forget The Incident—as you insist we call it—that made my sister go from sexy, sassy reporter extraordinaire to an ain't-getting-no-lovin', ain't-getting-no-nuthin' recluse." Erin exhaled audibly before adding in a voice that sounded a little too foreboding for Claire's comfort, "You don't have to go to their office. They'll come to you."

"What do you say we quit with the cock fights and get on with the picks, guys?" Shelley Lawrence breezed through Ecstasy Island's administration area door and into the first-floor meeting room. Thick, yellow client informational packets rested in the crook of the healing resort manager's arm.

Chris Cavanaugh tossed back the coffee in his Styrofoam cup in preparation of being called up front for first pick from the incoming, all-female client batch. A requisite week—time intended for regrouping and relaxing—had passed since the previous batch of women left. The way the bullshit tall tales and ensuing laughter and groans from the men seated at the tables around him came to an abrupt end, he wasn't the only one anxious to get back to work. He got along fine with most of the guys who called the private island home. Still, things got boring fast when the odds were a dozen males for every female, as was the case during their off week.

Shelley lined the packets up on the ledge built into the front wall. Photos of past clients interacting with the staff during far more enjoyable gatherings covered the wall above the ledge. Wall-mounted TVs dominated the corners.

Leaving over a dozen women to stare out from the photo

taped to each packet, Shelley turned around. She met Chris's eyes briefly, her smile as painfully tight-looking as her blond ponytail, and then glanced away. "Nic, you're up first."

Say what? The coffee cup compressed in Chris's hand. Speculation filtered through the room as every eye in the place outside of Shelley's zeroed in on him.

Coming to his feet two tables away, Niccolo Lombardi sent him a "take that, shithead" grin. "'Bout damned time."

Irritation speared through Chris, but he didn't bother to voice it. Nic was one of those guys who didn't care what others thought. Not even Treah Baldwin, Ecstasy's owner, since Nic figured he was too hot of a commodity to lose. According to Nic, his self-proclaimed Italian Stallion good looks were all it took to get a woman interested and his equally self-proclaimed godlike skills in bed were all it took to have her forgetting whatever fears resulted in her coming to the resort to beg for his touch.

Keeping his expression neutral, Chris waited for the group of men to gather at the front of the room and Shelley to return to the back of the building. Tossing the smashed coffee cup into a nearby wastebasket, he headed for the admin door.

"Going to piss and moan to big brother?" Nic goaded from behind him. "Seems to me there isn't anything to piss and moan about. Can't hardly blame a guy for not wanting a murderer heading up his team."

Irritation turned to a fierce clenching in Chris's gut. Slowly, he met Nic's smirk. Punching the dickhead in his too-pretty face was his first instinct. Since meeting his taunt with violence would make him look guilty as hell, he refrained.

Wearing a smirk of his own, he asked quietly, "What do you think you know?"

"Enough. More than enough, *cazzo*." Nic clapped a hand to Chris's shoulder. "Let me know when you've got my cabin cleaned out."

Like hell he would. Knocking Nic's hand away, Chris pushed through the admin door. Irritation rekindled only to quickly become panic.

Fuck. How could Nic have found out?

Quickening his steps, he moved down the short hallway to Shelley's office. The resort had been converted from a turn-of-the-century bed-and-breakfast and rental cabins when Treah bought the place and the accompanying five-mile-around island eight years before. All but Shelley's office and cabin, that is. Both retained the original pastel hues and vintage furnishings that typically matched her personality.

Today, her mood wasn't coming off so cheerful. She sat at a rosewood rolltop desk, attention fixed on her laptop screen and posture stiff. "What's going on, Shell?"

Her gaze flicked to his, brown eyes narrowed. "I'm just the messenger around here. Whatever it's about, Treah wants to see you."

"Before or after I stand in a damned line to get the bottom of the barrel?" Technically, it didn't matter to him which woman he spent the next three weeks with. It was simply a matter of principle that, as the resort's head healing coach, he got the choice cabin and first pick from the monthly clientele. So long as he was being technical, technically it wasn't Nic being given first pick of the women that was champing at Chris's ass. Not after that damned taunt.

"Now," Shelley responded tersely.

They'd been friends as long as they'd been coworkers. Any other day Chris would have asked what crawled up her ass to put her in such a pissy mood. Today, thanks to Nic the Dick, he was feeling rather pissy himself. "All right. Thanks."

Not expecting a reply, he continued down the hall to where a large receptionist area opened up. The space was decorated in the same cool shades of blue, green, and brown, with natural wood trim, as the remainder of the resort. The occupant of the space, Gwen Davis, Treah's sleep-in personal assistant, was anything but cool in a tiny black skirt and an equally tiny siren-red top.

Christian values had been instilled throughout Chris's youth. Hard-knock ones had been forced down his throat during his time in detainment. Both resulted in him making his fair share of vows. Thou shall not covet thy brother's woman wasn't one of them. Since Treah wasn't his real brother and Chris didn't want Gwen beyond the occasional look, he took advantage of the fact she stood with her back to him, stuffing folders into a three-high row of cabinets, and let the toned, tanned legs extending from the hem of her skirt to her spiked black heels work their soothing magic on his nerves.

Only, damn, the view didn't even touch his anxiety. "Hey, Gwen."

Brushing two-toned strands of blond and brown over her shoulder, she turned to flash a shiny red welcoming smile. "Morning, Chris." She pointed in the direction of Treah's adjoining office. "He's expecting you."

"Great. Thanks." With a parting nod, he went to Treah's closed door. Worry and anger mounted as he shoved it open with the flat of his palm. Treah was the only one on the island who knew Chris's past. While Treah *wasn't* his real brother, he was as close to family as Chris had these days and he couldn't see the other man selling him out.

Unless he'd caught some major hell for employing an ex-criminal in a business that centered on human interaction and ultimate trust.

Nah. He couldn't see him doing it even then. Still, his heart pounded like a jackhammer as he stepped inside the office and closed the door.

Treah didn't look up. Between the lack of acknowledgment and the way he sat at his desk—the fingers of one hand speared into his short, black hair while the others gripped the edge of the folder laid out on the desktop—something was definitely up. Even from ten feet away, Chris could feel the tension rolling off his body.

Since losing his brother, Chris's one-time best friend, to a cellmate's rage seven years ago, Treah didn't sweat the small stuff. Whatever was up, it had to be bad.

Chris moved to the edge of the desk, attempting to get a look at the folder's contents and see if they revolved around him. All he could see from this side were hand-scribbled notes and numbers.

The thrash of his heart eased a little, and he pulled out one of the chairs tucked under the visitor side of the desk. Turning it around, he straddled the back of the seat. "What's the deal, man? Nic's ready to clear out my cabin and move his shit in."

"Nic's an asshole."

Running with that topic held real appeal. Unfortunately, that wasn't going to get him answers. "An asshole who just accused me of being a murderer."

Treah looked up to reveal fatigue lines wearing on his face, making him appear older than his thirty-five years. "Christ, I don't know where he got that information."

Chris knew Treah would never have sold him out, and still the confirmation was incredibly relieving. "If my past leaking out isn't why I'm here, what is?"

Treah closed the folder on his desktop and pushed it aside. "Someone's been sneaking onto Gwen's computer and fucking with the accounting files."

"Fucking with them how?"

"In a way that takes money out of my pocket and puts it in theirs." He scrubbed a hand over his face, bringing Chris's attention to the dark stubble lining his jaw and upper lip. Treah was meticulous about shaving; his facial hair came in patchy and he hated to look anything but his best. Obviously, he was talking more than a few dollars to have him this consumed.

"I've been up since five going over the books, trying to find some pattern and getting no goddamned where. I don't have time to deal with this shit, Chris. I have a morning flight out for the Pacific branch opening. Earliest I can be back is Friday. That's if the batch of healers Mona picked out performs as well in person as they claimed to during their interviews and training."

Chris had met Mona—the woman Treah hired to manage Ecstasy Island's second location, which was due to open tomorrow afternoon—when he flew down to help with training last month. She seemed plenty competent. Even so, if it would ease Treah's anxiety, he would be happy to oversee things down there the next week. "You want me to go down there for you?"

"Yeah. But it's not happening. That would raise too many eyebrows, get people speculating something's wrong. I just need you to keep your eyes and ears open here. One thing you can count on with this group is their need to brag. Sooner or later, someone's going to get mouthy. I want you there when they do."

"You really think anyone's going to be shooting the shit with me after Nic opens his big mouth?"

"We're not the only ones who think he's an asshole, or know how much he feels insulted to be ranked second to you. Most of the guys will figure he's talking trash in an attempt to get you canned."

"Maybe." Probably not. Still it was possible, hopeful even, and Chris would take what he could get in that department. Of course, it would be a hell of a lot easier to remain hopeful if he had more to do than sit around with Nic's taunt eating at him. "Until I get the info you're after, I sit around on my ass clientless?"

"Shit, no. I'm already losing money. I can't afford to have your ass getting paid for sitting around." Treah lifted a thick, yellow packet from the corner of his desk and handed it to

Chris. A cute mid- to late-twenties brunette with spiky bangs and huge baby blues smiled at him from the photo taped to the front.

"And, no," Treah continued, "I'm not going to start pulling your picks for you either. This week was a no-brainer. She's got that innocent-bystander/believes-she's-scarred-for-life thing going that you can never resist." Amusement lightened the gravity in his eyes and tugged at the corners of his mouth. "If that isn't enough to convince you, her sister swears she's a hellcat in bed and way overdue for a scratching."

Typically, the victim type was Chris's favorite. Healing them served as a form of penance he would never get to make to the man he'd personally helped to become a victim. Now, with the sins of his past threatening to become common knowledge, a client with an intimacy issue or some other low-complexity fear would have been ideal—a distraction from his worries without stealing his thoughts completely.

Treah's pick might be both more difficult to cure and harder on Chris's peace of mind, but he wasn't about to turn her down. Not when doing so would make it seem Nic's words had disturbed him to the point of being unable to do his job. And not when he owed Treah his eternal gratitude.

Since The Incident, Claire had had too many nightmares to count. None had morphed from terror-filled dream to horror-packed reality. Not until now.

She emerged from sleep instantly. Felt the hands on her bare upper arms just as quickly. Nausea did a slow roll through her belly.

What the fuck? What the fuck!

Erin. Please be Erin playing some stupid, overblown trick meant to somehow magically fix her.

Not able to find her voice past the lump of fear in her throat,

Claire tested the hands on her arms. Her sister was smaller than her by a good three inches and twenty pounds. She could easily shake off Erin, particularly with the gut-punch of adrenaline currently on her side. These hands didn't budge with the shaking of her arms. These hands were far too big and strong to be Erin's. As her eyes adjusted to the shadows made by the moonlight bleeding through the fine lace of her bedroom curtains, she could see the profile of the person attached to those hands was far too big and strong to be Erin's, as well.

Too *masculine.*

Claire's pulse tripped into hyperdrive. He'd pulled back the warmth and weight of her covers and sheets at some point. She wore only cotton shorty pajamas—not enough to keep her warm on their own through the chilly May night. Sweat beaded on her skin regardless.

Panting for breath, she moved her arms again. This time no simple shaking, but shoving upward with both them and her knees as hard as she could manage . . . which wasn't all that hard at all. It was as if she had as little control of her body as her voice. Like she'd been drugged.

Oh, God. She'd been drugged. Rendered helpless. Impotent.

What was he going to do with her? Who the hell was he, even, to get past her state-of-the-art security system?

"Who . . ." she managed in a low, throaty voice that wasn't hers.

"Relax. There's nothing to fear."

Easy for him to sound calm when he wasn't the one under the influence of something undoubtedly illegal, about to have God only knew what done to him by an unseen stranger. Anything at all.

Anything like taking her out of this apartment. Hell, no. "But . . ."

The hands at her arms pulled up, lifting her into a sitting position. One of the hands moved away and an arm came around her back, supporting her body as he slid her to the edge of the bed. "Your sister sent for me, Claire."

The words whispered near her ear, calm again, gentle as the way he was handling her. Gentle because this was exactly what she first thought it. Erin playing some stupid, overblown trick meant to somehow magically heal her. The anxiety clawing at her belly lightened. Her sister tended to think in sensational terms, but when it came down to taking action, Erin tended toward the straitlaced side.

They'll come for you.

Aw, crap. The momentary ebb in panic flowed into a tidal wave of bile-rising anxiety as Erin's words from the previous month returned. Claire thought her sister had forgotten about the so-called top notch yet somehow amazingly cheap professionals almost certain to cure her when she hadn't brought them up again. But Erin had neither forgotten them nor was she taking a straitlaced approach. She'd had Claire scheduled into their books. And they'd come for her, just as her sister promised they would—with that ominous note in her voice.

If Claire survived this night, Erin was going to die.

The arm at her back tightened. A second one slid under her legs. Together they lifted her away from the safety of her bed. Against a hard body. A body that started moving from nearly the second she was settled in its owner's arms.

Claire's breath wheezed out, leaving her mouth dry and her throat achy and tight. He was moving toward the bedroom door. Moving through it. Down the hall. Her heart kicked lightning fast against her ribs. Tears stormed to the backs of her eyes.

She tried to move again, to struggle. Such a futile effort. She was so powerless. Not just an innocent bystander this time, but an immediate victim to be killed softly, slowly. One step at a time.

How could you, Erin? "Plea . . . don . . ."

"Shhh . . ." Soft lips feathered across her forehead. "Close your eyes and sleep, sweetheart. Everything's going to be all better real soon."

No, dammit, it would *not* be all better! Because he was still moving. And she wasn't. She could barely think now. Barely breathe. Barely hear Hot Stud's hissing and her captor's not-nearly-so-gentle curses that followed.

Good boy, Claire thought groggily, maliciously. *Tonight, you bite his balls off. Tomorrow, I'll feed you Erin, one rotten inch at a time.*

2

Erin had tricked her into agreeing to the kind of professional help that forced her out of her apartment in the dead of night. Claire could be sensible about it and understand that, in her own special way, her sister believed the kind of help that involved kidnapping was help all the same. She didn't have to scream or cry. Or puke her guts out over the idea someone had rendered her so completely out of it—to cart her from her apartment, to wherever the bed she'd just woken up in was, without her knowledge—that anything could have happened to her.

Might have happened to her.

No. She wasn't going to play the paranoia game. She was going to sit up, breathe deep, and take stock of her surroundings. The doublewide oak dresser butting up against an eggshell-white wall on her left. The cozy little breakfast table and chairs and the floor-to-ceiling vertical blind that let through the faintest of sunlight and invariably hid a sliding glass door to a deck or balcony on her right.

The half-naked man leaning casually against the bedroom's doorframe as he eyed her in a way that was anything but casual.

His gaze lifted from where the sheets and covers pooled at Claire's waist. Sliding his attention upward, he did the kind of slow-burn examination of her breasts that left the full mounds tingling and her feeling naked despite her shorty PJ set.

Bringing his gaze the rest of the way up, he stepped inside the bedroom. "How you feeling?"

Like screaming, crying, and puking. "Pissed."

A small smile quirked his lips. "Can't say that I blame you."

What about aroused, could he blame her for feeling aroused?

She wasn't dripping-wet-with-desire aroused, but her body was definitely aware it was within ten feet of a member of the opposite sex for the first time in months. A member of the opposite sex with the kind of raspy voice that made her panties want to instantly evaporate. That he was dressed only in faded jeans that rode dangerously low on his lean hips and not exactly what you would call hard to look at didn't help the desire.

With disheveled dark blond hair, nearly translucent blue eyes, and a body sculpted with just the right amount of muscle guaranteed to feel good rocking against hers without feeling bad, he had that rough-around-the-edges thing working well in his favor.

And she had that far-too-long-horny thing working well against her better judgment.

Pretending like her pulse wasn't racing for all the wrong reasons, Claire scooted back against what was presumably his headboard. The room had certain elements, like the spray of pink dogwoods in a vase on the dresser, that reminded her of a woman's touch, but the wildlife scene depicted on the green comforter and framed pictures of the same on the wall shouted masculine. "Is this your place?"

His smile deepened with the heat of sensuality. "My bed, yeah."

Her nipples pinged to life with how intimate his smile made this situation feel. How intimate was it? Had he had her naked last night? Had he done all sorts of wickedly carnal things with her body? Did she care if he had?

Hell, yeah, she cared. If not because it was the logical thing to do, then because she wasn't having her first post-incident man-supplied orgasm when she was too doped up to remember.

Claire winced with the memory the thought triggered. She couldn't recall being stuck with a needle or having a pill forced down her throat. Something had obviously been done to her last night though, to render both her body and voice all but useless.

His smile vanished. "Head hurt?"

"I'm fine." Truthfully, the verdict was still out, but she couldn't exactly rail into him for doing the job Erin had paid him to do.

"Want to take a walk along the beach?"

Instantly tense, she hugged her arms around her chest. "God, no!"

"The wind's a little brisk, but nothing we can't handle."

Wind? Was he nuts to think that wind was the problem, or just not in the know? "Do you know why I'm here?"

"Yeah." He sobered. "And I also know you're not fine." Moving to the dresser, he pulled out one of the top drawers to reveal bras and panties in an array of vibrant colors. "The left-side drawers are yours. Breakfast is ready, so get over the whole pissed thing, accept that you're here for a reason, and join me in the kitchen." With a last glance in her direction, he left the room, closing the door behind him.

Claire hurried out of bed and yanked a coral bra and matching boy-cut underwear out of the dresser. There was no telling how long he would stay away. If he hadn't seen her naked already, she wasn't going to give him that opportunity. Not when the uneven pitch of her breathing and the swollen state of her nipples suggested two things.

One, she wasn't exactly as pissed as she let on, or probably should be. And two, if he caught her in the buff and liked what he saw, she was liable to let her deprived pussy do the driving.

After grabbing a pair of jeans and a black sweater from the second drawer—at least Erin had the good sense to pack for comfort—she moved into the attached bathroom. A visual search while she dressed found her toothbrush and lotion on the sink basin and a makeup bag of odds and ends on the toilet tank. A more thorough check of the medicine cabinet revealed her deodorant and a box of tampons. He might not fit her imagined profile of a psychologist—between his buff body and not looking much older than her twenty-seven—but the guy was obviously a professional not to rebel against having her female products invading his personal space.

That he *was* a pro and, therefore, not any too likely to really force her on a walk down the beach, eased her nerves as she brushed her teeth and hair. Feeling almost calm, she returned to the bedroom and ventured out the door into the connected sitting area. A chocolate brown couch and recliner, with throw pillows sporting wildlife scenes similar to those in the bedroom, angled toward a wall housing a flat screen TV. On the far side of the room, beige carpet turned to the wood flooring of a kitchen. Past a short, two-stool bar, he stood with his back to her, doing something she couldn't distinguish.

Claire could see his backside just fine though, and the teasing flash of navy underwear—boxers she was guessing all the way—past the low-slung waist of his jeans. The divine way the worn cotton of his jeans molded to his butt cheeks reminded her again just how long it had been since she copped herself a feel of nice, firm man ass.

She started over to the kitchen and, oh, the view just got better and better. Her fingers flexed and her sex gave a decadent flutter she hadn't experienced in ages.

Seriously, no quack had a right to a back that broad and scrumptious looking.

Noting the two glasses of orange juice at the bar, she slid onto one of the stools and took a long drink. Whether it was the effect of all that gorgeous maleness on display, or a side effect of whatever she'd been given last night, she was seriously parched.

Setting the glass down, she observed, "You don't look like a shrink."

"I'm not." He turned around with a heaping plate of omelet and hash browns in either hand, which made for an excellent frame for his pecs.

He wasn't liable to have a shirtless tan in May and she couldn't see him fake baking. The golden brown cast to his skin was an *au natural* stunning contrast to the dark blond hair dusting his chest and arms and the morning stubble scruffing up his jawline.

Coming around to her side of the bar, he set the plates down and slid onto the stool next to her. His body was close enough she could feel the heat radiating off it. See the delicious play of his muscles as he reached for his glass and brought it to his lips. Appreciate the hell out of his strong, sexy profile as he took a drink of juice.

The tantalizing scents of garlic and butter wafted up, splintering her thoughts, and her stomach gave a low rumble. Apparently, she was hungry for more than just a good, long screw.

"So what, you're the prep guy?" Lifting the fork from her plate, she cut into the omelet. A mouthwatering melody of cheese-covered sausage and veggies oozed out. "You see that I'm well rested and fed for when the shrink arrives?"

"There's no shrink on Ecstasy Island. I'm the only one responsible for curing you and my knowledge is about as far as you can get from a six-figure degree."

She chewed a bite of omelet as she considered the words. Knowing he wasn't going to make her feel welcome just to hand her off to some textbook quack definitely added to her comfort level. As for their location . . . When he'd mentioned the ocean, she'd assumed he'd taken her somewhere near her waterfront apartment. Really, it didn't matter. Two miles down the road or two hundred or more miles away on an island, she wasn't going to make it past his front door without freaking out.

Much preferring to focus on the conversation—and, okay yeah, his naked upper half a touch away—than thoughts of the outside world, she asked, "Why Ecstasy?"

He ate a forkful of hash browns before looking over. Where his attitude had been sedate from the moment he'd left her in the bedroom, lust was in his eyes now, alive and sizzling hot. "Let's just say we believe in alternative healing."

Warmth rushed through Claire with the implication. "Alternative?"

He gave a curt nod, his lips tipping up at the corners, and the air between them seemed to spark about ten degrees hotter. Jesus, she really needed to indulge her sex drive more often. Maybe next time she would agree to let Erin hook her up with a gigolo instead of the therapist type.

Or had her sister already as good as done that?

She shivered with the thought, not from fear but anticipation. "You mean sex?"

His gaze narrowed. "You don't like sex, or why are you trembling?"

"I love sex." Was even now considering just how good his cock would feel sliding into her when he swept aside their plates and glasses to do her on the bar.

As if he could read her mind, the heat returned to his eyes. His gaze shifted to her breasts, giving them another of those all-but-panty-evaporating leers. "Then what's the problem, sweetheart?"

Her nipples peaked against the soft cups of her bra, answering the question without a sound. Since her famished pussy wasn't likely to be the problem he had in mind, Claire improvised. "I'm a recluse who, up until last night, hadn't set foot out of her apartment in months. Last night it was by coercion and, no doubt, some drug cocktail. What do you think the problem is?"

"The sedative you were given was very mild and all natural." Teasing glinted in his eyes as they returned to hers, and a shallow cleft came out to play amidst his chin stubble. "A lot like the sex you love. The natural part, at least. You don't strike me as a woman who goes for the mild, in bed or out of it."

Something about his expression—maybe how wet it suddenly had her—made one thing clear. He might not have a degree in psychology, but he knew precisely how to get into a woman's head . . . and panties. "You aren't cheap, are you?"

He wiggled his eyebrows suggestively. "Depends who's asking."

Oh, yeah, he knew what he was about. "I mean your services. Erin, my well-meaning PITA of a sister, said your fees were minimal. That was a lie, wasn't it? She paid a buttload to have me brought here."

"Not that much so far." His arm connected with hers at the shrugging of his shoulders, and the subtle brush was like the most intimate caress. He felt it, too; she could see the flicker of sensual awareness cross his face. "Ecstasy requires half pay up front," he continued in a voice even raspier than usual. "If our client's time on the island proves successful, the rest is due upon their return home. If they go home with the same fears they had when they came here, they don't pay another dime."

"Do you work on commission?"

"I get part of the half that's paid after the fact."

Bummer for him, he wouldn't be getting it this time around. He might be good at his job, but it was highly doubtful he could erase the effects of The Incident in a matter of days or even weeks. Would it be so wrong to throw in a consolation prize to offset his monetary loss? Celebrate her first post-incident trip outside the apartment and the fact she'd lived to be upset with Erin about it by ending her sexual dry spell? This could be her only chance to have a lover this year.

Or the rest of her life . . .

Glum thought, yet reality. The kind of cold, hard, empty reality that made this sexy stranger and this stolen opportunity too tempting to pass up.

Going with the heat spiking in her core, Claire lifted her hand from where it rested on her thigh and put it into his lap. The impressive bulge of a not-quite-flaccid cock stroked against her knuckles. Any doubts she had vanished as delicious tingles erupted in her sheath.

She grinned expectantly. "So with me you're counting on the sex being payoff enough?"

His smile flattened as he covered her hand with his own. She thought he meant to be a killjoy by lifting her fingers away. He turned her hand over instead. Turned it over and squeezed her fingers around the length of his thickening shaft through his jeans. "I'm counting on the sex being a bonus for a job well done."

Chris bit back a groan and the urge to beat the shit out of himself for not only allowing Claire to put her hand in his lap but encouraging further exploration. Friday morning, when Treah passed her file his way, he knew he was in for a challenge. Once Chris had time to look through her file and discover the details of the circumstances which brought her to the island, the enormity of that challenge became crystal clear. Last night just sealed the deal.

Normally, he went out of his way to avoid the mainland. Relied on the guys hired exclusively to bring clients to the island to deliver his women to his door. With Nic's taunt continuing to ride him, he'd embraced the escape the hour-long boat ride and another fifteen minutes of travel in Ecstasy's employee truck had afforded. Seeing Claire come awake scared to death for his actions had made him feel shady as hell. More so because, even with the edge of panic riding in her eyes and her bangs lying cockeyed across her forehead, she looked far hotter than what her picture let on.

She looked even hotter now, from her gleaming baby blues to the naughty curve of her lips to her bare feet peeking out from beneath the frayed cuffs of her jeans. Unlike her lips, her toenails were painted—a girlie shade of pale pink. Since spending over four years surrounded by men in uniforms as severe as their personalities, he was a sucker for anything soft like that, anything that spoke of femininity.

The sweep of her fingers along his cock was definitely feminine. Tilting her head to the side, she eyed his mouth. "How long did my sister buy your body for?"

Letting her believe their time together centered on sex would be both the easy and the feel-good way out. But it wouldn't be doing his job. Biting back another groan, this one about regret, Chris lifted her hand out of his lap and came to his feet. "This is a healing resort, Claire. I'm your mental coach, not your man-sized sex toy. I should never have implied otherwise."

Her gaze skipped to the bulge pressing at the fly of his jeans. "Just mental? You don't sleep with your clients?"

"Ecstasy takes a sensual approach to healing. So, no, not *just* mental. That doesn't mean I jump into bed with every woman that enters my home. If things get that physical, it's because the healing process calls for it. Even then, it only happens after I've had a chance to get to know a woman."

Her eyes returned to his face, skepticism filling them. "I look that stupid, huh?"

"There've been one or two through the years that I didn't know very well before things got hot," he admitted as he rounded the bar. He wasn't some horny teen that needed the partition between them to keep his hands to himself, but then he wasn't going to tempt fate and Claire's obvious desire to fuck him either.

"Years?" Amusement tinged her voice. "You've been doing this since you were what, fourteen?"

"Twenty-two, and I take my job seriously. I *will* cure you, Claire."

She seemed to consider the vow for a few seconds and then concentrated back on her food. Relieved she'd temporarily turned off the heat—no way did he buy that it was a permanent cool down—Chris pulled his plate and glass across the bar.

They ate in silence for several minutes before she pointed out, "You never said how long I'm here for."

"It's a three-week package."

A sultry smile returned to her lips as she cast her gaze down his body. "Fortunately, I already know it isn't a three-inch one."

She couldn't see past his waist with the bar between them. That didn't stop his shaft from perking right back up again. Ignoring the throb of his cock, he forced his mind on the issue that brought her to the island. "Since the shoot—The Incident—you haven't been outside even once?"

"Obviously I have that I'm here."

"Other than that?"

Her smile fell away. "You wouldn't understand."

"You'd be surprised what I understand." Claire's expression said she didn't believe him. Trust was a huge factor in the success of these sessions. Though he could already guess how she would respond, working on that trust issue was priority number one following breakfast. "Generally these weeks involve a good deal of outside time—taking advantage of Ecstasy's fleet of watercraft, socializing with the other women on the island, talking about your—"

"How many others are there?" she asked, bringing a bite of omelet to her mouth.

"A little over a dozen."

"Wow." The fork stilled in the air. "I never realized there were so many screwed-up women in the world."

"You're not screwed up, Claire."

She set the fork back on her plate and slid off the bar stool. Before he could guess her intention, she was around to his side, her body inches from his own. With the bulky black sweater covering her chest, Chris couldn't make out much about her breasts. He'd been able to tell plenty about them and the rest of her body when he'd carried her from her bed last night.

She was all lithe curves and valleys. Tall and long limbed. The kind of lushly sensual woman a guy could sink himself inside and forget his every worry. If that woman wasn't the guy's client.

Claire's head tilted to the side, brushing the blunt ends of her straight, shiny hair against her shoulder. Her lips parted a breath as her eyes returned to his mouth. "Not screwed up. Not fine." She leaned into him and placed her palms on his chest, fingers splaying warm and intimately against his bare skin. "So what am I?"

He let out a tense breath. Hell, he should have let her stay pissed. "Too close."

"Ah, c'mon. I haven't slept with a guy I just met in years."

Lifting her hands away, he set her back a couple feet. The last thing he needed was for his cock to jerk against her belly and have her realize he'd probably succumb easily at this point. "Like I said, you're not going to today either."

"You want to."

"I want to heal you more." He took a drink of juice, giving her time to return to her own side of the bar. When she didn't budge, he veered the conversation far away from the sexual. "How do you feel about one or two of the other women coming into the cabin for a visit?"

"Since I'm guessing Ecstasy doesn't get any murderers for clients, I should be okay with it. One at a time, at least."

No, Chris thought wryly as her words sent his gut into a vicious grinding, the resort didn't get any murderers. No reason to with a resident murderer on staff.

This was exactly his concern with Claire for a client. Her fear, stemming from a recent senseless shooting, would keep his resurfaced anxiety over a past senseless shooting right there at the front and center of his mind.

His appetite as gone as his erection, he grabbed his fork and plate and set them beside the sink. "All right. We'll work with that. First, I need to talk with my boss."

He was outside and about to close the door when the brisk nip of the wind registered against his bare skin. It was low sixties at best, cooler-feeling in the breeze. Not only had her words unsettled him to the point he'd failed to put on a shirt and shoes, but he'd forgotten about the whole trust deal.

Shit. Maybe he wasn't up to handling her right now.

But, yeah, he was. He could do this. He was the head healer for a reason, and, despite what Nic thought, it went beyond his friendship with Treah.

Drawing a calming breath, he turned around to find Claire had followed him nearly to the door. The sex-seeking siren from the kitchen was gone. Unconcealed fear filled her eyes as she surveyed the area around him, like she thought at any second someone was going to jump out of the trees and fire a pistol her way.

Her gaze fell on him, and her fear clouded over as a saucy smile formed on her lips. "Forget to kiss me good-bye?"

He couldn't have planned a better opening. Yet he hesitated to take it, unable to stop from wondering how quickly she would turn away if she knew what he really was.

Promising himself that all she would know him as was the man who eradicated her fears, Chris retraced his last steps and pulled her into his arms. "Matter of fact, I did."

Her lips opened a slice with her surprise. He pushed his

tongue inside to cut off any reply and taste the teasingly wet warmth of her mouth.

Claire's client file claimed she was a hellcat in bed. The way she boldly took his ass into her hands and rubbed her mound against his cock as she kissed him back with vigor, he believed it. She circled her breasts and pelvis against him with each silky swipe of her tongue. Her pubis connected with his erection and heady sensation slipped through him, tightening his balls as it warmed his blood.

The hot, soft press of her body was such a sweet contrast to the chilling wind he'd encountered seconds ago, he could just melt into her. Just let her keep going until they were both naked and writhing together on the carpet.

Nah, hell, he couldn't.

Before she made him forget his intentions a second time, he lifted her up his body. Her legs twined around his waist, and he did a slow backstep out the door. Not far, just enough so the morning sun could leak down on them. Just enough so she might hear the tidewater lapping at the sand past the fast-blowing wind.

Just enough that the second he broke from her lips, she was going to have a holy conniption.

Taking control of the kiss, Claire brought her hands to his back. Short nails, painted the same powder pink as her toenails, nipped and scraped at his skin. Rocking her pelvis against his abdominal muscles, she moaned into his mouth, and then went back for another rocking that jolted electric sensation straight to his groin.

And that was all the farther he dared to let her go without giving her the full-on primal scratching she'd gone months without.

Chris slid his hands to her ass, allowing a quick cup and squeeze of her rounded backside through her jeans. He took hold of her ankles then, and untwined her legs from his waist. She glided down his body, nails feathering along his back and her sex grinding torturously slowly along his. Releasing her lips at the last second, he made certain she was steady on her feet and then stepped backward.

Her eyes had fallen closed at some point. She opened them now to grin at him. "Mmm . . . That was— That . . ." The passion died from her expression. Gaze narrowed, she looked to her left and drew a sharp breath.

Claire's gaze snapped back on his. Terror burned in her eyes and her face was washed of the high color of seconds ago. "You. You." Her hand flew to her mouth. "Oh, crap. I'm going to be sick."

3

Hoping—make that praying—this wasn't really happening, that he hadn't used her attraction to him to get her outside his house, Claire looked around a second time. A cluster of huge, camouflaging trees rose up on either side of the house, which looked more like a cabin with its log siding, screened-in room off to one side of the structure, and smallish size. A hammock was tied to the trunk of two more trees, solitary and feet from where the sun shone on a white-sand beach with churning tidewater lapping at its fringes. The sun's rays bled down on her, warming her despite the blustery wind.

That wouldn't be possible through a window or wall.

A gasping sob broke past her lips with the realization that no amount of hoping or praying was going to help. They *really* were outside. Her stomach *really* was roiling bile straight to her throat and her heart was beating like it might come through her chest at any moment. And he *really* was a first-class asshole.

"Y-you asshole!" Claire fought to replace the breath voicing the words cost her, but her throat felt like it was collapsing in on itself. The wind seemed impossibly heavy as it whipped her hair across her cheeks. The sun against her back was hotter by the second.

Wildly, she glanced at the door. It was four feet away at most. Too damned far. "I—I . . ."

"Shhh . . ." Sympathy in his eyes, he pulled her into his arms and pressed her cheek to the groove between his shoulder and neck. "No one's going to hurt you, sweetheart. Everything's going to be all better real soon. I promise."

She knew this soothing voice. Recognized it as the same one that had spoken to her in her bedroom last night. He was the one who'd kidnapped her. The one whose balls Hot Stud hadn't managed to sever given she'd felt the stiffness of his cock moving against her less than a minute ago. And she'd wanted it. Wanted him bad. Believed he'd wanted her as well, when he turned back and pulled her into his arms, kissed her until she was grinding against him in an attempt to ease the heavy ache in her core. But all he'd wanted was to speed her fast-forward into a nightmare.

Ew! If she could move, he would be in such pain.

Claire couldn't move. Her limbs felt solid, her bare feet frozen in place on the pebbled walkway beneath them. His embrace was meant to comfort, she knew. But all it did was smother her, stole what little air she was managing to take in, and pitched her stomach to the heaving point. "Let go. I-I'm going . . . to puke."

His arms released and, for a second or two, she felt calmer. Then it all just grew worse again. Because she still couldn't move from this damned crippling spot just outside his door. Wouldn't move without his help.

As if he knew her thoughts, he nodded at the door. "Help yourself, Claire." Steely determination filled his eyes. "Get inside. You can do this."

Yeah, she could. Because it was so *freaking* easy. Maybe for him.

Fury pushed through her, tangling with the panic. She fought to shake her head. Fought and won. And immediately regretted the move as her mind filled with a pounding haze.

God, she was so helpless. So stupidly helpless. Maybe if Erin saw her like this, she would understand when Claire said she couldn't attend functions outside of her apartment. Maybe she would quit trying to fix her. "Can't. Move."

"Yes. You can."

"N-no. I—" Her stomach clenched as the bile rose up once more. Heat came along with it, fanning upward and outward from where the sun scorched her back to consume her chest and head and vanquish her thoughts. Tears burned at her eyes as she heaved out a dry, gagging cough.

"Do it, Claire," he commanded. "Get inside the cabin. Now!"

Can't. Can't. Can't.

Can't think. Can't talk. The pounding intensified, splintering pain through her skull and hammering at her temples. Shudders racked her body as the heat increased until her skin felt it would be forever blistered.

He spoke more words, maybe even shouted them. She couldn't tell. Could barely even make out his face as it swam before her as a flesh-colored fog. Could barely even see the ground as it came at her as a blur of grass and walkway.

Ooh . . . this was going to hurt.

"Help," a thin voice Claire loathed to think was hers cried out.

He said something else. A curse she could tell, as she closed her eyes and waited for impact, going only by the intensity of his voice. Another of the same followed, and then his hands were there. His mercifully strong hands grabbed hold of her arms and brought her descending body to an abrupt halt. One of those hands came behind her knees and he swung her up into his arms, holding her gently against his solid chest as he had last night. Then he'd moved her toward her greatest fear. Now he moved her to safety. He took them so goddamned easily into the cabin that she would have wept with envy if tears of terror weren't already streaming down her face.

He laid her on the couch and moved into the kitchen, returning with a damp washcloth in seconds. She could mostly make out his face now. Sympathy was back, brimming in his pale blue eyes as he sank down on the edge of the couch and applied the cool cloth to her forehead. "You're okay, sweetheart."

A hysterical laugh rolled out of her at the irony of his comment. She wasn't feeling sweet, not by a long shot. She was feeling furious as hell and like her body would go up in flames. At least the tears had stopped.

"Not okay. Burning." Strength slowly returning, Claire forced her hands to the hem of her sweater and pulled it up to her neck. The inside air wasn't exactly cool but even the moderate temperature was a relief to her fevered flesh. He brought the washcloth a couple of inches above her chest, wringing out the excess water, and she sighed with the blissful contact.

Smiling, he moved the cloth over her skin, tracing the contours of her breasts above her bra. "You're fine. Just like I said you would be."

Damn that smile. She could see his face picture perfect now, and the last thing she wanted was him breaking out that sexilicious chin cleft. It made the idea of closing her eyes and giving herself into his care far too appealing. She couldn't trust him like that, not when he'd been the source of her misery.

She let his ministrations continue another minute as she regained full control of her body. Anger surged higher with each step toward normalcy. Her mind finally clear and the heat mostly gone, she jerked the washcloth from his hand. "Don't you touch me, you dick. And don't you *ever* kiss me again."

He came to his feet. No quick bolt off the couch, but a leisurely stand that was accompanied by the broadening of his smile. "I take it the sex is off?"

The sex?

How could he even think about sex at a time like this? When she was lying on his couch with her shirt pulled up to her throat, her nipples taut from the stroke of the cool washcloth and pressing hard against her bra cups. And he was standing next to her with only his jeans on, probably sporting a semi from that little impromptu grinding she'd done outside his door. Both of them breathing hard . . .

Claire's nipples tingled as the decadent image painted itself in her mind. She sighed in understanding. He sighed back, a sound as amused as it was rough with arousal.

All the fight drained out of her as the truth of the guilty party returned. Erin's fault. All of this was Erin's fault. He was only doing his job by trying to desensitize her to the outside world. Whoever *he* was.

Ah, God. She'd almost slept with him and she didn't even know his name. During those first couple of crazy years of college, she wouldn't have cared. Now she didn't find the thought of sleeping with a virtual stranger—one who presented himself well, at least—to be desperate or slutty; rather, it was one more awesome step for Women's Lib. Still, a first name would be nice.

Pushing her sweater down, she swung her feet to the floor and moved into a sitting position. "What's your name?"

"Chris."

"Well, Chris, what happened to talking to your boss?"

His smile vanished. "Right. I should get to that." He went into the bedroom. He emerged a few seconds later, pulling a navy sweatshirt over his head.

Claire mourned the loss of the stellar view of his chest and torso even as she told herself it was a good thing. After what happened at his door, she could totally see him using her lust for his body against her for the next three weeks.

Going to a closet near the door, he grabbed a pair of tennis shoes and shoved his feet into them. Twisting the front door-knob, he glanced back at her. Her belly fluttered with the idea he would already try more of that desensitizing crap. Then her sex gave a fluttering of its own with the idea that he would use another sex-her-up approach.

In the end, he didn't do either, just tossed out a teasing grin. "I should be back in a half hour or so. Don't go too far without me."

Chris started down the quarter-mile stretch of beach that led from his cabin to Ecstasy's main office area. The trail through the woods would have been a lot quicker, but it also would have been devoid of the breeze, and his body needed a thorough cooling. His claim to Claire about talking to the boss had been just that; a claim for the sake of escaping her "murderer" comment. The truth was Treah had taken off for the Pacific opening yesterday morning. Even so, Chris was hoping this venture to the office would pay off as more than a reprieve for his mind and body.

Typically, at least one of the guys could be found hanging out in the meeting room, which doubled as a rec center for everything from Texas Hold 'Em tournaments during their off week to more intimate gatherings when the women were on the island. None of the men seemed liable to be stealing money from the resort, so Chris would start in on his covert interrogations with the most available of them.

Chris reached the set of docks that harbored the boats used both for bringing clients to the island and taking them out on pleasure cruises during their stay. Once the weather grew a little warmer, cabanas and a volleyball net would be placed in the sandy stretch of land in front of the docks. The beachfront was deserted for now, a fact he took comfort in as he veered toward the office, set thirty-plus yards off from the water to help ensure safety during hurricane season.

Arriving at the tan, two-story building—the second floor of which Treah, and lately Gwen, called home—he pulled open the meeting-room screen door. Ted Henner, one of the more recent healing recruits, was inside. The young blond guy sat kicked back in a folding chair, feet on the seat of a chair at the table across from him and his attention on the golf tournament playing on one of the wall-mounted TVs. Since Treah figured doing without certain luxuries meant they'd have more desire to stay focused on their clients, the lower-seniority coaches lacked for televisions in their cabins.

Chris went to the coffeemaker on the opposite side of the room. Shelley kept a fresh pot on throughout the day and, while he'd never been much of an afternoon coffee drinker, he helped himself to a cup. If nothing else, it would be something to do with his hands instead of fidgeting like an idiot when he attempted to search out Ted for information via the small talk he'd always sucked at.

He pulled out a chair at the table next to Ted's and straddled the back of it. "You get shorted a client, or what are you doing hanging out here this time of day?"

Ted glanced over. "I've got one. She works nights, so her schedule's off. She's sleeping right now." He looked back at the television, asking in a humdrum voice that said he could give two shits about the answer, "You?"

"Oh, I've got one, all right." Chris packed the enthusiasm into his voice that Ted was missing. The blond guy glanced over again, and Chris gave a smug smile. "Treah pulled her aside for me for fear no one else could handle her—if you catch my drift."

"That's why you get paid the big bucks, right?" Ted asked dryly.

Chris was feeling like a jerk more and more. At the very least Ted's indifferent attitude didn't seem to suggest Nic had shared his murderer speculation with him. "I'm not exactly hurting for money," Chris offered in his best Nic-the-bragster imitation. "Stick around a few years, pick up some tips from us seasoned experts, and you might be working for more than room and board, too, bro."

Something flickered through Ted's eyes. Bafflement over the way Chris was acting or annoyance over the assumption he made jack for a wage? Whatever it was, Ted didn't take the bait to do some defensive bragging of his own, just shrugged and concentrated on the golf tournament.

A half minute of silence passed that felt damned awkward to Chris. He was about to leave when Ted asked, "Treah took off?"

Why did he want to know? Was he hoping Gwen went along for the ride, leaving easy access to Treah's home and office? "I don't know, did he?"

Ted frowned. "The Pacific branch opened last night. At the last staff meeting, he mentioned heading down there to see things started up smoothly." He came to his feet. "I should get back to the cabin. See if Brenda's up yet."

Get away from the screwball way Chris was acting: Ted's frown clarified that much. Did it also say he wasn't guilty of stealing money? Hell, Chris couldn't tell.

Giving up on the act, since no other guys were around and he sucked at questioning anyone other than his clients, Chris went to the front of the room. After trashing the untouched coffee cup, he grabbed the communication clipboard and pen from the wall ledge. He scribbled a request for one of the other healing coaches to bring their client by his cabin at some point during the week, and then headed home to give Claire the sex he'd earlier denied her.

For a price.

* * *

"Ready to take that walk?"

Claire's heart kicked into high gear with the unexpected sound of Chris's voice. After he'd left, she'd familiarized herself with her temporary home. Checking out his closets paid off in that she found her laptop and, shortly thereafter, discovered that the island had wireless service. A snippy e-mail to Erin had done wonders for her mood. Starting a review article for the *Herald* had time slipping away and, obviously, place as well, given how completely his return startled her.

She saved her work and closed her laptop. Setting the computer beside her on the couch, she shot him a get-real look. "I'm ready to go home."

"No, you aren't." He smiled as he toed off his tennis shoes. "The change in venue is exactly what you need and you know it."

She eyed his feet as he started over. Bare again. Was there any chance his sweatshirt would go the way of his shoes? "Okay, so I don't hate it. I can't say as much for the thought of how I'll get home."

He didn't remove his shirt. He did move her laptop farther down the couch so he could sit beside her. *Right* beside her. Outer thigh rubbing against hers, he brought his hands to her shoulders and turned her upper half until her back was angled toward him. His fingers pressed into her muscles, kneading at knots of tension seven months in the making. "That's weeks away. Don't worry about it."

Claire's head lolled to the side as a shiver chased through her. Despite trying everything from meditation to masturbation, she hadn't been able to relieve the knots. But, oh man, he had some fingers. The knots were either unraveling, or the flush of desire caused by his proximity was making it feel that way.

Sensual warmth slipped over her as Chris's fingers continued their magic. With a happy murmur, she closed her eyes and sank into his touch.

Dare she keep going? Slip right back against his chest and onto his lap? Tip her head to the side so that her mouth could fuse with his and get another sampling of those dynamite lips? Yeah, she'd told him not to touch or kiss her again, but that was when her mind wasn't functioning on all cylinders. Now she remembered what a once-in-a-lifetime chance spending these next weeks indulging in ecstasy with him could be. The key was to not get lost in pleasure to the point that he could get her outside.

"Why do you call it The Incident?"

Claire stiffened. So much for the magic. She opened her eyes and attempted to pull away from him. He curled his fingers around her shoulders, making the move impossible. Fine. She could be a big girl about it. Maybe. "What should I call it— 'The day that seriously fucked up my life'?"

His fingers returned to their kneading. "You weren't hurt."

This time the knots stayed firm, her body tense as never-far-buried memories threatened to surface. Physically, she hadn't been hurt. Mentally, she'd been blown apart. "Like I said before, you wouldn't understand."

"Like I said, you'd be surprised what I understand." Chris's hands moved back to her shoulders, and he used his grip to bring her around to face him. Awareness filled his eyes. The kind of keen insight that suggested he really did get what was going on in her head. It had to be a trick of his training.

A slow, soft smile spread across his face. His hands left her shoulders to move down and take hers into them. "It's not survivor's guilt. Nah, it's the small-world complex. It always seemed so big and like no bad guys lived in your tiny corner of it. Then one day you were forced to wake up and realize the world isn't so big after all and the bad guys live right next door."

How could he do that—make things feel so intimate between them while speaking of a day that had all but destroyed her life? Claire's belly tumbled with lust even as her mind sought a defense. "Been witness to a lot of murders, huh?"

"Let's just say I've seen my share of evil. I've also seen things that appeared evil but when it came right down to it were little more than an accident at the hands of stupidity and boredom."

Was the passion in his voice another trick of his training, or did firsthand experience back up his words?

Even if he answered that question, she wouldn't have any way of knowing he spoke the truth. And even if he did have firsthand experience, what difference would it make in his ability to heal her? Likely, none. Focusing on the feel of his hands in hers, the strength of his body mere inches away, the warmth of his breath as it left his mouth . . . these things could make a difference. These things could get her through the countless long, lonely days and nights that lay ahead.

Looking at him from beneath lowered lashes, she circled her thumbs against his palms. "The sex doesn't have to be off."

"Better to fuck than talk?"

"We've been talking the last seven minutes. I haven't fucked anything more substantial than a vibrator in over seven months."

Chris released her hands and sat back on the couch. His smile returned, first slow and soft, and then in that broad, wicked way that made the enticing cleft amongst his chin stubble emerge. His gaze journeyed from her face to her breasts, eyes darkening to near gray. "What do you say to a compromise? Every question you answer gets a piece of clothing off me and us one step closer to doing the deed?"

How very tempting to sing out an emphatic yes. But was she ready for the stakes? "What if I can't answer?"

He met her eyes with a shrug. "A piece of clothing goes back on."

That didn't sound so bad. The worst that could happen was

she got his tasty man-candy on display only to have it covered up again. The best . . . the best she would be experiencing in a matter of minutes. "All right. Me first."

"I never said this was a two-questioner game."

"But you meant to." And Claire meant to get this game over with fast and a much more pleasurable one started. First came work. "You know I'm a staff reporter?" He nodded, and she peeled off the socks she'd put on in his absence. "Am I allowed to write an article about my experiences here for the *Herald*? It'd be a win-win deal. Ecstasy gets free promotion. I get paid."

"That'd be one to ask Treah, the resort owner. He had to take off after our meeting but should be back on Friday or Saturday." Curiosity entered his eyes. "Why would you want to write about this place when you're already convinced your time here will be pointless?"

Smiling, she tugged at the front of his sweatshirt. "Oh, no, buddy. Not without losing the shirt."

Chris sat dutifully forward and tugged the shirt over his head. Leaving it in a pile on her laptop, he raised a dark blond eyebrow. "Better?"

"A little." Truthfully, she was feeling a whole lot better and a whole lot hornier now that all that gorgeous, golden brown skin was back on display. Her pulse raced and if her pussy were a mouth, it would have been drooling.

Granting herself the right to touch, she brought a hand to his abs and stroked the lean, firm muscle at the waist of his jeans. He pulled in an audible breath as the muscles contracted beneath her fingertips. Laughing delightedly, she walked her fingers up to a dark nipple. The short white line she'd noticed when she confronted him in the kitchen this morning pulled her attention away from toying with the flat disc.

She ran a fingernail along the mark less than an inch above his heart. Maybe he did know a thing or two about evil and had the proof to show for it. "Is this a scar?"

"You owe me an answer, sweetheart."

"Right. The article. I don't think I'll be cured of my issues when I leave here. I do have every faith that numerous other women have been, or this place would have shut down long ago. Besides, your approach intrigues me. As does this." Giving the white mark another caress, Claire glanced up at his eyes. They still held plenty of heat, but also now caginess. "What happened?"

"You really want me to put my shirt back on?"

"Hypocrite."

"I'm not the one still fully dressed." He took the front of her sweater in hand and gave it a tug as she had done to him.

More than happy to oblige, she sat back and peeled the shirt over her head. She left it on top of his and then impulsively settled herself onto his lap. Mmm . . . What do you know, straddling a guy's lap still felt as incredibly good as she remembered. The press of a semihard cock against her ass upped the enjoyment factor by about a hundred.

Chris scooted down on the couch a couple inches. His wariness was gone for now at least. His smile went wolfish as he eyed her chest in that panty-evaporating style he had. "Orange suits you well."

Heat lashed through her breasts, spiking her nipples and warming her blood. She shook her head in mock disgust. "Men are so color challenged. My bra is coral and you've already seen it."

"Not when I was invited to look."

Yeah, and the difference was clear. Before, he'd appeared interested in her breasts. Now, he appeared as though he wanted to get his hands on them in a big way. She doubted he was the type to hesitate for long. Since she wasn't either, Claire tapped her fingernail against the mark she presumed to be a scar. "Tell me about this."

"My best friend from high school was in the wrong place at the wrong time." He kept his attention locked on her breasts as he answered in a sober voice. "I got knifed trying to stop him from being killed."

"Did you save him?"

Long seconds of silence passed before he lifted his gaze to hers. Playfulness glinting in his eyes, he wiggled his eyebrows. "You owe me some jeans."

Her mind on his friend as much as getting naked, she stood from his lap and quickly stripped the jeans down her legs. Chris let out a wolf whistle. Then he equally shocked and thrilled her by pulling her sideways between his thighs and swatting her butt. "Boy panties. Gotta love 'em."

Her ass tingling with awesome sensation, she goaded, "Like boys, do you?"

"Nope. But I like the way these ride up into your cunt when I pull on them." His fingers came around to the front, tugging the crotch of the panties between her labia and tight against her clit.

Moaning with the erotic chafe of the soft cotton, she sank back onto his lap and ground the crack of her ass against his cock. Between his grunt and the impressive feel of his member through his jeans, it was safe to assume he was no longer semi-hard but fully engaged and ready for action.

"So, did you save your friend?" she pressed before she either forgot or decided she no longer cared.

His eyes went steely. "That time I did. Why do you call it The Incident?"

Claire heard the words he didn't speak. Once he'd saved his friend, but another time he hadn't managed. Chris probably *had* been in her position. Probably did understand her better than most anyone else could. For now, she chose not to question him further on it, instead leaning forward to tug at a nipple with her teeth. The nipple hardened and his cock jerked against her butt. Taking her butt into his hands, he gave a chastising squeeze.

She reclined back to send him a cheeky smile. "According to my mental coach, I have a small-world complex." Her smile attempted to falter with her next thought, but she forced it to stay put. She got through this one last question and, quite possibly, a nice fat juicy cock steak would be her reward. "I wasn't blind to crime before—I don't think any reporter could be— but I wasn't so aware of it either. Now, every time I turn on the news, someone else is being shot or stabbed. Where there used to be sitcoms on, now it's all about the crime shows. Death is all around us."

Beyond her control, her tone went morose on the last words. Somehow that pulled his smile back to the surface. "So is life."

"Yeah, well, I suggest you get to life." She pushed to her feet, grinding her crotch against his shaft as she went and feeling a resulting burst of wetness in her pussy. "Off with the jeans."

"Promise you won't laugh at my boxers?"

Yep. She knew he was a boxer man. He had his gentle moments, but more so an attitude far too rugged to constrain with briefs. It also should have been too much for him to care if she laughed over his underwear. "Why would I laugh?"

Chris slid to his feet. With a hesitant glance her way, he unfastened his jeans and pushed them down his thighs. Before she'd only been able to see a strip of navy waistband above the rise of his jeans. Now she saw the rest of his boxers were white with a navy cat pattern and a tent pushing out the front of them.

He grinned in a smug way that said his hesitation had been for show alone. "I thought you might be missing Hot Stud."

Claire's smile was automatic. There he went mixing up her

feelings again. Her sex clenched with the desire to wrap around the object responsible for that tent even as gratefulness for his wearing the silly cat boxers to make her feel more at home warmed her through. "Is there anything my sister didn't tell you?"

"I'd say she pretty much covered it all"—wicked anticipation sizzled in his eyes—"including what a hellcat you are in bed."

Way to go, Erin.

No, really, way to go, Erin! She was about to end her sexual dry spell and, for the first time since waking in an unfamiliar bed this morning, she felt nothing but elation. Well, nothing but elation and a major case of lust.

Chris had helped himself to her underwear when he'd grabbed hold of it and jerked it up inside her pussy, so she helped herself right back. If she happened to get a fistful of cock in the meantime, hey, who could blame a girl?

She gave his erection a testing squeeze before gliding her fingers the length of it. His sex thrummed and her own responded in kind. "Will you really sleep with me once we're both naked?"

"I will," he vowed in a thick, smoky voice, and then glanced toward the bedroom door. "Out there."

She frowned as she followed his gaze. "Out where?"

"On the deck."

4

With the immediate way Claire's expression went from sultry to sickened, Chris felt like he'd delivered her a death sentence. Her fingers uncurled from his shaft and she took a step back, eyes narrowed. "I should have known this was a trick."

Lamenting the loss of her touch, he moved to the bedroom door. "At least come in here and take a look." She hesitated, so he added a pleading, "For me."

She looked shocked for about two seconds and then let out a dry laugh. "Erin really did tell you everything."

Her sister had included in Claire's file what a pushover she was when it came to begging, particularly if Erin was part of the equation. He hadn't intended to use that knowledge. But then, he also hadn't intended to use her desire to sleep with him and he'd since changed his mind on that note, as well.

She stood her ground the better part of a minute before her glare let up. "Fine. I'll take a look, but that's as far as I'm going."

Claire came to the doorway. She stalled when she reached him to send a nervous look at his tented boxers. "If you're thinking of skewering me as I pass by, then moving me out on the deck when I'm too stupid with lust to realize it, forget about it. I don't make the same mistake twice."

Chris brought a camouflaging hand over his cock. "No skewering, I swear."

With a nod, she continued past him. He'd been doing his best to ignore the fact that she hadn't pulled the crotch of the boy panties from her sex. He didn't have as much luck ignoring the hot way the coral—as she called it—cotton rode up between her butt cheeks. His dick jerked against his palm and, for the little bit of time it took for her to reach the bed and sit down, he had second thoughts about the whole skewering thing.

Ordering his head out of his ass and the blood back to his brain, he slipped between the bed and the two-person table-and-chair set to draw the floor-to-ceiling blinds. Past a sliding glass door, numerous trees were visible. None were close enough to the cabin to shade it. Sunlight streamed down from the deck's wood-framed screen roof, shimmering in the water that ran through a small, decorative fountain shrouded with dogwood seedlings and baking the dark oak floorboards.

Moving back around the table and chairs, he came to a stop in front of the sliding door. "As you can see, the deck's screened in with trees surrounding the outside perimeter. No other cabins are nearby either, so you don't have to worry about being watched." He grinned back to where she sat stiffly on the side of the bed, bare legs hanging over the edge and her hands fisted on the mattress near her hips. "Not that I think you wouldn't go for a voyeur if you knew they were harmless."

Claire didn't even crack a smile. "I'll admit it looks nice." She spoke quietly without meeting his eyes. "But I can't go out there."

"You *can*. You just won't."

Another of those dry laughs left her as her gaze lifted to his. The disappointment in her eyes was nearly palpable. "Somehow I thought that when you said you understood what I'm going through, you really did understand." Her voice wasn't quiet now but accusing. "You don't get it, though. You sound just like Erin."

"I do get it, Claire. Enough to know that, in this case at least, your sister's right." Adding some wicked to his grin, he held out a hand. "Try it. You have nothing to lose and a whole lot of me to win."

"Yeah. Nothing to lose. Just my breakfast and my mind."

"Suit yourself. I'm going out." Using the hand he'd offered to her, he slid open the glass door. Claire's breath dragged in loudly. Even before he turned back, he knew panic would be in her eyes. Knew it would reach out and grab him by the throat, make him feel like he was committing some grave sin.

Not about to let himself go there, he took a step backward through the door. The deck had been built at the best angle to avoid the wind. Barely a breeze lifted through the screened-in room, leaving the sun to render it almost steamy. Smiling in a way that wasn't almost steamy, but downright feral, he met her eyes and then slid his gaze to his groin. He slipped a thumb into either side of his boxers, easing the tacky cat shorts slowly down, gliding the soft material against the inclines of his hips. Lower to expose a teasing flash of dark blond pubic curls.

The rough edge of the waistband brushed the arousal-sensitized head of his cock. He lost his grin as electric sensation zinged through him and a sigh whistled past his lips. "Apparently, he has a weakness for hellcats."

Desire danced into Claire's eyes, knocking away all traces of fear. She sucked in a hot breath. "You don't play fair."

Reclaiming his grin in a rough chuckle, Chris skated the boxers down his hips another inch. "C'mon, sweetheart. Every step you take is another inch you get to see."

She shook her head in denial but then pushed to her feet. "I'm stopping the second it gets to be too much."

Nah, she wasn't stopping. The panties were still sucked up inside her pussy, wetness darkening the material and short dark, moist curls exposed on either side. She couldn't be that afraid and that turned on all at once.

She came a step forward, and he pushed the shorts down another inch. The head of his cock pressed furiously at the waistband with the move, building tension along the length of his shaft and spreading it down through his ass and around to his spine. "Thatta girl," he encouraged through gritted teeth.

One more step she moved, her gaze trained on his groin. Her breathing increased to steady pants that did a tantalizing thing to her breasts, making them heave and strain against the cups of her bra.

He eased the shorts down again, just a fraction of an inch this time. Any farther and the peekaboo show would culminate with his dick escaping its hiding place. Not a problem, unless the abrupt move was enough to trigger her mind out of the moment.

Right now, as she came another step toward him, she was as in the moment as it got. Eyes huge and sinful blue. Lips deep pink and parted a little. Her tongue flicked out of her mouth without warning, dabbing suggestively at her full bottom lip, and his cock bucked hard enough to push the waistband out of its way.

The head of his shaft sprang free of the cotton. Claire's eyes went wider still. Panting out a hasty breath, she brought her gaze to his . . . and came to a dead halt.

The air snagged in Chris's throat. Maybe she *could* be that aroused and that afraid at once. "C'mon sweetheart. Two steps. Just another two steps."

She wanted to take those last steps damned bad—he could see that much brimming in her eyes as dark, hungry need. Her gaze started to slip from his, to travel to the area past him. The area that was certain to be her downfall. "Look at me!"

Her eyes came back to his, hot and yearning, and then darted past him, out the open door. Panic replaced passion in the space of a heartbeat. Wildly, she shook her head, dancing her bangs across her forehead. "Dammit, I can't do this! I won't." She stepped backward quickly, forcefully, until her legs rammed into the side of the bed and she toppled onto the comforter.

Stopping herself from falling all the way back by planting her palms on the mattress, she set her chin and glared. "It's not happening, today or ever."

"Then neither is sex." Releasing a defeated sigh, Chris yanked his boxers back up. The far from graceful move proved near painful on his rock-solid shaft. Grunting, he moved inside the bedroom and closed the sliding glass door. Staying in the room with Claire so nearby and wet with arousal was a bad idea for both of their sakes, so he strode to the bedroom door.

"I should at least get a consolation prize for trying," she said when he reached the door. No anger colored her voice, no fear. Just that needful hunger he'd witnessed in her eyes seconds before.

Against better logic, he turned around to find she'd moved up on the bed. With her back against the headboard, legs bent and parted slightly, full breasts nearly overflowing the cups of her bra with each of her deep breaths, she looked thoughtful and too damned sexy.

Coral really was her color. The way the panties were still lodged up inside her pussy and damp with her juices was his undoing.

Not that he was about to cross the room and fuck her. But a consolation prize couldn't hurt. Rather, it could help them both. Get his mind off every other thought for a short time while relieving the knots he'd felt in her shoulders and back when he'd tried to give her a massage out on the couch. Too, it would help with building trust between them. Not to mention, it would feel damned good.

Chris moved a few feet back inside the room. "Something tells me you aren't thinking of a gift certificate to the jelly-of-the-month club."

A siren's smile curved Claire's lips as her gaze fell on his groin. "Close. I was thinking you could let me watch you stroke your jelly."

His cock pulsed with the suggestion. He would deliver her that want, but not without getting at least something out of her for his efforts. "Why do you want me so much, Claire? You're a beautiful woman. According to Erin, your last boyfriend was about as impressive as it gets. You can get a guy like that. Probably deserve one. So why do you want me?"

"Guys like that only stick around as long as things are running smoothly."

"I look like the type to last the long haul?" If that was what she thought, he had bad news for her. For one, no woman who knew about his past would want him. For two, due to the sensual nature of the resort, healers were required to be single.

"No. I can't see you as the settling-down kind," she answered seriously. Then the naughty spread into her eyes. "But you do look like the perfect guy to spend three weeks basking in ecstasy with. I haven't been with a man since before The Incident. After my time here, the only male I'm going to be with is the type that purrs and prefers a whole different kind of pussy."

"What it boils down to is that you're horny."

"Horny." Her hot gaze slid down his torso, feeling almost as good as a physical caress, before ending on the bulge of his cock. "And seriously attracted to you."

"My body maybe. Me, you don't know from Adam." She wouldn't be sitting on his bed in her bra and panties, let alone want to have sex with him, if she did.

"Fine. I'm seriously attracted to your body. Do I get my jelly now?"

"I'll give you jelly," Chris responded quickly, before the part about this consolation prize clearing his head of every other thought failed. "But you have to give me the same. And, Claire, this isn't a jelly-of-the-month club. This is a one-time, indoor prize. You want anything more, it either happens on the deck or outside of my home completely."

"Where do you want to do it?" Claire smiled at the wavering of her voice. Seven months ago, she would have taken advantage of her open-legged position on the bed, and already had been fingering herself until they were both too distracted for thought. Now, when she knew beyond a shadow of a doubt they were about to engage in mutual masturbation, she felt suddenly nervous.

Chris gave her another of those understanding looks that said he got what was happening in her head. After he tried to lure her out onto the deck, she wasn't convinced he did, but then she wasn't convinced he didn't either. Right now, she also didn't care.

He moved back to the bedroom door and took hold of the knob. "How about you make yourself at home and I'll come in after a while?"

Was he suggesting role playing, or just giving her time to relax? "Am I supposed to act surprised to see you?"

"You can act however you want so long as you're having a good time." With a parting glance at her crotch, he left the room, pulling the door closed as he went.

Claire scuttled off the bed. She didn't miss the irony of the situation as she hurried to the dresser and yanked open the last of the drawers he'd designated as hers. This morning she'd moved hastily so he wouldn't catch her in the buff. This afternoon she moved hastily to ensure she was well prepared for when he returned to the room with the purpose of catching her in the buff, or at least nearly naked.

Her earlier search of his home revealed that Erin hadn't just packed for comfort. The bottom dresser drawer held a selection of risqué clothes, as well as lingerie and a handful of sex toys. How her sister knew where she kept her toy stash, she had no idea. She didn't want to waste time wondering either.

Chris seemed plenty happy with the coral bra and boy-panty set, so she ignored the lingerie to focus on the toys. Or rather the lack thereof.

She pulled the clothes out of the drawer in the hope of finding her favorite vibrator hiding somewhere in the pile. Her heart sank a little when a thorough search yielded no pink vibrator with a built-in clit stimulator. She didn't need it to climax, but from the first touch the stimulator would have eased her nerves to the point that her bones felt liquefied and she had only his much-coveted return on her mind.

Accepting that she'd have to settle for her second-favorite vibrator, a short black bullet with a rotating head, she took the toy out and stuffed the clothes back into the drawer. She locked the sliding glass door for an added measure of comfort and then returned to the bed. Typically, masturbating in bed was a bit too tame for Claire's tastes. Knowing she wouldn't be doing it alone, but with a living, breathing, sexy-as-the-devil man for the first time in months added a whole new level of excitement.

Reclining against the headboard, she drew up her knees and spread her legs. She focused on the door as she turned the bullet on and brought it between her thighs. How far along the path to orgasmland did she want to be when he returned? Or was it better to give herself a quick climax via the vibrator now so that she could rely solely on fingering herself then?

The spinning head of the bullet brushed against her inner thigh. Not realizing how closely she'd held it to her body, she gasped with the unexpected touch. Her pussy clenched as the head whirred upward along her thigh, cream already welling and making her sex feel like it was melting with carnal heat.

Chris's boxer-dropping show and that partial view of his cock obviously had her body at full arousal. She wouldn't need the vibrator to reach a speedy climax today. She brought it to her slit and rubbed it against her sex past her panties anyway. The cotton still inside her pussy shifted with the vibrations, arcing heated sensation throughout her core. Warmth licked through the rest of her as she took hold of the crotch of the panties and dragged them slowly free of her sex. Her pussy lips resisted their loss, sucking at the sodden material and registering a tingling need in her clit.

Claire pulled the crotch of the panties to one side and answered that tingling with the head of the vibrator. The rotating tip eased past trimmed pubic curls to slip between her labia and stroke against her clit. Mini-vibrations shuddered into the swollen bundle of nerves, and she gasped as her hips bucked up off the bed. Parting her pussy lips with two fingers, she angled the vibrator. The thick, hard side rode between her labia with short, erratic bursts of speed. The rotating tip struck against her clit with each of those bursts.

Warmth turned to sizzling heat within the space of seconds. Orgasm took her over nearly as quickly. Her breath wheezed between her lips as she closed her eyes to visions of Chris standing naked in the doorway, one strong hand fondling his balls while the other pumped away at his cock.

The vibrations died away slowly, her breathing returning to normal pitch. It picked up again with the creak of the bedroom door. A wild thrill pushed through her, heating her pussy back into an inferno of aching need. She opened her eyes expecting to find him standing there, cock and balls in hand. But he wasn't there. The door was still closed, no further sound coming from the room beyond it.

Displeasure sailed through Claire. She displaced it with the thought he'd be here soon. Probably he was staying away with the idea of building anticipation.

She set the vibrator aside and pulled the panties down her thighs. Tossing the damp underwear onto the floor, she sat back and waited to give him the ultimate fingering show. And kept waiting for a good ten minutes.

Sighing, she brought her fingers back to her sex and petted the outer folds. The nervous tension had gone with her short but oh-so-sweet orgasm. She wasn't about to let it return because he was taking his time in getting back to her.

Another several minutes of petting passed without his return, and she glared at the door. Had he changed his mind about masturbating? Or had he never intended to go through with it in the first place?

If this was another trick, so help her. . . . "Chris?"

She hadn't shouted his name. In fact, she'd barely spoken it loud enough for him to hear beyond the door. Which meant he had to be waiting right outside, because the door burst open instantly. He wasn't wearing the cat boxers with the tented front any longer. He wasn't wearing a thing but a devastating grin and his hand around his cock. Except the action of his hand along his shaft was more of a stroking than a wearing. Not quite her vision come to red-hot life, and yet it was even better.

"Did someone call my—" His gaze latched onto her fingers caressing the folds of her sex. Appreciation mingled with the desire in his eyes as he met her gaze. "I don't know who you are, lady, but I'm certain you never asked to come in my bed."

So they were going with the role-playing game. That was one challenge she could eagerly rise to.

Chris slid his fingers to the blood-pink corona of his shaft. He rubbed his thumb in the silky moisture seeping from the tip, and then brought that same thumb to his mouth and sucked it between his lips.

Claire's breath dragged in with a pant. Her pussy went from warm and damp to scorching and drenched. With effort, she recalled that he was waiting for her to play her part in this sensual game. But, God, it would have been so much easier if he hadn't gone and tasted his jelly that way.

"Sorry," she said in a low, husky voice. "I was passing by and saw your bed. So big and warm and empty looking. I was just going to lie down for a few minutes but then my pussy started to ache." She stilled the easy petting to slip her fingers between the folds of her sex. A little moan left her as they pumped inside her channel. "Rubbing my finger around inside it helped but it's still aching something fierce."

He brought his hand back to his dick, stroking the hard length as he studiously eyed her cunt. "I can see the problem. It's juicy red and inflamed. You need more than a finger diddling, lady."

Excitement balled in her stomach. Was that an offer on his part? "I do?"

"Sure do. Lucky for you, I found this in the hallway." She hadn't paid attention to his left hand with all the good stuff his right one was doing. Now, she couldn't take her eyes off it as he held up her missing vibrator.

Her clit fluttering in anticipation, she innocently eyed the pink sex toy. "You think that will make it feel better?"

"Only one way to find out."

Claire pulled her fingers from her pussy to catch the vibrator. But he didn't toss it to her. He turned it on and brought the quivering clit-stimulator to the side of his shaft. His cock bucked wildly, his features contorting with maximum pleasure.

"Oh yeah," he said in a tight, raw voice. "I'd say there's an excellent possibility it'll work for you."

Oh yeah was right. More like oh hell yeah!

It took one confident man to taunt his cock with an object so blatantly phallic. None of her past lovers had had the balls to do so. Which just might explain why her sex was shuddering as violently as if it was the one being stimulated by the toy.

Chris's throat worked audibly as he teased the clit-stimulator the length of his erection. Muscles contracted visibly in his thighs. On a groan of pure pleasure, he brought the head of the vibrator to the weeping eye of his shaft and coated it with pre-cum. He tossed it to her then, the end shimmering with his own personal jelly.

Her jelly now.

His masculine scent lifted from the vibrator—strong, heady, and intoxicating. Claire's tongue moved restlessly over her teeth.

God, it had been so long since she'd tasted a man's seed.

She ached to take the vibrator into her mouth and suck his cum off. Her hungry pussy had other ideas, pulsing out a silent plea to put it inside. Ignoring both those needful aches in the hopes of getting something even better, she stared at the toy with feigned confusion. "I'm not sure I know how to work it."

He took his member back in hand, idly stroking the hard flesh. "It's pretty simple."

She tilted her head to the side and batted her lashes. "So am I. Show me?"

His hand stilled as hesitation slid into his eyes. "Will a hands-on sample get you out of my house?"

"Um. Maybe." It depended whether he meant that literally or as part of the game.

The answer had to be the game, because Chris accepted her neutral response by unhanding his shaft and joining her on the bed.

Her heart slammed against her ribs as he came up on his knees beside her, his erection so close if she straightened her right leg it would be rubbing against it. She wanted to risk it. Just not at the cost of losing his hands-on sample.

The heat in his eyes magnified about twenty times as he took the vibrator from her. Gaze intent on her crotch, he lightly touched the clit-stimulator to her labia. "It might seem like getting your pussy even juicier is moving in the wrong direction, but it's going to have to get wetter before it feels better. A little outer lip stimulation goes a long way."

Amen to that. Her sex fluttered madly as he moved the stimulator along her slit. The thumb of his free hand joined in, pressing between her damp folds. His thumb pushed deeper into her sex, opening her wide and, seconds later, exposing her clit to the stimulator's all-powerful touch.

Urgent, trembling need whipped through Claire. Her body singed almost as hot as it had when he'd coerced her outside this morning. The difference being this heat she wanted wholeheartedly.

Gasping, she fisted her hands in the comforter. "Should it get hotter before it gets better, too?"

His gaze lifted to hers. "Is it hot?"

Ah, hell. He looked so equally concerned and hungry for her that it was just impossible to stop from risking it all. "Scorching. I think it needs something to cool it off. A tongue maybe."

Chris's eyes narrowed accusingly. He jerked the vibrator from her body and left it to quiver on the bed. "First you come in my bed and now you want to come on my tongue. Lady, you're really something."

Something good or something bad?

Before she could voice the question, he had her ankles pinned in his hands and was jerking her down the bed on her back. Planting a palm on each side of her head, he came over her, looking huge and wicked and wild hovering inches away. "I wouldn't be much of a man if I left you suffering, now would I?"

The damp head of his cock nudged against her inner thigh. Her pussy pulsed with liquid anticipation. For just a second, Claire held out hope that he was so much of a man that he planned to give her far more than his tongue. Then he moved back down her body and buried his head between her thighs.

His fingers clamped around her upper legs as his lips pressed tight to her sex and his tongue speared deep inside her. And—what do you know?—she recognized that having his tongue in her wasn't so bad.

Matter of fact, it was downright glorious. So much better than even her favorite vibrator. So much better than what past lovers going down on her had done.

Of course, past lovers might not have been this orally skilled.

She'd defined his fingers as magical when they'd massaged the knots nearly out of her shoulders and back. His tongue was nothing short of a miracle as he licked, sucked, and ate at her pussy, and erased every knot in her body.

Chris scooped his hands beneath her butt and tilted her hips at an upward angle. His tongue slipped deeper inside her sheath, lashing at tender tissue until she lifted her pelvis and ground her cunt greedily against his mouth. "Yes. Fuck me more!"

His tongue retreated, and she considered her outburst had cost her dearly. Then his mouth moved to the nubbin of her clit, lips closing quickly around it, sucking hard as his hold on her butt intensified, short nails digging almost painfully into her ass.

Claire moaned against the decadent nip, felt it drive throughout her butt, leaving her crack feeling empty and untouched. His teeth closed over her clit, first twisting and then tugging at the tight bundle of nerves. Her thoughts splintered apart as shudders erupted in her core, small at first then growing into something fierce and delicious as one of his hands released her butt to toy with her crack.

Afraid to speak, she whimpered for more and lifted her ass off the bed completely. His finger lingered along the silky divide of her crack, taunting her for long seconds before dipping divinely into her hole.

Releasing her clit, Chris pushed his tongue back into her pussy. In tandem, he filled her, front and back, in and out, pumping her with ultimate pleasure until her entire body shook with tremulous force.

Her belly clamped tight. Her heart pounded. Frantically, she clung to the comforter, feeling helpless yet again because of him. Mindless.

At least this time it was for all the right reasons. Or at least reasons that felt right as the tremors coalesced into a hot ball of desperation.

"Yes. Please . . ." Words slipped from her mouth.

The hand on her ass left. She feared again that he would stop completely. He didn't stop. Just turned up the pace of his thrusts to savage devouring, expanding her desperation to the bursting point.

Claire shattered as rapturous heat slammed her eyes closed and caressed her to the soul. It left her trembling, panting, and weak. Unable to move, breathe.

Holy Jesus, his massages had nothing on his mouth jobs.

Chris's shout of release invaded the orgasmic haze shrouding her mind and body. The primal sound snapped her eyes open. Quickly, she discovered where his hand had gone. Eyes smoky and dark, the muscles of his throat and neck corded delectably, he pumped his shaft with a white-knuckled fist. He aimed it at her chest and bathed her fettered breasts with the warm, silky stream of his cum.

All thoughts of risk evaporated. Pulse pounding, she drew the cups of her bra down and released her breasts. She dipped a finger into the seed glistening between the slopes of her breasts and then rubbed the silky gel along her nipple. The shiny, pink tip went instantly hard. She repeated the move with the other nipple, bringing it to a matching crest. Giving each tight point a squeeze had a groan emerging from her bed partner. With a moan of her own, she went back for more of his cum.

He'd tempted her when he sucked his pre-cum from his thumb. She tempted him right back, slipping the shiny finger between her lips. Or maybe she'd tempted herself, Claire realized, as the hot, salty taste of him exploded over her senses, because she wanted more. More of his cum and more of his body.

She went back for more of the first, swirled her finger into the shimmering fluid, and then sucked it sensuously back inside her mouth. With a murmur of elation, she flicked her gaze to Chris's and let the digit pop back out. "My kind of jelly."

Dark desire rallied in his eyes. His cock jerked hard. Discounting them both, he climbed from the bed. "Too bad for you the indoor supply just ran out."

5

Chris breathed a sigh of relief with the knock on his cabin door. He needed a distraction damned bad. The mouth-on masturbation session with Claire two nights ago had helped to establish trust between them while momentarily taking his mind off both Nic's speculations and Chris's promise to Treah to help track down the person responsible for stealing money from the resort. But it also had made Claire more eager than ever to use him as her man-sized sex toy.

Each time she fell into one of her temptress routines, like "accidentally" walking in on him when he was showering and she just happened to be naked herself, he reminded her that she wasn't getting any more jelly unless it happened on the deck, or in another venue altogether. Regardless, she kept up her taunting. And, regardless, his desire to have another taste of her own jelly grew until the air in the cabin crackled with sexual electricity. It made going with the resort's typical approach of healing via the sensual almost impossible. Sleeping in the same bed wasn't even an option.

Not that he slept in the same bed with most of his clients.

Some, yes. More often, he gave the women his bed and personally made use of the queen-sized sleeper built into the couch.

Chris rose from that same couch and went to the door. Not caring who stood on the other side, so long as they could stay a while, he jerked it open. One look at the arrogant bastard responsible for the knocking, and he knew he was mistaken. He did care who stood outside his door. And the last person he wanted it to be was Nic.

Fighting the impulse to slam the door shut, Chris checked behind him for Claire. She'd been working on her laptop at the table in his bedroom the last hour. Apparently, she was still doing the same. Good. She'd made some slow-but-steady progress in the fifty-plus hours she'd been on the island. Once he'd even caught her sending the deck a coveting look and taking a few steps in that direction. Overhearing the damning accusations Nic was liable to toss at him would send her progress into a tailspin.

He looked back at Nic, not bothering to hide his disdain. "What do you want?"

Amusement filled Nic's dark brown eyes. "I heard your woman needs a friend."

For the first time, Chris noticed the short but voluptuous redhead in a low-cut blue sweater and skintight black jeans standing off to Nic's left. Nice. Just what he wanted. To be in Nic the Dick's debt.

It might not be what Chris wanted, but Claire could use some interaction time with another of the resort clients. One who was eager to get over the issues that brought her here and was following her mental coach's guidance in an effort to do so. Then there was the fact that sooner or later he had to spend time with Nic. The guy was as good of a candidate to be Treah's thief as anyone. Technically, he was probably the best candidate. His motivation: taking the money necessary to equal Chris's pay since he so obviously believed he had it coming.

Chris forced a grateful smile and spoke words of appreciation that tasted like shit. "She does. Thanks."

Nic smirked. "Anything to help out a subordinate."

Chris's smile evaporated as fury barreled through him. He wasn't a hostile guy. Never had been despite his criminal record and what some people liked to think. Even so, Nic had an uncanny way of making him want to beat the hell out of him. "You didn't get first pick." He forced his voice to remain calm. "Treah knew no one else could handle someone as messed up as Claire so he made certain I got her."

The laughter in Nic's eyes said he wasn't buying it. "Whatever gets you through the night, *cazzo*." His smile warmed as he nodded at the redhead. "This is Dawn. She knows how easily Claire scares of strangers and swore she'd save all her biting for me."

The woman had to be in her mid- to late thirties, but her giggle was pure schoolgirl. She sent adoring eyes Nic's way before smiling at Chris. "Hi."

Chris had to hand it to Nic. In spite of being a complete scumbag, in general the guy knew how to make his clients happy. With a welcoming nod, Chris returned Dawn's smile. "How's it going?"

She looked back at Nic and grinned. "So far I can't complain."

Nic gave the redhead's butt a swat. "I'm heading to the gym for an hour or two. I'll stop by to pick you up on my way back through. Be a good girl 'til then."

She let out another giggle. "Honey, if I were a good girl, I wouldn't be here."

Curious about what issue brought her to the island, but not enough to start in on an immediate conversation, Chris turned back to Nic. "Interested in company?"

Surprise filled Nic's eyes, quickly turning to speculation. He glanced at Dawn, then back at Chris and shrugged. "Why not."

"Great." So great, the idea of getting into a vehicle with the guy had Chris's guts roiling. "Let me get Claire out here to meet Dawn, and I'll be ready to go."

Not positive how she would respond to the idea of being left alone with a stranger, Chris went into the bedroom. Claire still sat at the corner table, but her gaze was focused on the door instead of her laptop. Her eyes were narrowed a fraction and were devoid of the naughtiness she'd repeatedly attempted to ply him with.

Shit, he hoped she hadn't overheard the conversation in the other room. Nic hadn't said anything to impede her progress, but Chris had all but called her a flake.

"Is someone here?" she asked in a tight voice.

Both her look and tone could have to do with nervous tension as easily as anger. Unfortunately, he'd have to wait until later to figure out which. "One of the other clients. You said you'd be willing to spend some time with one if she came here."

"Oh." She eyed the door warily. "Did I hear a man's voice?"

"Just Nic, her mental coach. He's leaving." He hesitated before adding, "I'm going with him."

"Oh." This "oh" sounded more like an "oh hell."

Smiling his encouragement, he held out a hand. "C'mon, sweetheart. It's just one woman with her own problem to overcome. She's probably as scared as you are."

Claire's gaze flicked to her laptop. She looked back at him after a few seconds, the caution in her eyes not quite so intense. "What's her problem?"

He let his hand fall at his side. "I don't know. I wondered, too, but don't have time to find out right now. Nic and I have some urgent business."

"So I guess I don't have a choice but to suck it up and go meet her?"

"Not really. But there's nothing to fear. She's short and mostly all breasts. You could take her in a heartbeat."

She didn't look exactly thrilled by that analysis. In fact, she seemed more pissed and less concerned by the minute. "Fine. I'll play hostess. But not until you guys leave. Have her sit on the couch. Once I hear the door close, I'll come out and make nice. A woman I can probably handle. I'm not so sure about a woman and two men all at once."

Chris let go a suggestive grin. "I figured a hellcat like you did a woman and two men all at once on a regular basis." Probably he shouldn't have brought sex up, even in a teasing light. He did so in the hopes of making her laugh.

She didn't laugh. Her eyes narrowed farther and she slapped her laptop closed with a fisted hand. "Yeah. I'm just a regular slut and a headcase all in one."

Well, that pretty much answered his earlier question. She'd obviously overheard the conversation with Nic. Speaking of the dick, he chose that inopportune moment to call from the other room, "You coming or what?"

"I'll be right out," Chris shouted back. He eyed Claire regretfully. "I didn't mean what I said out there. I was just trying to—"

"Go before I change my mind about meeting this woman."

"Her name's Dawn." He chanced another grin, this one far lighter. "Nic promised she wouldn't bite."

"Lucky me," she returned dryly as she stood from the table. She moved into the bathroom and closed the door. Not with a slam. But with a bang loud enough to ensure she was pissed in a way that was going to take some serious groveling, if not an in-cabin mouth job, to undo.

After leaving Dawn on the couch per Claire's request, Chris rounded to the back side of the cabin and climbed into the passenger's side of Nic's black Jeep. He cast aside thoughts of Claire as he did up his seat belt. Still, as Nic got into the seat beside him, he felt like her anxiety had followed him out the door.

How intelligent was it to put his life into the hands of a guy he knew hated him?

Without looking his way, Nic started the engine and pulled down a narrow path surrounded by a copse of trees and underbrush. A short distance down the path converged with the gravel road that surrounded the island. The terrain grew mountainous after the first mile, the road rising up sharply along with it. More of the camouflaging trees and sporadic bursts of wildflowers filled up the landscape on the left. On the right, the road's shoulder dropped off at an almost perfect ninety-degree angle. Jagged rocks protruded from the dark, wind-whipped waters fifty feet below.

"Someone was to get pushed down there, the body would never be found," Nic commented wryly.

Chris had planned to spend the ride in silence, wait until they reached the gym to attempt to get him talking. Now, he couldn't resist looking over and sneering. "Planning on pushing me out?"

"I'm not the murderer here."

Chris's rage returned in an instant. Fuck, he should have known Nic couldn't resist taunting him. "Whatever you think you know, I suggest you check your facts."

Nic glanced over, mouth curved in a shit-eating grin and humor gleaming in his eyes. "It's killing you, isn't it? Wondering who my source is and how much they told me? Like I said before, enough. A few words to the right people and you'll wish I'd pushed you out."

"Then why don't you speak them?"

"Big brother." Nic let the words linger as he turned off the gravel road onto the dirt one leading to several of the employee cabins and the gym that had been converted from a one-time pole barn. The steel structure appeared ahead, and he added, "It's just a matter of time before Treah sees the light. When he does, you can bet I won't be the only one standing in line to put a nail in your coffin." He pulled the Jeep into a parking spot in front of the gym. "Door-to-door service. So much for being an asshole, eh, *cazzo*?"

Chris climbed out. He frowned when Nic didn't make a move to shut off the engine. "You're not coming in?"

"Never planned to. I've got business to do." Barely waiting for Chris to clear the Jeep's front tires, Nic backed out of the spot and took off in the direction they'd come from. The office was in that direction. Of course, so were a good deal of the employee cabins. But what business would Nic have to do in someone else's cabin when the women were on the island and his wasn't along for the ride?

Whatever the business, something told Chris it couldn't be good.

From what she'd overheard when she'd been in Chris's bedroom, Claire hadn't thought she would like Dawn. She might be a redhead but she'd sounded like an airhead who couldn't stop giggling long enough to form an intelligent sentence. Once she met the woman and they got to talking, Claire realized she was actually quite smart. The reason for the whole airhead act when men were around was the reason she was on the island to begin with. In short form, she was a nympho. In long form, she was afraid of rejection and abused casual sex to avoid having to deal with it. Right now, she was enjoying the hell out of abusing her mental coach by trying to taunt him into sex.

The situation wasn't so different than what Claire was doing with Chris. Except Nic probably didn't think Dawn was a headcase. The last hour and a half Claire had managed to mostly forget her anger over hearing Chris tell his friend what a mental job she was. Now, her resentment resurged, balling her hands into fists along the arms of the recliner where she sat waiting for Dawn to return from the bathroom.

Chris's estimation wouldn't have been such a big deal if not for him lying about his feelings earlier in the week. Of course, he'd claimed he hadn't meant what he said to Nic. But then, who was he more apt to lie to? A man he'd probably known for years, or a woman he'd known less than three days?

A knock sounded on the cabin door, making Claire jump in the recliner. Dawn breezed into the room, a wide grin curving her lips as she affected a Southern drawl. "I do believe my stud has returned."

They'd spent the last half hour discussing their fears, so Dawn knew how she felt about having strangers enter her safe zone. Obviously, the redhead was too excited to have Nic back to remember Claire's fear because she hurried to the door and flung it open.

An olive-skinned guy easily befitting the label "tall, dark, and handsome" stood in the doorway. He stepped inside the cabin, exchanging a killer smile with Dawn before looking over and giving Claire one of her own. "Enjoying your time on the island?"

Nic was definitely hot, with his dark chocolate eyes and thick, wavy black hair. But something about him made Claire a little uncomfortable. Something more than the fact that he'd not only barged inside but failed to close the door behind him. Maybe it was just that she'd dated an Italian guy for a few months before hooking up with her last boyfriend and his temper had been for shit.

Claire pulled in a few calming breaths before responding with a partial smile. "More than I thought I would."

"Considering his shady past, Chris is an all-right guy."

"Shady?" Dawn's eyes widened. "Was he like a drug dealer or something?"

He winced. "Hell. Forget I said anything. He's worked too hard to get away from his felony record to have it biting him in the ass now because of my big mouth."

* * *

Showered and changed back into jeans and a sweatshirt, Chris slid into the passenger's seat of Shelley's red Blazer. The wind had picked up considerably since he'd entered the gym two hours before. Going by the pea green shade dusting the late afternoon sky, a storm was blowing in. Even if rain wasn't threatening, he hadn't been in the mood to make the cross-island trek back to his cabin.

A handful of guys had come and gone in the time he'd been at the gym. He'd attempted to chat up each of them in search of information and had gotten nowhere in the process.

Letting his frustration go, he smiled over at the resort manager. "Thanks for coming to get me."

"Not like I was doing anything else but sitting on my fat ass."

When he'd called her pre-workout to ask if she would come pick him up in a couple hours, she'd sounded like her typically chipper self. Now, she sounded the way she had every other time he talked to her this week. "Your ass is about as bony as they come. What's the matter, Shell?"

"Nothing's the matter," she snapped back as she pulled out of the gym parking lot. A few seconds passed and Shelley let out a long sigh. She glanced over with a contrite smile. "I'm just . . . over this place. I need to find a new job."

"Too much testosterone for one woman to handle?"

"You could say that." The sky opened up with her succinct reply. Hard, fat drops of rain splattered against the windshield and thudded against the roof. She set the wipers on high and then gripped the steering wheel with both hands as she maneuvered the slick, potentially treacherous stretch of mountainous roadway.

Chris let her focus on driving until she turned onto the half-mile stretch of blacktop that led to the main office. Tonight was the first of several client and staff gatherings in the meeting room. While Claire wasn't up to one yet, he'd figured she could still enjoy the food and had asked Shelley to drop him off at the office so he could get their dinners to go.

"Treah's not going to be happy to lose you," he commented when the two-story, tan structure came into sight.

"I know, and I feel bad for him. But, at this point, I don't think there's much that could get me to stay."

"What about a raise?"

"It would take more than a few dollars." Annoyance returned to her voice with the response.

Not wanting to irritate her further, Chris let the conversation drop. But her words refused to leave his head. Was it possible that it wasn't a man stealing money from the resort, the way both he and Treah had assumed, but rather a woman? Shelley would have easy access to the accounts. It didn't seem likely, considering all that he knew of her, including that she was as close with Treah as she was with Chris. Still, she'd been acting off about something lately.

She pulled the Blazer into the office lot and up to the meeting room entrance. He opened the passenger side door, but then looked over at her instead of getting out. "Are you in some kind of trouble, Shelley?"

She didn't look his way. She didn't need to: The stiffness of her body told a story all its own. "I know you're trying to help but I can't talk to you about this." The words came out uneven and he swore he heard her sniff. "Do you want me to stick around and give you a ride back to your place?"

"Nah." He stepped out of the Blazer, automatically ducking his head against the cool, biting nip of the rain. "I can borrow Treah's truck. If you change your mind, you know where I am."

"Chris?" Shelley called when he started to close the door.

He stuck his head back inside the vehicle. She faced him now. Even with his hair already drenched and dribbling rainwater into his face, there was no denying her eyes were heavy with unshed tears. Whatever was going on had to be serious. "Yeah?"

She smiled thinly. "You're a nice guy. Don't let Nic make you think otherwise."

Living along the Massachusetts coastline, Claire had been through numerous storms. Never had she weathered one inside a cabin less than thirty feet from the ocean. Between the blackness of the sky, howling wind, and driving rain, she couldn't make out the beach through the windows any longer. She'd been able to see it fifteen minutes ago. Already then, waves had beaten violently at the sand, the swells breaking halfway to the door and nearly whipping the hammock free of the huge trees it was tethered to.

Too jumpy to sit, she'd been pacing for the last ten minutes. Despite the hurtful comment Chris had made to his friend about her, and then the one his friend had made about Chris being a felon, she wanted him here. He had to endure this type of weather on a regular basis. He would know if she had a reason to be concerned.

As if her mind somehow conjured him up, the front door banged open less than a minute later. Chris hurried inside as a clap of thunder exploded overhead. Seconds later, lightning pierced through the blackness in a jagged line of yellow orange.

Claire's heart beat wildly in response to the furious sound, but she made studying Chris her staying point. His jeans and sweatshirt were soaked. His hair clung to his forehead despite the wild whip of the wind into the cabin. In his hands was a short stack of white plastic takeout containers.

She couldn't remember a man ever looking so good.

The urge to throw her arms around him hit her hard. She hurried over to him but bypassed the urge to take the containers from his hands. Turning around, he threw his weight against the door, shoulder first. He grunted with the contact, and then went back for a second attempt. This time the door slammed closed. He locked it and then turned back around to lean against it, drawing in a long breath before tossing her a quirky smile. "I wouldn't go out there if I were you."

Some of her tension drained away. His entrance had caused a stir, but now that he was inside, he seemed calm and not in any hurry to rush her out the door to higher ground.

"When did Dawn take off?" he asked as he toed off his saturated tennis shoes.

Claire's tension mounted all over again, right along with the shoulder knots, with the reminder of Nic's departure. More, his parting words.

Was Chris truly a felon and, if so, what had he done?

Bodily, she moved into the open kitchen and set the takeout containers on the bar counter. Mentally, she remained fixed on him. No longer as a staying point, but on the chance he would remove his soaked sweatshirt. She wanted another look at his body. Yeah, she'd seen him fully naked a few times now, but only when she'd been too horny to think to look for scars beyond the one over his heart.

Now she was too anxious to be horny, and she couldn't help but wonder where the chest scar had really come from and if others marred his body. "Nic came to get her a half hour ago."

"Sorry to hear that." He obliged her silent wish by pulling the shirt over his head and dropping it onto the floor. "Guy's a dick."

Claire swallowed hard as he continued to undress right down to nothing but damp skin. Blood pulsed between her temples, and her pussy surged to wet, aching awareness.

Apparently, she'd been wrong. She was neither too tense nor too upset to be horny.

Her hormones took a backseat as the heat in Chris's words registered. Nic obviously wasn't the friend she'd assumed.

Pulling plates from an overhead cabinet, she asked noncha-lantly, "Bad blood between you two?"

Grabbing his dripping clothes from the floor, he crossed to the bedroom. She gripped the plates hard to keep from drop-ping them with the nipple-beading view. Seriously, the guy had a killer set of hands and an awesome mouth, but his ass. Oh, yeah, his ass . . .

He disappeared into the bedroom. She set the plates down on the counter to fan her heated face. Maybe she could handle going out on the deck tonight. That she'd be drenched from the first step might even distract her to the point of forgetting she was no longer in her safe zone.

Yeah, right.

Chris emerged from the bedroom in black sweatpants. He came into the kitchen and grabbed a handful of utensils from the silverware drawer. Moving shoulder to shoulder with Claire, he opened the first of the takeout containers—a decadent-smelling wild rice blend—and rested a serving spoon against the box's lip. "You could call it bad blood." He glanced over with a sneer. "He thinks he deserves my job as head healer and would do or say anything to get me fired so that he can take over."

Much as the rice smelled incredible, the man smelled even better. Along with his natural scent, he carried that "air during a storm" aroma. The one she'd been missing for over seven months now. Between the scents and his yummy naked torso, which carried no more scars, she wanted to touch him in a seri-ous way.

All right, she wanted to do more than touch.

Since she still wasn't exactly pleased with him, and he wasn't likely to let her do the things her body ached to do, she opened a second box of food—this one stuffed with steaming king crab legs—and focused on the conversation. "If he's so bad, why doesn't he get fired?"

"Nic's good at what he does. And women love him."

"I'd be lying if I said he wasn't easy on the eyes."

As though he thought the compliment meant Claire wasn't as pleased with his own body, Chris's eyes narrowed. "Want to head over to his place and have a three-way?" His tone was pure defense. "Dawn can videotape."

"Are you for real?"

"Why not?"

"Because the last time you pulled me outside the door, I came about two seconds away from puking on your feet. Not to mention that there's a hurricane unleashing outside." Not to mention that while Nic was good to look at, she would toss him aside in a heartbeat to get her hands on Chris's divine body and her pussy wrapped around his cock.

Smirking, he leaned back against the counter. "Hurricane season doesn't come for another month. But I'm sure Nic would be more than happy to come back here in about a minute flat if it meant he got to do you."

She couldn't stop her disbelieving laugh. The guy was jealous. Too damned funny. "This is a pissing match, ego kind of thing, right? You want me to say I wouldn't do him if I was a nympho on a dry spell and he was the last guy with a hard dick left alive?"

"I don't care what you say."

"Bullshit."

"I don't. But you should, considering the sex ball's in my court."

Claire nodded toward the bedroom. "The sex ball's out getting soaked and knocked around on the deck." She looked back at Chris, remembering how many times he'd been gentle with her the last few days, and she couldn't let his ego suffer any longer. Even if he probably did deserve it for all those other times when he hadn't been nearly so gentle. "I wouldn't do him," she admitted. "Not because of your man tiff, though. I did some time with an Italian guy and their tempers turn to pure shit just a little too easily for my liking."

Shock widened his eyes. Then something truly strange happened given the topic under discussion. He smiled. "You did time?"

Not only was he smiling, but his voice rang with . . . dare she say happiness? Frowning, she clarified. "I dated him."

His smile vanished. Muttering an "oh," he turned back to the food containers and opened up a third one to reveal lobster prawns and oysters on the half shell.

Every box held food that Claire adored and that had her stomach quivering with an excitement to indulge. But her mind was quivering, too. With an understanding of what Chris thought she'd meant when she'd said she served time. "You thought I meant I was in jail." He didn't respond, so she pressed, "You liked the idea, didn't you?"

"Why the hell would I?"

He hadn't looked her way, but his snapping tone said plenty. He *had* liked the idea of her being a felon. Was it because it made him feel better about his own shady past, as Nic called it? Or were Nic's words nothing more than a lie to try to deface Chris's image? "You tell me."

He looked over, mouth set into a hard line. A hundred different thoughts seemed to pass through his narrowed eyes. The unyielding set of his mouth let up then. Lips curving into a light smile, he rounded to the opposite side of the bar and sat down on one of the stools. "We should eat. Seafood tastes like shit when it gets cold."

Could she eat sitting next to a man potentially convicted of who knew what crimes?

Oddly, Claire felt like she could. She hadn't come to know him all that well the last few days. But the gentle moments made it hard to believe he could be too bad. Then there was the heartfelt passion in his voice when he talked about the best friend he'd saved from death once but was unable to save a second time. If he was a felon at some point, he couldn't have done time for anything too serious.

The knots in her shoulders lessened. Grabbing a plate, she rounded the bar and slid onto a stool beside Chris. He reached across the counter for his own plate and piled crab legs on it. He glanced at her. "Up for some?"

She nodded, smiling at the consideration. Yeah, it seemed highly unlikely he could have such thoughtful moments and still have a sinner's past.

He grabbed two small plastic bowls of warm, melted butter from one of the takeout boxes and set them on the bar between them. They ate in silence for a few minutes. It was a comfortable silence, Claire recognized. She hated to ruin that camaraderie, but his hurtful comment to Nic about her was still in the back of her head. It just wouldn't do to have it lingering there for the next two and a half weeks. Not when she wanted to focus solely on driving him to the point of sexual frustration where he couldn't resist relenting to her right here inside the shelter of his home.

She gave him time to finish chewing the forkful of rice he'd just stuck into his mouth, and then asked, "Do you really think I'm a headcase, the way you told Nic?"

Apology weighed in Chris's eyes as he looked over at her. "I tried to answer that earlier. The only reason I said that was to piss him off. Like I said before, I think you're normal with the addition of a serious fear. One that you're making progress on."

If she'd had food in her mouth, she would have been certain to spew it with her laughter. "I'm making progress? How?"

A wolfish grin claimed his lips. He dipped a bite of crab

meat into the melted butter and brought it to her mouth. Her tongue flicked out on instinct, dabbing at the warm, salty meat and getting a taste of his thumb in the process.

Sensual heat sizzled in his eyes, rendering them nearly gray. "You almost have yourself convinced that the benefits of going out on the deck would far exceed the risks."

Claire took in his rain-cloaked scent again, the warmth lifting off his half-naked, deliciously hard body. The rise and fall of his chest with each of his slightly keyed-up breaths. She wasn't *almost* convinced. But maybe she was getting a little closer with each passing second.

She flicked her tongue out again, intentionally this time. Just as intentionally, she concentrated on licking the butter that dribbled onto his first finger and thumb. She took both his fingers and the tender meat into her mouth then. Sucking at the hot, salty combination, she eyed him with every ounce of the desire rocketing through her, flaming the wet heat in her core.

A muted growl escaped Chris's throat. Her pussy throbbed with the primal sound. Freeing her mouth from his fingers, she asked in a low, lusty voice, "If I were to try again, would there be another consolation prize?"

"No jelly samples," he responded in a voice equally as lusty and oh so thick and smoky with the sound of pure sex. "A little kissing and groping might be doable."

She slipped her hand into his lap as she'd done the first morning. This time she didn't brush her knuckles against the bulge of his cock, but turned her hand over and palmed his shaft—his wondrously solid shaft—through his sweatpants. "Five minutes per step?"

"Thirty seconds."

"One minute."

"Deal." Chris slipped his own hand into her lap, spreading her thighs and cupping her mound. She wore jeans and panties, yet he managed to make her feel naked and like the heat of his palm was singeing into her sex.

His middle finger moved, pressing hard against her pussy and shuddering tremors to her clit. Claire shivered with the sensation. She leaned toward him, intending to slide off her stool and transfer her mouth to his shaft. After all, he hadn't specified what kind of kissing and not all cock kisses guaranteed jelly. Though she was hoping more than a little bit that this one would.

"Quit worrying about the deck and eat up," he ordered. His grin turned goading, bringing her intended descent to a halt. "This stuff doesn't taste much different coming up than it does going down."

6

The look of stark fear on Claire's face when Chris pulled the vertical blinds open suggested he shouldn't have made her finish eating before giving the deck another go. He should have rushed her into the bedroom when her mind was thick with sexual thoughts. Not that he believed sex wasn't still on her mind, even if she did hover in the doorway looking stiff and afraid to take another step.

"It's really wet and wild out there," she observed, eyeing the area beyond the sliding glass door warily. "I don't think we should try this tonight."

Of course, she was right. The storm continued to wage its assault. The wind was so brutal it whipped around the sheltered back of the cabin as a low howl, plastering rain through the mesh of the screen roof and walls. Subconsciously, he probably never intended to let her go out on the deck even if she wanted to do so. Probably he'd just suggested that in the hopes of getting to offer her another consolation prize.

Probably he should have a hell of a lot better control of his body for a man in his late twenties and with a vast array of sexual experience.

"Just take your steps." Chris moved out of reaching range of the door handle. "I won't even open the door."

The rigidity left Claire's stance. With a knowing smile, she took a first step toward him. "You want the consolation prize."

"I want more than that, but I'm not getting it tonight."

The naughtiness from back in the kitchen returned to her eyes. Smile wide and wanton, she quickly traveled the remainder of the steps across the room. She didn't spare a look out the door, but wrapped her arms around his middle and slid her hands to his butt.

Both her speed and her move surprised him. It clearly showed on his face, because she let out a throaty laugh and squeezed his ass. "Let the groping begin."

She dipped her head, silky brown bangs teasing along his bare chest and quickening his pulse. The soft press of her mouth connected with one of his pecs for the space of a heartbeat, just long enough to have his breath sucking in. Her lips lifted away and her own breath, warm and moist, feathered against his skin. Then her lips were back, soft again, warm again, as they closed around his nipple.

Sighing, Claire took the small nub between her teeth and tugged. Another tug, harder. This one jolting raw sensation through him, arrowing it to his loins, to his cock.

Her mouth lifted once more, moving to his other nipple on a hot puff of air. Her hands moved in succession, releasing his ass only to grab it right back up seconds later. This time beneath his boxers and sweatpants.

Her fingers curved around his naked flesh, molding to the lines of his buttocks. She used that grip to jerk his pelvis flush to hers. The flare of her hips rose up, circled, ground. She sucked his nipple back between her teeth. Gave another hard tug. And then immediately relented to her tongue.

The tip swiped, hot and damp, over the erect nub. Licked across his pecs. Zinged another current of electric sensation from his chest to his groin.

Chris grunted with the fervent bucking of his cock. The layers of their clothes weren't nearly enough to mask the feel of her pussy's greedy press. He'd all but lost his brain to his dick each time she'd reached into his lap and stroked him during dinner. With the sweet, hungry press of her cunt, his brain was attempting to go the way of his dick all over again.

He fought to think straight enough to reprimand her. "I never said naked groping."

Claire's hands pulled free of his sweatpants and her arms released from around his middle. She took a step back. But no way did he believe she was giving up.

She didn't give up. Just changed tactics by going down on her knees, with her mouth level to his crotch.

Tipping her head back, she wet her lips and flashed a vixen's grin. "You meant to." Her gaze returned to his crotch and an eager moan rolled out. "Just like you meant you wanted me to kiss your cock."

Did he want that?

Christ, what a question. Of course he did. But that didn't mean he should let it happen. It also didn't mean he was going to tell her to stop. For now, he just waited, just watched. Just stood with his muscles taut and his heart pounding nearly hard enough to beat a hole through his chest.

Tension blazed through him as she took hold of the sides of his sweatpants and dragged them and his boxers down to midthigh. She eyed his erection for long seconds, amorously, adoringly. Like it was the finest piece of meat ever set before her.

Deep blue eyes shimmering with lusty appreciation, she parted her lips and leaned forward. He held his breath waiting for her lips to close around his cock. The air nearly sucked right out of him when she bypassed his shaft to cup his balls in one hand and feed them into her mouth with the other.

Abdominal muscles clenching with the exquisite heat swelling through him and pressure skating along his spine, he watched her suckle at his balls. She was neither groping nor kissing, but then Chris had already determined he wasn't doing all that much in the way of thinking.

He was just feeling. Like he would come in her mouth the second she closed her lips around the head of his cock.

He didn't have long to wait. Another suckle of his testicles, and Claire turned her attention to his straining shaft. "Here comes the kissing."

She wasn't kidding. She also didn't go for subtle. No licks of the pre-cum gelling at the tip of his dick. No toying around with the blood-reddened head. Her mouth just closed around his shaft and sucked him deep inside the warm, wet cavern.

Feeling almost helpless against her sensual assault, he shoved his fingers into her hair. Her tongue wrapped around his rod, licking at the thickly corded vein lining the underside. Her mouth fell into a fast, furious pumping. She started to hum then. A low, sweet melody that rippled vibrations of erotic sensation throughout his groin.

Blood blistered through his veins. His thighs tensed and shuddered. On a curse, he pulled his fingers from her hair.

Now that he'd relented to a mouth job, he didn't want to come nearly so soon.

Apparently, Claire didn't want him coming yet either. Her lips pulled from his cock. Gripping a thigh with either hand, she shoved him toward the bed. Half trapped by the jeans riding midway down his legs, he stumbled a few steps and then fell back onto the mattress.

Grinning like a madwoman, she came over him. Her hips straddled his lower thighs and the ends of her hair feathered tauntingly light against his chest. Lust sparkled in her eyes as she dipped her head for another tug at his nipple. "Don't think I'm through kissing you yet."

"I'm counting on it," he returned in a rough, deep voice, and was amazed he'd gotten even that much out for how mindless she had him.

Far past time to drive her just as mindless, Chris made a grab for her arms. He intended to drag her down beneath him to grope and kiss every lithe curve, every supple valley, every straining peak of her rocking hot body.

She moved first.

Back down between his thighs, she pulled his cock between her lips for a long, lingering suck. As her mouth worked, her fingers stroked over the muscles of his torso. The femininity of her powder pink nails was almost as arousing as her teasing touch. Moving lower, her fingers traveled through the swath of his pubic curls and then closed around the root of his cock.

Pumping her lips and hand in reverse directions, Claire fell into another of those sweet, sexy hums that did him in, in a major way. Every cell in his body went on full, standing alert. The blood roared between his temples. The tension knotting at his spine was nearly unbearable, and his cock jerked in her lips with the urgent demanding need to release. Her free hand dipped to his sac, massaged the weight for a few seconds, and fondled his perineum.

Pleasure exploded like dynamite, wrapping around every inch of his body, jerking his breath out in ragged wheezes, rocketing his seed into her mouth.

Claire continued to pet his perineum as she swallowed back his cum with happy little murmurs. The suction of her mouth stilled with the last drop, and she let his cock slip free of her lips to lap at the hot flesh until his shaft went flaccid and his breathing returned to almost normal. She climbed up his body then, placing her cheek against his chest and stroking his torso with her fingertips. Before, the touch had been meant to take him higher. Now it soothed, brought him down from orgasm the rest of the way.

Made him realize what a selfish bastard he'd been.

She'd chosen to take the kissing and groping to the next level, but what kind of man left a woman wanting while he got off?

Chris slid a hand beneath her shirt and rubbed her back. "What about you?"

Her eyes—the darkest blue and filled with satisfaction—darted up to his. "You really think I spent all that time sucking your cock and didn't get off?"

He grinned guiltily. "I guess I was enjoying myself a little too much to notice."

"Good." Her gaze sobered before traveling back to his chest. He looked down to find her finger running along the scar above his heart and the hand at her back halted. Quietly, she asked, "How old were you?"

The last thing he wanted was to throw up walls that would hinder the growing trust between them. But this was one hell of a serious wall. His body tensed before he could stop it.

Thanks to Claire's wicked whims, he'd managed to forget about the conversation he'd avoided back in the kitchen. Now, all the words he hadn't said bombarded him. Somehow she was on to him. Considering that Nic had returned to the cabin before Chris could get back, that somehow—or rather some-one—wasn't too hard to guess. She couldn't know the whole of Nic's speculations, though. Not and be lying here with him, having just finished sucking his cock.

"Fifteen," he supplied, not yet sure how much he planned to reveal. Learning more would probably be worse for her healing progress. But, at the same time, if she learned of his past through Nic's half truths, there would be no *probably* about it. She would assume the worst-case scenario, as Nic intended for her to do.

"How bad?"

"Could have been fatal." Tense as he was, he felt her body go even tighter. Resuming the rub of his hand over her back, he added in a lighter voice, "It wasn't."

She relaxed a little, but just a little as she tipped back her head and looked up at him. Questions were in her eyes. Questions that guaranteed she knew something, all right. "Have you been in a lot of fights?"

"Just that one. I didn't want to be in it either but—as you well know—life doesn't always go the way we plan."

Claire's eyes narrowed. Her body regained the lost trace of tension plus some. "How *off* did yours go?"

His hand stilled again. He wanted to tell her something, needed to, but right now he couldn't think of words light enough to appease her without frightening her further.

Near-deafening thunder shook the cabin as Chris hesitated. He recalled the maelstrom raging outside and took it as the easy out he needed.

"Enough." Slipping his hand from beneath her shirt, he rolled to the side of the bed. He pulled the jeans and boxers up his thighs before offering an easy smile. "Get some sleep. I know it's early yet, but the storms around here are a lot like an aching pussy. They get wetter, not to mention louder, before they get better."

She nodded but didn't smile back. He was not exactly surprised about that, but not exactly prepared to do anything more about it tonight either, so he started for the bedroom door.

"I'd sleep better if you stayed," Claire said when he cleared the door.

Stunned by her words, he froze. How could she still want him in her bed after his nonresponse to what should have been a relatively simple question? How could he want so damned badly to go back there himself, when it would mean granting her the opportunity to probe further? "I can't."

"You *can*. You just won't."

Chris hadn't turned around, didn't want her to see how much her invitation weighed on him. Still, he could hear the taunting in her voice. Remember, when he'd spoken the same words to her. The difference was she'd tried to deny them. He didn't even attempt it. Just tossed out "You're right. I won't," and then closed up temptation behind the bedroom door.

If the person attempting to shake her awake from one of the best wet dreams of her life didn't knock it off, Claire was going to slug them. Even half-asleep and with her eyes closed, drags of fatigue pulled at her, telling her it wasn't morning. Sure as hell not yet nine.

The hands around her upper arms gave another shake. She growled at their owner. Erin. The only person it could possibly be. "G'way, 'Rin. It's not nine."

"Wake up, Claire!" A raspy voice that was far too masculine to belong to her sister snapped through her subconscious. "It's me. Chris. We need to move."

Mmm, yeah, Chris. The studilicious man of her dreams. He could put that tongue and those hands on her body any time he wanted. And that ass. Mmm hmm . . .

"Goddammit, Claire!" Fingers bit into her arms as the hands gave another shake. This one jarring, almost violent. Too violent to be a dream. "Wake the fuck up."

She jerked to full alertness with the snarling command. Opening her eyes found the bedroom lights on and Chris fully dressed and kneeling on the bed. His hands gripped her upper arms to the point of severity.

She glared at his fierce grip. "I'm up. And you're hurting me."

Relief slid through his eyes. Releasing her arms, he came to his feet beside the bed. "Sorry, but you were sleeping like the dead. If I knew how hard you were going to be to wake up, I would have moved you asleep."

Claire forgot all about the residual tingling sensation in her arms as panic clawed at her belly. She shot to a sitting position. "Moved me?" she gasped. "Where?"

"The storm's getting worse. This cabin's one of the best for the view and amenities, but it's the worst when it comes storm time. We need to go to the office. Treah lives over it. He's still not home, but he's a good friend of mine and I always stay at his place when the weather gets this severe."

The office? She hadn't seen the building but she knew for a fact that it wasn't attached to this cabin. The clawing turned to a painful roiling. Bile started to rise in the back of her throat. "What are you saying?"

Instead of responding, Chris dragged open her second dresser drawer and plucked out a sweatshirt and jeans. He threw them on the bed next to her hip. "Put those on. We're going to get drenched regardless, but at least you'll be warmer to start."

She stared down at her shorty PJ top as the words sank in. Moving to the office. Drenched.

Thunder broke through the cabin. The ceaseless hammering of rain on the roof and the thudding of something much larger registered.

Oh, God. No. No, he could not seriously be suggesting she go outside. "I can't," she whined in a tiny, pathetic voice.

Compassion flooded his face. He hurried to the side of the bed. Grabbing the sweatshirt he'd tossed her, he pulled it over her head and stuffed her arms into it like she was a rag doll.

Claire *felt* like a rag doll. Helpless again. Impotent again. With the furious way her heart was pounding and the air trapped in her throat, she didn't even know if she could move a muscle let alone dress herself.

Chris whipped back the portion of the comforter and sheets still covering her. He worked the jeans up her legs as far as he could while she was sitting, and then lifted her off the side of the bed to her feet. Her legs wobbled, gave away. She swayed to the right and squeaked out a cry.

He pulled her back against his chest, righting her as he soothed, "It's okay. I've got you."

Holding her against him with one hand, he used the other to tug the jeans up over her pajama shorts. Not bothering with the fly, he slid the jeans button into place and scooped her into his arms. Up along the solid chest she was becoming well acquainted with being held against—far too often when it felt like her sanity was walking the thin line of permanent dismissal.

"Just relax and I promise this will all be over with soon," he vowed in a rough, tender voice as he moved for the bedroom door.

The breath wheezed sharply between her lips as he cleared the door. That wheezing turned to a painful, burning screech of air when he cleared the sitting area and was partway to the front door. She realized it was no longer a matter of *if* she could move, but that she *had* to move.

Move . . . or die.

Screeching out a "No," Claire fisted her hands and pounded at his chest.

Chris's arms loosened. In the space of a heartbeat, her fear morphed from that of being forced out the door to that of being broken into pieces when she landed square on her back from five feet up.

Yelping, she threw her arms around his neck and clung for dear life. His hold on her strengthened again but not before he went down on his knees. The hard muscles of thighs pummeled against her ass. His pained-sounding grunt suggested his own body had taken even more of the brunt.

"Son of a bitch!" His fury-packed gaze bored into hers from three inches away. "I'm trying to help you, here!"

"I can't go outside!" she snapped back. "I can't even go outside on a good day without feeling like I'm going to die. This . . ." She glared at the door six feet away. Six crippling feet. Six feet that if she made it past would lead to even more feet. Even more misery. "No. No freaking way!"

Chris released a weary sigh. Taking her chin in his hand, he forced her to look at him. The fury was gone from his eyes. The compassion back, along with a silent pleading. "Listen to me, Claire. Going out there might make you feel like you're dying. But staying here could well guarantee it."

Whatever had been thudding on the roof in the bedroom slammed into the front of the cabin. Only this thing sounded bigger, like it could take out the entire wall. Like he was right. That if she stayed here, there might not be a morning for her. And then how would she ever get home to kick Erin's ass for putting her in this fucking predicament?

The truth of what she had to do lifted the bile into the back of her throat. Heat seared through her veins. She ignored both sensations to yank her chin from his hand.

Shoving herself away from his arms, she stood on legs that felt like rubber and turned her glare back on the front door. On the rain battering the windows, plastering them with more of the grit and shredded leaves that already covered them. "How could anyone be stupid enough to build a cabin so close to the water?"

"They didn't." Chris pushed to his feet. "This cabin was remodeled, along with the rest of the resort, when Treah bought the island but the original structure was built decades ago. The island's eroded a lot in that time." He moved partway to the door and held out his hand. Then he had the balls to grin in that devastating way that broke out the chin cleft. "C'mon, Claire. Treah's place has a deck, too."

Typically, his grin was devastating to the dry state of her

panties. Now, she wanted to devastate his nuts by kicking them in. "Fuck the deck."

His grin disappeared. He left his hand extended, fingers curled and urging her forward. "Okay, fuck the deck. Let me carry you out to Treah's truck, drive a few seconds, and then carry you into his home, and I'll sleep with you wherever you want."

Like he honestly thought sex would be enough to motivate her outside when all hell was unleashing. Pulling in deep breaths, Claire hugged her arms around her chest and searched for something, anything to make this unavoidable trip even a fraction less of a nightmare. She let out a huge sigh of relief with the obvious answer. "Use whatever you used to make me unconscious when you stole me from my bed Saturday night."

"You weren't unconscious. You were just in a deep sleep. Besides, I don't keep that stuff in my house."

Well, shit! The sigh sucked back in, bringing every bit of her tension back. She could no longer disregard the bile pulsing at the back of her throat or the heat spearing through her, feeling like it was burning her alive from the inside out.

Bending at the waist, she heaved out a dry gag. "I . . . I'm going . . . to puke."

"No. You are *not!*" Chris snapped. "There's no time for you to be sick. We have to get out of here, now."

Working her burning throat vigorously to keep the contents of her stomach inside, she straightened. Nodded. Searched her spinning mind for answers. There had to be some other way to make this bearable. Something . . . "Just . . . let me think for—"

"No more thoughts." In a blur of movement, his arms jerked out and yanked her against him. His mouth crashed over hers in the next heartbeat. Hard, unyielding, near crushing in intensity. His tongue pushed past her lips, waged a dark, sensual explosion. Hands slid to her ass. Cupped. Lifted her up his body. Wrapped her legs around his waist.

Pelvis rocking into hers, he ate at her mouth with need, urgency; quiet demand that was somehow screaming.

Desperate need unfurled a little more with each forceful lash of his tongue, turning her body's blistering heat into something yearning, wild. Primitive.

She fell into it. Fisted her hands in his shirt and hungrily ground her pussy against his body. Just tasted. Just explored. Just experienced.

Chris's body shifted around her. Once. Twice. His rising cock pressed against her heated sex with each move. She dug for the hem of his sweatshirt. For his hard muscles. His hot skin. Rain slashed against her back before she could make contact.

Huge, freezing bolts of rain.

Her fingers froze. Her lips and tongue stilled. The shifting of his body transmitted as what it had been. Him walking them out the door.

No. No fucking way! The bastard.

With his fierce possession, Claire had forgotten all about getting sick. The bile rose up again now. Lingered there at the back of her throat. She tried to drag her mouth from his. Tried to pound at his back so he would drop her on her ass and she could somehow scuttle inside. But he just hung on. Just kept kissing her. Just kept going.

Killing her with each step. Killing her so softly. So slowly.

The rain was suddenly gone from her back. The heat of his body left hers. His mouth left her as well and, for one heart-stopping moment, she was alone. Freezing. Scared to the point she truly believed that she would die. Then his hand returned to her, shoving between her thighs. Squeezing her pussy through her jeans.

Lust lashed through her even as she took in her surroundings. The near-black interior of a truck. A running truck. "Just hang on, sweetheart." Chris's voice piped in from somewhere to her left. "We'll be at the office in less than two minutes." The staying point of his hand left her sex. "Sorry. Tonight I need these both to drive."

Claire slammed her eyes closed as sizzling pain erupted in her head. Made her feel like she would keel over in the seat from the extreme pressure. She had to have his hand back. Had to have his touch. "No! I can't! I. Need. You."

Brakes screeched above the brutal wail of the wind. Her eyes slammed open as the truck fishtailed toward the edge of the narrow road. The headlights shone against a thick copse of trees bent at all angles from the force of the storm. A thousand fervent prayers jumbled through her head in the seconds before the skidding came to an abrupt end and the truck settled with a snap that nearly threw her against the windshield. Wearing a seat belt had been the last thing on her mind.

"Get over here!" Chris's voice rang with turbulent command.

She stared at him wide eyed. Movement at his waist had her gaze wrenching downward. His jeans rode low on his hips, the length of his erect cock sticking up from his open zipper.

"Get over here!" he growled again.

She didn't move, just continued to stare, trying to comprehend his meaning.

"Son of a bitch. Listen to me when I talk to you." His hand crossed the space between them with the order. His fingers shoved into her hair and yanked hard. She moved out of desolation, half-crawled/half-dragged across the seat.

Chris pushed her head into his lap, her face inches from his dick. "Suck it."

What? Was he nuts? Had he lost his fucking mind?

His hand pushed harder, pressed her face tight to his groin, forced her mouth against his shaft. Forced her lips to open.

She took him inside on a trembling gasp. The familiar taste of his salty flesh erupted over her mind, her senses. Her head swam again, this time with sensation. Electrically charged sensation that brought with it understanding.

"Listen to me, Claire. Listen to me and you'll survive this. We're still in my bedroom. You're still giving me a blow job. Just keep going, sweetheart. Keep your head down, remember we're still in my bedroom, and just keep sucking my cock."

Yes. She could do that. She wanted this. Wanted him.

Gripping his thigh for balance, Claire closed her eyes and let visions of his bedroom and his naked body beneath her flood her mind. His shaft pumped into her mouth as a glide of hot, savory steel against skin that was now becoming cool and clammy. Willingly, eagerly, she sank her lips farther onto his cock. His hand left her hair and his hips edged forward, driving his rod deeper, delivering his silky pre-cum into her throat. Chasing back all urge to be sick. Mixing her feelings like only he could do. Converging passion and panic until there wasn't a nerve in her body left untouched.

The truck lurched again, all but jerking her mouth from his shaft. Chris's hand returned to her hair. Her mouth did jerk free then, with the force of his tug. His arms closed around her wrists and he dragged her onto his lap.

Feeling like she was trapped in some howling, swirling fog of ecstasy, she stared at his face bathed in the dim lights of the dashboard. The strong lines of his jaw dusted with a fresh growth of stubble. The wild desire flaming in his eyes. The hot breath leaving his parted lips as hungry, hasty pants.

His mouth came closer, came over hers. Kissed her hard, savagely. Drugging. Dimly, she was aware of his body shifting. Lifting.

The rain returned. Plastering into her back as an ice-cold wash of undeniable reality.

Claire went still, hissing against his mouth as fear resurfaced as a coiling snake of panic. His hand pushed back between her thighs to palm her sex. "Just a few more steps, Claire." The words feathered against her ear as a hot caress. "A few more steps and my cock will be inside you. Filling up this sweet pussy."

He reclaimed her lips on a bruising kiss. Each jarring step he took pressed his hand against her sex, boiling her blood, blistering her soul. A lifetime of misery and rapture seemed to unfold in tandem. And then suddenly the jarring steps ended. The tangling of his tongue grew awkward as he squatted and fumbled with something behind them.

Long seconds passed before Chris's sigh flooded her mouth. His tongue returned to a knowing, needful lash. Finally, finally, the rain's tormenting pound left her back.

His lips lifted to her ear, nibbled on the lobe as he set her on her feet. Both arms came around her, holding her close when her legs felt unable to stand on their own. "We're home. You made it." He hadn't turned on a light, but she could hear his pleased grin. Past that, the same dark, primal arousal that coursed madly through her veins. "Do you have any idea how proud I am of you, sweetheart?"

His tongue stroked into the shell of her ear. Life-conforming shivers trembled through her. Real, freezing shivers quickly followed. "N-no."

One of his arms left her middle. Deft fingers moved to the hem of her drenched sweatshirt, dragging both it and her pajama top up her body and over her head. His mouth returned to hers as a warm brush that felt suddenly scalding against her icy skin.

His fingers went to her jeans. Coarse words of sensual heat and promise issued against her lips as the button slipped free. "I'm proud, Claire. And you're incredible."

7

Despite knowing Claire enjoyed a hard, fast screw just as much as he did, Chris had intended to go slow the first time they had sex. Relish each breath, each kiss. Each glide of skin against hot skin. He meant to reward her for a job well done when she met her fears head on by going out on his deck. It might have been against her will, but tonight she'd come well past his deck. She stood clinging to him just inside the darkened doorway of Treah's home, teeth chattering and her breathing ragged.

The heavy rise and fall of her breasts against his chest had nothing to do with fear. Rather, lust. Quaking anticipation as he stripped her of her jeans and panties.

Not yet sure her legs were ready to stand without support, he set her against the wall. He slipped his arm from her waist to pull his soaked sweatshirt off. Her body was pressed against his the moment the shirt cleared his head.

Arms around his middle, she rubbed her breasts against his chest so furiously it was like she was trying to burrow inside his skin. "I'm cold. So cold."

He was cold on the outside, as well. Inside, his body burned.

On the drive over, he'd only been able to half concentrate on the feel of her lips closing around his cock. Even half concentrating, and with the wickeder forces of nature at work around them, Chris had been walking the tightrope edge of climax when he pulled the truck around back of the office and into Treah's driveway. Mounting the stairs to the second-story home with his hand on her pussy and then having to screw around with fumbling the spare key into the lock had nearly done him in.

But it hadn't. He'd made it inside. Inside and on the verge of proving himself a liar in saying he wouldn't be getting more from Claire tonight than kisses and gropes. Circumstances had changed. He was getting it all and giving back as much in return.

Sliding his arms around her, he rubbed her back and butt briskly. "Cold is good. Cold I can fix."

She rose up against him, pressing her mound along the ridge of his shaft through his jeans. Her lips touched at his as a soft caress. A caress that became suddenly, demandingly hard.

"Let me in," she commanded when he didn't open his mouth against the pressure. "I need to come in."

"We're both coming in. Just give me ten seconds." Setting her against the wall again, he stepped back and pulled a condom from his jeans pocket. Just in case they got carried away during the doling out of one of her consolation prizes, he'd been carrying the rubber in his pocket since the conclusion of that first prize Sunday night.

Palming the condom, Chris worked the wet jeans and boxers down his thighs and kicked them aside. He'd left the lights off to give her time to adjust to the unfamiliar surroundings. Now, he wanted to see her in full detail. Wanted to see the heat darkening those sexy baby blues as she watched him roll the condom on. The rapture claiming her features as he bore her up against the wall and sank into her heat.

Next time.

This time, he ripped open the condom package, hurried the rubber on as fast as his nearly numb fingers would allow, and then pulled her back into his arms. She sighed with the blissful contact of skin upon cool, clammy skin. He sighed right back with the renewed brush of her nipple-hardened breasts against his chest and the provocative wriggle of her hips.

Slipping his hands into the wet silk of her hair, he found her mouth in the dark and pushed his tongue inside. Claire met him at the ready—licking, sucking, pulling at his tongue with such force it literally took his breath away.

He pulled back panting. "Getting warmer?"

Her hand slipped between them. Fingers closing around his cock, she guided his erection to her sex and rubbed the tip between her folds. "Not fast enough."

White lightning zinged through his balls, drawing them tight and hard. He couldn't feel the slickness of her pussy with the rubber on, but it didn't matter. He smelled her arousal on the air just as strong as his own, and knew she was dripping wet in a way that had nothing to do with the dousing they'd taken to and from the truck.

Groaning with that knowledge and the continual glide of her pussy along his dick, Chris took her ass into his hands. She released his shaft to wrap her arms around his neck as he lifted her up his body. They'd been in the same position, both when he carried her out to the truck and brought her up the stairs. Then, they were fully clothed with only his legs for support. Now, they were buck naked with a wall at her back.

"Hang on," he ordered in a voice as rough and ragged as he felt.

Claire's grip on his neck increased. Her hips moved against his until the head of his cock was again sliding between her folds, nudging up inside her opening. "Now!" she cried out. "Make me warmer now."

How he'd managed to put off fucking her this long was a mystery, because he couldn't resist the carnality of her low, throaty tone or the hedonism in her seeking pussy. Using the wall to its fullest advantage, he pressed her tight to it and pushed his cock deep inside her warm, welcoming body.

Sex clenching around his shaft with her elated gasp, she brought her mouth back to his. Back to that hard, demanding press. This one he opened to easily, eagerly. Parted his lips and met the hot, silky swipe of her tongue. Squeezed the cheeks of her ass and met her pistoning hips, thrust for greedy thrust.

Way in the hell too fast, Chris felt orgasm nipping at his heels. His balls pulsed and heat scorched through his groin, thundering his heart as it sizzled through his back.

Not about to get off until she did, he dipped his face to her breasts and drew an erect nipple into his mouth. He pressed the nub up against the roof of his mouth in time with the shove of his cock. Nipping her nails into his back, Claire panted out a little moan. He captured the nipple between his teeth, gave it a hard tug, the way she'd done to him earlier tonight, and turned that moan into a much bigger and louder one.

Her hips bucked hard. Her pussy squeezed. "Ah, God. Yes. I'm going to come!" Her sex gave another fierce clenching as she lived up to her vow, tight muscles milking his full-to-bursting cock. Commanding him to come along for the ride.

He went gladly. Bellowed out a moan and fell headlong into her openmouthed kiss as orgasm swept through him to rival the tempest carrying on just outside the door.

Claire slipped from his arms slowly, her body disconnecting from his in the process. He regretted that loss. Would have preferred to stay buried inside her throughout the night. She was just so warm and good. So easy to lose his thoughts and mind in the way he knew she would be from that first day.

Her mouth came back to his on a soft, teasing rub. "Thank you."

He let out a shuddering laugh with the sincerity of her tone. "Trust me, sweetheart, you aren't the only one who enjoyed yourself."

"I meant for making the trip bearable."

"You're okay now, even being in a strange place?"

"No one else is here. Are they?"

Anxiety ate at the passion in her voice, making him wish he would have kept his mouth shut about her unfamiliarity with their surroundings. But then, she would have remembered on her own as soon as he turned on the lights. "Like I said, Treah's gone. I'm not sure if his girlfriend went with him, but I haven't seen—"

The overhead lights flared to life, near blinding after spending so much time in the dark. Chris blinked against the burst of light. He caught Claire blinking, as well, before she looked over his shoulder and the breath rushed out of her on a sharp gasp.

Securing her between the wall and his body, he glanced to the light switch ten feet away. Gwen stood there, wearing a skimpy red nightshirt and a fierce glare.

"What are you doing here?" she snapped.

A whimper left Claire. Swearing, he held her even tighter and tried to forget about their naked state. "I always come up here when the weather gets this severe."

Doubt crept into Gwen's eyes. "Since when?"

"Since I moved into the head healer cabin three years ago." Something she well knew. The continued cool skepticism in her gaze seemed to suggest otherwise, and left him wondering if he'd missed the memo that all staff were supposed to act weird as shit this month.

Claire felt so loose. So languid. She felt like she'd had sex with a real, live man for the first time in over seven months.

The first and the *second* time.

Rolling onto her back, she smiled up at the bedroom ceiling.

The room was as foreign to her as the rest of the house and the office and meeting space below it. Chris's scent made it seem otherwise. His natural, familiar male scent cloaked with that revitalizing "air after the rain" smell surrounded her, clinging to the sheets and covers, soothing away any knots of tension that hadn't been erased last night.

Gwen coming upon them naked and fresh from orgasm had lifted her panic. But only long enough for the woman's glare to defer to an apologetic smile and admittance that they'd startled her, and Chris to explain her as a friend and about as harmless as they came. Claire had relaxed after that. Relaxed and let him bring her up here, to Treah's spare bedroom. And then he relaxed her some more by dragging her wrists over her head, slipping inside her body, and loving her with the tenderness he normally only showed in her moments of distress.

Sighing with the delightful twinge of far-too-long-unused muscles, Claire tossed back the covers and slid to the side of the bed. The clothes Chris had worn last night were hanging over the back of a chair at a small table similar to the one in his own bedroom. The man himself was nowhere to be seen.

Oddly, that didn't worry her. Or maybe it wasn't so odd. Maybe she really was beginning to heal, the way he'd suggested last night. Maybe he, with the aid of a past she just couldn't believe to be shady, really did hold the strength to cure her in a few weeks' time.

Or would any good he did be forgotten the second she left the resort?

Not wanting to think about that, she stood and stretched. Before, the back of the chair had blocked her view of the tabletop in front of it. Now, she saw clothes piled on its surface along with a note. Crossing to the table, she lifted the note and started to read. A high-pitched meow stopped her mid-sentence.

The noise came from somewhere behind her and sounded frantic. The same way Hot Stud cried when he got himself closed up in the apartment bathroom and couldn't get back out again. She finished scanning the rest of the note quickly, laughing—and all right, getting a little sappy—when Chris ended with a vow to be back from checking on storm damage as soon as possible with her favorite feline-covered boxers in tow.

Setting the note aside, Claire turned her thoughts back to the real feline somewhere in the near distance. Within seconds, the frantic meowing came again. She followed the sound to the wall that faced the ocean. Beige mini blinds covered the set of windows lining it. Behind the first blind, the window was sealed and locked. Behind the second one, the window was unlocked and cracked a couple inches.

Instant gooseflesh rose on her nude body as the cool draft seeped in. Shivers joined that gooseflesh as she spotted the cat out the window. Not a cat though. A calico kitten barely bigger than her hand lay on the first-floor roof overhang, an errant shingle trapping its small body in place. From six feet away, his blue gray eyes flicked to hers. He released another of those mewing wails, and her heart stuttered a beat as compassion swept through her.

He looked so helpless. So feeble.

She knew those feelings, knew that terrified gleam in his eyes. She had to help him. "Don't panic. You'll be okay. I promise."

Not sure if she'd spoken those words to the cat or herself, Claire hurried back to the table. She pulled on the gray, drawstring flannel pants and matching top on loan from Shelley—the resort manager, per the note—and then flung open the bedroom door. Someone had to be around. Someone who could help before it was too late.

If it wasn't already.

Refusing to accept that as a possibility, she charged out into the hallway and down to the next door. When pounding against it accomplished nothing, she flung it open and darted her gaze around inside. Another bedroom. This one bigger and with an attached bathroom. Probably Gwen and Treah's room. Neither of whom were inside.

Well, fuckity fuck.

Darting back out into the hall, she continued down through the living room and then the kitchen and attached dining room they'd walked through last night. No one was in any of the rooms. No one was in the whole damned house.

What about the office? Could she get to the first floor without going outside? Somewhere there had to be a stairwell, but where?

Ew! She didn't have time for this. The kitten could be dying while she dinked around because she was too afraid to go out and get him herself.

She could call Chris. Assuming he had a phone. But then, even if he did have one, she wouldn't know his number or whether his service had withstood the storm. Or, for that matter, if he was still at the cabin.

No. She couldn't call Chris. She had to do this herself. Somehow.

Heart slamming, Claire rushed back to the bedroom. To the window. To the sweet little calico kitten waiting for her to save him.

She pushed the windowpane up the rest of the way. Icy cool air breezed inside. She huffed out a hot breath and planted a hand on the roof's rough, nearly flat surface.

The kitten's eyes met hers. A pitiful mew left his mouth. Her heart turned over even as her belly clamped tight. "Hush now. It's okay, baby. I'm coming to help." She stuck a second hand on the roof. Her guts roiled and she looked out into the distance, at the waves crashing along the deserted beach, for comfort.

Too bad it didn't help.

"Oh, God. If I survive this . . ."

No. There were no "ifs" about it. She'd gotten through the storm last night. Made it all the way here from Chris's cabin. She could make it six feet out the window.

Of course, it would help if she had a cock to suck. Or maybe not, given that type of distraction would probably make her forget her purpose and have her falling off the roof.

Realizing her mind was drifting, Claire reined it back in. She sucked in a deep breath and then another, forcing herself to focus. "You can do this. Hand over hand. One inch at a time."

Breath held, she pulled herself out the window. Her knees contacted with the roof's hard surface and her breath came whooshing out on a gasp. "I'm okay. We're okay. Almost there."

The kitten meowed again, more cheerful sounding this time, almost like he was offering his encouragement. Going with that idea, because she damn well needed support, she moved gingerly along the roof. Hand over hand. Inch by inch. One breath at a time.

It felt like an hour that she was out there, moving those six feet. An hour or an eternity. Finally her fingers touched the renegade shingle's edge. She hauled the rest of her body forward on a yelp. With a low purr, the kitten lifted its head the inch of space the confining shingle's weight would allow.

Hope surged through Claire. A purr had to be a good sign. It had to mean they weren't going to die up here, together and yet still so completely alone.

Allowing only positive thoughts, she carefully lifted the shingle up and away from the kitten's prone body. He lay still for long seconds, time where she almost grew negative again, and then he came up on his paws and let out another purr.

A louder one. A happy one.

He nuzzled his little pink nose against her knee, and her heart just about melted. She remembered where they were then, and that they weren't out of danger just yet. Scooping the kitten up in one hand, she fumbled her way back to the window like a human tripod. The trip wasn't nearly so long this time. Less than a minute passed before they reached the window and moved inside.

Claire's feet touched against the carpet. Clinging to the kitten, she let out a whoop of relief and then one of pride. "We did it, buddy."

Holy Jesus, I did it!

Tears welled in her eyes as she sank trembling onto the edge of the bed and soothed the calico using Hot Stud's favorite ear-scratching technique. "You're going to be just fine now. Maybe we both are."

"I see you've met Bosco."

While she hadn't completely freaked out during the trek out the window, Chris's voice had her jerking so hard she almost fell off the bed. It definitely chased away the tears. She scowled to where he stood in the bedroom doorway. She'd planned to yell at him for scaring her, but she couldn't manage it when he wore that slow, sweet smile and looked as proud as she felt.

Had he seen what she'd done?

He came over to the bed and sat down a few inches away. "Treah found him on the beach last week. Looked like someone just left him there to die."

He had to have seen her. His smile was huge now, his eyes gleaming with happiness. Just in case that smile was for another reason and he really hadn't seen her, Claire wanted to tell him every detail. But then, part of her didn't want to tell him, too. Just in case it wasn't a sign that she was getting better.

"Treah might as well have done the same if this is how he plans to take care of him." She spoke without any true censure, because she knew Treah wasn't around to point the finger of blame at. "He was on the roof, trapped under a shingle that must have come off during last night's storm."

Chris nodded toward the open window. "You went out there?"

He didn't sound surprised. He did look even more pleased

with her, though. Pleased in a gentle sort of way that, coupled with his admiration, felt incredible, warming her through, easing away all trace of nerves, making her feel cared for and like she wasn't alone, the same way he'd done last night. Had been doing, despite her occasional snits and name-calling, since she woke up in his bed Sunday morning.

Erin tried to make her feel this way. Mom did, too, when her hectic schedule allowed for it. But neither had accomplished it with their best attempts the way he could do with what generally seemed his most simple.

An automatic smile tingled along Claire's lips. She held it at bay to shrug, as though the near miracle of going out on the roof was no big deal. "I didn't have a choice. No one else was home. I don't even know if you have a phone. I couldn't leave him to suffer."

With a look that said he knew exactly what a big deal it was, he brought his hand to her free one and squeezed. "You did great, Claire." He turned his smile on Bosco. "What about this guy? Is he okay?"

"I think so." Was *she*? It couldn't be good how impeccable his fingers felt twined with hers in such a nonsexual manner. "Probably just hungry."

"Sit tight and relax. I'll grab his food from the kitchen." Freeing her hand, Chris started to rise. He leaned over at the last moment to brush her lips with his.

Such a little kiss. Such a soft kiss. Such a tender kiss it sent frissons of sheer delight rippling through her as he made his way to the door.

Did he make all his clients feel this way? Or was there some truth to her last night's theory that he'd been jealous of her attraction to Nic?

Maybe there had been some small truth to it, but even if there had, he still probably treated all his clients the same. After all, he only got his commission if he sent women home happy and healed. A few days ago those two things seemed interchangeable. Now, she wasn't so sure. A few days ago she also thought sex and emotions could be unrelated. Now, when every smile he tossed her way had her emotions running faster, she wasn't so sure about that belief, either.

Recalling why she was in Treah's home, she asked, "Was the cabin okay?"

Chris reached the door and looked back. "Mostly. One of the trees on the beach was taken out. It took the hammock and a window with it and did some damage to the roof, so it'll be a couple days before we can move back there. In the meantime, I brought your laptop, and clothes for us both."

Another easy consideration that made her feel cared for. Another one that sighed through her, making her want to smile.

Claire did smile. Not in the silly, soft and dreamy way that wanted to creep onto her lips. But in a wide and naughty way that suggested her attention was back in her panties. "Do these clothes include my favorite feline boxers?"

His smile hitched into a playful grin. "Like I could forget them."

She couldn't forget either. Couldn't shift her mind onto sex, as she'd insinuated it was, no matter how hard she tried. Wonder over the way he made her feel, and whether he was feeling anything for her in return, still tumbled through her head when he returned with Bosco's connected metal dishes of food and water a few minutes later.

Chris nodded at the kitten on her lap. "Guess he doesn't need these, after all."

She looked down to discover the kitten had fallen asleep. So much for her vigilance. "I guess he was just tired."

"More like in the hands of an inborn nurturer."

There was that pride again, alive in his eyes and voice, making her feel just too good. "Actually, there's nothing inborn about it. I had years of experience raising Erin while Mom put in eighteen-hour days."

"And Dad?"

"Walked away long ago."

His eyes narrowed with contemplation. "That part wasn't in your file."

"I want to see it."

He set Bosco's dishes against the wall. When he straightened the reflection was gone from his eyes, replaced with heat too wickedly sensual to miss. He wiggled his eyebrows. "Lucky for you I want to show it to you."

Claire laughed as a portion of her thoughts dipped to her panties. Or rather to her sex. She hadn't had any dry underwear to put on. "I meant my file."

"I meant my jelly." With a wolfish grin, he lifted the tail of his shirt to reveal her favorite vibrator tucked halfway into his jeans pocket. "This guy was just humming for some loving."

Pulling the pink dildo out, he flicked it to shuddering life and started toward her. The remainder of her thoughts moved to her crotch with the anxious thrumming of her pussy. Apparently last night's double helping of sex had her more anxious than ever for her man-sized sex toy.

Going with that want, Claire set the kitten in the center of the bed and hurried to meet Chris halfway across the room.

He touched the vibrator's pulsing tip between her thighs. The flannel pants were thin. Without underwear on, the clit-stimulator attachment felt as though it buzzed directly against the part of her labia, awakening the bundle of nerves hidden within on an anxious flutter.

Sweeping her mouth across his, she slid her hands past his jeans and boxers and fisted the silky length of his cock. "You drive a hard bargain."

"Trust me, sweetheart, it's about to get a whole lot harder."

* * *

"A panty party? You're joking, right?" Claire's stunned question followed Chris out of the bathtub, where they'd gotten dirty before showering clean.

"No joke." He grabbed a bath towel from a short stack on the sink basin and scrubbed it over his dripping hair. He'd expected her anxiety when he suggested it was time to take her healing to the next level by attending the drinks-and-hors-d'oeuvres gathering in the meeting room downstairs. The fact that everyone would be in their underwear was supposed to be the drawing card to make the event tolerable. "There's not a much better approach to stripping away a person's fears than sticking them in a room full of people in their underwear. Besides, it ought to appeal to you."

Pulling back the shower curtain, she frowned. "Because it's kinky?"

Kink had been the last thing on his mind, but now that she was standing there in the buff, with water droplets glistening all over her lush body, kinky thoughts were gelling in short order. "Actually, I was thinking you wouldn't have to fear someone carrying a weapon since there won't be anywhere to stick one." He eyed her newly hairless mound and licked his lips exaggeratedly. "The kinky angle works, too."

Laughing, Claire stepped out of the tub and swatted his arm. She sobered as she lifted a towel from the sink basin. "My overzealous sister seems to have given you the wrong impression with her "hellcat" comment. I'll admit to loving sex and even enjoying my kink, but it's not the only thing on my mind." She bent over to twist the towel around her hair. "Even if it was, I can't go down there. I'm not ready."

With her ass plumped up with her positioning and so near to his hands, Chris gave serious consideration to forgoing the party and the need to continue his shitty attempts at the interrogation game. The lack of conviction in her voice stopped him from reaching out. "That's it," he groused.

She straightened to wrap a second towel around her body before eyeing him with a fresh frown intact. "What is 'it'?"

"Your overuse of the word 'can't.' It's officially out of your vocabulary." Dropping his towel to the tiling, he skimmed his thumb along the seal of her lips. "If I even hear it whisper across these lips, your jelly supply is gone. You *can* go down there, Claire. You can do anything you put your mind to if you focus hard enough."

"Or someone sticks a cock between my lips."

Was it any wonder he associated her with sex when things like that had a routine way of coming out of her mouth? "That might work on this island, but I can't think it's going to go over so well once you get home."

Claire moved her mouth away. Grabbing a brush from a bag of toiletries on the back of the toilet tank, she turned to face the mirror over the sink. Stiffness took her over as she pulled her hair free of its wrapping. He could see it in the reflected view of her eyes and the sharp set of her shoulder blades against the body towel's top edge.

It had to be thoughts of her inevitable trip home wearing on her. That was still over two weeks away. To him, most of the time, two weeks felt like the fourteen days it was. During his years in detention, two weeks had felt like they would last forever. Now, two weeks seemed like it would pass in a heartbeat.

It wasn't that he was falling for Claire. He just loved watching her feisty spirit engage and seeing the pride in her eyes each time she managed something she never thought she'd be able to do again, like going out on the roof to save Bosco. And, all right, it got to him that she knew something unpleasant and likely evil resided in his past and she wanted him in her arms and bed regardless.

Not wanting to think about his past now, when it was a near guarantee he'd have the displeasure of running into Nic at some point during the party, Chris took the brush from her hand. He sat down on the toilet seat and pulled her onto his lap. "I don't expect you to charge downstairs and declare yourself the center of attention." Slipping an arm around her middle, he ran the brush through her wet hair. "Shelley mostly sticks in the kitchen and helps out with the food. You can start by spending some time with her. Thank her for loaning you clothes yesterday."

He slid the hand at her waist slowly upward as he brushed. His fingers closed over a breast through her towel and she tipped her head to the side on a breathy moan. "Fine. I'll go downstairs"

"Really?"

"Yeah." The rigidity melted from her body. "I'll start with Shelley."

And finish.

Claire didn't speak the words, but when she turned on his lap to take the brush and rake its beaded ends along his chest, he could see it in her eyes.

Unfortunately for her—or fortunately, the way Chris saw things—he had other ideas, and friends to help him realize them.

8

The thought of Chris introducing her to another woman while she was wearing only underwear didn't exactly set well with Claire. She'd had him take her to the kitchen's stock entrance, which thankfully didn't involve going outside, and then go on to the panty party on his own. Before kissing her good-bye in that awesomely tender way that ate at her mind and made her think pointlessly crazy things, he'd said he expected to see her out in the meeting room within the hour. Five minutes had passed and she'd yet to budge from the stock area, so she wasn't counting on it.

She hung tight another couple minutes before working up enough bravado to move to the stock area's front entrance. A glance around the corner, into a good-sized kitchen arranged galley style, had her nearly doing a face plant into a pair of black lace–covered breasts.

Claire reeled back on a gasp, and the owner of those breasts released a short laugh. "I thought I heard someone in here." A slim, bare hand extended to her. "Hi. I'm Shelley. It's Claire, right?"

The anxious beat of Claire's heart slowed with the familiar name. Trying not to stare at the other woman's half-naked body, she met her eyes with an awkward smile. "Yeah. I'm Claire." Even doing her best to avoid it, she was infinitely aware of their state of near undress. Not a big deal if they were longtime gal pals instead of strangers. As it was, she skipped her gaze to the woman's blond ponytail to mutter, "This is weird. What am I supposed to say, nice panties?"

Shelley let out another laugh, this one ripe with understanding. "There's a reason I help to cater these things. Keeping busy in here means not having to flaunt my stuff out there." She inclined her head to a set of windowed doors twenty feet away. "These gatherings do seem to help some of the women, though, so I guess they're worth it."

"I guess." With soft brown eyes and a friendly smile, Shelley exuded warmth that had put Claire at momentary ease with the woman's last laugh. The idea anyone could peer in the windows had her anxiety riding right back up again.

"The food's already been taken out, so it's just you and me in here until it comes time to refill the platters." Shelley moved to a large, stainless steel refrigerator several feet from the stock area. She opened the door and pulled out a glass pitcher of something froufrou pink. "Do you drink?"

Back when Claire had been attending various social events as a staff reporter for the *Herald*, having a drink now and again had been like part of her job. But lately, holed up alone in her apartment, she'd mostly avoided drinking for fear its thought-numbing effects could become an ugly habit. "Sometimes."

Shelley set the pitcher onto the counter that butted up against the fridge. She grabbed two clear plastic cups from a stack at the back of the counter and poured the pink drink into each. "Try this."

Warily, Claire eyed the drink Shelley pushed her way. "What is it?"

"Courage in a plastic cup." Shelley took a drink from her own cup. "It's really good and has zero side effects come morning."

Like the natural sedative Chris administered to her Sunday night? If it was, then she had a complaint. The sedative had one big side effect. It forced her into cohabitating with a man she wanted to leave behind a little less each day. She still believed he cared about her well-being, the way she'd perceived yesterday, but he couldn't care about her beyond that. Not when he'd sounded so detached when he talked about the time when she would return to the mainland.

Claire picked up the offered cup and took a long drink. For one, she loved the froufrou shade. Second, Shelley was drinking it so it really did have to be safe. Third, she needed courage outside of her own if she was going to join the panty party.

The refreshing twist of raspberry and something snappy popped on her tongue in a totally tasty way. She took another drink before smiling at Shelley. "Wow, this is really good."

"Addictively." Cup in hand, Shelley started for the double doors. "C'mon, let's check out the view."

Claire took another drink and then followed the blonde—not quite to the doors but close enough if she leaned forward, she could probably see out.

"There's Nic," Shelley observed with a note of female appreciation.

"Then it's safe to assume Chris isn't anywhere nearby."

Shelley glanced back, surprise in her eyes. "Chris told you about their ongoing clash?"

"Sort of. Nic shared his client with me for a couple hours on Wednesday. When he came by the cabin to pick her up, Chris was gone and Nic said some stuff. Then when Chris got home and speculated on what Nic had told me about him, he said some stuff of his own."

Myriad emotions crossed Shelley's face before she focused

back out the window. "Sometimes Nic can be a real charmer. And then he can be a complete ass."

"I'm sure his current client isn't helping the situation."

"What do you mean?"

"She's a nympho who came to the island in the hopes of getting over the issues that made her that way. Only, now that she's here, she's taking great pleasure in trying to taunt Nic into bed. So far, he's done all that he can to resist."

Shelley's eyebrows rose. "Nic resisting a nympho? I don't buy it."

Maybe not, but the hope in Shelley's eyes made it clear she wanted to. Did she have the hots for Nic, or was there more to it than that? "I got the information from the woman herself."

"He had first pick from the clientele this month. I just can't see him taking on a woman who's trying to give up sex. I'd much easier believe that it's his past coming into play, making him jerk Chris around."

Claire forgot her wondering about Shelley's relationship with Nic at the mention of Chris. In the hopes of learning more on his past, she risked moving the rest of the way to the door. Whatever was in her cup was doing its job. The idea of people peering in at her through the double windows barely even riled her.

Pretending to observe the scantily clad partygoers, Claire said, "I didn't realize he and Chris had a similar past."

"I don't know that they do." Curiosity entered Shelley's eyes. "Chris told you about his past?"

"I asked about the scar over his heart. From there one thing led to another."

"Interesting. I had to learn about his past from someone else, and we've been friends for years. Maybe he just needed to get it off his chest and you were convenient."

Well, crap. So much for learning more about him. Claire drowned her disappointment in a cup-draining drink.

"Or maybe he really cares about you and doesn't want any secrets to emerge and ruin things."

Claire sputtered as the last of the froufrou drink went down the wrong way. She'd already determined Chris didn't care about more than her well-being. She was just another client to him. Wasn't she? "Has he cared about—"

"Didn't anyone ever tell you two that wallflowers have less fun?" a familiar female voice questioned.

Claire glanced over her shoulder to see Gwen standing behind her in screaming red lingerie that left next to nothing to the imagination. The woman had obviously slipped in the back way. She also obviously wasn't nearly as nice as Chris had led Claire to believe. Laughing debauchedly, Gwen planted her hand in the center of Claire's back and shoved her out the door into the meeting room.

The plastic cup flew from her hand. The air gasped out of her throat. She worked her feet double time to keep from doing a face plant. Coming to a jolting standstill, she surveyed her surroundings. Bluesy music drifted in the air along with the mixed scents of Cajun-themed hors d'oeuvres. The room itself was dimly lit; the people who occupied it a little fuzzy looking.

From panic? Or from the drink Shelley gave her?

Claire didn't feel panicked in the body-consuming way this scenario warranted, so maybe it was the drink.

Dawn's familiar face swam into view near the wall a couple dozen feet away. Claire latched on to it, for now deciding to be happy she wasn't spazzing out for whatever reason. Nic stood beside the short, stacked redhead, his olive skin and tall, muscled physique remarkable in black silk boxers. Probably going over to them wouldn't thrill Chris. But then, she'd been brought to Ecstasy to get better. Not make a guy "really care" for her, even if the idea had her heart pounding and her palms sweaty.

Or maybe that was the drink. Or the panic.

Concentrating on placing one foot in front of the other, Claire started toward Dawn and Nic. She reached the halfway point and was in the process of giving herself a mental "atta girl" when a hand grabbed hold of hers and jerked her around.

Her pulse quickened. The breath rushed out of her once again. Chris was standing a foot away. His face was picture perfect, as was the return of his silly white-and-navy cat boxers and his beam of satisfaction.

He squeezed her hand. "Look at you. Mingling."

Heat danced up her arm and her sex warmed in turn. What was it about his smile that always got to her? That even now, in this room full of strangers, made her want to lean forward and lick the exposed cleft in his chin? "I wasn't mingling. I was pushed out here."

"Still, you're out here. And you're eager to dance."

She eyed the handful of couples moving in time with the smoky blues rhythm on the far side of the room. That half was darker, lit only by a few tapered candles and the dim light encroaching from this half. Darkness could be a friend that would relax her even further, or a bitter enemy that could panic her in spades.

Chris didn't give her a choice to decide which, but took her silence for agreement and pulled her across the room.

In the circle of his arms, she felt a strange sort of unity—liberation from her fears and vulnerability to know they still existed even if she wasn't much aware of them right now. She also felt the press of his cock cradled against her mound. Blame whatever it was Shelley had given her to drink, but her sex went from warm to pulsing with hungry, horny want.

Claire tipped back her head, feeling the swipe of her hair against her shoulders as she eyed him accusingly. "You lied."

He frowned. "About what?"

"When you said there wouldn't be any weapons at this party." Sliding a hand between them, she grabbed his shaft through his boxers and gave it a long, leisurely fondle. "Sure feels like you're packing to me."

His cock went near instantly hard, jerking against her fingertips with his grunt. "Keep up the stroking and I'll be going off."

"Going to share your jelly with the whole resort, huh?"

"You make that happen and you'll be sharing your naked ass with the whole resort when I throw you over my lap and paddle it."

Mmm . . . Now, that sounded good. Daring. More than she should be able to handle. Yet it wasn't, going by her wet, quaking pussy. "Is that acceptable?"

"You tell me."

"I mean do you guys end your panty party by segueing into an orgy?"

"Never have before." The panty-evaporating leer appeared, and the hand at her back came down to pet her ass. "But I'd be willing to start a new tradition."

Chris was pleased to see Shelley's mystery drink—seltzer water blended with fresh raspberries—affected Claire the way he'd hoped it would, making her believe she had liquid courage coursing through her veins when in truth she was just focusing on something other than her fear enough to operate under her own strength. Gwen's shove had also played out well, looking so natural he would have guessed she'd have wanted to do it even if he hadn't asked her to. What pleased him more than anything, though, was the anxious heat in Claire's eyes.

Technically, pleased was too mild to describe the way her bold, explorative fingers had him feeling. In the near blackness, with the crush of their barely clothed bodies masking her hand, it was doubtful that anyone knew she was stroking his cock. Even so, the exhibitionist possibility had his blood spiking hot and his dick rock solid.

He slid the hand at her ass to her back, turning her a bit, as he brushed his mouth along her ear. "See that corner?"

She followed his gaze to the corner fifteen feet away. "It's dark."

The chairs that had been removed from the floor to make room for dancing were stacked to one side and the tables leaned up against the wall a few feet away. Those few feet made for the perfect place for a fuck. Probably, no one would even realize they were doing anything more than kissing with the potential for a little heavy petting. That the extent of their actions *could* be discovered was all it would take to prove she was past the point of fear at least where inside gatherings were concerned.

"Dark enough." Chris lifted her hand from his cock and twined their fingers together. Covering the bulge of his erection as discreetly as possible with his other hand, he guided her to the corner.

Claire settled against the wall, giving him just enough time to place the flat of his palms on the wall around her, before pushing her fingers into the opening at the front of the tacky cat boxers and pulling out his shaft.

She pressed her mouth to his, her lips a hot, moist seal, as she thumbed the fluid leaking from the tip of his cock. Her fingernail flicked against the hypersensitive eye. Red-hot sensation whipping through his groin, he pressed a guttural moan against her mouth. Her lips parted, gobbling up the sound before her tongue pushed into his mouth and slipped against his own tongue. Stroking his torso with her free hand, she kissed him first light and easy, then hard and forceful before letting up entirely.

She moved her head back a few inches to look up at him. And, damn, what a sight she made. Thick lashes half lowered with lust. Full breasts rising and falling against the dark blue of her bra. Stunning face and body masked in shadows and still so incredibly on display.

His blood fired hotter and his shaft jumped against her touch. With a dirty-girl smile fit for *Penthouse*, Claire moved aside the crotch of her panties and stroked the head of his dick against her bare slit.

"I used to love having sex in public." The confession came with the damp flick of her tongue against his chin.

Leaving one hand against the wall for support, Chris curled the other around her hip. "You're about to again." He impaled her mouth with his tongue, intending to do the same with his cock in her sex. The press of her hot, wet pussy against the head of his shaft stopped him dead. He ended the kiss on a grimace. "Or not."

"Definitely do." She wrapped her arms around his neck and encouraged him with the rub of her breasts against his chest. "There's something magical working through my veins tonight and I'm not about to let it slip by without taking advantage."

"I don't want that to happen either, sweetheart, but I don't have a condom."

The X-rated smile disappeared. She leaned to the side, scanning the whole of the meeting room. Her smile returned with carnal promise. "You worry about getting me off. I'll worry about where you go off."

Chris had no idea what she'd seen during her scan. But he knew that wasn't an invitation his throbbing cock had plans to resist. Slanting his mouth back over hers, he pushed his tongue between her lips in time with the shove of his hips. Her eyes widened and she gasped into his mouth as his dick slipped inside her bare, open body.

All that heat, all that silky tissue. Rarely had he screwed without a rubber—never in recent years—and he wanted to keep on pushing to her womb.

But he could get just so deep the way they were standing, and he wasn't sure she would go for it if he lifted her up his body the way he had two nights ago when they'd been upstairs, in supposed privacy. Their actions would be overt with her legs wrapped around his waist, ankles locked, and his ass pumping hard.

Claire's arms moved from his neck to his back, roping around him tight. She yanked him forward as she arched her hips toward him. He slipped that much deeper into her sheath. Deep enough he broke the kiss to grit his teeth against the pressure hardening his balls and cording the tendons in his neck and thighs. Still, it wasn't deep enough for where he wanted to be.

Later, he'd get that deep.

Now, Chris took what he could get, lifting his hand from the wall to drag down one of the cups of her bra just past her areola. He took the erect nipple between his fingers, rolling, tugging, pulling with each of his thrusts until her mouth opened into an O. Tepid air cruised against his chest. Her pussy went glove tight around his cock.

He bit her lower lip gently and then pushed his tongue back into her mouth with a commanding stab. She came hard and suddenly, eyes flaring wide and breath feathering hot and jerky into his mouth. His blood pounded and his cock shuddered, more as her juices flooded around him, making for a slippery, sexy ride that would have been incredible at any level of penetration.

Gripping her hips with both hands, he increased the rhythm of body and mouth. Pleasure coiled deep in his belly, built into a blazing inferno in his groin, lashed through his body and into his soul as orgasm crashed down upon him.

Claire jerked his cock free of her pussy at the last second. She went down on her knees, hands gripping the cheeks of his ass through his boxers as her mouth closed around his length. She sucked back his salty fluid while her tongue swiped greedily, hungrily, like she didn't care who witnessed her taking down his cum.

She might not care, but suddenly he wasn't all that keen on it. Not with the idea that the voyeur could be Nic. Chris had exchanged stares with the guy a few times as he made his way around the room, chatting up coworkers in an attempt to learn at least something useful before Treah returned to the island. But they hadn't exchanged words and he could just see the bastard coming over now and spilling everything he thought he knew about Chris for Claire and everyone else to hear.

The instant the last of his cum drained from his body, he pulled her to her feet. He took her mouth in a ravenous kiss, tasting his seed and the sweet nip of raspberry on her tongue, before covering up the nipple he'd exposed and setting her back against the wall. He smiled like a man well sated. "Not that I'm complaining, but you just upped the odds of people guessing what we were doing by about 100 percent."

"Good." Even in the near blackness her eyes sparkled with wicked thrill as she wrapped her fingers back around his shaft. "Since that was the idea."

Against the desire to stay spooned against Claire's warm, naked, sleeping body, Chris climbed from bed with the abrupt knocking on the bedroom door. She'd been great last night. Stayed strong even after they returned to the better lit area of the meeting room to a number of speculative glances. He was proud as hell of her progress and wanted to spend the morning continuing her healing trend by convincing her to go out on Treah's deck. Which he could get started on just as soon as he got rid of whoever was on the other side of the door.

Opening the door a couple inches, he camouflaged his nudity behind it as he peered into the hallway. Gwen stood there, a catty smile curving her vivid red lips. "Am I interrupting something, or do you two only screw with an audience?"

Automatic defense shot to Chris's lips. He kept the words inside to say calmly, "We were sleeping. Just a second." Closing the door, he pulled on a pair of boxers and then slipped out of the room. "What's going on?"

"Treah got in late last night." Her smile went cattier with the narrowing of her eyes. "He's in his office and demanding to see you."

Demanding? Had more money gone missing while Treah was away and he blamed Gwen for it, or what was going on to have her acting so bitchy? "All right. Tell him I'll be down in ten minutes."

Gwen left with a huff and a glare about as uncharacteristic as it got. His mind racing with wonder, Chris moved back inside the bedroom to pull on jeans and a sweatshirt. He was heading out the door for the bathroom down the hall when the sheets rustled behind him.

"Leaving me?" Claire asked in a sleepy, sexy voice.

Hand on the doorknob, he turned around only to wish that he hadn't. She sat in bed, her dark hair mussed captivatingly and the sheets and covers pooled at her waist to reveal her nude upper half. Atop those full, stunning breasts, her nipples peaked and arousal stirred in his groin.

He'd slept with some of his past clients—as he'd told her that first day—but only once or twice throughout the duration of their stay and, almost always, because doing so lent itself to the healing process. Claire he couldn't get enough of. And he hadn't exactly been thinking of the recluse issue that brought her to Ecstasy when they'd tumbled into bed last night, tearing off each other's underwear along the way.

Chris wasn't exactly thinking about it now either, as he brought his attention to the soft press of her lips.

Hell, he wanted to kiss her. Taste those lips as they welcomed him to a new day. Let her reap consolation prizes for whatever she damn well pleased for the next eight or nine hours.

He closed the bedroom door in case anyone happened to be

walking by but otherwise stood his ground. "Treah's back. He called me to his office."

Unease passed through her eyes. "To kick us out of his house?"

"No. Like I said, we're good friends and more than welcome here. There's a problem employee he wanted me to keep tabs on while he was away. He's probably after a status report."

The unease turned to interest. "Nic?"

"Could be. We know there's a problem person but haven't quite narrowed it down to whom it is yet." He also shouldn't be discussing any of this with her. The thing was it felt good sharing at least a portion of his stress. At the same time, it made him remember the other reason for it. Nic hadn't approached them last night, but the odds were favorable he would soon. Chris's gut tightened with the knowledge that he had to give Claire some glimpse at his past ASAP, before the guy dropped a fabricated bomb that left no room for her to still consider him a good guy worthy of her trust.

"Is something going on with him and Shelley?"

The tension in his gut let up with his laughter. "Not a chance. She's way too smart to get wrapped up with that dick." He sobered to say, "I should be back in a half hour or so. I was thinking about some deck time when I return."

"Oh. Maybe." Anxiety edged into her eyes and had her sitting a little stiffer. She didn't appear ready to either throw up or beat the hell out of him, though, the way she would have just a few days ago.

Maybe that threat to take away his jelly the next time she used the word "can't" had worked. Or maybe, in the morning light, she realized she hadn't been drunk last night, but stone sober and doing what her body craved instead of what she was too afraid to attempt.

Whatever the reason, it gave Chris hope that before she left the island, she would be cured in full. Ready to face the world again, take back the high-ranking reporter position she used to have with the newspaper. Have a male other than Hot Stud to occupy her time and her bed.

That last thought returned the tightness to his gut. After all, what man liked to think of his lover's future sex partners?

Telling himself he would leave Claire with plenty for other men to live up to, he crossed to the bed for a quick kiss. She grabbed hold of his sweatshirt as he bent over, taking him off guard and jerking him down on top of her.

Her legs spread, embracing his lower half as their tongues met, fusing in a kiss way hotter than he'd intended and way, way hotter than his cock could handle and still remain flaccid. Moaning, she wriggled her pelvis against his and moved her hands beneath his shirt to caress his torso. Sliding his palms up the soft skin of her belly and beyond, he took her breasts in hand, massaging the heavy globes as their tongues continued the reckless dance and his heart beat a wild stampede.

He's in his office and demanding to see you.

Gwen's words and the catty look in her eyes surfaced. Swearing to himself, Chris lifted his hands and mouth away from the sweetest and sexiest of temptations. Backing away from the cradle of Claire's thighs and off the bed, he came to his feet, just a bit shaky and just a whole lot hard and just wanting to say to hell with Treah for the rest of the morning.

Since he couldn't do that, he returned to the head of the bed. He brought his mouth back to hers for the quick, brushing kiss he'd first intended and then straightened again with a smile. "Keep that thought."

She returned his smile with an eager one of her own. "I'll be right here waiting for you."

Christ, that sounded just too good.

Flushing the words from his mind, he went to the door. He closed it behind him and headed for the first floor, using the outside stairwell so the crisp morning air could work its way over his heated body.

Breathing easier and with his cock mostly relaxed, he stepped into the receptionist area outside of Treah's office a few minutes later. Gwen was nowhere to be found so he went ahead and knocked on Treah's door. An invitation to come inside mumbled from the other side. He pushed open the door to find Treah standing with his back to him, staring out the glass patio door on the other side of the office. Gwen occupied one of the visitor chairs in front of Treah's desk.

Chris crossed to the desk. He pulled out the chair next to Gwen's, turned it around, and straddled the back. As was true when he'd walked into Treah's office just over a week ago, he could feel the atypical tension rising off the other man from ten feet away.

Had more money gone missing, then?

When Treah continued to stand silent at the window, Chris glanced over at Gwen for answers. She sat facing him, wearing that same bitchy look she'd had outside the bedroom. What was she doing in here anyway? Treah and he had shared plenty of shitty moments and never needed a chaperone before.

He looked back at Treah. "How'd the opening go?"

Treah hesitated another few seconds before turning around with a folded piece of paper gripped in his right hand. Patchy black stubble dusted his jawline and upper lip, and dark circles rimmed the underside of his eyes. "The trip was fine."

"You going for fucked up, insecure, neurotic, and emotional with that? Or why do you look like hell?"

"I haven't slept since yesterday." The words came out gravelly as Treah sank down in the chair behind his desk. His gaze skipped to the paper clenched in his hand. "Gwen's discovered more money is missing than we first realized."

Chris eyed the paper. Treah never backed down from a battle. He sure as hell never looked away from Chris when doling out bad news. Unless it was so bad he couldn't stomach the thought of looking at him when he shared it. "Sorry to hear that, man. I did get a couple potential leads, but for the most part I can't play the spy for shit."

"Might help if you looked in a mirror," Gwen bit out.

He looked over at her again. Now, she wasn't just eyeing him bitchily. Now, she sat cross-armed, scowling down her nose at him like he was the equivalent of shit.

Or maybe a murderer.

Is that what this was about? Had Nic not bothered with dropping a bomb on Claire last night because he'd been too busy filling up Gwen's ears? Even if Nic had tried to convince her of the worst, he couldn't see Treah not clearing things up.

"What are you getting at?" Chris tried to keep the defense from his voice, but his tone still rang hard and guilty.

"This came for you," Treah said in a low, rough way so far removed from the easygoing man that Chris knew it roiled his gut.

He looked across the desk to find Treah holding the folded paper out to him. What could be on it to have them both acting so off? "What is it?"

"Evidence," Gwen supplied shortly.

"It's a letter that came for you yesterday," Treah said. "It came to the business address and Gwen opened it by mistake."

Aware whatever awaited him inside had to be damning, Chris unfolded the sheet and scanned the words within. They made no sense. Christ, he'd never even heard of the woman who'd written the letter. There was no way he could have deposited his sperm in her to make the baby she was claiming as his and requesting child support immediately unless he wanted to reacquaint himself with the criminal side of the justice system.

Money. Thousands of dollars. Like the bundle of cash that had so recently disappeared from the resort's accounting system.

Fury cruising through him with the implication, he looked

from Treah to Gwen, then back to Treah. "Is this supposed to be a joke?"

"Do we look like we're laughing?" Gwen clipped.

No. They didn't look like they were laughing. They looked like they believed every word. Even Treah, who he thought considered him as close to a brother as he had these days believed he'd stolen the money. "Then it's a big goddamned lie."

"Are you sure?" Treah pressed.

"Shit, yeah, I'm sure." Chris shot to his feet, sending his chair skittering backward. He waved the letter. "This woman claims to be from California. When the hell would have I gotten there? In the last three years, I've been off the island twice for more than a few hours at a time. When my dad passed away, and then when you had me fly down to the Pacific location to help train the new healing coaches two months ago."

"What about your tracks on my computer?" Gwen sneered. "I had it looked into. Your information's all over the back end."

Chris snorted. "You're nuts if you think I hacked into your system. I barely even know how to work the Internet."

"Then you won't mind if someone looks into your bank accounts?"

"Someone wants to invade my privacy so damn bad, let them."

"No one's looking into your bank accounts," Treah said in a relatively calm voice. "Just . . . figure it out, Chris. Give her a reason to believe you."

Treah's voice might be mostly sedate, but his eyes held the cutting edge of betrayal. Well, guess what? He wasn't the only one feeling sold out.

All these years Chris had felt indebted to Treah for giving him a life and a job when the odds of anyone else doing so were next to nil. All these years he'd considered the man his family after his blood family cast him out as an unforgivable sinner and cut off all ties. All for nothing, because the moment things got ugly, the even uglier truth of how Treah really felt reared its head and gnashed its bitchy teeth.

"You mean you, right?" he snarled. "Give *you* a reason to believe that I'm not guilty. After all, what would a little theft to appease the mother of my bastard baby bother me when I've already got two deaths on my hands?"

9

Claire sucked in a breath and prepared to face what could well be her demise.

Okay, so she didn't really think Shelley would let her step outside the meeting room's beachside door, be swallowed up by panic, and tip over in a lifeless heap. Not after they'd spent the last hours sharing lunch in her office, chatting and drooling—Claire drooled, at least—over the room's turn-of-the-century furnishings. And, too, they'd seen each other in their bras and panties and shared froufrou cocktails. Shelley couldn't possibly let her die after that.

"Ready?" Shelley asked, gripping the screen door's handle.

Claire nodded, and the blonde pushed open the door and stepped out onto the sidewalk. Holding the door open, she smiled encouragingly. "You can do this, Claire."

Pulse thrumming and tension knotting in her shoulders, Claire moved to the inside edge of the doorway. She pulled in a breath, sucking back the salt air like a long-lost friend, as she took in the view, for once not obstructed by either glass or mesh.

It was still cool, in the low sixties, but the breeze was nearly nonexistent and the early afternoon sun shone on the beach, undoubtedly warming the sand she'd always loved feeling between her toes. A hundred or so feet ahead, gulls played along the water's edge. Beyond that, four large white and green cabin cruiser boats bobbed at twin wood docks. She'd always loved boating, as well.

Thanks to Chris pushing her when she could have so easily succumbed to her fears, and successfully battling her anxiety to save Bosco from the roof, she'd already come far with her healing. Truthfully, farther than she'd believed possible. Maybe one day she would get out on a boat again. Or, more precisely, get out on a boat again when she wasn't under the influence of a sedative-induced sleep. One day soon . . .

For now, she needed to fortify her courage and withstand this trip outside. Chris might not "really care" about her the way Shelley had guesstimated, but he at least liked and trusted her enough to recount what happened in Treah's office yesterday morning. Claire might not "really care" about him either, but she knew and liked him enough that he didn't have to tell her how badly the accusations stung for her to feel his pain. And he didn't have to tell her the only reason they were still sleeping under Treah's roof was because he didn't want to force her into making the ride back to either his nearly repaired cabin or Shelley's place, where she'd offered to let them crash.

As he'd done yesterday, Chris was spending the morning and afternoon helping to finalize his cabin's roof repairs. By tomorrow, the repairs would be complete and Claire was determined to see they were moved back in.

"Here goes nothing." Hoping that "nothing" didn't turn out to be her lunch, she held her breath and lifted a sneakered foot that felt like it was made of lead.

"Wait!" Shelley cried. "I have to tell you something."

Claire slapped her foot back to the floor to eye the other

woman. Only half joking, she asked, "Is it one of those things you tell people when they're on their deathbed because you know they'll never be able to repeat it?"

"You will be absolutely fine," Shelley admonished with a laugh. "But, no, it's not one of those things. It's about the other night at the panty party."

In case Shelley planned to broach that whole "really caring" thing again, Claire said quickly, "About your feelings for Nic?"

Shelley's brown eyes went wide. "Why would you think I have feelings for Nic? Like I said, he's an ass."

Claire smiled knowingly. She'd had a lot of free time the last couple days. Part of it she'd filled with work for the *Herald* and dropping Erin an e-mail to check in on Hot Stud and remind her sister she still wasn't happy with her—even if the trip was going far better than imagined. The rest of the time she'd spent thinking—about her life, Chris's life. Shelley's life and how Nic might fit into it. "Actually you said he was an ass *and* a charmer. Then there was how obviously bad you wanted to believe he wasn't sleeping with Dawn, his nympho client."

"Yeah, well . . . he's a lost cause. He's also not what I wanted to talk to you about. It's about the drink I gave you."

Claire lost her smile. "What about it?"

"It wasn't alcoholic," Shelley admitted sheepishly. "Just a berry and seltzer mix I like. Chris asked me to make you believe otherwise so you'd think you had liquid courage and not fear your fears, so to speak. But you didn't have liquid courage, Claire. Everything you did was under your own strength. He planned to tell you himself but—"

"Shit happened," Claire supplied, even as her thoughts raced back to two nights previous. Back to the way she'd danced with Chris in a room filled with people. To the way she'd thrown caution to the wind to go down on her knees and swallow his cum in the darkened corner of that same room.

If he wasn't already so upset, she might be pissed at him.

Since he was already so upset, and she could see how well his plan worked, she wasn't pissed. Rather, she was more determined than ever to make this trip outside successful.

"Yeah, shit happened. The point is you can do this." Shelley regained her encouraging smile. "Just remember, a few small steps today means getting to salivate over my cabin full of antiques tomorrow."

Claire didn't need the added benefit of a visit to Shelley's home to make her take that first step onto the sidewalk, but it didn't exactly hurt matters either.

After washing away the sweat and grime accrued while finishing up the cabin repairs, Chris returned to the bedroom to find Claire sitting cross-legged on the end of the bed. Her smile held a teasing edge that typically he would be a sucker for. The last couple days he'd been too frustrated with too many people to be a sucker for her smile, or most any other part of her body.

Since he couldn't ignore her, he dropped his dirty clothes into the paper bag that was serving as their temporary hamper, then continued over to the bed. He sat down a foot away. "Something on your mind?"

"Mmm hmm. A game. You up to playing?"

No. But again he couldn't just ignore her because accusations made by others were riding his ass to the point he hadn't slept more than a few hours since they'd been flung his way. "Sure."

"If you win, I go out on the deck."

Chris raised an eyebrow with the unexpected stakes. He'd never gotten around to following through on his plan to get her outside. That she was volunteering to go out on the deck had to be a good thing. Then again, maybe not. "What about if you win?"

Claire's smile dipped away. "You tell me about the evil in your past."

Yeah, maybe not, considering he hadn't gotten around to telling her anything more on that either. "What's the game?"

"To see who can get out on the deck the fastest."

What the hell . . . ? "Am I missing something here?"

Coming to her feet, she taunted, "What's the matter, afraid you'll lose?"

"Hoping," he corrected, because he wanted to believe she was so far along in her healing, she would breeze out onto the deck. Only, the longer his response lingered between them, the more he wondered if he wasn't hoping she'd win for another reason, as well. He hadn't told her everything that happened in Treah's office, but she'd taken his side in a heartbeat over the stuff he had told her. He wanted to tell her more.

Hell, he wanted to tell her everything, Chris acknowledged. Ached with the need to get it off his chest. Would she turn away from him after that? Her first day on the island, he would have been certain that answer was an unequivocal yes. Now, he wasn't so sure and he suddenly had to find out.

He slid to his feet and nodded at the door. "On your mark."

Amusement glimmered in Claire's eyes as she stood from the bed. "Get set."

"Go!" they shouted in unison.

He watched her dart out of the bedroom. Apparently, he wasn't completely frustrated anymore, because he appreciated the enticing way her ass bobbed as she ran. After giving her a few seconds head start, he hurried down the hallway. The deck branched off from the living room through a set of double hardwood and glass–encased doors. Those doors were already open and Claire was already standing on the deck, grinning like she'd taken Olympic gold.

He grinned back automatically. The warmth of pride swept through him as he moved out onto the deck and pulled her into his arms. She was breathing fast, but whether from the short run, the fact she was outside, or the needful way he dropped his mouth to hers and kissed her long and hard was anybody's guess.

Lifting from her lips, he accused, "You've been practicing."

"Not on the deck but outside the meeting room with Shelley's help." She slid her arms around his waist and hugged him. "I was wrong that first day. You *can* cure me. I'm already so much better, Chris, and it's all because of you."

He sighed with the goodness of those words. Between the pleasure she brought to his body and the balm with which she soothed his frayed nerves, he could so easily become addicted to this woman. It wasn't something he'd ever planned to do. He hadn't thought any woman could be truly interested in him if they knew of his past. But maybe time had changed that. Or maybe Claire was just different from most women. Maybe it was okay to be addicted to her.

Maybe, if he didn't hold a job that strictly forbade real relationships.

Not trusting himself to respond to her compliment, Chris slid his arms from around her and stepped back from her own. "Does Shelley seem depressed to you?"

Disappointment flickered over her face with his withdrawal. She let it go to respond. "You mean about putting her two weeks' in?"

"Yeah. Did she say why she's quitting?"

"Too much testosterone. Frankly, I don't know how she's lasted this long with Gwen the only other woman here full time."

The mention of Gwen raised his hackles. He ignored the sensation to study Claire's face. She wasn't telling him something. "There's more to it, isn't there?"

"Yes. But nothing that affects you in any way. Nothing bad." Her eyes narrowed. "Nothing like feeding me a nonalcoholic drink, then letting me act like I'm operating under the influence of liquid courage."

Ah, hell, Shell. Way to blab. "I planned to tell you about that the next morning. Then Treah called me into his office—"

"I know." The narrowing of her eyes let up with her saucy smile. "As I recall, we were both left feeling very happy for that little lie."

Feeling safe with the topic of sex, Chris moved a step forward and pulled her back into his arms. He ground his hips against hers. "We could be happy again."

Claire pushed her pelvis into his, throwing in a bump and grind maneuver that brought to mind thoughts of stripteases. "We could." She tipped back her head to brush his lips with a feather-light touch of her own. "And will." Her mouth returned, pressing a bit harder this time. "Right after you pay up."

He winced with the reminder of what her coming out on the deck had cost him. Damn, he'd been starting to enjoy himself, too. His cock was semihard and his mouth anxious for a whole lot more than her teasing touches. "I actually planned to tell you some of my past the other morning, as well."

"You should have. Waiting a few days means paying the penalty of not withholding details."

Chris's stomach clenched with the thought of telling her the whole sordid story.

Lowering his mouth to hers, he brushed her lips in the same simple fashion she'd done to him. He didn't stop with that brush, though, but peppered her lips with little kisses until her mouth parted on a sweet sigh and he swept his tongue inside to move against hers in a warm, slow, decadent dance.

He lifted his mouth away to find her eyes had drifted closed. Opening them on a blissful murmur, she smiled. "What was that for?"

"Just in case you don't want to touch me again after hearing what I have to say."

Her smile went reassuring. "I trust you, Chris. No matter what happened before, I know you're a good guy now."

No matter what, though—really?

It didn't appear anyone else was within earshot. Even so, he wasn't about to risk someone overhearing the impending conversation. Taking her hand, he guided Claire back into the house and down the hall to their temporary bedroom. Now that the cabin was fixed and she was making great progress, they could get out of this house where he'd come to feel like both a criminal and an intruder.

Chris planned to stay in it tonight in the hopes of getting lucky.

Not with sex, though he would be a liar if he said that hope wasn't there, too, but by watching over the office area the way he'd done the last several nights.

Claire settled on the bed with her back to the headboard. He couldn't stomach the thought of sitting still while he talked, so he closed the bedroom door and paced around the room. "What did Nic tell you that day he came to collect Dawn?"

"He said you have a shady past. That you're a felon."

Nic had said that much and she still wanted him and trusted him? He almost smiled. Instead, he admitted, "He was telling the truth."

"Okay."

She didn't even flinch so he pulled in a breath and segued into the gritty stuff. "Treah and I grew up in a dinky town in New Hampshire. I don't know how much you know about hick towns, but they don't come with a lot of entertainment. At least, not to a seventeen-year-old's way of thinking. Drinking and sex was about as good as it got. Neither of which I did much of because I knew my parents would never forgive me. I was right about that much. They never have forgiven me."

Sympathy filled Claire's expression, but otherwise she remained quiet and still, her blue eyes wide and attentive.

Chris's heart wasn't nearly so quiet or still. It slammed in his chest as he sucked in a few, jerking breaths of air in preparation of continuing. "My best friend, Blair—Treah's younger brother—and I were out with a couple other guys. We got hammered and then someone made the stupid-ass suggestion to add a little excitement to the night by pretending to hold up the mini-mart." He snorted. Yeah, "someone," all right. "The guy who ran the place was always a real ass to us and, with alcohol in our systems, scaring the shit out of him seemed like the perfect payback. No one planned on him having a gun. Or for Blair to panic and try to take it away from him."

Her breath caught, hurtling his mind from ten years in the past. "Blair was killed?"

"No," he said simply, needing to get back to his confession if he was going to make it through. "I wasn't in the store. My job was to serve as the getaway driver so that after they were done spooking the guy we could get out of there quick." He smiled deprecatingly. "We were real clever in that idiotic way only drunken teens can be, sticking panty hose over our heads and thinking that would mask our identity. Never mind we were four of only about ten boys our age in the area. Dumbasses."

"Anyway, when they came tearing out of the store, looking like they all just pissed themselves, I figured the guy had made them and threatened to call the cops. It wasn't until we got well out of town that I learned Blair had gotten into a scuffle with the guy."

Bile charged up the back of Chris's throat and heat stung his face and neck as the memory surfaced full force. Was this sickened, helpless feeling how Claire got when she went outside? Or at least used to get. Her progress brightened his spirits before dropping way back downhill with his next words. "Blair ended up fatally shooting the guy while trying to get the gun away."

Her breath sucked in again, eyes shuttering closed with the sad shake of her head. "How awful. For the guy who died, yeah, but for you guys, too."

Sympathy. He'd told her all of that and she was giving him sympathy.

Shaking his own head, he fought off the urge to pull her into his arms. There was a lesson for her to learn here. "People do stupid shit, Claire. Every day they do. But you can't stop living because of it."

She opened her eyes on a nod, but then bypassed her issues to head right back to his. "Were you tried as an adult?"

"*I* wasn't. They considered me an accessory since I wasn't in the store and had no idea what was happening when I took off. I was stuck in a juvie center for four years."

"And Treah's brother?" Claire's gaze fell to his chest, and he knew she was thinking of his scar. "You said you saved him once. But you couldn't save him a second time, right?"

Right. Chris had been the bastard who'd led him into hell and hadn't been able to lead him back out. "Blair and the rest of the guys weren't so lucky." The admission came out thick with the emotions Chris was trying to keep inside. "The guy that was killed came off as an asshole, but he ended up being a devoted father and husband."

"Your friends went to jail?"

"Yeah. And, yeah, Blair died in prison." Looking away, he scrubbed a hand over his face. Fuck, it all felt so fresh again. In an unsteady voice, he finished, "One of his cellmates went off in a rage and Blair paid the price."

"You blame yourself for his death."

"I should." He turned back to her, needing to face her for this last, gravest admission. "It was my stupid-ass idea to hold up the mini-mart."

Surprise flashed over Claire's face. And then right on its heels came empathy. "You were drunk and the idea was to only *pretend* to hold it up."

God, how could she still be on his side after what he'd just admitted; this woman who, less than ten days ago, was scared to even open her apartment door for fear someone would harm her? "It doesn't make a difference," he retorted. "Two people are still dead because of me. I'm not a murderer, but I'm something real close to it."

"It obviously matters to Treah for him to employ you. Not as a peon either, but his head healer."

"He was there to pick me up the day I was released from the detention center. He was the *only* one who was there." The only time Chris had seen his father since the day he'd left for the center was when they'd placed his body in the ground two years ago. His mother had tried to come around a bit, giving him a hug during the funeral, but after a decade of disowning him, he couldn't give in that easily. Maybe one day . . .

Feeling like total shit, he paced to the blind-drawn window and looked out, not seeing a thing but his own misery. "Now, even Treah's convinced I'm a criminal."

"I'm convinced, too."

Claire's hard words snapped his head around. He met her eyes unable to stop the question from entering his own. Had he finally said enough to push her away?

"I'm convinced that it's time you get over feeling guilty for a past you can't change." Her hard tone relented to a soft smile. "If you were thinking my trust would falter after hearing this, you were wrong. I still trust you, Chris. I know you would never intentionally hurt someone and I also know that you didn't take any money from this resort, or leave some baby in another state without a father. You're way too good of a man for that."

She did, too. Even after all he'd said, she trusted him, believed in him. Cared for him. Her feelings were blatant, right there on her face, and way more than he could handle when his emotions were already so raw.

Going to the bed, he sank down beside her and forced a carnal grin. Only, it didn't take all that much forcing. He needed to feel her in his arms, ached for the warm slide of her supple body against his. "This is about getting more jelly, isn't it?"

Understanding entered Claire's eyes. Her smile moving from soft to sultry, she reached her hand into his lap to find his cock through his jeans and give it a stroke. "Funny you should mention that. I was hoping to help myself to some PB and J."

"PB and J?"

"Mmm hmm . . ." Licking her lips, she crawled onto his lap and slid her hands around to his ass. "Three of my favorites. Penis, butt, and jelly."

Chris ensured that Claire was asleep, and then rolled out of bed. He might not last the entire night playing the vigilant, given how little he'd slept the last few days, but he was still going to put in as much time watching over the office as possible.

After storming out of Treah's office the other morning, all he'd been able to see was the way Treah had sided with Gwen. All he'd been able to feel was how damn much that felt like betrayal. Sharing with Claire what a critical part Treah played in helping to get his life back on track had stuck with Chris long after their conversation ended. Treah's continued weariness and how unlike himself he was acting burned through Chris's mind until he could no longer ignore how upset, and quite likely powerless, Treah felt about the situation.

Forced to choose between his live-in lover and a friend who was like family, Treah had taken the detached route and listened to the evidence. And then he'd all but pleaded with Chris to invalidate that proof. Chris could be pissed at fate for dealing him another shit hand, but no longer at Treah for being logical.

Adrenaline cruising through his system with thoughts of catching the real thief, Chris slipped into dark jeans and a black T-shirt. He used the private, indoor stairwell to descend to the first floor. The last few nights he'd watched over the administration area from inside the storage room the stairwell led to. Tonight, he planned to do the same. At least, he did until he cleared the stairwell to find light filtering in through the window of the door on the opposite end of the storage room.

His pulse accelerated. Moving soundlessly between metal floor-to-ceiling shelves of filing boxes and office equipment, he made his way to the door. Shelley's office was directly across the hall. The door was open and the room was pitch black inside.

Chris breathed a sigh of relief. Claire had told him Shelley's odd behavior as of late was nothing for him to worry over. Still, after Shelley made that comment about needing a good deal of money to fix whatever was wrong in her life, part of him had feared unveiling her as the thief.

Of course, just because the light wasn't coming from her office didn't mean she wasn't the thief. For that matter, just because a light was left on somewhere in the office area at all didn't mean someone was down here. The light could have been left on as an easy oversight. Much as he wanted to catch the real thief and clear his name, Chris found himself hoping for that oversight option as he tucked into the small space between the corner and where the door's window started. Breath held, he followed the source of the light to the receptionist area.

Shit. The space was occupied. And not by Nic, his favorite candidate for the role of thief, either.

From this angle he couldn't see much, just a portion of a woman's slender back and the tips of her two-toned hair: blond and brown waves that fell against her siren red top. If the hair wasn't a giveaway, there could be no mistaking her signature shade of red.

Gwen.

She sat at her desk and, from what he could tell, was working on her computer. The question was, why? It had to be close

to two. Could she not sleep? Or had something far less innocent brought her down to the office?

Chris twisted the storage room doorknob and slowly pulled
the door in. Heart beating faster, he darted through the doorway to the wall on the opposite side. His breath feathered out,
sounding like a roar to his hyper-aware ears, as he moved along
the wall the short distance to the receptionist area.

This close he could hear the occasional click of her finger-
nails against her keyboard. Taking the sound to mean she still
faced away from him, he stepped from the cover of the wall. He
didn't spend much time on computers, but he saw her doing so
enough to recognize the accounting software pulled up on her
screen.

She could be working. More likely, she was either looking for
additional evidence to pin on him, or preparing to make money
disappear by transferring it into her own account. Chris's gut
told him it was the latter, and that the bitchy glare Gwen had
been tossing his way for the last two days was nothing more
than a front for her own misdeeds.

He moved up close enough to touch. "Taking out a deposit?"

She jumped with a gasp. Her body went visibly rigid, then
with her snapping, "Go away, Chris. You've already done more
than enough to screw with this resort."

"You're half right. Someone's been screwing with it." Grabbing the back of her chair, he spun her around. Her eyes narrowed to a glare. Hands on the chair arms, he bent down and
glared back from a few inches away. "It's you, isn't it? You're
the one who's taking the money? And that letter you supposedly intercepted from some chick I knocked up, nothing but
pure shit?" Quite likely, she was also responsible for learning of
Chris's past through Treah and filling Nic in on the details as a
crutch for her cause.

Denial flared in her eyes only to melt on an amused smile.
"What do you say we take a walk and I'll tell you all about it?"

He would rather call Treah down and get on with the unveiling. But then, Chris didn't want to point fingers her way
without irrefutable evidence. He was disappointed with her.
Treah was going to be both ticked and hurt.

He released the chair arms and straightened. "Let me get a
coat."

"I don't think so." Shutting down the computer, Gwen
stood to pull on a black pouch-style sweatshirt hanging from
one of the desk drawer knobs. With a nod for Chris to follow,
she went into Treah's office and crossed to the patio door. She
lifted one of Treah's coats from the rack beside the door. "Wear
this. He's not going to be waking up anytime soon and needing it."

Dread slammed into Chris as he took the coat and slid his
arms into the sleeves. That she could be dangerous had never
crossed his mind. Now, he caught the gleam of malice in her
eyes and had to fight the urge to grab her around the throat and
shake the answers out. "What did you do to him, Gwen?"

"Nothing bad." She pushed open the patio door and stepped
out into the moonlit night. "Just gave him some of his own
medicine."

Breathing a little easier, he followed her out. By "his own
medicine" she had to mean the sedative given to those clients
too afraid to make the trip to the island any way but asleep. "Is
that how you've been doing this? Feeding him that stuff every
night so he has no chance of catching you in the act?"

Shrugging, she moved off the patio and started toward the
water. "It's harmless and works like a charm."

The wind had kicked up since nightfall. Between its low,
keening wail and the loud crash of the surf against the sand
when they reached the shoreline, Chris had to shout to be
heard. "Why, Gwen?" He took hold of her arm, jerking her
around to face him with his demand. "Just for the money?"

Her eyes regained the catty glare he was quickly coming to

know and hate. She shook off his hand. "It's not like I'm going to get it any other way. I couldn't even afford to live on the mainland with the joke of a wage I pull in here. Treah will sure as hell never marry me and share his nest egg."

"Why not get a job somewhere else?"

"I like living here. I love fucking the boss. I just need a little stipend to go along with it." One of her hands shoved into the pouch at the front of her sweatshirt. "You're not going to keep your mouth shut, are you?"

Chris tensed with the disappearance of her hand. Just as he hadn't thought her dangerous, he hadn't considered she could have a weapon. Something told him that was about to be a serious oversight. "I owe Treah everything."

"He believes me over you. You said so yourself."

"It doesn't matter. He gave me a chance at a new life when everyone else turned away. I can't knowingly stand by while you chip away at his livelihood."

Gwen's smile fell flat. She looked truly saddened for the seconds it took to pull the anticipated gun from her sweatshirt and point it his way. "Then it seems we have a little problem, because I can't let you tell him."

10

Claire woke with her heart pounding and the breath wheezing between her lips. The panic she hadn't experienced when going out on the deck with Chris earlier tonight had emerged as a hellish nightmare. Pulling in calming breaths, she rolled over to cuddle against his warm, strong body. Only, his side of the bed was empty.

Sitting up, she reached to the nightstand and flicked on the light. A soft brushing sound near the foot of the bed had her attention whizzing down. Bosco pounced onto the end of the mattress with a happy little mew.

"Where do you suppose he went?" she asked as she reached for the calico kitten.

He sidestepped her hand to jump onto the floor, then leap up to the windowsill. She laughed as he burrowed his little body between the slats of the mini blinds. "You're definitely feeling better. Not to mention frisky."

Claire climbed out of bed and went to the window. She pulled the blind open to retrieve the kitten before he hurt either the blind or himself. Something flickered from the beach, pulling her attention from the kitten to the sand. The moon was almost full tonight. Glinting off the choppy water, it made the couple on the beach nearly as visible as if it was daylight. Gwen... and Chris?

Oh, God, were they lovers?

Her belly twisted with the thought. Then twisted so much harder when the thing that had first caught her attention snagged the moonlight and flickered again.

Her heart raced. Tension knotted through her body. The franticness of her nightmare seemed suddenly gentle by comparison.

What the fuck was Gwen doing with a gun? Or was it not real? Was this a test? A way to draw Claire outside and a good distance from the house?

The moonlight gleamed against the barrel of the gun, making it look so big and real as Gwen pointed it Chris's way. Gwen's arm jerked suddenly, and she rammed the snout of the gun into his shoulder. He shifted with the impact, his face turning so that Claire could see it. Even from thirty yards away, his body language showed fear.

Claire fought off the urge to gag as two realities swamped her: what was going on down on the beach was no test, and she really did "really care" for Chris.

Leaving Bosco to his own defenses, she bolted for the bedroom door and then the one just down the hall. Shoving the door open, she shouted, "Treah! Wake up!" She could see him lying in the bed, but he didn't move with her yelling. She hurried to the side of the bed, took hold of his arm, and shook with every ounce of her strength.

"Wake up," she pleaded again when he remained inert. "Please, wake up!"

His eyes didn't open. His breathing stayed shallow. Now,

she knew how Chris had felt the other night when he said that she was sleeping like the dead. Eventually, she'd wakened. She prayed Treah would eventually do the same.

The kind of eventually that came before his psychotic girl-friend pulled the trigger.

Ignoring the dull ache in his shoulder from Gwen slamming the gun into it, Chris kept up with his reasoning attempts. "This is crazy, Gwen. You're going to shoot me just so you can bring in a few extra bucks a month?"

"I'm not going to shoot you." She waved the gun. "This is just to help you into the water. And it's not a few extra bucks, Chris. It's thousands. Something to keep me warm when Treah dumps me."

"What makes you so sure that he will?"

"He's head up his ass in love with his ex." She waved the gun again, this time at the rolling ocean. "Enough talk. I want this over with."

Because she didn't really want to do it.

If there was one thing Chris knew from his time in deten-tion, it was how to recognize the eyes of a killer. With only three feet separating them, he could read the reservation in Gwen's eyes loud and clear. She might have had the nerve to turn a gun on him, but the only way she would be able to see his death through was by the same kind of accidental approach that had cost the mini-mart guy his life ten years ago. "You're not going to let me drown. You're too moral."

"You don't know what I am," she sniped.

"Yeah." Smiling, he took a slow step toward her. "You aren't going to—"

"Shut up! Just shut the hell up before I change my mind about giving you the easy way out."

With a wry laugh over what she called the easy way out, Chris shifted his body to the left and made a jerking grab for the gun. Gunfire tore through the night seconds before his fingers connected with the cool metal barrel. Gwen screeched as her body slammed into his, and they both went down hard on the sand.

She landed with a wheezing inhale beneath him. Keeping the weight of his thighs pinned against hers, he sat up and did a frantic search for the gun. It wasn't in her hands. It wasn't in his. Who the hell fired it? And were either of them hit?

"Chris!"

He jerked his head in the direction of the office with Claire's trembling shout. She stood thirty feet away, nude aside from the gun shaking violently in her hands. Damn, he was one twisted SOB. Because he couldn't stop from thinking she looked incredibly hot with the moonlight streaming down over her. Not even with the knowledge she held that gun pointed directly at his groin.

"Oh my God." Horror widened her eyes as they moved to Gwen's prone body. "Did I . . . Is she . . . ?"

Gwen pushed up on her elbows to fire an icy glare at Claire. "You shot at me, you crazy bitch!"

"She's fine," Chris assured in a calm voice. He scowled at the woman trying to wriggle out from beneath him and added for Gwen's ears alone, "I mean in a fucked up, insecure, neurotic, and emotional sort of way." Finally spotting Gwen's gun on the sand a few feet away, he pushed to his feet and grabbed it. Confident she wasn't going anywhere—after all, they were on an island and the boat keys were kept inside the house—he left Gwen to pick herself up out of the sand and started over to Claire.

He stopped midway to where she stood. "Are you okay?"

"Yes. I mean . . . okay, yeah."

"Then can you put down the gun?"

Claire's gaze darted to her hands. As if she hadn't realized she held it, she let out a yelp and tossed the gun to the sand. "I didn't think," she blurted. "I just saw her out here pointing that gun at you and . . . and Treah wouldn't wake up. I was going to grab the lamp to knock her over the head with, like they do on the crime shows, but then I saw the nightstand and I remembered in the crime shows people like to keep their guns there. And I found the gun and I came down here—"

"Shhh . . ." Chris ended her rambling with the press of his finger to her lips.

After dropping Gwen's gun in the sand beside the one that came from Treah's nightstand, which meant it was loaded with blanks meant for show alone, he lifted Claire into his arms. "You're in shock, sweetheart. Just relax and let it pass." She nodded numbly, her silky brown hair brushing against his jaw. He smiled as that "goodness" feeling she had a way of bringing out in him emerged. "You were incredible, Claire. I'm proud of you. Not just for potentially saving my life, but for facing your fears by coming out here."

Her gaze skipped to the office, and she shivered. "I'm not sure I can get back."

He hauled her tighter against him. "Then it's a good thing I have no intention of setting you down."

11

Claire stood outside the meeting room door, feeling the sun beat down upon her and make the day seem almost hot. Feeling like the last three weeks had passed in an instant. Feeling like she was about to be sick. Not because she was standing outside, but because she was about to leave Ecstasy Island behind.

Ecstasy . . . and Chris.

In the nearly two weeks since that middle-of-the-night incident on the beach, he'd helped to turn her reclusive ways around to the point that she'd worked up the courage to take a walk down the beach with him yesterday. She still wasn't ready to charge into a crowd of strangers, but maybe one day, in the not-so-far-off future, she could manage a trip to the mall with Erin again.

Standing beside her, with that soft smile she'd come to both trust and adore, Chris asked, "You ever talk to Treah about writing an article on this place?"

"No. I kind of like the idea of putting it off. Gives me a reason to come back sometime."

Shelley came out of the meeting room and grabbed Chris up

in a hug. With a promise to visit soon, she released him and started for the boat loaded down with her possessions that hadn't been taken off the island already. Claire's stuff was on that boat, as well. She wasn't ready for a mall quite yet, but somehow she'd convinced herself she *was* ready to take a boat ride when not under the influence of sedatives.

"You sure you'll be okay on the ride to the mainland?" Chris asked, as though her uncertainty was painted on her face in neon green.

She forced a confident smile. "I have Shelley to keep me company. And if I do end up puking, I can always call it seasickness."

With a raspy laugh, he pulled her into his arms. "I know I've said it a hundred times in the last week alone, but I'm proud of you, Claire."

A hundred times at a minimum and those words still felt wonderful. His mouth felt even better as he brought it to hers for another of those sweet, slow, drugging kisses like he'd given her that night on the deck and that had her heart slamming with secret desires. She'd never told him that she really cared. Earlier this week, Shelley had mentioned that the healing coaches were required to be single, and Claire refused to make him choose between a job he'd had for years and a woman he'd known less than a month. Maybe if he'd given her an indication that he really cared, too . . .

"Time to shove off," Shelley shouted from the boat.

Something rose up in the back of Claire's throat. For once not bile, but emotion that felt thick enough to choke on. She stepped back from Chris's arms, smile plastered on so hard it hurt. "I'm proud, too. Of both of us. Take care of yourself, Chris."

"You, too, sweetheart."

She turned for the boat, but then turned back to do a stupid little wave thing. Stupid because he was only four feet away. "Bye."

"Bye."

She went another ten feet and looked back again, gave another of those stupid little waves. Three weeks ago, she'd believed each step he'd carried her toward her apartment door had the potential to kill her softly, slowly. Today, each step he took away from her felt like it would strike her down on the spot. "See ya."

He laughed. "You bet."

Claire turned back again, this time making it all the way to the boat. She moved into the cabin and sat down, somewhere she couldn't see Chris and somewhere he couldn't see the tears in her eyes that proved just how much she really cared.

"Pansy ass," Nic chided, coming up beside Chris.

Chris fisted his hands at his sides to keep from sticking one in the dick's face. Claire had disappeared inside the boat's cabin. Still, she could stick her head out at any moment and the last thing he wanted her to see was violence.

Keeping the same feigned smile on his face for Nic as he had for Claire, he asked, "What the fuck is your deal, man? Do you have nothing better to do with your life than piss with mine?"

"Actually, I do. I put in my notice."

Chris's eyebrows rose. "Why would you?"

Nic smirked. "I'm not some pansy ass who's afraid to be with a woman more than a few weeks at a time."

Chris wasn't afraid to be with a woman long term. He *couldn't* be with one and retain this job. Between his record and how many other, more qualified people were vying for work these days, it would be inane to think he'd find employment for similar, or even substantially less, pay elsewhere. Letting Claire go, no matter how much the idea of staying addicted to her forever appealed, was his only option.

Apparently, Nic felt he had other options and a woman worth his exploring them. "You're quitting so you can settle down?"

"I'm already done. The boss man said to consider my notice time served." Nic looked down at the boats and smiled in a way too replete with meaning to be contrived. "Shelley isn't any too keen on me sleeping with other women while she's pregnant with Nic Junior."

Chris sucked in a breath, feeling like he'd taken a sucker punch. Claire had suggested something was going on between the two of them, but he hadn't seen this coming. It did explain Shelley's need for money, and Nic could make anyone's attitude run hot one second and cold the next. Chris had figured the guy was up to something bad when he'd said he had business to attend to that day he left Dawn at the cabin to visit with Claire. Now, he could guess that business involved spending time with Shelley. "Funny. I always thought she had better taste than you."

"Are you coming or what?" Shelley shouted from the boat, this time her focus on Nic.

"Yeah, yeah, yeah," he called back, affection clear in his voice. "Just give me five seconds, *amore*."

Chris's smile went from forced to real. Despite every bad thought he'd had about Nic—and, all right, the bolt of envy that struck through him—he and Shelley clearly had a promising future. "Treat her right."

"Don't worry, *cazzo*. I'm not about to do anything to get your gun pointed my way."

Chris's smile fell flat as the anger only Nic could rile surfaced. He looked over at him with a mouthful of four-letter words, all of which were forgotten the moment he caught the amusement in Nic's expression. "Whatever. Just be good to her."

"Be good to yourself. Shelley says you deserve it, and I promised to agree with her on that much at least." Nic clapped a hand to his shoulder before pushing off and starting for the docks. "See you around. I have a woman to please."

*   *   *

Treah had forewarned that, even though Chris had filled the job vacancy left with Shelley's departure, with Nic gone and so many clients booked well in advance, he may have to do double duty for a while. Last month, he was able to concentrate on resort management duties alone, leaving time to strategize his plan for getting Claire back in his life. Both times that he'd gone to her apartment in the hopes of putting that plan into action, she was away for several days, per her elderly neighbor. Now, it was a new month, and Treah's double-duty warning had come to fruition.

Ecstasy's pick-up guys had delivered a woman to the cabin in the middle of the night, explaining another of the healers had come down with the flu, leaving Chris to take on the guy's client. The woman had been sedated into slumber, and Chris hadn't cared to get an early look at her. He had her put into his bed, and then crashed on the couch the moment the pick-up guys took off.

With morning's arrival, he had no choice but to open the bedroom door and greet her. No matter how much thoughts of sensual healing with any woman but Claire ate at his gut, he had to set aside aversion and get to work on his newest client.

Of course, it would help if he'd been provided with a client file.

As part of his managerial position, Chris was responsible for booking clients and then spending some time reviewing each woman's information to ensure she didn't end up with a bad healing-coach match. Still, he couldn't remember every little fact about each woman, or probably even place a name with a face.

Later, he would head to the office and grab the resort copy of the woman's file. Now, he accepted his fate by opening the bedroom door.

The woman was awake and sitting up in bed. Not checking out her surroundings with a mix of panic and eagerness in her eyes, like most of the clients who came to him by way of sedation, but mouthwateringly nude and smiling expectantly at the door.

Claire's gaze latched onto his and her smile grew wider. "Good morning."

Funny thing, but all of a sudden it *was* a good morning. At least, he was hoping it was about to become one.

Afraid he wouldn't stop at a few steps if he were to move farther into the room, Chris stood his ground. Externally, his expression remained passive. Internally, his pulse raced like mad. "Morning to you. Enjoy having the bed to yourself last night?"

"Not really. I was too knocked out on sedatives to appreciate it."

A new client being sedated for the trip to the island was common. Claire shouldn't have needed it. Not when she'd seemed well on her way to being perfectly healed when she left the island last month. "Has your progress slowed?"

"No. Thanks to you, I'm getting better every day. Just not yet to the point of taking a car trip, then a boat ride with complete strangers."

He didn't want to smile until he knew why she was here. But between her breaking out that compliment and her glowing grin of pride, he couldn't help himself.

They stared at each other that way for nearly a full minute before the room was overtaken by nervous tension. Not bothering to hold onto a smile that no longer felt natural, Chris broke the silence. "What are you doing here, Claire?"

"The same thing the rest of the clients are. Getting over my fear." She looked down and locked her fingers together over her lap. "My *new* fear."

"Which is?" Obviously nothing that revolved around nudity. Her joined hands mostly covered her crotch but the rest of her lush body was on full display, increasing the already hasty beat of his heart while enlivening his cock.

"According to Erin—by the way, she totally freaked when Shelley and Nic dropped me off on her doorstep—rejection." Legitimate fear quavered in Claire's voice as she lifted her gaze to again meet his.

He'd caused this new anxiety, but for reasons that were logical and that had seemed his only option. Reasons that were no longer an issue. He could guess that she already knew about his career move through the man who had to be responsible for bringing her to his home: Treah. Ever since learning Gwen was his thief, Treah had been going out of his way to apologize to Chris for what happened that morning in his office. Chris had forgiven him long ago. Even so, he wasn't going to complain over this latest offering.

Nah. He was going to be thankful as hell and return the favor at the first opportunity.

Chris risked taking a lone step toward the bed. "You'll have to give me more to work with here. I didn't get a file."

"The fear you won't deliver my last consolation prize."

Hope-filled anticipation kindled, a partial smile slipping out as he took another step forward. "What did you have in mind?"

"Nothing much. Just a permanent spot in your bed, panty parties for two at least five times a week, Shelley's vacated cabin or at least some of the furnishings. Mmm . . . a playmate for Hot Stud . . ." Claire tipped her head to the side and her eyes went enchantingly warm blue. "I could go on. Or you could stop me now by saying you really care about me as much as I really care about you."

"How about a kiss instead?"

Discontent passed through her gaze. "Okay."

Not about to let her stay disappointed for long, Chris moved the rest of the way to the bed and climbed onto the foot of the mattress. Grabbing her ankles, he pulled her flat onto her back and crawled over her. Her gasp of surprise ended with the hot press of his lips against her own.

She sighed into his mouth, a happy little sound that made him feel just too good. Her arms slipped around his back. Holding him tight, she shifted her hips against his and stroked his tongue with a needful, hungry urgency that made him feel even better yet.

Before he forgot his intentions, the way she was so incredibly good at making him do, Chris lifted from her mouth to confess, "I've missed you."

Claire's answering smile was huge and full of affection. "Me, too."

"But I don't really care about you." Bringing his lips back to hers, he nibbled at the corners. "What I am is addicted and, to quote Gwen, head-up-my-ass in love. My head must have been stuck up my ass to let you leave."

Her mouth parted, tongue slipping out to stroke against his and pull him into another blood-heating kiss. She eased her lips away to reveal her smile back in place, happy still but also now undeniably naughty. "You know what's good for that?" He shook his head, and she added in a teasing tone, "Jelly. Lucky for you I have one gift certificate left for my personal jelly-of-the-month club."

Grinding his erection against her mound and stirring both of their jellies, he laughed. "You drive a hard bargain, sweetheart."

"Yeah, and something tells me it's about to get a whole lot harder."

IN LIVING COLOR

1

"Treah?"

The lone word drifted from the speaker of Treah Baldwin's office phone, slipping around him like an old favorite love song. Warm and inviting, soothing yet smoky. Hers was a voice he could never forget.

Unlike breathing.

Hearing Dana Lancer's voice now, after eight years of no contact, had the air stilled in his throat and his body stone stiff in the desk chair. This call shouldn't come as such a surprise. They hadn't spoken personally, but she'd contacted the female-targeted, sensual healing resort last month to book an appointment for her twin sister, Deanne.

Apparently, knowing that she'd called and hearing her voice were two very different things.

Letting his breath out, Treah grabbed the cordless phone off the receiver. He would be damned if she hung up because he was too dumbstruck to say hello. He also didn't want Sonya Grigg—his recently hired, incredibly reserved personal assistant, who was stationed in the receptionist area outside his closed door—overhearing the conversation. The young blonde came highly recommended, but something about her timidity rubbed him the wrong way. Honestly, though, it could be nothing more than losing Gwen, his previous PA and one-time lover, to her greed, that made him leery of anyone handling resort information outside of himself and Chris, the resort manager and a long-time friend.

With Gwen's deception still so fresh, frustration added to his surprise, making his response sound near breathless. "Hello, Dana."

Soft laughter pealed from the other end of the phone line. "Sorry to disappoint you but this isn't Dana."

Of course it was. Had to be. Or had endless thoughts of her, piqued by Gwen's accusation that he was still in love with his ex, made him so eager to hear from Dana that he made another woman become her?

Regardless of the answer, he needed to regain control of his emotions.

Relaxing in the chair, Treah looked across the office to the patio door. He kept the storm door in place for when hurricane warnings went up. On days like this, when the temperature was nearing eighty and the sun blistered down on the private island's white-sand beach, the screen door was more than enough protection against the elements.

The warm salt breeze drifted in off the ocean, slowing the rapid beat of his heart as it almost always managed to do. "No need to be sorry. I was just expecting a call from someone else. What can I do for you?"

The woman's laughter sounded again, lighter and with a teasing edge that called him a liar despite his relaxed tone. "Someone else, huh? Someone who happens to sound exactly like my sister?"

"Deanne." Not Dana but close enough to his ex to bring a smile of familiarity to his lips. "How are you?"

"Good. Just not good enough for Dana's liking." The amusement vanished from her voice. "She signed me up for a trip to your resort."

Dana knew that he owned Ecstasy Island? How did she feel about it?

Hell, he shouldn't care and, yet, he had to know more. "How did she find out I own this place?"

"She didn't. We read about it in the *Herald* last month. There was no owner name listed, but you know how Dana and I tend to think alike?"

"Yeah." Most of the time they did. Deanne had never agreed with Dana's leaving him.

"We obviously both thought the resort worth trying out, because I called to schedule her an appointment and found out she'd already booked one for me. I don't need to come there. Dana does. I asked your manager to arrange a swap, but he said I would have to speak with you. There aren't too many Treah's out there. Probably only one Treah Baldwin."

Their self-assurance was another way in which they differed. Deanne he could see potentially needing help with getting over a fear. Dana, not unless she'd changed drastically. The woman he knew had confidence in spades. Not to mention obstinacy and passion. She took life on full speed ahead, with no thought to fearing the outcome. "Why do you want her to come here?"

"You're there."

"You didn't know that when you called."

"No. But I do now. You're exactly what she needs."

Why? Because this was the first time Deanne had managed to track him down in eight years and she was still anxious to see them end up together?

In Dana's mind, they hadn't had enough in common to make their relationship worthwhile, once she'd finished her master's degree and gotten herself situated in a pretentious career he didn't have. It was crazy to think they would have a chance now. Crazy enough that he'd lost sleep more than one night while he turned over Gwen's words: If there was a chance that he still loved Dana, he should do whatever it took to give them another try.

Even if he wanted that, the odds were next to nil that Dana would. "What about you, Deanne? What does Dana think this resort has to offer you?"

"A lesson in self-esteem," she admitted grudgingly. In a more upbeat tone, she added, "She's wrong. I'm not. She needs you, Treah."

Damn, it wasn't right how much he wanted to believe those words and have Dana believe them, as well.

Needing more than a tranquil view of the ocean from afar, Treah pushed back the chair from his desk. He moved through the patio door and sat at one of several picnic tables, his back to the table and front to the quartet of boats that bobbed along twin docks a hundred feet away. "I'll admit it's a tempting offer, but I don't do the healing."

"I don't need you to cure her of any fears. I just need you to show her that her fiancé doesn't have what it takes to make her happy."

The lightened beat of his heart falling by the wayside, he pulled the phone from his ear to glare at the receiver. Dana was engaged? Like this call, the news shouldn't be surprising. At one point, he'd written her off as married with children. But she wasn't. She was just engaged. Engaged but not happy, at least to her sister's way of thinking.

Treah brought the phone back to his ear. "What makes you think he doesn't?"

"Professionally, they're perfect. As lovers, she's always left wanting."

No matter what his feelings for her were these days, he didn't want to think of her sleeping with another man. Even so, hearing she wasn't pleased by that man's sexual prowess brought a measure of both comfort and conceit. Personally, he'd never left her wanting. Of course, maybe if he'd pleased her a little less and acted like he understood her work a little more, she wouldn't have walked away.

Old frustrations rising up to taunt him, he pointed out, "Dana's career is her life. At least, the Dana I remember. If he's a perfect career match, then she's happy."

"You don't believe that. I know you better."

"You knew me eight years ago, Deanne. Time changes most everything."

"Are you still single?"

He winced with the soreness of the subject. "At the moment."

"Then what's your price?"

Time did change most everything, but not Treah's lack of love for money. It was at the root of far too much evil in his life, including the primary reason behind Gwen's deception. "You can't pay me enough to seduce your sister into breaking things off with her fiancé."

"You *have* changed." She sounded disappointed. "There was a time when you would have done anything for Dana's happiness."

He didn't like to disappoint people, least of all a woman who'd gone against her own twin to take his side. Like his feelings on money, those on Dana's happiness hadn't changed. They still mattered, as did finding out if he loved her before it was too late. "I never said I wouldn't help you. I just won't take money for it and I won't play the seduction game."

"How else are you going to show her what she's missing out on?"

"I'll think of something." Something that didn't involve

greeting her in his bed and proceeding to make her wish that she'd never left it.

When Treah got his hands on Chris, he was going to wish he was dead. Per Treah's approval, Chris had arranged the swapping of the two sisters and then promised to personally see a sedated Dana delivered to Treah's spare bedroom. But she wasn't in Treah's *spare* bedroom. She was in *his* bedroom. In his bed. Her face was buried in his pillow and, somehow, she still managed to snore loudly enough to wake the dead, just the way he'd remembered her doing.

He'd been exhausted when he'd mounted the stairs from the administration offices and meeting area that made up the first floor of his house. He'd considered coming up earlier but he hadn't been tired, what with thoughts of Dana's arrival thick in his mind. Then he'd gotten into work and the hours had slipped away until it was after three in the morning.

Now it was close to three thirty, and he wasn't feeling exhausted any longer. He was feeling like his heart might slam through his chest for its fierce pounding.

Drawing in calming breaths, he moved to the side of the bed and allowed himself to do what he hadn't been able to for so long. Watched her sleep. Her hair was longer and the once dark brown shade was streaked with golden highlights. He curled his fingers at his sides to keep from reaching out and sliding them into the silky waves.

Pulling back the top sheet and a thin blue cover brought an immediate smile. She still slept semicontortionist style, with her knees tucked up under her belly and her ass in the air. Such a nice ass it was, too. A little rounder than it used to be, in white cotton pajama shorts. Now, it would be all the better for gripping while he stroked his cock into her and met her thrust for eager thrust.

Not the thoughts he should be having, Treah acknowledged. They had his shaft rousing against the fly of his trouser shorts as he bent and scooped her off the bed. She'd always been a heavy sleeper. Between that and the natural sedative she'd been given for her trip to the island, moving her into the spare bedroom and, in turn, himself away from temptation, should be a cinch.

It should have been. But it wasn't.

With a soft sigh, Dana curled her arms around his neck and nuzzled her face against his shoulder. "Missed you."

His heart stuttered a beat. If only she really had. But she was asleep, probably dreaming of her fiancé. Lucky bastard. At least, the guy was lucky for now. Maybe before her time at the resort was through . . .

It wasn't a maybe he should contemplate now any more than he should consider her lusciously curvy butt. "It's time for—"

Her head lifted to reveal her copper-laced brown eyes partway open and her smile so bright it stopped his words on a dime. Her lips parted. He thought she would say something until her mouth contacted soft and warm against his own.

Her tongue pushed inside with his surprised breath. The damp, lusty sweep of it against his own took one hell of a potshot at his good intentions. Her fingers kneaded at the back of his neck in such a familiar way that Treah sank into the kiss without thought, without care. Just sank his tongue against hers and let his head spin with how incredible she still tasted. Warm and sweet with a generous coating of brazen.

Dana's mouth pulled from his. Eyes once again closed, she snuggled back against his chest and murmured a low, throaty, "Yummy."

God, yeah, it was.

He'd vowed not to seduce her. He wouldn't let her seduce

him, either. Not while she was out of her rational mind. Her eyes had opened for a second or two, but he didn't buy that she knew what was happening.

Tipping his head back so that she couldn't get her mouth on his again, he started for the bedroom door. "Time to go to your own bed, sleepy girl."

"Want you."

He groaned with the toll her breathy disclosure took on his body. "Trust me, you don't want me."

Or maybe she did.

Her hand moved between their bodies to cup his crotch. Through his shorts, her fingers closed around what was quickly becoming a full-blown erection, and she let out another throaty murmur. "Do."

Before his judgment could be swayed by his dick, Treah hurried down the hallway to the spare bedroom. Not bothering to turn on the light, he crossed to the bed, whipped back the covers, and lay her down.

At least, he tried to lay her down. She still had ahold of his cock with no apparent plans to release it.

Moving them onto the bed as a unit, he laid her back while he hovered over her, the weight of his thighs around hers pinning her in place and a hand on either side of her head. Far too intimate of a position. Particularly now, when he could see all of her.

The bedroom light wasn't on, but the light from the hallway bled in to throw shadows across her face. Dana had always thought her nose too straight and uppity to match the softness of her mouth and eyes. Personally, he thought it fit her well, particularly considering her tendency for snobbery that had emerged toward the end of their relationship. Only, in the shadows, her nose didn't look uppity and not an inch of her came off as snobby.

Her body was hot beneath his. The contrast of her smooth, bare upper thighs as they contacted against the crisp hair of his legs was more intimacy than Treah had known for months. Too much intimacy when coupled with a woman who was his ultimate temptation.

As if she knew his thoughts and was granting leniency, her grip on his shaft released. He breathed a sigh of relief for the second it took her to wrap her legs around his ass and wrench him forward. Caught off guard, he went down fast and hard, losing his handhold on the bed and then quickly replanting his palms before his face pummeled into her breasts. His mouth still brushed against a hard nipple through her thin pajama top, but the fall could have ended much worse for his peace of mind.

She made it much worse on his mind then, by tightening the hold of her legs around his butt and pressing her groin flush to his.

The heat of her sex warmed into his despite the layers. On a needy whimper, she wrapped her arms around his back, trapping him entirely while she wriggled her pussy against his solid cock.

Fuck, he'd always loved how passionate she was. If her fiancé was missing out on this part of her personality, then Deanne might just be right. Dana might not be happy. She couldn't be happy with a guy who catered to her professionally only. Just as she hadn't been happy with Treah for catering to her physically while professionally he was a clear miss to her way of thinking.

That cold slap of reality had him risking the full press of his face against her breasts so that he could use his hands to get her arms unlocked from his back. Focusing on anything but the nipple pressed against his mouth, he grappled for her hands. He found her fingers interlocked and damned impossible to get unhooked.

Moaning, she segued her pelvis into a circling grind. His cock gave a savage throb and he muffled against her breast, "Stop, Dana."

"Nah uh. Want you, Treah."

Oh, hell. Not his name in that sexy, smoky voice. She still had to be sleeping, dreaming, just not of her fiancé, the way Treah had presumed. But of him.

She was going to kill his good intentions yet.

2

Dana was dreaming about Treah more and more. It had to be normal, though, to dream about past lovers with the wedding only months away. But was it normal to want to keep on dreaming until she experienced the kind of Technicolor passion that came to him as easily as breathing?

It had to be normal and nothing to guilt over. It was a dream, after all.

She'd only opened her eyes for a few seconds, but when she had, her surroundings hadn't been familiar. And her mind felt so sleepy, her thoughts lackadaisical. All but those of making love with Treah.

Dream love.

"Let me go, Dana." His lips caressed her right breast, almost closing over her nipple as he struggled against the bindings of her arms and legs around his back. "Before we do something you'll regret."

Almost sucking her nipple wasn't good enough. This was her dream and, now that she'd decided it was okay to have, she was going to play it out as the taboo fantasy she craved.

Tepid breath sifted through her thin pajama top. Taking it as a cue that Treah was about to say more, she strengthened her hold around his back, lifted her breasts, and drove her nipple between his parted lips. His mouth circled the crown, damp and warm, and tiny bursts of pleasure zipped from her breast to her core.

In a sleepy, lusty voice, she vowed, "No regrets."

His attempts at getting her hands unlocked faltered, and he brought his palms back to the bed. Stealing the glory of his mouth from her nipple, he lifted his chest away from hers the inch she was allowing. "Good God, girl, what's it going to take?"

Dana could feel his gaze boring into hers and wished she had the strength to open her eyes. But if she was going to keep her dream lover captive within her embrace, she had to channel every ounce of her power into her limbs.

Imagining his eyes, more yellow than green and raw to the point of predatory with desire, she shifted her hips to rub her sex the length of his cock. Treah groaned, a pant of sultry air against her throat, and her pussy went soft and liquid.

She shouldn't have to be ordering him around to get the job done as she wanted. Since he wasn't complying, she did it anyway. "Touch me!"

"I am."

Grinding against each other through their clothes was nice. But this was a stolen moment. A taboo dream. She wanted it all. "Inside. Put your cock inside me. Or quit fighting me, so that I can release you and do it myself."

He let free another groan, then added in a rough voice that spoke of frayed control, "Listen to me, Dana. You don't really want this. You're sleeping."

God, she loved how gravelly he sounded when he was worked up.

The thickness of his tone slid along her spine and down around her ass, bringing every nerve in her body shuddering to life as her pussy flooded with cream.

"Please, Treah." If ordering didn't work with this dream version of him, she was ready to resort to pleading. "Just once. Just touch me. Make me feel good. Make me feel the way only you can."

"Ah, hell." The words whispered against her throat. A whisper and, yet, so feral and rough they echoed through her like a scream. "I never could resist your begging."

His face planted tight against her breasts again. This time, his lips didn't tease against her nipple but parted over the crown and sucked it into his mouth through her shirt.

Skin on skin, Dana silently chanted as a whimper of sweet relief cruised from her lips and she released his back to grip his shoulders. His hand pushed between their bodies to dive beneath the waist of her shorts, and that whimper became a moan of pure gratitude.

Treah's fingers slipped through the moist curls covering her mound. Panting with anticipation, she unlocked her ankles and slid her legs from around his ass. Now that he was giving in, he wouldn't stop. Now that he was giving in, he also wouldn't deliver her to climax with a few simple finger fucks. He would touch and stroke and tease every inch of her to the nth degree before he finally slipped his fingers inside her dripping wet pussy and offered up orgasm.

At least, that was the way he used to operate. But then, a lot of years had passed since he last brought her to climax, and this man wasn't even the real Treah. This man was her dream lover. A figment of her imagination.

In her mind, she obviously wanted him to forgo the teasing and get right to the fucking.

His fingers petted her mound for the space of a heartbeat before one slipped into her center. Not exactly a fast penetration, not near to the girth she was used to filling her sex. But he pulled her shirt up and drew the bare point of her nipple into his mouth in time with that impaling, and the combination felt as good as, if not better than, what she was used to.

Sucking hard on her nipple, he joined a second finger with the first and rocked them up inside her cunt. His knuckles hit against her clit, rubbing the hard bundle with such force that she gasped.

His lips shifted against her nipple, feeling like they formed a smile as he repeated his knuckles move, this time with even more pressure. Bolts of sensual electricity charged from her clit throughout her pussy, swelling the tender tissue near to the point of explosion.

Dana gave up her hold on his shoulders to fist her hands in the sheets and fall into the decadent rhythm of his fingers. "Oh, yes," she panted. "God, yes. This is what I needed."

Even as she thought it, she knew it was a lie. She needed more. Wanted to feel additional girth pushing up inside her. Wanted nothing but skin separating their bodies as he slipped his cock into her and drove her mindless with rapture.

Uncurling one of her hands from the sheet, she groped for the waist of his shorts. Her fingers connected with the fly and she quickly jerked down the tab of his zipper.

Treah's fingers went still inside her sex. His mouth pulled from her nipple. "No," he growled. "You get my fingers. No more. Not tonight."

Since when did dream lovers ration out their sex acts? It was almost enough to make her open her eyes to glare at him. But her eyelids just felt so heavy. And her pussy felt even heavier. She didn't want to make him cross to the point he quit his fingering. If this was all she got tonight, then it was just more to look forward to tomorrow.

Could she keep conjuring him up without guilt?

Yes. Until she was married, doing a guy born of her imagination couldn't be a sin. After she was married . . . That was still four months away. "Just your fingers. Just your mouth. Just fuck me, Treah. Just make me happy."

Finally, he moved without reservation, without requiring an order. Without hesitation, he brought his mouth to hers and sank his tongue inside. So good he tasted, so familiar. His fingers regained their pace, driving into her pussy with purpose, knuckles hitting against her engorged clit with that same purpose.

Keeping with the purpose theme, Dana sucked at his tongue and rode his fingers for optimal pleasure. Orgasm exploded over her as a sizzling, shining thing of beauty. Tremors burst in her belly and her core, rocking her eyes open for a split second, just long enough to see him looking back at her. So hungry. So passionate. So loving.

She was definitely loving every moment of this. Loving his tongue right down till a last tiny shudder quaked in her sex.

She freed his tongue on a giddy sigh. "Mmm . . . yummy."

Treah's fingers left her body. His weight shifted on the bed and then disappeared completely. Her smile went along with him. At least, until she remembered he wasn't real. He was a figment of her imagination that she would call upon again soon.

Just as soon as she got over this feeling that she wanted to slip into a coma and sleep for about fifty years.

Though she no longer felt tired, which meant morning had to have arrived, Dana kept her eyes pinched closed against her pillow and attempted to summon her dream lover. She wasn't a nympho, but last night had seemed so incredibly authentic. She'd woken up with her pajama shorts still damp in the crotch.

Was *she* damp in the crotch?

She slid a hand from beneath her pillow to move it between her thighs. Every man whose bed she'd shared had commented on the way she slept. Maybe it was a little unusual. But having

176 / *Jodi Lynn Copeland*

her knees curled up under her definitely had its advantages. Like now, all she had to do was spread her thighs the tiniest bit and her pussy was off the bed a good four inches, making it easily accessible.

Slipping her hand inside the leg of her shorts, she fingered the length of her slit. Still moist. Her clit still aroused, going by the way her ass bucked with the casual brush of her fingertip against the bead.

She needed to get the day started, had a hard-and-fast schedule to stick with. At the same time, a wake-up orgasm could only be good for her, particularly since her every-other-Saturday sleepover-and-sex date with her fiancé was still six days away.

Digging her forehead into the pillow, Dana pulled her finger free of her shorts to raise up on her knees and tug the shorts down her thighs. Leaving them bunched at her knees, she relaxed her face back against the pillow. No barriers kept her from her sex now. Between how much she'd enjoyed that imagined hasty climax last night and the fact that she really should get her day started, she went right to her pussy, pushing her fingers inside and fingering the slick, warm walls with abandon.

For a long time after ending things with the real Treah, she hadn't taken another lover. That solo time had given her a thorough appreciation for masturbation and a deft awareness of how to get herself off in short order.

She used that knowledge now, pumping her fingers up inside her cunt, hard and fast a few more times before forming them into a fist. Biting the pillow, she dragged her pussy against her fist, feeling that same delicious chafe of knuckles against her clit as she'd known last night—or at least felt like she'd known.

As with her dream, climax built hot and swift, whipping through her as tremulous heat that erupted as a muffled scream of rapturous release.

Gasping for air, Dana lifted her head from the pillow and flopped onto her back as gracefully as her shorts-bound legs would allow. She kept her eyes closed, pleasuring in the residual vibrations in her sex until her breathing was back to normal.

She opened her eyes then. And then she opened them even wider as a gasp of disbelief burst from her mouth.

"What the hell?" Her ceiling and walls were buttercup yellow. Her sheets a brighter shade of the same. She had curtain-covered windows on three sides of her bedroom. This bedroom had eggshell white walls, pale blue sheets, and two side-by-side windows flanked in beige, half-drawn mini blinds.

This bedroom wasn't hers. It wasn't a room she'd ever been inside.

Her breathing returned to erratic on a ragged inhale. Her stomach went queasy. "Oh, God."

What the fuck had she done?

Dragging her shorts back into place and the unfamiliar sheets up to her throat, Dana recalled the day before. A new exhibit had opened at the fine-arts museum and she'd gone out to celebrate its sterling first-day attendance with several of her colleagues. The champagne had flowed freely.

How freely?

So freely that she'd forgotten about her fiancé—who'd done his usual thing and stayed at the museum to catch up on his curator work—and went home with another man?

Swallowing hard, she lifted the covers to get a better look at her body. There were no telltale marks to suggest what might have happened. But there was something unusual and that she would have noticed before if her mind hadn't been so strung out on thoughts of her dream lover.

She was wearing pajamas. To cut down on her air-conditioning bill, she wore only underwear to bed during the steamier of the summer months. Had the owner of this bedroom dressed her?

"Is this Treah's room?" The question rushed into her mind and out of her lips before she had time to digest it.

Normally, she would never have considered such a possibility. But that dream had seemed so real last night. And now here she was, in someone else's bed. That someone might be Treah.

"Who the hell cares!" a panicked voice shouted from her mouth. "Just be glad he isn't here now and leave!"

Dana did her best not to act on instinct these days, but that voice seemed to know exactly what it was about. Throwing back the covers, she scurried out of bed and did a quick search for other clothes. Or shoes. Or a purse. Or something.

The sight out the half-covered windows froze her to the spot. A beach and water. Lots of water. Water that appeared to have no end. Which meant it was either a really huge lake or . . .

No. Not an ocean.

She lived almost two hours from the Atlantic Ocean. In her most drunken state, she wouldn't have come home with a stranger who lived hours away.

Unless that stranger wasn't a stranger at all. Then she might have. Now she had to know immediately if that was the case and if this was Treah's bedroom.

Forgoing the personal-item search, Dana hurried to the closed door and flung it open. A hallway extended out on either side of the door. Veering to the left, she moved to the next door. This one was closed, as well, and when she opened it a second, larger bedroom came into view.

Mini blinds cloaked each of the room's four windows, shutting out all but a trace of the morning sunlight. Still, enough light bled through the blinds and in from the hallway that she could easily see the body in the bed fifteen feet away. The body that was covered with a sheet alone from the waist down and whose profile became distinctively male as she drew closer.

That became distinctively familiar when she reached the side of his bed.

In the pure light, he might look different, a bit older perhaps. In the low light, he looked exactly the same. The same as he'd looked eight years ago. And the same as he'd looked in her dream. Which it now seemed highly unlikely was a dream at all.

"Treah?" The lone word shuddered out as a throaty whisper.

His eyes opened instantly. "Dana." He blinked and then shook his head as if disbelieving the sight of her. "What are you doing here?"

"I, uh . . . I . . ." What *was* she doing? Not here, but acting like she was guilty of something? If she was in his home, it was because he'd brought her here.

Annoyance funneled up past her panic. Crossing her arms over her chest, she scowled. "No. I don't buy it. You know damn well why I'm here."

On a yawn, he tossed back the covers to climb from the bed. Naked. Three feet away. "You have something you need help moving past?"

"Yes." The sight of his body when he put it on full display that way.

Dana gulped down a hard breath, far too aware of the arousal pitching through her blood and warming her core. Muscles in his thighs and arms, developed to the point of perfection, flexed and shifted with his moves. His black hair was cropped near military style, the way he always wore it during the summer months. The faint shadow of dark stubble rose along his jawline and was patchy over his upper lip, lending an air of imperfection that somehow made him more appealing.

Time had been far too good to the man.

Time, or all the women he'd spent the last eight years screwing.

Sex was Treah's only true passion in life. It used to be and she needed to believe that it was still, to use it as the cold rush of reality her burning body craved. "My arrogant ass of an ex."

Smiling, he went to the closest window and pulled open the blind, casting the light in to detail his sun-bronzed skin. He looked back at her with amusement lighting his eyes. "Jesus,

Dana. You'd think you hadn't seen me naked a thousand times before for how red your face is."

"You'd think you have all the civility of a caveman for parading around that way in front of me." Why *did* his body have to bother her so much? Her fiancé might not be big on nudity outside of a darkened bedroom, but she'd seen every inch and angle of plenty of other men's bodies, from those of flesh and blood to the breathtakingly beautiful statues in the museum.

"You know what they say"—humor was in his voice now, as well—"looking's free, so go ahead and ogle."

Realizing that she *was* ogling brought even more heat to her cheeks. She forced her attention away—to the wall, to the dresser. As though her gaze was a beacon for his body, Treah moved to the dresser and pulled black briefs from the top drawer.

Turning back to face her, he worked them up his legs. Over his thighs. Past his—

"This is *my* bedroom," he pointed out.

Yes, and it was such a better thing to focus on than the part of his anatomy his briefs came to rest against. The part she'd probably held in her hand last night. The part she'd begged for him to put inside her.

Oh, God. Oh, God. Oh, God. What would Claude say when he found out?

He wouldn't find out. She didn't even know for sure if she'd done anything with the living version of Treah. She would get out of this house, wherever it was, and get back to her fiancé. Life would be fine. Just fine.

If she could get the image of Treah's cock lying soft against a thatch of black curls out of her head, it would be.

Dana looked around his bedroom in an attempt to flush the vision away. The room looked familiar. A carbon copy of the one from her dream.

Had she said "Oh, God" yet?

"You can't honestly believe I was an ass to you?"

She brought her attention back to his. Jeans were in the process of camouflaging his lower half. Much, much better. Safer. Less temptation.

Temptation?

No. She didn't want him. Not when she was fully awake. She also couldn't disagree with his question. "No. You weren't an ass." Going to the window, she stared out at the water. It had to be the ocean. "Where are we, Treah? Your home, but where is that?"

"Ecstasy Island."

"Ecstasy . . ." Oh, no. This was so not good. She wasn't even on the mainland. She was at the sensual healing resort she'd arranged for her twin to visit in the hopes the resort's healing coaches could relieve her of her fears. Deanne was supposed to be brought here while she slept last night. Had the resort pick-up guys somehow mistaken her for her sister? Was Deanne supposed to be the one with Treah as a dream lover?

Not caring a bit for the way the thought churned her belly, Dana rushed out, "Deanne's supposed to be here, not me."

Concern entered Treah's eyes. "What's the matter with your sister?"

"Same old, same old. Self-esteem issues that have her pretty well convinced she has no chance with the male population. Now that I'm getting married, it's even worse."

His concern turned to displeasure, and Dana realized what she'd said. If not for her big mouth, he would never have had to know since they didn't believe in engagement rings in Claude's family. Still, that she'd let it slip shouldn't be a big deal. Treah shouldn't be upset over the idea of her with another man, not after so much time apart. Not when his job as a healing coach had to pit him with other women on a regular basis. Maybe not long term but the point remained.

He went to the closet. "Who's the guy?"

He *shouldn't* be upset, and yet, there was definite irritation in his voice. Well, he wouldn't have to worry over it for long. She had no intention of staying on the island beyond the time it took to find a boat and a driver. "No one you'd know."

He pulled a white polo shirt off a hanger. Slipping the shirt over his head, he asked, "Let me guess, he has a real job and passion that extends beyond sex?"

The cut in his words was sharp enough to have her bringing her arms back around her chest, this time for comfort. "Did you have me brought here, Treah?"

"If I did—" A cordless phone chirped from the nightstand at the head of the bed. Putting his first finger in the air, he moved to the stand, grabbed the phone, and punched the "talk" button. He spoke a few words that were undecipherable to Dana from ten feet away, cursed near silently, and then set the phone back down. "Sorry, but you're going to have to hold that thought. I'm needed at the office."

What? Was he out of his mind? Just hold her thought and stay in his home while he ran off to work?

What work could he even have to do away from here? According to the resort pamphlet, the healing coaches each had their own cabin, which the clients stayed in with them during their time on the island. Taking another look around the room, remembering the bedroom she'd woken in and the hallway that brought her to this room, she frowned.

This wasn't a cabin.

Treah was already to the bedroom door. Accepting she only had time for one question, she asked, "What am I supposed to do while you work?"

"Make yourself at home. Your clothes are in the dresser in the other bedroom. There's a bathroom down the hall. Towels are under the sink. I'll be back as soon as possible." He stepped out of the room, then poked his head back in. "If you don't hear from me by eleven, head down to the beach for the ice-breaker volleyball game. I realize it's not exactly a sophisticated way to spend a morning but, for the sake of the other clients, try to pretend like you're having a good time."

3

Treah took the stairs to the first floor two steps at a time. He reached the storage room the stairwell ended in and continued his fast clip past metal, floor-to-ceiling shelves of filing boxes and office equipment to the door on the opposite side of the room. Crossing the hall, he shoved open the manager's office door.

Chris Cavanaugh looked up from behind his desk. His gaze connected with Treah's and a slow, knowing grin spread across his face. "Good night?"

"Yeah, and it's an even better morning to kick your ass." Treah's gut burned with the memory of coming upon Dana in his bed last night. Of what he'd allowed her to talk him into doing. Of how much more he'd wanted to do. Goddamn, Chris. "What the hell were you thinking having her put in my bed?"

"They put her in your bed?" He sounded shocked.

Treah snorted. "Nice try."

With a laugh, Chris rocked back in his chair and rested his

neck against his bridged fingers. "Payback's a bitch, man. As you might recall, you put a woman in my bed not so long ago."

"A woman who loves you and that you wanted there."

"You don't want Dana in your bed?" Chris sounded shocked again. Only, this time it was legitimate, going by the way his expression matched his tone.

"No. Probably not. Not right now, at least." Treah groaned. Christ, why couldn't he have left it at a simple no?

Because nothing about this morning had been simple. Not the arousal that turned Dana's eyes from soft brown with copper flecks to solid smoky copper when she'd ogled his naked body. And not the call he'd gotten immediately after that ogling came to an end.

Stepping back, he grabbed hold of the doorknob. "I don't have time to argue. Sonya woke me up with the cheerful news that Dad called."

Chris's expression went from surprised to disappointed. He rocked forward, planting his palms on the desktop. "Sonya woke you up? What happened to Dana?"

"She's in the spare bedroom. Where she *belongs.*" Treah stressed the last word, though he wasn't sure if it was for Chris's sake or his own. She'd felt too good in his arms last night, her damp body loving his fingers. Her lips soft and hungry against his own. Way in the hell too good.

"Your dad seriously called?" Chris asked, his displeasure over the Dana scenario gone. "Why now, after so much time?"

"Claire's article."

Chris flinched. "Shit. I'm sorry, man, but you did agree to let her do it."

"I'm glad she did." No matter how much tension may result from this morning's call, Chris's newspaper-reporter-girl-friend's feature article on the healing resort had both this location, an hour's boat ride off the coast of Massachusetts, and the recently opened Pacific location booked through the end of the fall. "It's been great for business, particularly on getting word out about the Pacific location. From what Sonya deciphered from Dad's message, disguised as a ten-minute tirade, he just never knew what the resort was about until the article."

"A name like Ecstasy Island does make it hard to guess," Chris said dryly.

"Apparently it did for him." Per Sonya, his dad had as good as accused Treah of running a gigolo service. They'd barely spoken in the seven years since his brother Blair's death, so that his dad was unimpressed by his business venture shouldn't bother him. But, like seeing Dana again, it got to him bad.

Channeling his frustration into his grip on the doorknob, Treah divulged, "He thinks this place is catering sex by the oceanside and wants back the money he gave me to help get it off the ground by the end of the week."

"The man he was before Blair died wouldn't have cared what the business was." Chris's voice rang with both support for Treah and guilt for himself. "He would have been proud of you for making it a success."

Treah tackled the guilt half because he knew part of Chris still did and possibly always would blame himself for Blair's murder while in prison. "This isn't your fault, Chris. Or Claire's. It also doesn't have to be a big deal. I have the money to give him. It's just going to take a hell of a lot of juggling to get it all in one place by Saturday."

Time might have made Treah's body even easier on the eyes, but his feelings for her were clearly the same as they'd always been.

"Pretty shitty," Dana mused aloud as she took stock of the contents of her bathroom bag, which she'd found on a small oak table, flanked by a set of chairs, in the bedroom she'd woken up in.

At least, his feelings that revolved around her career and the influence that it had on her life were pretty shitty.

Going by his "volleyball isn't sophisticated" remark, he still believed her work had turned her into a snob. She wasn't a snob. She liked culture. Loved her job as Under-Curator of Abstract Art for New Hampshire's prized Fine Arts Galleria. The position meant spending the majority of her time surrounded by people who ate, drank, and breathed class, and, most of the time, she loved her work even more for it.

Treah never had.

The few times he'd agreed to attend museum-sponsored events, he'd been a complete ass, whispering wisecracks in her ear about her colleagues or the food or the art itself: pretentious. Stuffy. A foolish way to blow a shitload of dough.

"Too damn bad if he feels that way."

After all, not everyone could be as lowbrow as he was. Not everyone could toy around with "play" jobs as the mood suited them and spend the rest of their time focusing on sex, sex, and more sex.

Speaking of things not everyone could do. She couldn't spend another day on this island. Even if that was exactly what her colleagues—her fiancé included—expected her to do.

Not ready to speak with Claude, she'd called Jane, the Galleria's assistant director, to let her know she couldn't make work. Dana had been prepared with an excuse of a bad viral bug. But she hadn't needed an excuse. According to Jane, the museum had been informed nearly a month before that she was being whisked away for a surprise getaway on a private island.

"What a brilliant treat!" Jane had gushed with her typical panache. "A three-week sojourn before the wedding planning and festivities become intensive."

Dana wasn't sure what stunned her more: that someone had scheduled her time off and had gotten it approved, or that they'd scheduled her three *whole* weeks off. She rarely took time off, so she had plenty of vacation hours to use up. When *she* chose to use them. Which wasn't right now.

Tomorrow, they'd find that out at the museum firsthand, when she showed up for work at eight o'clock as usual.

Today, this morning at least, she would do her best to enjoy unwanted time away.

Setting her bathroom bag on top of the dresser that Treah said she would find her clothes in, Dana did a quick check of the dresser's contents. The top drawer held her underthings, socks, and a couple of bikini swimsuits; the second drawer shirts; and the third drawer shorts and jeans. They all had one common theme.

"Sensuality."

Lovely. This day kept getting better and better. Whoever packed her stuff had brought along her most scanty clothes. Those things she rarely had an occasion to wear.

Not eager to wear any of them in front of Treah, she grabbed out the shorts with the most coverage in the ass and a lacy white strapless bra and matching thong with the most coverage in the—well, the most coverage possible given it was a thong. Unable to decide between a teal, halter-style top and an orange, off-the-shoulder, midriff-baring one, she took both, grabbed the bag from the dresser top, and headed out into the hallway in search of a shower to wash away the remnants of orgasm.

Heat swept through her as the memory of Treah's mouth clamped around her nipple came charging back. Urging away that nasty thought, which wasn't nearly as nasty as it should be, she hurried down the hall.

Past his bedroom, two closed doors occupied the end of the hallway. She pulled open the one on the right, groped the inner wall to locate and snap on a light switch, and found herself staring into a five-by-ten storage closet.

Rows of shelves lined the wall on either side. Boxes filled

those walls. Ecstasy's logo, which Dana remembered from the resort brochure, was stamped on each of the box ends. She took a step inside the room to read the words beneath the logo. It differed on nearly every box but, like her clothes, each of them had a common theme. It wasn't sensuality, either. Rather, they had to do with resort operations.

"Taxes. Payroll. Repeat Clientele." She read each label aloud.

Why would Treah have all this stuff in his house?

Well, he did say to make herself at home. Sating her curiosity would be as good as doing that.

Feeling a little guilty regardless, Dana pulled a box with "Taxes" and the previous year's date on it from the shelf. She sank cross-legged onto the closet floor and lifted the lid off the box. Olive green files hung neatly inside. She tugged out the one labeled W-2. A scan of the tax document had her eyes widening with the resort's profit margin, and then nearly popping out of her head with the name of the person who reported the earnings.

Apparently, she'd been mistaken about Treah. His attitude *had* changed with time. At least, his business-sense attitude, because he didn't just work for Ecstasy Island, doling out his time and inborn sensuality to the all-female clientele as a healing coach; he owned the place.

"So what?" a stunned voice asked from her mouth. "He cares about more than sex these days. That doesn't change the way you feel about him."

"Good point," Dana agreed for the sake of appeasing that voice.

Silently, though, she couldn't help but wonder if, despite his volleyball remark, he would value her own business sense these days. And, silently, she had to acknowledge that she really didn't have any idea how she felt about him.

She hadn't ended things because she'd fallen out of love with him. It had been because she thought he could never love her as a whole—person, partner, and professional.

Was the fire still burning between them? And, after how strongly he'd affected her both last night and in his bedroom this morning, did she have the fortitude to ignore the heat long enough to get off this island?

Treah took one step into his bedroom and froze with the lyrics drifting through the connected bathroom's closed door. Dana had a great singing voice. Her naturally low, smoky tone came through as a sultry seduction. Slipping over him. Refreshing him after the stressful-as-hell last hour down in his office. Inviting him to come inside the bathroom and do exactly what she was suggesting he do.

"Come a little bit closer." Her voice raised a few octaves as she reached the song's refrain. "You're my kind of man. So big and so strong."

She wasn't really singing to him. Probably.

And, probably, he shouldn't pretend like she was and get closer. But then, she had gotten to see him in the buff. It seemed only fair that he got a peek at the same. Frankly, he could *use* a peek at her most excellent goods since just as soon as he told her what he'd come up here to tell her, he had to get back to the headache in his office.

She beckoned with the promise of a long night spent alone. He couldn't let that happen. No woman who felt so right in his arms should need to sleep alone. Before she could invite José, who seemed too good of a euphemism for her fiancé, into the song, Treah opened the bathroom door and crossed to the bathtub.

Pulling the shower curtain aside a foot put a stunning rear view of Dana on display. She stood with one foot poised on the ledge near the bath spigot, shaving a thigh as she belted out the lyrics. Like he'd noticed last night, her butt was rounder than it used to be, in all the best ways. The kind of ways that had visions of taking her from behind spinning through his head and hardening his cock.

The part of the song where José made his entrance was just about to arrive. Before either that happened, or he helped himself to her shower and her body, Treah asked, "Is this close enough?"

On a scream, Dana dropped both the razor and her foot from the ledge to swivel around in the tub. She grabbed hold of the shower curtain, whipping it back against her body. The shower spray pelted the curtain's edge and was redirected against his chest, drenching his polo shirt nearly instantly.

With one hand holding the curtain in place, she used the other to switch the water from the showerhead to the tub head. She looked back at the shirt plastered to his chest and smiled spitefully. "Serves you right." Her gaze lifted to his. "What the hell are you doing in here?"

Apparently, getting soaked and aroused.

Treah returned her smile with a seductive one of his own. "I thought you were serenading me."

Her eyes narrowed, and he laughed. A real laugh that felt like exactly what he needed. Or, at least, exactly what he needed and had a chance of getting from her. He could go for a duo shower, a thorough scrubdown from her skilled hands. A thorough hand job. So much more.

Since he wasn't getting any of those things, he focused on his reason for coming upstairs. "The volleyball game starts in a few minutes. One of the guests is battling jet lag and is still asleep, so they could really use another player to even things out. Unfortunately, I have more work to do."

Dana's glare changed to an intrigued look. "Running this place is a huge time investment?"

"Been snooping, have we?" The real question was how did she feel about her find? Did it raise him up in her eyes? Bring him to a level closer to the high-and-mighty rank of her friends and colleagues? Make him worthy?

"You said to make myself at home. If your stuff is my stuff, you can't technically call it snooping."

Technically, he could call it whatever he wanted. Maybe later he would call it misbehaving and consider a proper reprimand that involved the swat of his hand against her lush ass. Now, he had to get thoughts of her out of his head, and the best approach was to reallocate his assets in short order into it. "It can be a lot of work. But it's worth it."

"For the money?" she pressed in a voice edged with hope.

Maybe later he would ask why she wanted to believe he only valued this place for its income. For now, Treah pointed out what she should have already known. "Some things change in time, Dana. How I feel about wealth isn't one of them."

Slipping a wolfish smile into place, he slid his gaze to those succulent curves now masked by the shower curtain. "Neither is how I feel about your body."

A breathy gasp escaped her before the glare reclaimed her eyes. Laughing to himself, he headed for the bathroom's second door, which led out into the hallway. A white lace strapless bra and a nearly invisible matching thong lay on the toilet lid, quickening his pulse when he'd almost reached the door. A pair of small tan shorts and two even smaller shirts hung from the towel rack.

His smile grew with the reminder of her indecisiveness. She'd always had a problem deciding what to wear. He'd always been eager to help her out, on the condition he got to assist in removing the chosen item later in the day.

The odds were slim that he'd get to help her take either of these shirts off. He offered his help anyway. "Go with the orange. It brings out the copper in your eyes."

* * *

Wearing the orange, off-the-shoulder, midriff-baring top, Dana made her way through Treah's second-floor home in search of an exit. She wasn't wearing the top to please him. But, rather, because he had a great eye when it came to style. Which was just one of the reasons she'd never understood how he could not get her work. Between that and the culture of his heritage, they should have been a superb match in every way.

But he hadn't embraced his heritage by working alongside his affluent father in the hotel ownership industry, and she and Treah hadn't been a superb match. Even now, when Treah had a real career, they would probably go together like oil and water. She would never know for certain, since she already had a full-time man who was a superb match.

Mostly a superb match. No, Claude *was* a superb match.

Mostly.

"Oh, shut up!"

When Dana had spoken to the resort manager about how they got women onto the island who might not be thrilled about the prospect of being there, he'd told her they used a natural sedative. Obviously, she'd been given that sedative last night. Obviously, too, it was still in her system, making words come out of her mouth and thoughts fill her head, because she never talked to herself this way.

A door appeared ahead as she cleared a homey-looking living room and moved through a kitchen that had an attached dining area. She forgot about the sedative in order to hurry through the doorway and down wooden steps to a blacktopped driveway with a forest green truck sporting Ecstasy Island's logo on its side.

She cleared the shadow of the two-story, tan structure's roof overhang, and sunshine fell against her highly exposed skin.

Tipping back her head, she closed her eyes. "Mmm... nice."

She felt a little like a cat preening in the warmth of the summer sun, but it was so rare that she got outside this time of the day. Never on a Sunday, since the weekends were when the museum was at its busiest.

Voices carried on a light, warm breeze laden with the briny scent of the ocean. Dana opened her eyes to follow those voices around to the front of the building. A hundred feet away, a couple dozen people, most of whom were wearing bathing suits that covered even less than her clothing did, stood gathered around a volleyball net. The ocean was there as well, a lone sailboat dotting the horizon and a gentle surf slapping against the white-sand beach. Gulls dove into the sparkling, blue-green water. A few more tottered along the shoreline, pecking at the sand.

She was on this island by deception, not on vacation; still, it was just too gorgeous not to smile and jog toward the crowd gathered around the volleyball net. She wasn't playing to please Treah or to prove she wasn't a snob. All right, maybe it was a little to prove she wasn't a snob. More so, though, it was because she'd always hated idleness. It was either the game or snooping through his house some more. After her last find and the questions it raised, volleyball seemed the much-preferred alternative.

"Glad you could join us," an attractive shirtless guy in black canvas shorts, who looked a handful of years younger than her thirty-two, said as she joined the half of the group on the nearest side of the volleyball net.

With wind-whipped dark blond hair and pale blue eyes, the guy seemed remotely familiar. Before Dana could question if she knew him from somewhere, the tall woman with short black hair standing next to her offered a warm smile. "Hi. I'm Gena."

Dana smiled back. "Dana. It's nice to meet you."

"So what are you in for?" Gena asked.

"In for?"

"You know, here for?"

"Oh." Right. These women were all resort clients, the men their healing coaches. "Nothing. I'm not supposed to be here. There was a mistake made."

Gena's smile grew understanding. "I feel ya."

"How about you?" Dana bit her tongue around the question. What if she didn't want to know the answer? The resort was dedicated to helping women overcome their fears via sensual means. Those fears could be wide ranging and maybe more than she would be comfortable with.

"I'm not exactly keen on men," Gena supplied.

As feared, Dana wasn't comfortable with that response. It wasn't because she was snobby, but just a matter of course that she didn't have much experience with lesbians. How was she supposed to act? "Uh, right. I feel ya."

Gena moved closer, almost close enough their bodies touched. A suggestive smile curving her lips, she thrust out her breasts, which were barely contained to begin with in a red and blue handkerchief-patterned bikini top. "Go right on ahead and feel me, honey."

Oh, God! Dana felt her eyes go wide. A gasp escaped before she could stop it.

With a burst of laughter, Gena regained her normal posture. She stopped laughing to give Dana a friendly smile. "Kidding. I love men in the physical sense. I just have issues when it comes to trusting them."

"Oh." Oh, did she ever feel hugely out of place! Did Treah feel this way, too? Or did he fit in here, but had felt the way she was feeling now those times she'd exposed him to her career world? Her thoughts hadn't been much better than his whispered wisecracks.

"Welcome to Ecstasy Island," the blond-haired guy who'd greeted Dana shouted above the crowd. "I'm Chris, the resort manager. Before we get started with the game, let's make some quick introductions. It's up to you if you want to share why you're here or not, though doing so will help to kick off your healing."

The mix of men and women on the other side of the volleyball net took turns announcing themselves. Then Gena started off for the group on their side. "Hi, everyone. I'm Gena and I'm here because most every guy I've ever been with has morphed into a faithless asshole about the time I'm ready to get serious." A few snorts, laughs, and nods of agreement followed, and she continued, "My goal is to leave here not afraid to trust a guy for more than sex." She looked over at Dana. "And this is Dana. She's in denial about her fears."

What? "I'm not in denial. I'm not supposed to be here!"

From his referee post at the side of the volleyball net, Chris smiled compassionately. "If you have to be somewhere by accident, then you picked the right place."

"But I'm really not—"

"Who's next?" he cut her off.

The rest of the players introduced themselves while Dana felt like an even bigger outcast than before Gena accused her of being in denial. Maybe it wasn't too late to opt out of this game. . . .

She glanced at the beach behind her. Several cabanas sat in the sand twenty feet from the water's edge. A brunette lay in a chaise under one of the cabanas. She was watching the players, an odd sort of look on her face. The brunette's gaze shifted to Dana and went instantly cool. Or was it snobby?

Is that what she would look like if she opted out? Is that how Treah saw her?

"You're up for first serve," Gena said.

Dana looked over at the black-haired woman to find her holding the volleyball out to her. She hadn't played in years, but she *did* know how to play. Damn good, as a matter of fact.

Forgetting most everything but the game, she served the ball. And as it came back to her a few spikes later, she really did forget everything. Forgot all her concerns to have simple fun with a bunch of strangers.

A win for each side later, Dana bowed out due to sore muscles and a sunburned nose. Several others had quit playing after the first game and were either swimming or lounging on the beach. Dana headed for one of the open cabanas to relax in the shade. As she was settling in, a male voice said, "Hi, Dana."

She looked up to find Chris, the resort manager, squatting in front of her. Even with black sunglasses on, he looked too familiar for their paths to have not crossed at some point. "Do I know you from somewhere?"

"We met a few times. Back when you were with Treah."

A friend of Treah's, she should have known. Or was he more of an accomplice these days? Had he been involved in "Operation Exchange Deanne for Dana"?

Dana searched her memory to come up with a last name. "Cavanaugh, right? Chris Cavanaugh?"

He nodded. "How've you been?"

"Good until I woke up here." She let her displeasure come through in her voice. "I was serious before. I'm not supposed to be here."

"I handle all the reservations. Deanne seemed to think otherwise."

So it wasn't Treah who was responsible for her being here then, but her own twin! She shouldn't be surprised. It wasn't the first time Deanne had done something in an attempt to push Dana and Treah together. And, too, it explained why the museum had approved an "outsider's" request for Dana to have time off. Still, the news left her momentarily speechless.

Finding her voice, she asked, "Is my sister here?"

"She called to make you an appointment and found out

you'd done the same for her. With Treah's permission, she swapped herself out for you."

She narrowed her eyes shrewdly. "I knew he had to be involved somehow."

"Deanne was very convincing with her worry over your fear."

"What fear?"

"You'd have to ask Treah."

No, she wouldn't. Because she didn't have any fears. Ready for a topic change, Dana searched her memory for more on Chris. "You're friends with Treah's brother, Blair, right?"

"I was."

She couldn't see his eyes behind the shades, but his tone sounded suddenly morose. And that left her feeling uncomfortable all over again. "Sorry. I didn't realize you two had a falling out."

"We didn't."

"Oh."

"That's another question for Treah."

Apparently, there were a lot of those. And she didn't plan on sticking around to get the answers to any of them, either. "How about this one: when can I get off this island?"

"The pick-up guys—the ones who bring clients to and from the island—only come every three weeks. Treah or I could take you to the mainland, but not today."

"In the morning?" One more night she could handle. Given the sedative was well out of her system by bedtime and she didn't conjure any more dream lover Treahs who weren't dream lovers at all.

God, that polo shirt had looked amazing clinging to his chest in the bathroom. Or, rather, his chest had looked amazing pressed up tight against the soaked, white cotton. It had almost been as good as when he'd climbed from his bed completely naked.

"There's a good possibility," Chris responded.

His voice dragged Dana'a mind back to the present, with the realization her thoughts were dipping down to her thong and straight to her pussy. Treah *had* looked good both in the bathroom and in his bedroom, but that wasn't something she should be considering. She also wasn't going to spend another second considering whether the fire still burned between them.

She was going to get off this island, just as she'd planned to do before learning of his true position with the resort.

Not tomorrow morning via Chris or Treah. But today, when either Deanne finally answered her phone and arranged Dana a ride home, or Dana tracked down a water taxi and, then, a real taxi with a driver happy to take his passengers long distances.

Or, hell, if it came to it she would call Claude and explain the whole crazy situation. Minus the bit about Treah fingering her to orgasm, of course.

The dream lover version of Treah, that is. Because starting now she was going to assume the denial role Gena had given her, and know that he hadn't touched her or kissed her for years in any manner outside of her mind.

4

With not nearly as much accomplished as he'd hoped for, Treah threw in the towel on his workday. Saying a quick good-bye to Sonya, who tossed him an awkward smile from the receptionist area desk, he headed for the stairwell to the second floor.

Anticipation at seeing Dana mounted with every step he took. He'd done a good job of getting her suggestive lyrics and naked, shaking ass out of his mind when he returned to his office after dropping in on her shower. For about twenty minutes, he had. Then he made the mistake of looking out the patio door and saw her down on the beach playing volleyball with the resort clients and staff.

She hadn't looked sophisticated or snobby. She looked like she had the day they'd met in the cocktail lounge of one of his father's hotels, carefree and high on life. Treah had been killing time bartending and Dana had been enjoying a glass of wine while she waited for her friends to join her to celebrate their graduation from undergrad school.

Then, she'd worn her hair pulled back in a ponytail. Earlier today, she'd worn another of those high, flirty ponytails, along with the small tan shorts that barely covered her butt cheeks.

At the time, Treah had forced his attention off her ass and on to his work. Now, she *was* his work. More specifically, he needed to learn how she really felt about her fiancé. And how she really felt about Treah.

Heart beating fast, he pushed in the door at the top of the stairs. The living room was directly in front of him. Dana lay on the long end of a tan, L-shaped couch, reading a magazine. Her hair was free of the ponytail and fell in loose, brown and gold waves against the couch pillow. He would have liked to have stood there and watched her for a while. But the door *snicked* shut, and she looked up from the magazine to frown.

After she had such a good time on the beach, he'd hoped she would be in a better mood this afternoon. Clearly, she was still ticked at him.

He crossed into the living room and smiled at her from the end of the couch. "Hungry?"

"Bored." Sitting up, she tossed the magazine onto the wooden coffee table situated central to the couch's two sides. "Who packed my entertainment bag?"

"I would guess Deanne." Treah could also guess that her sister made the bag as dull as possible in the hopes that Dana would come to him for a better distraction.

"Ah, the evil twin," she said dryly.

"I take it that means you found out who had you brought here?"

Her frown turned to a scowl. "I found out that she dangled 'Dana bait' and you were only too eager to bite."

"Your sister has very real concerns about your welfare. Ones that need more immediate attention than your concerns about hers."

"Let me guess: they involve me getting married in four months?"

His smile attempted to evaporate at the ugly reminder. Forcing it to stay in place, he moved up in front of her. "I'm not at liberty to divulge that information just yet. Fortunately, I am allowed to see you fed." He offered his hand. "Help me find something for dinner?"

She sent his hand a wary look, but then took it and let him pull her to her feet. It should have been a casual move, a simple lift and release. But Dana's fingers in his didn't feel casual to him. They felt like her body had last night, like her kisses had.

Familiar. Right. Like no matter how she felt about him, there was becoming an increasingly good chance that Treah still loved her—occasional uppity tendencies and all—as much as he ever had.

He didn't want to let her go. Her irritated look forced his hand, literally, making him free her fingers and gesture for her to precede him into the kitchen. Which actually wasn't so bad in the long run, given the enticing way her butt cheeks winked at him past the tiny cuffs of her shorts with each of her steps.

She turned around, stealing his view as she settled against the counter near the sink. Crossing her arms over her breasts, she gave him another view to consider. She still wore the orange, off-the-shoulder top that brought out the copper in her eyes and showcased her navel and the trim line of her belly. No straps were visible on her shoulders, which meant she likely still wore the lacy white strapless bra, as well.

And the thong?

He slid his gaze lower, to the crotch of her little tan shorts, and Dana said in an indignant voice, "I'm not for dinner, Treah."

With a guilty laugh, he brought his attention to the refrigerator and pulled open the door. "Tuesday night's a seafood dinner gathering in the meeting room downstairs, so we should probably stick with meat or pasta tonight."

"I won't be here Tuesday night, so it really doesn't matter to me."

Treah's gut tightened with the thought of her leaving so soon. Thanks to his dad's shitty timing, he'd yet to spend more than an hour total with her. Not responding to her comment one way or the other, he closed the refrigerator door and opened the pantry next to it. He loved to cook, many times found it as relaxing as the view out his windows and patio door. Tonight, he wanted to concentrate on Dana as much as possible.

Pulling out a box of spaghetti and a jar of sauce, he set them on the counter. Aware that she hated to be inactive, he nodded at the cupboard near her thigh. "Can you grab me a couple of pots and a strainer?"

He really had asked for her help to be nice. But then, he discovered it came with the added benefit of her ass being put back on display, as she turned and bent over to grab the requested items. It would be nearly impossible to see the scrap of white lace covering her mound from this angle. He swore he caught a glimpse of the thong anyway. Between the already stellar view and that glimpse, his blood was running hotter and his cock was giving serious thoughts to rising to the occasion.

Dana swiveled around with the pots and strainer in hand. Treah quickly busied himself reaching into an overhead cupboard for wineglasses and one of several bottles of Rothschild merlot he'd picked up specifically for her visit.

Setting the glasses on the counter, he looked over. "Do you still favor red?"

Hesitation entered her eyes as she set the pots and strainer on the counter. "Are you trying to get me drunk in the hopes it will have the same effect as the sedative?"

Though he knew exactly what she meant—his cock, as well, going by the way it gave into its rousing urge—he asked, "What effect?"

She searched his face a few seconds before shaking her head. "Never mind. I'll have some wine. And, yes, I still favor red."

He uncorked the bottle and poured them each a glass. She sank back against the counter again and sipped at her wine while he started the water boiling for the noodles and poured the sauce into a pot to heat.

Treah was reaching for his own wineglass when she said, "Chris said maybe tomorrow morning one of you can take me back to the mainland."

His fingers curled around the glass's stem. Damn, he wished Chris would have come up with some plausible-sounding lie that required a delay in her departure. It would have saved Treah from doing the dirty work himself. Or not so dirty, since he actually did have a good reason not to take her back in the morning. "If I can get the mess straightened out that I was dealing with today and will probably be hammering away at again after dinner, I'll take you."

"Thank you." Gratitude shone in Dana's eyes with her smile.

It was the first real smile she'd given him since being reunited, and it made him wonder if Deanne wasn't mistaken. If Dana was so anxious to get home, then maybe her fiancé did have what it took to make her completely happy. Maybe she wore lacy bras and almost invisible panties for the guy on a regular basis.

And where did that leave Treah?

Licking his wounds for the second time in eight years. At least the wounds wouldn't be so deep this time, since he wasn't even certain that he still loved her.

Dana sipped at her wine and tried to ignore the hurt look in Treah's eyes. The irritated look he'd gotten over mention of her marriage this morning, she could handle. But he looked upset in a dejected way now, like the thought of her leaving got to him deep down inside.

She didn't want to think about his feelings. Her own feelings, either. If she'd gotten off the island today as hoped, she could have continued to play the denial game. But she hadn't gotten off the island. For reasons Dana could well guess, and that had to do with caller ID telling her sister who was on the other end of the line, Deanne was answering neither her cell phone nor her home phone. As for her own attempts, Dana had zero luck finding a rental boat to come pick her up and deliver her back to the mainland on such short notice. She would have to accept Treah's offer of a ride for tomorrow as sincere and, in the meantime, appease the hurt look in his eyes.

Setting her wineglass on the counter, she smiled reassuringly. "It's not that I don't want to spend time with you."

"Yes, it is."

"Okay. Maybe in a roundabout way it is. But I'm engaged, Treah, and—"

"Already having second thoughts. You don't need me to make them bigger."

Second thoughts? Where would he have gotten that idea? Claude was perfect for her.

Mostly. No, not mostly. He was.

Almost.

Oh, geez, stupid voice, quit already!

"Whatever Deanne told you, she was wrong." Her sister had to be the source for his speculation. "She just doesn't like Claude."

Treah turned around to stir the sauce. "Nice name. Very cultivated."

He might be facing away, but Dana still caught his snort. She'd wondered if he would take her business sense more seriously nowadays. Given how quick he was to mock her fiancé, the answer was a big fat no freaking way.

Resentment funneled through her. She wanted to let it out vocally, but doing so would be pointless. Tomorrow, their lives would again go separate ways. Tonight, she might as well keep the peace as much as possible.

She waited until he turned back around and had a sip of his wine to start in on a safer topic, in that it had nothing to do with either of them. "What's the deal with Chris and Blair?"

The wineglass's descent stilled in midair. "What do you mean?"

Treah didn't sound morose the way Chris had, but he didn't sound pleased by the question, either. Since she'd already broached the subject, she continued, "When I recalled that he's a friend of Blair's, Chris responded that he *was* a friend. Then when I said I hadn't realized they'd had a falling out, he said they hadn't and that what did happen was a question for you."

His expression went blank as he set the wineglass down on the counter. In a deadpan tone, he confided, "Blair was killed seven years ago."

Dana couldn't do the deadpan thing. She wasn't even sure if her trembling legs were going to keep her upright. "Oh, my God." After setting her wineglass safely on the counter beside his, she brought a hand over her thudding heart. "I had no idea, Treah. I'm so sorry."

"Of course, you didn't." He turned to stir the sauce again. "It's old news, Dana. Don't let it ruin your dinner."

Old news? How could death *ever* be old news, especially when Blair had been so young? How could Treah act so unaffected? "But he was your *brother*."

"Was and always will be," he agreed as he spun back. "I'm not saying I don't still think of him every day or miss him like hell. It's just something I've accepted and done my best to move on. Having Chris around helps."

"What happened?" she asked unsteadily.

"He was fatally stabbed by a cellmate." Emotion came into his eyes, weighing down the greenish-yellow shade and sounding in his voice.

Her heart clenched for his loss. As with any sibling, Deanne could be a pain in the ass—by sticking Dana on an island with her ex-lover, for example—but she couldn't imagine life without her.

She wanted to pull Treah into her arms and soothe him the way she hadn't known to do seven years ago. But she'd caught the hungry way he'd been eyeing her when they'd first come into the kitchen and she also caught the heated way her body responded to that eyeing. She didn't dare risk getting too close. Not when their emotions were already running high.

"I forgot about the shooting," she admitted. "Has Chris gotten past it?"

"He's still working on it. Having a good woman helps."

"He's married?"

"Not yet, but I can see it happening sooner rather than later." Warmth returned to Treah's eyes with his smile. "Up until a few months ago, Chris was my head healer. Claire was his client. Actually, I'm surprised you didn't meet her during the volleyball game. She's a good-looking brunette in her mid-twenties with big blue eyes and bangs."

Relieved to see him smiling again, even if that relief was a little too acute for its own good, Dana recalled the women she'd met today, both while playing volleyball and then while sharing lunch with the group in the meeting room downstairs. None of them fit his description.

Then again, one did. One that she hadn't met and didn't think she had any longing to do so in the future. "Might have she been hanging out in a cabana?"

"Probably," he supplied as he opened the box of spaghetti noodles and emptied its contents into the pot of boiling water.

"Interesting."

Giving the sauce another stir, he glanced at her. "What is?"

"Chris just seems so lively and friendly, and she seems . . . not so nice. She didn't bother to come to lunch at all and the whole time we were playing volleyball, she sat in that cabana, watching everyone. Then when I looked over at her, she gave me this rather, well, snobby look."

Amusement flashed in Treah's eyes. "I hate to suggest that you don't know snobby when you see it, but this time you don't. Three months ago, Claire was a recluse. With Chris's help, she's not afraid to go outside anymore but a crowd full of strangers still makes her nervous. Just watch: by the middle of the week, she'll be mingling with the rest of the group."

"I guess I misjudged her." Dana would probably feel bad about that, too, if her thoughts weren't focused on his implication that she would still be here come Wednesday. He'd better have misspoken.

"Everyone has faults," he returned, humor back in his eyes now, as well.

It was the kind of humor that was cleverly disguised as sensuality. The kind that a woman not in the know of his methods would probably grow damp over.

Dana knew all about his methods—how easily he could insinuate himself into a woman's shower and make her believe that some part of her really had been serenading him to come a little bit closer—and she didn't get damp.

Much.

Treah lifted his wine from the counter. He eyed her over the rim as he sipped. The sensuality in his eyes wasn't so secret any longer, but raw and intense, and hot enough to electrify the air between them.

In search of safer territory, she shifted her attention to his mouth. And discovered the slow suction of his lips against the rim of the wineglass wasn't near to safe. It brought back memories of last night again. Of his lips sucking her nipple into a hard, achy point. Of his mouth crashing against her own. His tongue slipping inside. Licking at hers. Stroking. So wild and hungry.

"Want to know what yours are?" he asked.

My what?

She had no clue what he was talking about. Frowning over the way her mind had drifted, Dana focused on locating plates. She pulled open three overhead cupboards before one offered up a plate bounty. Taking out two plates, she crossed to the attached dining room. An oval, wooden table and chairs filled up the majority of the space. Three red pillar candles sat in a silver stand in the center of the table and a lacy, white curtain with red trim fluttered against the open window facing the beach.

Treah wasn't someone who'd decorate his home with lacy white and red curtains. "Do you have a girlfriend?"

She regretted the question instantly. Not just because her voice rang with the same displeasure his had when he asked over the lucky guy she was marrying, but because she remembered how adamant he'd been about not touching her last night and how even when he'd given in it had been on a curse. It was bad to think she'd climaxed for another man. She couldn't stomach the idea she'd climaxed for another woman's boyfriend after that boyfriend tried to deny her.

His fingers brushed against hers as he relieved her of the plates she'd been standing and holding like an idiot. With a knowing smile, he set them on the table. "Don't worry. She's not in the picture anymore." His smile faltered a bit. "Hasn't been since she decided to embezzle resort money and pin the blame on Chris."

For the second time in the last ten minutes, Dana's heart clenched for him. It had been so easy to dismiss him as a guy whose only passion was passion itself. But he was more than that, now and, admittedly, eight years ago. "Life hasn't been easy for you, has it? First, me leaving you, then Blair's death and, now, this woman's stunt."

Treah shrugged. "It's had its ups and downs, but hasn't everyone's?" His smile returned to that amused, knowing one. "You don't honestly think I forgot about your faults?"

Is that what he'd been talking about the last time she'd let her mind drift to thoughts of kissing him? The last time as opposed to this current time. Damn, maybe she wasn't as immune to his methods as she wanted to believe. "What about my faults?"

"Do you want to know what they are?"

That depended on his definition of faults. If he meant whatever fears Deanne supposedly told him Dana had, then she was all ears. But if he meant her overall shortcomings, and number one on the list was Claude, then, no, she really didn't want to know. "No. I'd rather you take that information to your grave."

Dejection shone in his eyes before he moved back into the kitchen to attend to the food, and Dana realized what she'd said so fresh on the tail of learning about Blair's death.

Obviously, she did have faults. More than she'd ever realized, she wanted to make up for her big mouth by not only pulling Treah into her arms for the comforting hug she'd earlier disallowed, but the kind of all-body kiss guaranteed to soothe the ache growing in her core.

5

Shit, he couldn't sleep again tonight.

Treah wanted to believe it was his dad's demand for the return of his money that had him too edgy to doze off. But shortly after sharing dinner, Dana had excused herself for an early night to bed and he had gone down to his office to work. It had taken until two in the morning and tapping into the money he'd been left from Blair's wrongful-death suit, but he'd gotten every penny either into one common account and ready for transfer, or scheduled to be deposited into that account come morning.

Now it was almost three again, and here he lay, wide awake and unable to stop thinking that it had been nearly this same time when he'd found Dana in his bed last night. He should have given in to her request and fucked her.

No, he shouldn't have.

He wasn't some asshole who took advantage of a sedated woman. He was some asshole who wanted to go wake up that same woman with the feel of his lips on her body.

Only, he wasn't even that much of an asshole.

She'd given off strange vibes tonight. Making it seem in one minute that she was head over heels for her fiancé and, in the next minute, that she wanted nothing more than to get naked with Treah. It had to be learning of Blair's death that had her warming to him. That, and the wine. Red wine had always made her easy, which is why she never drank it in the wrong company.

Pity and alcohol had been at work on Dana tonight, making it seem she wanted something she didn't.

Pity and alcohol were at work on Treah tonight, too. Making it clear he was never again going to get the woman he wanted, so he might as well take it upon himself to expel the sexual frustration that being this near to her without being able to touch her caused.

Tossing back the sheet, he unveiled his nude body and took his cock in hand. Lying here in the dark, thinking about her for the past half hour, had his shaft semihard. A few quick pumps of his fisted hand and his dick was rock solid.

He'd never been much on envisioning a woman's mouth wrapped around his cock in place of his fingers, because he'd never had much reason to. Up until Gwen's deception, he'd almost always had a woman in his life. But now it had been over three months since he'd had a woman in his life or his bed. Closer to six since he'd had a lover give him oral sex. The appeal of imagining it was Dana's warm lips closing around his cock, her passion-fogged gaze rapt on his own as she sucked and licked at his hard length, was too great to ignore.

Treah brought his hand to his mouth, thoroughly wetting his palm and fingers before circling his thumb and first finger and slipping them around the head of his cock.

Moist, soft skin gripped his shaft as the circle of his fingers slid slowly downward. He closed his eyes and groaned her name with the contact.

Almost. Almost, he could imagine it was her supple lips, her warm mouth. The damp flick of her tongue as he dabbed the first finger of his other hand into the pre-cum weeping at the tip of his cock, and then traced the fluid along the bulging vein at the underside.

He wrapped the rest of the fingers of his right hand around his rod. They were nearly dry, knocking away the impression they could be Dana's lips and mouth. But he could still pretend they were her fingers. Her hand that held his cock tight and pumped it hard and fast. Her other hand that massaged his upper thighs, stroked his balls and the root of his shaft, teased along his stomach muscles and up to his chest. Her fingers he licked the taste of his pre-cum from as his blood warmed and his sac grew heavy and tight.

There was no pretending about her name. That fell from his lips a second time, an instinctive and amorous shout, as electric pressure sizzled through his groin, cording the muscles in his thighs and ass, and racing his heart as he found his release.

Treah realized only as the seed shot from his cock that he hadn't taken any precautionary steps to keep the bed dry. He opened his eyes as it rained down upon his thighs and legs and, undoubtedly, the sheets, in a hot, thick stream.

He shouldn't have been able to see in the dark. And he couldn't see perfectly. But he could see well enough to tell that he'd hit the bed with a magnum-sized load of cum. And he could see well enough to know that his bedroom door had been opened to let in light from the hallway and that Dana was standing at the foot of the bed, watching him masturbate.

Like a wet dream turned to flesh and blood, she wore only the lacy white strapless bra and matching thong. The crotch of the thong was all but translucent. Last night, short dark curls had covered her mound. Now, it was shaved bare, the slit of her labia a delicacy on filmy display. Her breasts were equally enticing, rising and falling so violently with each harried breath the right cup of her bra slipped to expose the top half of an areola and a hint of erect nipple.

It was the same nipple he'd had in his mouth last night. His hand was automatically stroking his cock hard again with the idea he'd been wrong about not getting to make love with her ever again. He might get to spend this night loving both that nipple and every other part of her beautiful body.

Dana swallowed loudly. He lifted his gaze from her breasts to her face. Unbridled want shimmered in her dark eyes, passion burning higher with each pump of his fingers. Her tongue flicked out, dabbing hungrily, teasingly at her lips.

His shaft pulsed. Hell, he couldn't go on like this. Either she retreated or he reached out for her. "Dana, what are you doing?"

Her eyes jerked to his with the parting of her lips. Out came a breathy, little gasp. She took an awkward step back. "I, uh . . . heard my name."

Another step followed that first. Treah released his cock with the knowledge she was about to make her getaway. His shaft might not agree, or his arms, which had been empty for far too long, but her leaving was a good thing. The red wine would be out of her system by now. The pity would remain, and he didn't want it swaying her.

She *would* sleep with him. The needful want in her eyes left little room for doubt. But it would happen when she was stone sober and aware she was doing it because she loved him in a way she could never feel for her fiancé.

To help her out the door, he risked making an even bigger mess of his cum by pulling the sheet over his lower half. "Sorry. I'll be quieter next time I shout your name when I climax."

"Good idea." She quickly moved the last steps to the door. Then, with a last look in the vicinity of his groin and a " 'Night," she disappeared into the hallway.

*　　*　　*

Dana had had some doozy Mondays. But none that ever went this badly.

First, she'd woken up with the image of Treah stroking his cock with one hand while he licked pre-cum from the fingers of his other hand burned in her mind. Then she'd learned he couldn't help her until after noon because he had to make some final arrangements on whatever he'd been working on the previous day and night. And now, just a few short minutes ago, Chris had tracked her down with the news that no one would be going anywhere for a day or two, because every one of Ecstasy's four cabin cruisers' motors had been vandalized.

He'd said it was a part that they didn't have extras of on hand, but that could be delivered to the island along with someone to perform the repairs in a decent amount of time. He'd looked too serious for her to think he might have done the vandalizing himself for the sake of keeping her around longer. She'd barely given a passing thought to the idea Treah would harm his own boats.

Someone else had done the damage. As a side effect, until the repairs were made, she was stuck living with Treah. Stuck dreaming about Treah. Stuck waking to find Treah coming with her name on his lips. No man had done that in years. Even if they had, it wouldn't have been the same. Not in his rough, sexy voice. Not with such intense passion blazing in his eyes and straining his muscles.

Dana had wanted to climb onto the bed and over his cock so badly her pussy was damp and throbbing even now, just from the memory.

She had to call Claude. ASAP.

So far, she'd been taking the offer to make herself at home to heart by using Treah's phone. For this call, she wished she had her cell. Since Deanne hadn't included it in her entertainment bag, Dana sucked up her valor, grabbed his cordless from the receiver in the kitchen and returned to her bedroom.

God help her sister's safety if this line was the same as Treah used in his office and he picked up midway through her conversation with Claude.

Or maybe he was already on his way upstairs for lunch; it was close to noon. Which just made her fingers shake all the more as she punched in her fiancé's direct extension at the museum.

"Claude Rainer, Curator," he answered on the second ring. "How may I help you?"

"Claude. It's me. Dana." Her voice wobbled as she dropped down in a chair at the bedroom's small table.

"Dana, darling, it's good to hear from you. How is the sabbatical?"

The context of the words was warm, but his detached voice made him sound distracted. Of course, he was often distracted by the demands of his job and how much he thrived on meeting them. This time, it worked in her favor because it made him oblivious to her anxiety.

Now, if he would just stay oblivious. "Not so good. I, um . . ." Need something to do with my hands.

Spotting the pad of paper and pen she'd used last night to jot some work-related notes, she grabbed them from atop the dresser and dropped back down at the table. Claude had informed her that random doodling—actually, he'd called it artistry—was a great way to ease her nerves during high-stress conversations. It worked, too, though oddly only when the conversations were between the two of them.

Not that they had a lot of high-stress conversations. They didn't. Much. Not enough to worry her anyway.

Much.

"Dana?"

Right. Talk to her fiancé, not the nut trying to overtake her mind. "I never made it to the planned getaway spot. Actually, I didn't even know there was a planned getaway spot until I spoke with Jane."

"Then where in the blazes are you?" His question snapped through the phone line.

Oh, goodie. She had his full attention. "It's a long story."

"I have ten minutes."

Since when was ten minutes long? Too aware of how much was riding on this conversation, she fixed her gaze on an imaginary crack in the wall and doodled harder. "Remember how I signed Deanne up for that healing resort?"

"The place with the New-Age approach?"

Dana had assigned the term "New Age" to the resort's sensual healing technique. It sounded much more sophisticated than saying "I'm sending my sister off for therapy that could include anything from co-ed naked back scratches to full-blown sex." "Yes, that place. The resort pick-up guys were supposed to bring her to the island Sunday night but they brought me instead."

Claude's breath sucked in loudly, then whooshed out again on a blast of words. "That's preposterous! You live ten miles apart and look nothing alike."

"Nothing" was pushing it, given that they were twins. Still, they didn't look enough alike to easily confuse them. Regardless, she would rather he think badly about the resort than admit that Deanne was responsible for the exchange. "It's unbelievable, I know. Maybe I put down my address on the form by mistake."

"How could you have?"

"Everyone has faults." Dana gasped with the words, for just an instant thinking that Treah had picked up a secondary phone to speak them. But they were hers, today. His, last night. Which was not a good thing to be thinking about.

"Yes, but that's just foolish."

It sure was. Thinking about Treah while she was talking to her fiancé, that is. On the contrary, owning up to her faults was a good trait, wasn't it?

Fairly certain Claude wouldn't agree, and irritated about that for reasons she couldn't explain, she moved her hand over an inch on the paper and scribbled some more. "It was dumb of me, you're right. The thing is, now that I'm here, I can't get home unless someone comes to get me."

"They took you. Have them bring you back."

"That was the plan, but there was a boat motor issue."

"The resort only has one boat?"

"No. They have several. All of them have problems." He made a huffing sound, and Dana winced. She really didn't want him to think the worst of Treah's resort. After all, Claude did have influence in some pretty high places. Later, she would explain things better. Now, she had to focus on what mattered most—getting away from Treah, who was serious temptation whether she liked it or not. "Can you come get me?"

"Where is this place?"

"Um, on an island. Off the coast of Massachusetts."

"Are you serious, Dana? You're hours away and you want me to drop everything to drive to the coast, rent a boat, and track you down in the middle of the ocean?"

Well, geez, when he put it like that . . . When he put it like that he sounded pissed and like she wasn't important enough to drop everything for.

Maybe she *should* be having second thoughts.

No. That was nonsense. They were a great match.

"I just miss you," she rushed out before that stupid little voice could interject a "mostly" or "sort of" or "you used to think that you were until Treah reentered your life" retort.

"And I miss you, darling," Claude said in a calmer voice. "But I can't get away today or tomorrow. Thursday or Friday I might be able to work something out."

A calmer voice that was deceptive.

Was he out of his mind? Dana shot the imaginary crack in the wall a death glare and doodled like mad. *Thursday at the earliest?* A whole freaking three days away? By then, she could have succumbed to temptation a dozen times. "You know what, don't worry about it. Deanne didn't answer the first time I called"—or the fiftieth or the hundredth—"but I'll try again and see if she can't get here sooner. If that doesn't work out, they should have the boats fixed in a couple days."

"Sounds good." He was back to sounding distracted. "Try to enjoy the time away."

"I will." She started to jab the END button, then realized she'd forgotten those three little words. Even when she was angry, they deserved to be spoken. "I love you."

"You know the feeling's mutual."

The line went dead on his end, and she scowled at the phone. She'd *almost* forgotten those three little words, but he'd never said them to begin with—angry, happy, or postorgasmic. He'd implied that he loved her but it wasn't the same. Not when she didn't even have an engagement ring to symbolize his affection.

Feeling a massive pity party coming on, and not in the mood to stop it, Dana let her chin droop to her chest. Her gaze fell on her random "artistry," and she was torn between laughing and crying.

Like a silly little lovesick teenager, she'd drawn a heart with a guy's name in the middle.

It was really too bad that it was Treah's.

"Hi, Dana," a female voice said from behind Dana.

Dana frowned over her disappointment that the speaker wasn't Treah. She'd woken this morning to find a note on her bedroom table that he had an issue come up with Ecstasy's Pacific branch and had to spend the morning dealing with it. The morning had turned to afternoon with no sign of him and she'd gotten bored.

Or so she'd told herself at the time.

Going by her disappointment now, when the seafood dinner gathering had begun in the downstairs meeting room and he'd yet to emerge from his office, it was more than boredom she was feeling.

Not ready to diagnose what else it might be, Dana turned from refilling her hors d'oeuvres plate from a steaming, rolltop chafing dish of crab cakes to greet her visitor. She'd expected to find one of the women she'd met on Sunday. Instead, Claire smiled at her. Even more surprising than the brunette's identity was that she knew Dana's own.

It was probable that Chris had discussed Dana with her. Even so, without Claire having seen a picture of her, Dana shouldn't have stood out in a crowd of over a dozen other women, several of whom shared a similar hair color and style.

"Have we met?" Dana asked.

"No. You just look a lot like your sister."

Not according to Claude, Dana thought crossly. She forgot her continued upset over yesterday's call with the oddity of Claire's remark. "You've met my sister?"

Claire's eyes widened. "Oh." She sent a nervous glance at the clear plastic cup filled with something pink in her right hand. Bringing the cup to her lips, she took a long drink. Her smile slipped back into place as she returned the cup to her side. "I sometimes help Chris with the client files. I saw the photo you supplied for Deanne's."

Dana eyed Claire's cup. Were its contents some sort of instant anxiety killer, or why had she acted so suddenly nervous, then fine again right after she had a drink? "What are you drinking?"

"I don't know if it has a name, but it works." Claire's gaze went to where Chris sat at a table across the room, visiting with one of the clients and the woman's healing coach, and her smile took on a hint of naughtiness.

Looking back at Dana, she held out the cup. "Want to try it?"

Did she want to try a drink that, going by Claire's smile, was spiked with something that would stoke her libido? Yeah, that sounded like the worst thing she could do since walking into Treah's bedroom two nights ago. "Thanks, but I'll pass."

"Are you sure? It's really good and has no side effects come morning."

It did look good and smelled rather incredible. Having a sip would probably go a long way in showing Claire she trusted her and, in turn, make the woman more comfortable around her. Considering the not-so-long-ago recluse tendencies that made Claire anxious in the first place, it seemed unlikely she would consume the drink among mixed company if its aphrodisiac power was too strong.

"Okay. I'll try it." Dana took the offered cup. "But just one sip."

Bringing the cup to her lips, she sipped at the pink liquid. She'd been expecting either sour and tangy, or sweet with the nip of citrusy alcohol. The drink was sweet, but the alcoholic components were masked to the point of being undetectable. The taste of raspberries and something else popped on her tongue. "Wow. This stuff is great."

"That's what I said the first time I tried it. Would you like a glass of your own?"

A sip was one thing, but a whole glass? Ah, what the hell, Treah wasn't here for her to do something ridiculous, like throwing herself into his arms and asking for a repeat of Saturday night's fingering session. "Okay. But just one glass."

Treah cleared the door connecting the administration area with the meeting room and Dana's low, smoky, completely unforgettable and completely inebriated-sounding laughter froze him on the spot. She sat at a table twenty feet away, tossing back drinks of something pink in between chatting with a couple of the resort clients so loudly and animatedly it was like the women had been friends for years.

Seeing her interact without prejudice again was great. Seeing her take another drink from the cup had his gut tightening.

Chris crossed the room to join Treah near the admin door. "Finally get things straightened around?"

The bulk of the day all that had been on Treah's mind was easing the frustrations caused by Ecstasy's Pacific branch manager accidentally overscheduling the month's clientele and leaving two women without healing coaches. Now, all he could think about was Dana and whether she believed she had liquid courage cruising through her veins. That, and whether the person who gave her the drink and made her believe it was alcoholic was the same person responsible for sabotaging his boats yesterday morning so Dana was forced to stay on the island a while longer.

After what happened with Gwen—how she'd convinced Treah that Chris was stealing money from the resort when in truth she'd been the guilty party—he hated to accuse Chris of anything. Even so, he couldn't stop his scowl. "Who gave her the drink?"

"Don't look at me, man. I barely even know what goes into those things."

"Where's Claire?" Fingers curled around Treah's arm, pulling him around before Chris had a chance to respond.

Dana stood less than a foot away, smiling way too brightly and way, way too friskily. The placebo effect obviously had her well in its grip, making her think she was drunk and ready to take full advantage of her heightened libido and lessened rationality.

"Having a good time?" he asked casually.

"I am." She leaned into him until her breasts brushed against his chest.

Her yellow tank top and white cottons shorts were like the

rest of the clothes she'd worn this week. Small, tight, and too revealing for his cock to remain flaccid when she was rubbing up against him that way.

Her gaze drifted from his eyes to his mouth. "What happens after we eat? Are there games or dancing or something sensual?"

"Not tonight." Thank God. "At least, not on a group level."

She pressed tighter against him, bringing her pelvis flush with his on a slow, sinuous grinding of her hips. "Is that your way of asking me back to your place?"

Treah groaned as desire stabbed in his groin. He hadn't been trying to proposition her. He'd been saying that when the clients and healing coaches returned to their cabins, sensual things might happen as part of the curing process. "Do you feel okay?"

"Great." Returning her gaze to his, she dabbed the tip of her tongue against her lower lip, leaving it shiny and wet. "I taste even better. Wanna go to your place and see for yourself?"

When she was licking at her lip, reminding him of the hot way she'd done the same while watching his masturbation show two nights ago, he wanted to say a big "Fuck, yeah."

But he wasn't going to. Not so long as she believed she was operating under the influence. He should tell her the drink wasn't alcoholic. He would if not for the risk of getting Dana pissed at Claire for insinuating it was, presuming that she had.

Sonya and a couple of the healing coaches emerged from the set of windowed kitchen doors at the side of the meeting room, trays of steaming food in hand. They placed the trays onto the tables at the front of the room, and Treah nodded in that direction. "Dinner's ready. Eat up, and if you still want to go to my place when you're done, I'll take you."

Considering that they were technically already at his place and she was already staying in his spare bedroom, not much harm should come of that offer. Unless, of course, she realized she wasn't drunk by the time they reached the second floor and wanted him regardless.

Then maybe he would give in. Then maybe he would get some sleep at night again. Then maybe the only harm would be that which she would have no choice but to inflict upon her fiancé by calling an end to their engagement.

6

Dana pushed her nearly empty plate aside and smiled suggestively across the table at Treah. "I'm full. And ready to go."
And crazy to even be considering going back to his place for
the express purpose of having sex.

But she'd thought about the move long and hard as she
downed the delicious spiked drink Claire had given her, followed by two more Dana had helped herself to after finding a
pitcher of the pink stuff in the large kitchen's refrigerator. With
the aid of the alcohol, she'd loosened up enough to dismiss
guilt and admit what a perfect match Claude wasn't. Treah
might not be perfect for her, either, but he was a hundred times
warmer than Claude. He'd never been shy about telling her
how much he loved her. He'd never been afraid to make love in
the daylight hours. He would have come to pick her up in a
heartbeat if the situation were reversed.

And she'd missed him. God, how she'd missed him.

Earlier, she hadn't been able to own up to what she was feeling while she waited for him to finish his work. Now, she ac-

cepted it for what it was, along with the truth that she could never miss Claude so much.

Caution filled Treah's eyes as he stacked her plastic plate onto his empty one. "You're sure?"

As sure as she could ever be. Nerves unfurling in her belly, she rose and reached across the table to offer her hand. "I'm sure."

"And drunk?"

"No. Like I said earlier, I feel good. Better than good. But I'm not drunk."

With a slow nod, he stood and rounded the table to take her hand. Like when he'd helped her to her feet from his couch the other day, carnal heat sizzled from the tips of her fingers to her core as he guided her toward the exit. He stopped near the admin door long enough to toss their plates into a wastebasket, then pushed in the door and led her down the hallway to the storage room housing the stairwell to the second floor.

Dana's heart beat into galloping terrain when they reached the top of the stairs and he opened the door. The living room was directly across from them, but all she could think about was his bed. About the sight of his strong, scrumptiously nude body both of the times she'd encountered him in that bed. About getting both of their bodies naked immediately, whether that bed was in sight or not.

Stopping short, she tugged on his hand. Treah turned around, acceptance in his eyes along with enough scorching sensuality to have her pussy flooding with cream. "It's never too late to change your mind. We could head back to the party."

"I did change my mind." She laughed as displeasure flickered through his gaze. "I thought I wanted to go to your bed, but now I realize how long it's been since a man fucked me against the wall."

"Dana..." He sounded equally pained and eager, like he ached for her but at the same time felt he shouldn't have her.

Maybe he shouldn't. Maybe, despite her long, hard thinking and vow she wasn't drunk, it truly was alcohol making everything about this moment and the two of them seem about as perfect as it got. Maybe she was just going to go with the moment and give into what her body craved.

Freeing her hand from his, she moved up against him as she'd done downstairs. Only this time she went even farther, by sliding her hands beneath his shirt with the slow, sensual circling of her pelvis against his. Palming his warm, bare sides, she brushed his lips with hers. "We should, Treah. We really should."

"Ah, hell. We should." His hands cupped her ass as he parted his mouth on a shaky sigh and let her tongue move inside to explore his rich, dark, masculine flavor.

His was a taste she could never forget.

Unlike breathing.

Kissing him stole her breath away, made her feel like she was floating on a cloud of pure rapturous heaven. Not alcohol induced. She'd rarely been drunk when they'd kissed in the past and it had always been its own kind of breathless intoxication. The kind that had her pussy swelling and throbbing, and her fingers jerking from beneath his shirt to yank it up his torso.

Crisp hair and hard muscle caressed Dana's fingertips as she stroked them along his chest. She pulled away from the nirvana of his mouth to jerk the shirt over his head. Leaving his arms trapped in the sleeves, she flattened her palm against his chest and playfully shoved him against the wall.

Heat, want, and teasing glinted in his eyes. "Paybacks."

Oh, yeah, paybacks. She could hardly wait.

Trembling with the thought of Treah pushing her up against the wall and stripping away her clothes, she took hold of the fly of his shorts and tugged open the button. His zipper jerked down with a hiss. Her clit tingled with the telling sound. Her sex went soft and molten as she squatted to shove the shorts down his thighs and over his feet, along with his briefs.

From a nest of black curls, his erection jutted out thick and long, the tip near purple and inches from her mouth. She'd felt a hard cock a handful of times in the last months, but she hadn't seen one in over three years.

Seeing his shaft so close, the plump head shimmering with a silky drop of fluid, made her pulse go wild and her tongue desperate to taste.

On a needy whimper, Dana reached for his thighs, intending to lock them in her hands as she took his cock in her mouth. Before she could make contact, his shirt dropped to the floor and his hands grabbed hold of her shoulders. Pulling her up from her squatting position, he spun them around until it was her back against the wall.

"Paybacks." Treah's eyes flashed primal yellow-green as he voiced the word a second time in that rough, gravelly tone she could never get enough of.

Taking hold of the hem of her tank top, he tugged it up and over her head, leaving the shirt to pin her arms at her back. She'd relied on the tank top's built-in bra for support. He planted his hands on the wall around her head as his heavy gaze singed her bare breasts, telling her exactly how much he loved their nudity.

Then his mouth was on her breasts, his tongue lashing hot against her tits, swiping across her nipples. Sucking them between his lips as he pushed his hands into the sides of her drawstring shorts and dragged them down her hips.

His dark head bucked back an inch as he cupped her thinly covered mound and gave the nipple in his mouth a hard twist. Erotic sensation burst through her breast. That same sensation answered in her cunt as a quaking, urgent need that dampened the crotch of her thong and slid a moan past her lips. The fingers at her mound lifted to dip beneath the thong's side straps.

Treah's mouth left her nipple. His breath feathered hot and

sultry against the deep pink tip as he moved his head back and met her eyes with his. His fingers slipped from beneath the side straps of her thong. His lips parted.

Dana held her breath. Every nerve in her body felt like it was standing at hyper-aroused attention as she waited to feel his magnificent mouth on some other part of her body. Her other nipple. Her belly. Stroking deep inside her soaked sheath.

Anywhere, just so long as it was soon.

"Tell me to stop," he commanded.

Her breath stuttered out on a broken cry. What the hell? Was he out of his mind?

"Stop," a thready voice that sounded just like hers said, then added, "Regrets."

What? Was she out of her mind, too?

Or had she been drunk all along? Was she coming down from an alcohol high and realizing she'd been out of her mind to ever allow things to go so far?

She was engaged, for cripe's sake! To a guy who was almost perfect for her. All but when it came to sex and the ability to put voice to his feelings. But those were such little things. Weren't they?

Treah searched her face. "Are you really telling me to stop?"

Yes. But no. Or maybe. "I think so."

"There's no thinking about it, Dana. Either you are, or you're about to get a stiff cock in your pussy."

Her sex thrummed with his dirty talk. Claude never talked to her that way even with the lights out. But that was such a little thing, too. They had so many bigger things going for them. Even if those bigger things eluded her just now.

Keeping her gaze locked on his face, because God forgive her actions if she looked at his naked body again, Dana fumbled with her tank top until it was worked back down over her breasts. Ignoring the sensual chafe of the cotton against the straining points of her nipples, she yanked up her shorts. "I can't, Treah. I never really wanted to in the first place. You were right. I'm drunk and you know how easy that makes me."

Only, usually it took red wine to make her easy. Whatever was in the drinks she'd had downstairs had to share the stimulating component of red wine.

"You're not drunk, Dana. There was no liquor in your drinks, just blended seltzer water and raspberries."

"Oh." Uh oh. "I need to go to bed. *Alone*." Hugging her arms to her chest, she hurried the fifteen feet down the hall to her bedroom door.

"You do have a fear, Dana," Treah called after her, halting her in the doorway. "It's called happiness."

"I *am* happy," she argued without turning around, without allowing the annoying voice in her head to suggest to the contrary.

"No, you're not. I've seen you when you are and you don't look like you do now."

It didn't matter how she looked. It shouldn't. But she had to ask anyway. "How do I look?"

"Now, you're beautiful. Then, you're so completely stunning everyone who passes by feels instant envy because it's clear you have life by the balls and nothing can stop you. Then, you're way too easy to love."

But now, she wasn't. Now, he didn't. It was what she needed to know. What made moving inside the bedroom and closing the door the right thing to do, even when it felt so incredibly wrong.

"It's time to go."

Dana purred with the sound of Treah's voice. He was in her dream again, stroking her breasts, her parted thighs, deep inside her. Getting her ready to go for a nice, long ride on the Treah Express. "Mmm . . . On top."

"Home, Dana," he bit out on a groan. "It's time for you to go *home*."

She came instantly awake with the grim words. He wasn't in her dream, but standing beside her bed. Clean-shaven and dressed in an olive shirt and khaki shorts that complemented his tan, he should have looked sexy. And he did look sexy, but he also looked irritated.

Good. Coupled with the knowledge he didn't love her anymore, his irritation should make leaving this place as simple as packing her bags and getting on a boat.

She tossed back the sheet and thin cover to climb from the bed. "The motors are fixed?"

Treah's attention fell on her body. She wore shorty pajamas but the sudden heat in his eyes made it seem she was naked. "The one we need is." Sounding surlier yet, he strode to the door. "Meet me down at the docks in an hour."

"Okay. Then—" The door slammed closed, cutting off her words of gratitude.

So he was ticked. So what?

It was because she'd acted like a cock tease, not that she was leaving his island and would probably never see him again. And if that thought made Dana feel a little unhappy, then it was exasperation for her behavior last night.

She was just going to forget that it ever happened. Just going to remember she would soon be home. Back to Claude, who made her deliriously happy regardless of Treah's claim she was afraid of feeling that very thing.

Liar.

"I'm not lying!" She didn't fear happiness. As for not feeling it with Claude . . .

She didn't have time to waste on such an inane idea. Even if they weren't a perfect match, they were as close to it as she'd ever known.

Shutting out the voice that dared to call her a liar a second time, she focused on getting washed and dressed and packed. The only problem was that getting washed made her think of the first shower she'd had in Treah's tub and that made her think of how he'd invaded that shower and looked like he wanted to invade her body while he was at it. And that made her think of how badly she'd wanted him to do that exact thing last night. When she hadn't been drunk.

Dressing didn't go much better. She couldn't decide what shorts to wear and she couldn't help but think how good Treah was at picking clothes out for her. Claude knew art, but he didn't know a thing about fashion.

Packing took forever. She found the heart "artistry" that she'd done while on the phone with Claude tucked in the bottom of the drawer with her underthings and swimsuits. The doodle had frozen her on the spot, left her staring at it, wondering if she wasn't slipping into denial the way Gena had told the group she was that first morning.

Did Claude truly not make her happy? And had she really wanted to sleep with Treah last night? Did she still?

"You okay?"

Dana jumped with the sound of Treah's voice. She banged her shin against the bedframe and winced as she spun to look at him. He stood in the doorway. His earlier aggravation was replaced with concern that suggested that while he didn't love her any longer he obviously still cared at least a little.

Enough for her to turn the spark into a flame?

Damn, she didn't know what she wanted anymore. The only sensible thing to do was leave this island and return to Claude. If thoughts of Treah remained with her then . . . then she would deal with it at that time.

"Yeah. I'm all packed." Smiling in an eager way she hoped looked less of a sham than it felt, she tossed the strap of her bathroom bag over her shoulder and rolled her wheeled suitcase to the door. "This place was a nice getaway, but it will be great to get home. I might even stay off from work the weeks Deanne scheduled me to be here. I could use the time to figure out where things are at with the wedding planning. Claude's usually big on details but I guess, like most every other guy, that doesn't extend to weddings." Or saying I love you.

"Dana?" The word snapped out as Treah took the suitcase from her.

She met the resentment in his eyes, and her smile wobbled. "Yes?"

"I really don't want to hear about it."

Treah swore as the cabin cruiser's engine sputtered a few times and then died. Two miles out from Ecstasy Island and a great deal farther from the mainland was the last place he wanted to be alone with Dana after the harm that had come of taking her back to his place last night.

He tried to restart the engine. It wouldn't even turn over. Going by the way it had sputtered to a stop, he wasn't surprised. "Shit."

She looked over from the passenger's seat. The ends of her brown and gold ponytail whipped into her face with the breeze and worry filled her eyes. "What's the matter?"

What the fuck did she think? She was marrying some guy he'd never met but hated.

Knowing she meant with the boat, he shrugged. "It acts like it's out of gas, but I filled the tank myself before I came upstairs to see if you were ready."

Speculation entered her eyes. "Did you?"

The vehemence he hadn't quite been able to contain when she started in on talk of wedding planning barreled up once more. "Yes, Dana," he growled. "I did. You want to be home, planning your wedding. I might hate the idea but I'm not about to force you to stay with me at Ecstasy."

"Oh."

Yeah, oh. Oh, he never should have allowed Deanne to talk him into letting Dana come to the island in the first place.

Since Treah had, he flexed his fingers around the steering wheel and, past the dark lenses of his sunglasses, searched for solace in the water surrounding them.

"Sit tight while I call Chris," he managed almost calmly thirty seconds and several deep breaths later. He grabbed the marine radio off the panel mount beneath and to the left of the wheel. "He can be here in a half hour. We can make the mainland by noon." *I can be back home and well on my way to forgetting you by four.*

The only flaw in that logic was that he hadn't forgotten her in eight years, so there was no way in hell he was going to forget her in a few hours.

And then came a second flaw, when he turned the radio dial and heard neither static nor talking.

Son of a bitch!

Holding his breath, he flipped through the stations. None of them made a sound. None of them were going to make a sound, Treah knew even before he pried off the radio's faceplate and found the cut wiring.

"Something else is wrong, isn't it?" Dana asked.

"Someone screwed with the radio." Chris he could maybe see siphoning out the gas in an attempt to help keep Dana around longer, but he wouldn't go to the lengths of damaging the radio.

Was this Sonya's handiwork? Was she the one who'd vandalized the motors, as well?

His assistant came off as reserved and mousy, but she rubbed him the wrong way while doing it. Hell, he didn't know a thing about her. The employment agency he'd found her through had only glowing feedback, but then, they made money when they placed someone in a job so the feedback could have been bullshit.

What rationale would she have to hurt his business, though? None that made sense outside of being a friend of Gwen's and that was highly unlikely.

"You didn't do it," Dana observed. "You wouldn't look that way if you did."

"It's not a big deal." Treah slapped the faceplate back on and hung up the radio. "I was supposed to get my assistant a report by the end of the day. When she doesn't get it, she'll ask Chris where I am. He'll know something must have gone wrong with the boat and come looking for me. In the meantime, we might as well relax and enjoy the sun."

If the Chris theory didn't pan out, there was always water patrol, or other boaters. The shipping routes were still a half mile away but it was possible that if he sent up a flare, one of the freighters would spot it and come to their aid. It would be more possible if he saved the flares for nightfall, when they wouldn't be all but invisible between the brilliant sunlight and the luminous water.

Accepting that he was stuck alone with Dana a while longer, Treah did as he'd suggested she do, and relaxed. He pulled off his shirt, angled back the captain's chair, and closed his eyes.

"I guess it's a good thing I planned to rent a car instead of having someone pick me up when we got to the mainland," she muttered.

He waited for more muttering, or more of the damned talk about her upcoming wedding and schmuck of a fiancé who was so sophisticated even his name reeked of refinement. But she didn't say a word. Just repeated his move, by pulling off her shirt, angling back her chair, and closing her eyes.

He cut her a glance from behind his sunglasses and groaned. She wore another of those tiny tops, this one a strapless black bikini top that thrust her breasts up against the cups, exposing almost half of the generous mounds.

Damn Deanne for packing only clothes guaranteed to rouse his cock.

He tipped his head back and closed his eyes again, thought about anything but Dana's breasts or the feel of her damp pussy when he cupped it through her thong last night. He tried anyway. Tried and failed, and gave up after ten minutes.

Reopening his eyes, Treah looked at the sky. A handful of clouds dusted the blue, the largest of which was about to overtake the sun. The thing was huge and resembled one of those paintings Dana was so thrilled by, in that it looked like a blob of nothing.

Smiling, he pointed it out. "There's something you don't see every day."

She opened her eyes and followed the direction of his finger. "What?"

"Come on now, don't tell me you of all people can't see it. The wounded dove crying out for mercy. The hunter hot on her trail. The look of terror in her eyes is so real I can feel it deep down in here." He knocked his fist against his heart. "Power expressed that stunningly just does me in."

Her eyes narrowed in disbelief. Amusement flashed on its tail. "Hah hah."

"You really aren't seeing it?"

"What I see is you trying to ruin a perfectly decent moment."

If that was true, why was she attempting to fight a smile? "By trying to see things from your point of view?"

"All I see when I look at that cloud is that I'm going to need to put my shirt back on until it passes." She let her smile blossom. "I *do* appreciate your effort."

Hell, it was her happy smile. The one Treah told her last night she didn't have these days. He'd been serious. And now it seemed he'd been wrong.

It was possible the smile was because she was going home to

her fiancé. Only, they weren't going anywhere right now. They wouldn't be going anywhere soon. And that meant it was even more possible the smile was on her face because she was beginning to understand how good they still went together.

The irritation he'd been feeling since last night melted. Hope, and the knowledge he owed someone big-time for sucking the gas tank mostly dry, kindled. With a wicked grin, he glanced at her barely contained breasts. "I *do* appreciate the way your body looks with your shirt off."

7

Lounging on the cabin cruiser's wraparound, bench-style backseat, Dana peered over the edge of a crossword-puzzle book at Treah. For lack of a better way to spend their time, while the boat drifted in an ocean that seemed endless and otherwise void of human life, she'd pulled the book from her entertainment bag. This was puzzle number three, and she was surprised to be having a good time, considering how angry he'd seemed with her this morning and how foolish she felt about her behavior last night. Not to mention that she was supposed to be en route to her home and a fiancé she was having serious second thoughts about.

She was having serious second thoughts about Treah, as well. The kind that had her wondering why he'd admitted to hating the idea of her marrying another man if he didn't still have strong feelings for her himself. The kind that had her blood warming, right along with the rest of her, as he graced her with an expectant smile from where he reclined shirtless in the swiveled-around captain's chair.

Doing her best not to ogle his sun-bronzed chest, the same

way she'd been trying not to do for hours now, she offered the next clue. "A four-letter word for fox."

His lips curved higher. "Dana."

Laughing in a way she hoped sounded carefree, she filled in the correct answer. "You know this is the first time we've had to visit longer than it takes to eat or . . ." *Screw.* Yeah, that was not a good subject to bring up.

"Or?" Treah prompted, pushing the sunglasses up on his head.

The quick dip his gaze took to her breasts suggested he knew exactly what that "or" represented. She disregarded the pinging of her nipples against the scanty cups of her bikini top to go the ignorant route. "Read."

He grinned in a way that called her bluff. Losing the grin, he said, "I planned to mostly be off work this week and the next two so I could spend the time with you."

Dana's pulse increased. Tensing, she set aside the puzzle book and swung her feet off the bench to sit up. "Why would you?"

"Deanne asked me to."

Oh. Really, though, what had she been expecting, him to confess that he still loved her and had planned to spend the three weeks she was on his island convincing her to give them another chance? Not Likely. But then, his answer didn't seem completely logical, either. "You hadn't heard from my sister in years. Yet the second she called, you felt obligated to do her bidding?"

"What makes you think we don't keep in touch?"

"She would tell me." Wouldn't she?

He shrugged. "Deanne offered to pay me for helping you move past your fear of happiness but, like I said, I don't run the resort for the income."

"Like I said, I'm not afraid of being happy. If Deanne honestly believes that I am, it's because she has a different definition of the word than I do." One that clearly involved Dana spending her life with Treah. "If you don't run this place for the income, why invest so much time and energy in it?"

"That's why." At her frown, he explained, "I started the place eight years ago as a way to occupy my time and get my mind off the negative. I keep it going because I like to see people happy and I can't think of a better way to get there than via the sensual." Curiosity entered his eyes. "How about you? Still at the Galleria?"

He'd started it eight years ago? Was it just a coincidence that was the same length of time they'd been apart, or was her leaving him the negative thing he needed an escape from? Was his definition of happiness the same as Deanne's? And if so, did it mean he still loved her despite his comment last night?

Her heart pounded with the need to know. But she didn't dare blurt the questions. Not when she no longer had any idea of her own feelings. For Treah or Claude. "Yeah, I'm still there. I'm Under-Curator of Abstract Art now."

"That's great." He smiled encouragingly. "I might not always get your work, but I know it's where your heart is."

Then that made one of them who knew its whereabouts. "Thanks."

He nodded and they fell silent for a few seconds before Dana asked, "If you don't run the resort for the profit, what do you do with all the money it brings in?"

"This week I paid my dad back every penny he invested in this place." Revulsion bled into his words, then gave way to a wry smile. "I suppose it's my just deserts that he doesn't understand what I do."

As little as a week ago, she might have agreed. Might have even gotten a gratified kick out of the fact that Treah finally understood how she felt. Now, to know that he wasn't getting along with his dad when he'd already lost his brother made her want to comfort him with a hug and a kiss again.

She settled on a sympathetic smile. "I'm sorry."

"Don't be. It's taken care of." His eyes betrayed that he wasn't so over it before he covered them with his sunglasses. In a more upbeat tone, he shared, "Most of Ecstasy's income goes back into operations and then a youth-betterment program the resort sponsors in Blair's name. He wasn't a bad kid, but I figure he'd still appreciate my helping out those kids who do get a rough start."

"He would like that," Dana agreed solemnly. Personally, she loved knowing that Treah was hanging on to his brother's memory far more than he'd originally let on. She also had to wonder why he was divulging the information now.

Was it just because she'd asked where the resort income went, or was it part of a last attempt at winning her back before she returned to Claude? Or was that wishful thinking on her part because she had no longing to ever return to Claude?

Needing to do something more than sit idle on this bench and let her thoughts roam, she stood and nodded out at the water. "Do we have fishing poles?"

"There's a couple in the cabin." Amusement colored his voice. "Were you hoping to snag the shore and reel us in?"

"I was hoping to catch some lunch. Or dinner." She looked at his wrist and found no watch. She took hers off before bed each night, so it was at home on her nightstand. "What time do you think it is?"

"Two or three. Maybe a little later. How are you planning to cook the fish after you catch it?"

"I wasn't. How different can it be than sushi?"

Treah's revolted look suggested the taste would be the polar opposite. Without responding vocally, he went down into the cabin. He returned after half a minute with a fishing pole in one hand and two brown-wrapper, couple-inch-thick and several-inch-long rectangles in the other.

He handed her the pole. "Enjoy. Personally, I'm going to help myself to the meat loaf."

Placing the brown-wrapper rectangles on the back bench, he returned to the cabin. He emerged a few seconds later with two green bag chairs. Setting one near her feet, he pulled the other from its bag, opened it, and sat down in front of the bench. He peeled open one of the brown-wrapper rectangles to reveal plastic silverware, a couple more wrappers, and a small, rectangular cardboard box with the words "Meat Loaf Entrée" stamped on the outside. The other wrappers were clear and contained bread with jam, and—hello!—a chocolate chip cookie!

Leaning the fishing pole against the side of the boat, Dana grabbed the bag near her feet, tugged out the chair, and set it up beside his. She sank onto the chair and grabbed the other brown-wrapper rectangle of goodness. "I've never been a big fan of sushi."

With a knowing laugh, Treah watched her dig into her food, which didn't contain the same items as his. "Still set on going the cold route?"

"I have another option?" More importantly, where the hell was her cookie? Cheese tortellini, mashed potatoes, and crackers with cheese spread sounded great, but it wasn't fair trading her cookie for pound cake.

"You do." He grabbed his cardboard box and opened it to reveal a solid gray pouch that presumably held meat loaf inside. He ripped the top off a second pouch, which resembled a narrow, clear plastic bag with a lot of black writing on it, poured a tiny bit of water in from the bottle he'd opened earlier, and slipped the meat loaf inside. After quickly curling the plastic pouch's top down, he stuck it inside the cardboard box, and then leaned the box against the side of the boat at an angle.

Dana repeated his steps with her own food. Except she wasn't planning on steam lifting off her pouch nearly the instant the water made contact, or precisely how hot the clear plastic bag would get in a matter of seconds.

"Holy cow!" she gasped, shoving the pouch into the box

and all but throwing it against the side of the boat beside Treah's.

He let go another laugh. "Pretty incredible, huh?"

"Seriously. Claude would never know to do something like that." She bit her lip too late. Talk about killing a moment. She'd totally obliterated his smile. "Honestly, I don't think he's much for boats," she added in an attempt to make it clear he had nothing on Treah in this setting.

Apparently, he didn't get her point, though, because he scowled at the cardboard boxes. "What do you say we just watch the food cook?"

They could do that. Or she could kiss him to make up for her stupid big mouth. "Or we could finish the crossword puzzle."

He nodded, then said emotionlessly, "The puzzle it is."

But the puzzle it wasn't. Because Claude it wasn't.

Maybe it wasn't Treah, either. Dana just knew she couldn't any longer deny how many ways she and Claude weren't a match and the singular way in which they were. A shared passion for art was not enough to build a marriage on. She also couldn't ignore how right it felt being here with Treah. How all it took was a puzzle book and a brown wrapper bag of food to make her happy when he was around.

The kind of happy that had her beaming as she slid onto the bench seat.

She scooted along the seat until her hip brushed against their side dishes, and he frowned. "Trying to crush my cookie?"

"Nope. Trying to crush my mouth against yours."

Surprise flared in his eyes as she grabbed hold of the arms of his chair, climbed on to straddle his lap, and crushed her mouth to his. After her hot then cold attitude last night, she'd expected hesitation. He didn't hesitate. Jerking the ponytail holder from her hair, he opened his mouth and pushed his tongue between her lips.

Her hair spilled around her bare shoulders, tickling her sun-warmed skin as it danced on the breeze. He buried his hands in her hair, trapping the strands in place, using the fierce grip to keep her head in place, as well, while he attacked her mouth with demanding licks, bold caresses, hungry sucks.

Her head spun. Her belly warmed. The heat bolted down to her thighs, her pussy. She smiled against his mouth with the knowledge it was back. That deliriously breathless intoxication, no alcohol needed. No nothing but Treah and his Technicolor brand of seduction that made her feel alive like nothing else and no other.

His fingers left her hair to slip down her back to her butt. Cupping her ass, he ground his swelling cock against her mound. She moaned with the contact. So good. Always so good. She craved more immediately, all of his hot body pressed against all of hers. But not at the risk of him thinking this was a spur of the moment decision.

Dana let the kiss go on, let her pussy dampen and soften and her mind spin nearly out of control. Then she broke from his mouth to pant a cease-fire.

"Let me guess. Regrets?" Treah asked in a rough voice before she could speak.

She swooped in for another quick, openmouthed kiss before sliding from his lap where a full-blown erection had surfaced to taunt her famished sex. "Nope." Concentrating her hunger elsewhere, she dropped down onto her own seat and tore into her crackers and cheese spread. "Empty stomach."

"So that's it? I get a little tongue action and a dry hump, and then we eat?"

The desire in his voice was thick enough to slide down her spine and tease along her crack. Not feeling up to seeing that same desire reflected on his face and stay in this chair, she focused on spreading the cheese onto her crackers. "Are you complaining?"

"Hell, I don't know what I'm doing."

"That makes two of us," she mumbled as she shoved the cracker into her mouth. She chewed the cracker down, then nodded at the heating pouches. "Are they done?"

"Close enough." He stood to open the plastic pouches and remove the cardboard boxes.

Dana kept her attention trained on his chest as she accepted her box. She took out the inner pouch of tortellini and scooped out a forkful of noodles. She murmured as the first bite of cheese sauce hit her tongue. "This is actually quite good."

Treah dropped back down in his chair. "They're made much better than they used to be."

Sexual tension rode thick in his voice and carried like a current in the inches of space that separated them. It called to her like a living, breathing entity, keeping her sex moist and her pulse fast as she ate her tortellini. Needing an excuse to look at him—any excuse—she reached across to stab a forkful of meat loaf from his pouch.

Her fork skimmed his hand as she lifted it free of the pouch. Her mouth watered with the want to lick the trail of sauce from his skin. Better yet, to cover his body with it so she had a valid excuse to lick every inch of him.

He looked over at her as she popped the bite into her mouth. Strain weighed in his eyes. "Would you like my cookie while you're at it?"

Cookie. Cockie. Close.

Ready for his cookie, not so sure yet about his cockie, Dana grabbed the former and tore into its packaging. "I thought you'd never ask."

He gave a short laugh that eased the tension a fraction. Enough for the meal to finish out in silence. When they were both done, she grabbed up the empty pouches and boxes, leaving the heater packets for him to dispose of since she had no idea if they were burnable. Tossing the trash into a wastebasket in the cabin, she couldn't help but stare at the bed.

As she retook the seat beside him, Treah looked over at her expectantly, much the same way he had when they'd been doing the crossword. Then she'd been eager to hand out a clue. Now, she didn't have a clue where to go next. "I really am sorry that your dad is being negative about the resort. It hurts when people don't get the things you love."

He smiled self-deprecatingly. "I should have given your work more attention."

She sighed. So much for compassion. "I didn't mean that in reference to you not getting my work."

"I still could have tried harder, or at least made it clear how much I supported your love for it."

"You could have kept your wisecracks to yourself," she conceded.

"I could have."

"Would it have made a difference?" Dana clamped her mouth around the question. As badly as she wanted to know the answer, she hadn't meant for it to slip out.

He didn't skip a beat but responded as though he'd been hanging on the answer for years. Eight, to be exact. "I'm not the one who walked out."

Treah returned to the lit cabin after sending up a second set of flares. The first ones he shot off shortly after dark a half hour ago, apparently without a captive audience.

Dana lay on the bed the same way she slept, with her knees pulled up under her belly and her face burrowed against a thin pillow. "I could use a me-size pouch like the ones we used to cook our dinner," she mumbled.

Or she could stay in that position, lose the jeans she'd changed into after the sun set, and let him warm her up by sliding his cock between her butt cheeks. If he knew what her earlier kiss was getting at, he would do it. But he didn't know what that kiss or the flashes of her happy smile were about, and he wasn't going to torture his body or his mind by starting something she had no plans to finish.

"There are plenty of blankets." Squatting in front of the cabinet beside the bed, he pulled open the door. A single blue blanket sat where there should have been four. He grabbed it out and tossed it to her. "There *should* be plenty of blankets, but whomever we owe for stranding us out here apparently took the blankets along with the gas."

She situated the blanket over her, then lay on her side and opened her arms. "I'm cold. Lie down and hold me, please."

Talk about the mother of all temptation. He didn't know if he could be that close right now and *just* hold her. He also wasn't about to turn her down.

Toeing off his shoes, Treah climbed onto the bed and pulled her into his arms. And she pulled up both of their shirts and pressed their chests together. Make that her bare breasts to his chest. Her nipples pressed into his chest as rigid points, and his cock went rigid in turn. "Lose your bikini top?"

"It's much warmer this way," Dana muffled against the crook of his neck.

Her mouth was inches from his ear, close enough he could both hear and feel each of her moist, warm breaths. They were coming fast, her breasts rising and falling rapidly against his chest. Which made him think her nipples weren't just hard because she was cold. Which made him think of about fifty other, far better ways to get warm. All of which involved their naked bodies. "You know how they say extreme situations lead to great sex? Well, I figured that was mostly bullshit until I saw a documentary on the subject last year. According to the interviewees, you'll never top an orgasm achieved during or right after a high-stress experience."

"I'm not that stressed." Her head lifted from the crook of

his neck. Eyes saturated with copper and lust met his. "I kind of do want to sleep with you."

His shaft pulsed with her sexy, smoky tone. He recognized the hunger burning in her eyes from seeing it a thousand times before, in reality and in his dreams. There was no "kind of" about her want. Once upon a time, there also wouldn't have been any hesitation about it. But then, once upon a time she hadn't been engaged. "Just kind of?"

"Maybe a little more than that. Maybe just not quite all the way."

He could work with that. Now that she was sober and admitting she wanted him, Treah could happily—make that ecstatically—oblige. "I'm pretty sure that documentary mentioned that the sex didn't have to be full consummation to be explosive."

"What are you suggesting?"

"A repeat of Saturday night." He unfolded his arms from around her to slip his hands along her back to her ass. "Only, this time I won't stop you when you try to stick your hand down my shorts."

Defensiveness came into Dana's eyes. "I thought I was dreaming."

"You were. Of fucking me." Using his grip on her butt, he ground her mound against his erection. "Lucky for you I was feeling polite that night. Of course, if I hadn't been you wouldn't be lying there battling with guilt. You would have had to face the fact we go together better than you and your fiancé ever could."

She looked surprised by his words. Then her arms wrapped around his middle and she took over the grinding game. "Sexually we do."

Arousal bolted through his groin and along his shaft with the sensual rub of her pubis. He reared back his hips and shoved them forward again, grunting with a second, more intense bolt. "Sexually's a start."

Her breath dragged in on a whimper. "No penetration?"

"Not with the good stuff."

She snorted out a laugh about as unrefined as it got. The rubbing of her sex died along with her laughter, and she mused aloud. "Maybe I shouldn't do it. But I'm so cold. And doing it would warm me up fast. Probably if we don't do it now, we'll have to do it by morning or end up freezing to death."

Sighing, Treah released her butt and rolled to the opposite side of the bed.

"Where are you going?" Dana gasped.

"To sleep. Wake me up when you've decided that it's okay to be happy."

A handful of silent seconds passed where he waited for her to press the issue that she was already happy. Instead, she said, "Sexually, at least."

"At least," he agreed as relief swept through him. Only, it wasn't going to be an at least. Now that she'd admitted sleeping with him would make her sexually happy, he had every intention of seeing there was a lot more than sex between them.

A few more silent seconds passed. Her hands came to his back then, and she dragged up his shirt to press her breasts against his bare skin. Slipping an arm around his side, she splayed her fingers, warm and teasing, across his chest. "Okay."

His cock bucked against his zipper with her breathy tone. Grinning, because he already knew the answer and his pulse was racing with anticipation eight years in the building, he questioned, "Okay, you're going to wake me up when you've decided?"

"Okay, I've decided. Make me happy. Sexually."

8

_____

Heart slamming with expectation, Dana ran her hand down Treah's muscle- and lightly hair-lined torso in search of his shorts' zipper. She wasn't going to feel guilty. She was going to acknowledge that when it came to sex she could find no better match, and enjoy every breathless moment to come. And she would come. With him, she never had to worry about obtaining orgasm. She had only to wonder how many times he would bring her to climax before he surrendered to his own release.

Her fingers trembled as they connected with the tab of his zipper. Before she could drag it down, his hand folded over hers. He rolled onto his back to meet her eyes. "Tell me right now if you're going to have regrets."

It was a tall order, because she already knew that she would. She was going to regret not having all of him while the offer was on the table. But he didn't mean that kind of regret, so she rose up over him to slide his shirt farther up and press her mouth to his naked chest. "No regrets. I swear."

"Just remember you said that." A wicked grin winked at her as Treah caught her free wrist in his fingers. He took both of her hands into one of his, and dragged them together above her head.

In a flash, he exchanged their positions. Keeping her arms above her head, he trapped her onto her back with the weight and press of his strong thighs around hers. Primal heat seared in his nearly yellow eyes as he bent his dark head. Nudging her shirt up and away from her breasts, he sucked a nipple into his mouth.

Dana sighed with the warm, wet contact. After years of very little sex, and then only in the dark, watching his mouth work at her breast alone was exquisite enough to ignite tremors in her pussy. A few little tugs and she would be coming in her jeans.

But he didn't give her those tugs.

He freed her nipple from his mouth to again sit back on her thighs, the bulk of his weight concentrated on his own thighs. Warning, dark and sensual, narrowed his eyes. "I don't like being teased hard and then left wanting, Dana. You realize you're going to pay for last night?"

Delicious sensation rippled through her with the threat. Always she'd been a sucker for his paybacks, the kind that were drawn out to the point of being nearly torturous. Arching her breasts off the boat's small bed, she wriggled her crotch against his and tugged at the hand binding her wrists. "You'll give me what I deserve."

"You deserve to have your ass spanked. You're not getting that tonight."

She didn't have to get it tonight. Just the idea of feeling Treah's hand swatting against her backside, which had neither been spanked nor loved in so long it was like virgin territory, had her cheeks tingling and her pussy clenching.

The hand that gripped her wrists tightened as he returned his mouth to her breast. His free hand played along the sensitive skin surrounding her navel, and the rest of her body tingled to aching awareness. Unlike last time, his lips didn't close over her nipple, but nipped at the puckered skin of her areola until his mouth traveled a complete circle and her nipple went blood red with the want for the same treatment.

Without touching the nipple, he moved to the other breast, nipping at this areola in the same slow, circling fashion. His tongue flicked back to the first breast, retracing the path of his mouth in a hot, damp swipe, but always avoiding the hard, throbbing peak at the center. The fingers at her belly circled around her navel in tandem, stroking, caressing, never dipping inside. Never venturing beneath the low-rise waist of her jeans where her sex grew ever damper and soft with desire.

Treah's tongue retreated from its circling game. Watching her face, he blew on the damp skin surrounding her nipple. Shivers of pure erotic sensation whipped through her, coiling needful warmth in her belly and contracting her cream-slicked cunt.

Arching her breasts off the bed again, instinctively this time, Dana moaned and struggled to free her wrists from his hand.

God, how she wanted to touch. To drag his mouth to her breast and demand that he suck her nipple until she was coming from the forceful pull of his lips. He could do it. He'd done it many times before.

He laughed, dark and delicious, and his hot breath caressed her nipple a second time. "You act like you haven't been made love to in years."

"I haven't. Not by you. No one else does it right." No one else had ever driven her crazy with mindless desire. No one else had ever made her feel so cherished.

Cherished? But, yes, it was the only word to describe how she was feeling.

Gratitude touched his lips as a soft smile. His voice contrasted, coming out in that sexy rough pitch that was a verbal nirvana. "Trying to convince me to go easy on you?"

"Please don't do that. I'll lie and tell you that you're a rotten lover if it means you'll keep punishing me."

A mix of relief and conceit shone in Treah's eyes before he dipped his mouth to her other nipple and lapped his way around the erect crown. The fingers at her belly moved to her hip, gliding just beneath the waist of her jeans and caressing with pressure so light it was almost nonexistent and yet maddening, because it made Dana want more of his touch.

So much more.

She got more then, as his hand slipped from her jeans to join his mouth. Together, they waged a sensual assault on her breast, cupping and rubbing its fullness. Squeezing the flesh and then feeding it between his lips. He sucked at the tender, aching mound, and then repeated the move on its partner. Always still ignoring her poor, craving nipples. And then, too, ignoring her breasts to work his mouth down her torso.

Back and forth he moved, tongue and lips and teeth, licking and sucking and nipping at her hot skin, side to side, along her navel. Around her navel.

Finally, inside her navel.

Treah's tongue thrust into the shallow indent. She jerked off the bed with a moaning gasp, wrenching at her bound hands captured in his as her pussy squeezed tight.

His tongue retreated and he moved lower. Always he'd been meticulous about keeping his facial hair shaven, but now stubble was coming in and he used the short, coarse hair at the waist of her jeans. Dusting over the soft skin of her lower belly, dragging his chin back and forth, deliciously chafing her flesh to the point of pinkness. Making her cunt yearn for the same rough caress.

He lifted his head and darted his mouth to her mound without warning. He nipped at her sex through her jeans and thong. Dana reared up on the bed and panted out a desperate cry as vibrations of impending orgasm shook through her core.

Just before she would have peaked and fallen over the edge, his mouth lifted away.

She whimpered her dissatisfaction. He was building her up for a monumental orgasm, she knew. But a dream lover version of him who gave in to her unspoken command to come immediately sounded incredible about now.

He looked up at her on a chuckle. "Impatient?"

"Yes! Undress me."

"You're being punished."

"Then punish me naked."

The same dark warning that had come into Treah's eyes with his last threat returned. "Just remember you asked for it."

It couldn't leave her any more wanting than she already felt. Only, she realized that wasn't true as he peeled off her jeans and thong in tandem. His mouth started back for her sex, acting like it would nip at the freshly bared folds. But his lips parted without making contact, and he blew on her hairless mound from a couple inches away until her cunt quaked with creamy pleading.

The hand not holding her wrists moved everywhere, stroking, petting, fondling every inch of her. His tongue soon followed, licking, lapping, flicking. No curve or valley did he leave untouched. No part of her naked, trembling body but those she felt she might literally die from ecstasy if he didn't touch.

His mouth journeyed back to her breast and he toyed with the mound again. Toyed and taunted and started to draw away.

Dana yanked at her hands but his grip only tightened. "Just a nipple," she pleaded on a ragged sigh. "Just one nipple suck."

He lifted his mouth away to sit back on his haunches, and every nerve in her body screamed its raw, aching displeasure.

Treah smiled like some feral animal who'd found the most succulent of prey. "I love it when you beg."

He bent forward again. His mouth closed over her nipple in the next second, his lips soft and sucking without reprieve, and she nearly came on the spot.

She could have climaxed. She clenched her sex and fought

off what promised to be a soul-shattering orgasm because she knew he had something even better in store for his next move. She knew because she was going to beg for it.

"Just one pussy," she panted. "Just one pussy suck."

His mouth went to her other nipple, taking it between his lips and twisting it with a furious tug that nearly did her in. She curled her fingers into fists and held on. And was rewarded as he lifted his mouth and moved down the bed, down her body, down to where she was molten and dripping with want.

His eyes shimmered with that same molten desire as he asked thickly, "Did I mention I love it when you beg?"

They'd agreed to no penetration with the good stuff. And when he freed her wrists to take hold of her thighs, press his mouth to her slit, and lick his tongue up inside her cunt, it wasn't good.

It was the most amazing thing Dana had experienced in eight years. "Oh, God, Treah!"

He lapped at her pussy, tenderly, delicately, and then faster. She grabbed hold of his shoulders, panted for air, and hung on as she watched every glorious move he made.

Fingers joined his tongue, slipping inside her sheath, moving back and forth against her slick, fiery flesh. First, like his mouth had done, as a distraction, a tease. Then harder, driving up inside her tantalizingly with each push of his tongue. One of his fingers found her clit. Her breath snagged, hips twisted, thighs quivered wildly. The finger pressed, his tongue swirled. Heat licked from her toes to her core to her breasts to her mind.

Again, he had her there, at the breathless point. This time, it was more than intoxication. More than need. More than she could take without exploding.

This time, she dug her nails into his shoulders and cried out. Crested. Fell.

Treah's mouth stayed her constant. Licking. Sucking. Devouring her pussy with each of her shameless grinds. Keeping the vibrations going until she was frantically gasping for air and the orgasm was wrung from her system.

God, she felt so liberated, so alive. She felt like she needed more of him instantly. All of him.

Condom. They needed a condom.

But no. Not that far. Not real sex. Not yet.

Soon?

Not important right now. And, still, Dana trembled with the want to feel Treah buried deeply inside her, the need. She harnessed the anxious energy and used it on him, releasing his shoulders to bound up and knock him onto his back. Mostly on his back. Even using her full strength coupled with a mountain-sized adrenaline rush, she couldn't take him when he was primed to be the one in control.

Not with her body. Words might be a worthy adversary.

He'd never made a secret of what a victim he was to her voice. Smiling like the wondrously naughty woman she felt, she pressed her palms flat against his chest. "Lay on your back so I can suck your cock."

Unbridled desire for that very thing skipped through his gaze. "What about no penetration with the good stuff?"

"You think sticking your tongue in my pussy wasn't good? It was good. So good." She gave his chest a light shove. "Lie down, Treah."

He hesitated a beat, and then started to shift to the side of the bed and onto his back. She flung herself over him, dropping him fully onto his back with a whooshing breath, and then flattening her body against his.

Treah's heart beat against hers, fast and perfect. She could have stayed there and listened and been perfectly content for hours. But he was still hard and she still ached to relieve him of his erection.

Dana came up on her knees to drag his shirt over his head, kissing him openmouthed when it slid past his lips. His eyes reappeared, and she sat back to flash a seductress's smile. "This isn't a clothing-optional exercise. There's no clothing allowed, period."

"Sounds like my kind of exercise."

Thoughts of him lifting weights while muscles bulged and strained all over his nude body had her pussy flushing with heat and dampness again. She slipped down his body and cradled his knee with her labia as she went to mad work at removing his shorts. The zipper gave way. The shorts eased down his hips. One inch. Two. More. His long, thick cock burst free and slipped right into her waiting mouth.

Rocking her crotch against his knee, she gave his shaft a hard sucking. His pre-cum was another taste she could never forget. Never replace. She eased back far enough to take the root of his cock in hand and lapped greedily at the silky fluid gelling at the tip.

So, so good.

Moaning, Treah shoved his fingers into her hair. "Good God, girl. You act like you haven't sucked a dick in eight years, either."

Not his. Not in the light. "Not like this." Her heavy-lidded gaze fastened on his, she licked up another drop of pre-cum with a happy little sigh. "So there's no confusion, you're not being punished. You're being thanked."

Twisting the hand at the base of his cock, she opened her mouth and took his shaft nearly to the hilt. His cock surged, fingers tightening in her hair. "Get yourself off, Dana."

She worked her mouth up and down his length, sucking forcefully a few times, before letting him slip free. "I already had my turn."

"Take another. Play with your clit."

As much as she enjoyed sucking his dick, and with the continual press of his knee against her pussy, she didn't need to play with her clit to come. She swiveled her hips to the side for his sake, because she knew he loved to watch her masturbate as much as she loved to watch him do the same.

Taking his cock back into her lips, so that the greater width was pressed against the roof of her mouth and tongue, she pulled her knees up under her and fingered her clit. Juices leaked from between her labia as she thumbed the aching bud in time with the downward slide of her mouth around his shaft.

Still so fresh from orgasm, her pussy required very little stimulation. She gave the bead of her clit gentle strokes to keep the pressure building without overflowing as she petted the base of his cock and the sac of his balls.

His testicles grew taut in her hand. His cock pulsed. She worked her mouth and the finger at her clit faster. Watched each alluring shove of his dick between her lips until she couldn't keep her eyes open any longer for the heat and tension spiraling higher and higher. Building into a blistering inferno no longer able to be tamed.

Treah's hips lurched up and his cock shoved deep, nearly to the back of her throat. "Now!" he bellowed. "Come for me, now!"

Gasping around his rod, Dana slipped two fingers into her pussy and let the fire take her over. Juices rushed out around her impaling fingers as his seed flooded her mouth and slipped down the back of her throat.

The fingers in her hair kept her mouth working when she didn't have the stamina or state of mind to carry on. She gave herself over to total pleasure, total ecstasy, total perfection. Sexual perfection if nothing more, though it felt like more.

It felt like everything.

Strength returned with the thought and how much she wanted it to be accurate. She slipped her mouth free of his shaft and moved up and over his body, settled her face into the crook of the neck, back to where this had all begun. Full circle. Like their relationship?

His hand came up to stroke her back. "Regrets?"

She lifted her head far enough to find his lips and seal hers over them. His tongue slipped into her mouth in an enticing game of flick and retreat. Arousal pitched through her system again. He was going to turn her into a nympho yet.

"No regrets." Dana smiled lazily and then returned her head to his shoulder. "That was . . . yummy." Completely inadequate word choice, but how far did she dare to go? How much did she dare to hope they could make a second go of it and actually have it work this time? How did she even know he wanted a second chance at a relationship?

"Better than my cookie?"

"Mmm . . . Chocolate chip *is* my favorite."

"And me?"

"Gingersnaps," she answered, knowing it wasn't what he'd meant. "Because your grandmother made them with you and Blair every Christmas before she passed away." It *wasn't* what he'd meant, and yet her response felt even more intimate than admitting where he stacked up on her list of favorites.

Intimate in a way she'd never experienced with Claude. Not with any other man.

Was that her fault? Had she not let enough of herself come through to make them want to do the same? Or was it because she didn't have all of herself to give another man because part of her had always been with Treah? That part still beating fast against his chest, even with the soothing rub of his fingers along her spine.

"Sleeping?" he asked after a full minute of silence passed.

She nodded sluggishly. For all her heavy thoughts, his familiar embrace was soothing and warm, and she nearly had dozed off. "Almost."

"Me, too." His fingers left her back. Stealing away his warmth, he eased her off to the side of the bed. "I'll be right back."

Dana eyed his luscious butt as he stood. He didn't work out

to the point his body was too hard to enjoy, but he worked out to the point he was so hard she wanted to grab hold of his tight ass and never again let go.

For now, she would settle on Treah coming back to hold her. The bed wasn't very big, but it still felt huge and empty without him in it. "Going to tinkle?"

"Tinkle?" Amusement warmed his eyes as he turned back to tug his shorts up over his softening shaft. "No, Ms. Refined, I'm not going to *tinkle*. In case someone happens by the boat, I don't want them to think we're anchored out here for the night. I'm going to make it obvious we're broken down and in need of help."

"Okay. I'll be here when you get back."

"I hope so." Sincerity rang in his words.

His smile was just as sincere. He wanted her in his bed. But for how long? And did that want extend beyond sex? Did he still love her?

She pulled the lone cover over her and rolled onto her belly. Resting her face on the thin pillow, she drew her knees up under her and let all the questions sink, let herself wonder over her own feelings for him.

"Dana?"

She turned her head far enough to see him standing in front of the molded stairs that led up to the deck. "Yeah?"

"You look happy."

Oh, God. Her heart skipped a beat. Did that mean she was too easy to love again? Did that mean that he did?

She couldn't ask it. Couldn't ruin this night. She sent him a satiated smile instead. "You look like a guy who knows he's just left a woman well satisfied."

Without responding, he mounted the stairs and pushed open the cabin door. The door closed again, and he disappeared from view. She snuggled her face back into the pillow. Lethargy tugged at her subconscious. Not surprising she was so tired after all the fresh ocean air and sunshine today, and then the last hour down here in this boat. Incredible.

More incredible would be when Treah returned to the cabin and pulled her back into his arms, keeping her tucked up against his strong body as they slept.

It probably even happened that way. Dana didn't know for certain. She fell asleep before he returned, not waking until daylight glared against her eyelids so brightly it almost burned.

Still feeling tired and with no desire to move away from the warmth of Treah's arm around her, his chest spooned against her side while she slept in her usual fashion, she opened her eyes. She blinked against the light too close and white to be the sun. Sliding a hand from beneath her pillow, she raised it to shield her eyes. The light moved off to the side a couple inches. Chris's face came into view and, beyond that, the darkness of night.

Not the sun. Rescue. "Thank God. We thought you'd never find us."

"I didn't realize you were missing until an hour ago. Treah will sometimes go onto the mainland and not get back until after dark. When it got to be after eleven and he hadn't called, I figured something was up. What happened?"

"Someone sabotaged the boat." She'd considered it could have been Chris in an attempt to give Treah more time with her. But, as he had when the motors were vandalized, he both looked and sounded too concerned to be guilty.

"How?"

"They siphoned out the gas. And cut the radio wires so we couldn't call for help. At least, you found us before we hit a sandbar or something." Dana started to rise, then remembered Treah's arm was around her body. Her *naked* body. She looked down to where one of his hands covered her otherwise bare breast, and so did Chris using the flashlight as his guide.

Jerking her gaze back up, she stuttered, "Um, can you give

me a few minutes to wake up Treah and get dressed? It was cold. Skin to skin contact was the only way we were sure to keep from freezing to death."

"There isn't a chance in hell you could have frozen to death," Chris observed as Treah poured gas into the tank's side vein from the spare container kept on the jet-boat moored to the cabin cruiser. "It's almost sixty out. Closer to sixty-five in the cabin."

Treah glanced over his shoulder to make sure Dana was still downstairs getting dressed before glaring at Chris, who sat in the driver's seat waiting to fire up the engine. Hell, he shouldn't be glaring after how well things went, but then he didn't like being manipulated. "You set the stage. I just took advantage."

"I didn't set the stage."

Treah wished he *had* been the responsible party so that he could stop wondering what else might go wrong with one of the boats or some other part of the resort. But Chris looked too serious to be lying. "Whatever. We didn't fuck."

"Hey, that's your business, man."

It was, but Chris's smile said he wasn't buying that they hadn't slept together. "I'm telling you for Dana's sake. She would never be able to handle thinking you caught her post-coital with a guy other than her fiancé." He set the empty gas tank on the deck and twisted on the rail cover. "Give it a try."

Chris turned the key and the motor roared to life. Flipping on the boat's running lights, he came to his feet. "Gwen was right. You still love Dana, don't you?"

"I don't know. Probably." Definitely.

Treah couldn't doubt it anymore. He also couldn't believe she didn't feel the same for him, after how completely she'd given herself to him tonight. She'd even quit with her snoring and the mini-contortionist position to curl up against him when he'd first returned to the cabin after setting up a makeshift SOS.

Chris slipped over the edge of the cabin cruiser to drop down onto the slightly lower deck of the jet-boat. "Want me to wait around and follow you in, just in case?"

"Go ahead. If we aren't back by morning, come looking for us."

Treah unfastened the ropes securing the two boats together and tossed them to Chris before giving the jet-boat a push away from the side of the cabin cruiser. Chris gave the jet-boat more throttle and took off in the direction of Ecstasy Island.

The cabin door opened as Treah was sliding onto the captain's seat. Dana emerged at the top of the stairs, wearing the blue blanket wrapped around her shoulders with the ends draping to the knees of her jeans. Her hair was pulled back in one of those high, flirty ponytails that made her look carefree and her smile was wide and so inviting he gave serious consideration to stalling the boat and then acting like gas hadn't been the issue after all, just so they could be stranded alone together a while longer.

But they couldn't be stranded for the rest of their lives. For both of their sakes, it was better to figure out where her feelings lay as soon as possible. "We have gas, but not enough to make it to the mainland."

"That's okay." She dropped down onto the passenger's seat and snuggled the blanket up around her throat. "We can try again tomorrow. Unless you have business you need to attend to, in which case Friday or Saturday's fine."

Treah had business, all right. The kind that involved making her see she wanted to remain with him long after Friday or Saturday.

Dana's visitors left her table and she fought a smidgen of guilt.

She wasn't supposed to be hanging out in Ecstasy's meeting room, tapping her foot to a blues rhythm while partying in her panties with people whose names and faces were quickly becoming common. She should be in New Hampshire, helping to pick out tuxedos, making final food decisions, ordering invitations . . .

Instead, she'd called Claude and said Deanne was arranging to have her picked up this weekend and that she would either call when she got home or drop by the museum sometime next week. He'd agreed without hesitation. Without saying he'd missed her. Without even noticing, or if he noticed than not caring, that she failed to say she loved him before she hung up the phone.

God knew he didn't say the words to her.

Treah had, plenty of times. And if what she overheard him tell Chris on the boat last night was true, then probably—dare she think hopefully?—he would again. It was the reason she'd lied about Deanne arranging a ride for her. And the reason she'd told Treah this morning that she didn't need to get home today.

Speaking of Treah, he appeared beside the table in hunter green briefs and nothing else but a smile. With a suggestive smile of her own, Dana glanced at the eye-level bulge at the front of his briefs. "I like your outfit."

He scanned the visible portions of her matching black strapless bra and thong, and let out a low whistle. "Yours isn't half bad, either. Or half there."

Obviously the nonalcoholic drinks were going straight to her head again, because she stood from her chair, lifted her arms, and turned in a slow circle to show off exactly how much her thong didn't cover. She'd considered wearing a bikini. But this wasn't a bikini party. She didn't want to feel like an outcast, so she'd worn all that she had: the barely there scraps of underwear Deanne had packed for her.

When she'd first come downstairs, she'd felt a little uncomfortable. But there were a couple of other women in thongs and no one had given her a condescending look. And even if they had, it would have been worth it to see the raw sensuality in Treah's eyes as she turned back around.

Teasing joined the heat as he glanced at the clear plastic cup on the table that held her pink drink. "Getting drunk?"

"Mmm hmm . . . And that makes it totally acceptable for me to do this." Closing the foot of space between them, Dana wrapped her arms around his neck and ground her pelvis against his. And, ah God, that connection was pure bliss. "I have a secret to tell you."

He brought his arms around her waist. "Yeah?"

"Oh, yeah."

Rising on tiptoe, she flicked her tongue across his ear before whispering, "I wasn't being nice earlier when I said the trip to the mainland could wait."

He tipped his head back to meet her eyes. The kind of keen insight that was laced with carnal promise sizzled in his gaze. "I know."

Her smile grew as excitement danced through her belly as a wave of arousal.

Last night, she hadn't been quite ready for his cockie. But today, after that phone call with Claude, and now, when Treah had spent the last few hours working in his office, and she'd spent every minute wishing he would get the hell back to her already, she was ready for his cockie in a big, wet way. "I figured you did."

His mouth descended slowly, lips brushing with bare touches and then a bit more pressure. She parted her mouth on a sigh, and his tongue slipped inside as the sweetest of indulgences. Slow licks and caresses mimicked the sluggish circling of their hips. A decadent dance that again made Dana feel as cherished as she was desired.

She pulled back, a little breathless and a little more giddy. "I have another secret." He shifted his head so that her lips brushed his ear. She'd done away with jumping in headfirst quite some time ago. Now it seemed exactly the thing to do. "I want to take you upstairs and fuck you until you can't see straight."

Treah exhaled audibly, his breath hot and erotic against her bare shoulder. His arms slid from her waist. He unwrapped her arms from around his neck, as well, to step back a half foot and ask soberly, "What about him?"

Him, aka Claude, she would handle another day. Tonight, she only wanted to handle the man standing in front of her. Handle him. Fondle him. Make love with him until they were both too exhausted to move, let alone question regrets.

Purposefully misunderstanding, Dana sent the growing bulge at the front of his briefs an anxious smile. "He's in for a long, wet night ahead."

9

Treah's heart pummeled like he was about to score his first lay as he took Dana's hand and the old familiar heat of intimacy lifted from where their fingers joined. Nodding at a few people as they passed and giving Chris's knowing look from across the meeting room a mental finger, he guided her toward the administration area door. They reached the door and he pushed it in. She halted to tug on his arm.

Christ, if she'd changed her mind . . .

Almost afraid, he looked back at her. With desire dilating her pupils and flushing her cheeks past the tan she'd obtained this last week, she appeared every bit as eager as he felt. Still, he held his breath as he raised an eyebrow in question.

"I don't want to go upstairs to your bed," she explained.

Hearing the "but" in her voice, he released his breath. Not up to his bed, *but* she did still want to sleep with him somewhere. And it wouldn't be just sex in Dana's mind. That she was taking this step assured that much. "Then where?"

"Somewhere you've fantasized about having me."

"What makes you so sure I've fantasized about you?"

"Great minds are known to think alike."

In other words, she'd been fantasizing about him. Since before she'd come to Ecstasy? Not needing to know the answer, at least for now, Treah pulled her through the admin door. "We're not going upstairs."

"Then where?" she tossed his earlier question back at him.

He left her to wonder for the half minute it took to reach his office, grab a condom from the stash in his desk left over from when Gwen had been working for and living with him, snap on the patio light, and move through the door. He'd come out here for solace the first time he'd heard Dana's voice after eight years of no contact. In the end it had been Deanne's voice, but still this place was where it had all begun again.

The moon was little more than a slip of yellow-orange tonight. The nearby crash of the waves and the salt lading the warm breeze were the only signs the ocean was a hundred feet away. Knowing it was there helped to slow the hasty beat of his heart as he guided her to the picnic table.

Releasing her hand, he set the condom on one of the bench seats and then took hold of her bare sides and lifted her onto the end of the table. She flashed a smile packed with naughty as she spread her legs and opened her arms. "Come a little bit closer, Treah," she beckoned, her tone half indulgent smoke, half sexy song.

Damn, how he wanted to relent, both to her stunning body and her unforgettable voice. But that there was another man in the picture was also unforgettable.

She had to feel something for Treah to be allowing this. But did she get that he felt more than just "something"? Did she understand that once they made love he would never let her marry some other guy? The second he sank his cock inside her warm, welcoming body, he was going to become a possessive ass. "You're sure?"

"Oh, yeah. You're my kind of man." She kept up the smoke

and song game, eyes sizzling copper and her fingers curling with a silent summons.

His shaft pulsed with her beauty and bravado, both drawn out to the extreme beneath the overhead floodlight. Sliding his hands up her smooth, silky legs, he moved between her thighs, just not close enough that their pelvises would touch.

Dana lifted her hands to his chest. Her fingers feathered against the muscle and toyed with the dusting of black curls. Leaning forward, she bent her head to flick her tongue across his nipple. "So big and so, so strong."

He fought to ignore the way that damp, sultry lick pebbled his nipple. The way her gaze shot to his briefs when his cock bucked for a lick of its own wasn't discountable. Amusement curved one side of her mouth higher. Before she could grab hold of his shaft, he asked, "Do you still want to go home tomorrow?"

"Only if you don't convince me to stay."

Just for the day, though? Or far longer?

Hell, it didn't matter. Not in the short run. No matter her response, Treah was going to have this night. He was going to have her naked and clenching around him with orgasm. He was going to have every one of his red-hot memories of the two of them brought back into the flesh.

Moving snugly between her thighs, he took her face in his hands and kissed her, soft and easy. In that slow, lazy way that made her taste spill over his senses and him crave her more than any hard, frenzied feasting could have accomplished.

The Dana who'd never been known for holding back emerged, gripping his sides and rubbing her pussy against his cock through their underwear.

His underwear, at least. The bit of black lace she wore over her mound barely counted as clothing.

If he was a jealous guy, he might have been annoyed by the way she'd put her decadently rounded backside on display for the entire resort. As it was, he'd been damned proud to see her throwing sophistication so far to the wayside. At it was, too, he wanted to bend her over the end of the table, get that lush ass sunny-side up, and give her the paddling he'd forgone last night.

Treah kissed her a second time. Just a little faster. Just enough to have heat arrowing through him and his heart pounding like a jackhammer again. Then he let go of her face and stepped back from the cradle of her thighs. "Get off the table, Dana."

A frown line crossed her forehead as she slipped off the edge. "I thought doing me on it was your fantasy?"

"It is." He grabbed her arm and spun her around with a quick jerk. "Now get back on it. Just your belly and breasts. Ass in the air."

The frown line disappeared as anticipation brought a jubilant grin to her lips. Crossing her arms over her chest, she channeled it into a dry look. "The man gives me a couple orgasms and thinks he has the right to order me around."

So she wanted to play games? He could do that. He could enjoy the hell out of doing that.

Taking Dana's arm back into his hand, he pulled her partway around and brought the flat of his free hand smacking across her naked backside. She contracted her butt cheeks on a mewling whimper he felt as a needful stabbing in his balls. "Get on the table *now*, or I'm swatting your ass twenty times instead of ten."

The overhead light caught the twinkle in her eyes that said she would be thrilled to have him spank her all night long. Vocally, she grumbled, "So much for thinking you aren't an ass."

"Don't be confused. I am an ass." Hoping she would never have to find out what he meant by that warning, Treah gave her a little shove toward the picnic table.

She whirled toward the table a shade on the dramatic side, and planted her hands on its surface. Bending at the waist, she pressed her breasts, belly, and cheek against the wood. Her thighs parted and her butt cheeks spread to expose the thong's thin black strap sheathed against her crack.

Treah sucked in a shaky breath and ran his hands up her thighs to palm the globes of her ass. His thumbs pressed against the scrap of lace at the rear of her mound. Heat and moisture raced through the thin material as she tightened her pussy against his probing.

His breath hissed in with the twinging of his cock. "Fuck, are you hot."

"Does that mean I get all twenty swats?"

That meant he wanted to forget the swats and get right to the part where he tore aside the tiny scrap of damp lace and shoved inside her.

But Dana wanted the swats. And, as he lifted his hands away and then brought one soundly back down across her butt, he knew he wanted them, too.

She cried out with the contact, and his shaft gave a savage throb that grew twice as intense with his next spanking. Pale scarlet fanned across her cheeks as his swats continued. She grabbed hold of the sides of the table and wriggled her mound against its edge with the fifth slap. Juices shimmered along her thighs in thin rivulets and her breath came as short bursting gasps.

Struggling to keep his own breathing controlled, Treah shoved his left hand under her and dipped his fingers beneath the cup of her bra. Trapping a nipple between thumb and forefinger and squeezing, he lifted his other hand into the air.

His pulse pounded and his balls went taut as his palm fell in slow motion. He twisted the hard point of her nipple as flesh smacked against sweaty, stinging flesh.

Dana's fingers went white-knuckled around the table's sides. Her hips shot back on a keening moan. Pressing her butt tighter against his palm, she rubbed her pussy along the table's edge. "Not gonna make twenty. Gotta come."

Desperation shook her words and shimmied along his spine. Rolling her nipple between his fingers, he slipped a finger of the other hand beneath the thong's butt strap and petted her anus. Her breathing went ragged, her hips twisted for more. He brought his probing finger lower, under the black lace and up inside her sheath.

And, hell, what a glorifying move that was.

Only five swats and she was already so soft and hot, dripping with cream. His blood thrummed and his cock jumped for release with the implication. "No one's spanked you in eight years, either?"

In wait of her response, he added a second finger and pumped them together inside her soaking cunt. She pressed her face flat against the table and muffled out, "No one." Canting her hips, she rocked back and clenched around his fingers. "Love me, Treah. Please. Now. Get inside me."

He'd planned to draw this out, have them both trembling and desperate with the need to come before he entered her. But she'd used the word love and he wanted to believe she did feel that way for him so damned badly that he gave into her request, releasing her nipple to free his swollen cock from his briefs.

Lifting the condom from the bench seat, he quickly unwrapped it. His cock jerked with the subtle tremble of his fingers as he worked the latex over his shaft. Sex had always been the last thing to make him nervous. But then, this was so much more than a casual fuck, and his breath feathered out anxiously as he pulled back aside the crotch of the thong and pressed the tip of his cock to her opening.

"More!" Dana demanded, pushing back and bringing him an inch inside her heat.

On a groan, he released the thong and fed his shaft inside her the rest of the way, inch by awesome inch.

She tensed for a second as he shoved to the hilt and then loosened again on a thready sigh. "You feel so good, Treah."

Yeah, and she felt like coming home.

Taking her hips in his hands, he pulled out a couple inches and then pushed deep again. Electric sensation coursed from his groin to churn riotous heat through his body. "This is way better than a gingersnap."

She laughed, then stopped short to suck in a hard breath as he drew out almost all the way only to slam back inside her with a gasp of his own.

Both the view and positioning from this angle were spectacular, but Treah wanted to see her face. He wanted her to see the love on his own.

He pulled from her sex again, this time all the way out. He sidestepped a couple feet to the table's bench seat, worked the underwear down his legs and off, and then dropped down on the seat. With his breathing sounding like a whirlwind, he tipped his head to the side and smiled into her equally hungry and bewildered eyes.

Dana lifted her cheek from the table. "What are you doing?"

He looked down at the cream-slicked condom covering his aching cock. "You're needed on my lap."

She followed his gaze and her mouth regained its smile. Keeping her eyes on his, she moved in front of him and eased the wet thong down her legs. He groaned at the sight of her bare cunt, the lips plumped up and glistening pink with arousal. Before he could make a grab to get all that sexiness wrapped around him, she was straddling his lap.

Her thighs slid over his, her ass cheeks caressing his balls and her breasts pressing into his chest through her miniscule strapless bra. Taking hold of his face, she touched her lips against his in time with the mouth of her pussy brushing against the head of his cock. Her tongue pushed inside then, and she sank onto his shaft without reprieve.

And he was home. Exactly where he wanted to be. Exactly where he'd never stopped wanting to be.

Last time, he'd relented to her wishes and let her walk away. This time, Treah wouldn't. This time he was going to be as big of an asshole as it took to keep her at his side.

Dana speared her tongue into his mouth and stroked his back as she licked at his inner cheeks, over his teeth, against his tongue, all while her hips lifted and fell, and her sex squeezed urgently around his. He let his thoughts go to answer her urgent demand. Kissed her back until it was his tongue in her mouth, her soft inner cheeks he swept along, her ass he took hold of and lifted her along his rod.

Again and again, she contracted around him, nether lips sucking wet and wanting around his shaft and barely contained breasts slapping against his chest. Then her tongue went still and her sex shuddered with a clenching too violent to be practiced.

She moaned into his mouth as her inner walls clamped tight. He slipped a hand from beneath her butt to move it between their bodies and part her labia. He rubbed his finger against her clit, just once, and she exploded around his cock.

Yanking her mouth from his, she tipped back her head and puffed out a series of little "Ohs," while he alternately kissed and licked and sucked on her ears and throat and down to what parts of her breasts he could reach. And when her spasms ended, he reached down again and stroked her right back to the peak of climax.

"I'm coming again!" Dana's fingers coiled around his shoulders. Her eyes squeezed shut as she squirmed up and down his cock, her cunt pulsing with a dozen little vibrations and then a much larger one.

With a satisfied grin, Treah pulled the hot, salty skin of her neck into his mouth. Grinding hard and deep inside her, he gave into a shout-worthy climax.

Sucking on her neck, he rode out the orgasm to the last pump. He returned his mouth to hers then for a long, wet kiss.

He softened it as he slowly eased his tongue back, wanting her to understand that just because the sex was over it didn't mean he was done holding her or touching her or kissing her.

As if she could read his mind and hated where it was going, she released his sides and broke off the kiss. He waited for her to climb from his lap. She leaned back, but otherwise stayed in place as she studied his face.

A dazzling smile surfaced. "You look happy, Treah."

"I am." And he would continue to be. Just so long as she didn't give him a reason to spend another eight years licking his wounds.

10

Treah had always been a master at sensual persuasion. He'd convinced Dana to stay on the island throughout the weekend, and she'd convinced herself, with the aid of the better part of a bottle of merlot at dinner tonight, that it wouldn't make one bit of difference to stay even longer than that. She already had the time off work and Claude wasn't tracking her down to declare his undying love.

She might as well stay right here, with her hands and feet bound to Treah's head and footboards, while he took advantage of her easy state of mind and body by driving her nuts with slow seduction.

Slow but not exactly sweet.

Kneeling between her spread-eagled thighs, he teased the head of a flesh-colored vibrator along the outer folds of her labia. He'd been at the taunting game for a good twenty minutes, ever since he'd used the sheets to tie her naked body to his bed. The unmasked desire in his yellow-green eyes and the way his gel-tipped cock stuck straight out said his actions were taking as big of a toll on him as they were on her.

Dana lifted her hips off the bed and attempted to bury the head of the vibrator inside her soaking sex. He pulled the toy away, and she huffed out a breath.

Rough, pleased laughter rolled from his lips. "You'll get it, just as soon as you agree to a favor."

"What?" she panted, trying not to sound irritated but, geez, she'd already offered every sexual act under the sun and he wouldn't give in and do her already.

Unease flashed in his eyes. "Go to the Pacific branch with me tomorrow."

Oh. Guess that explained why he hadn't given in. He wanted her desperate for climax in the hopes of swaying her into doing something he seemed to think she wouldn't want to do. Did she? It would mean missing even more work and lying to Claude again. But then, work really wasn't an issue and Claude . . .

Thoughts of Claude totally killed the heat of the moment.

She had to call him. Talk to him. And tell him what exactly?

That he was a slouch as a lover and a bore in pretty much every other regard? That outside of work they didn't come close to connecting? That she'd fallen back in love with her ex?

Only, Dana didn't know if she had fallen for Treah. Or maybe she'd never stopped loving him in the first place and was afraid to admit it for fear of what would happen when this retreat from reality reached its end. "For how long?"

As if he took the question as agreement, a confident smile reclaimed his lips. Dipping his head, he nuzzled her sex. His tongue darted up inside her sheath quickly and unexpectedly, and she was flung headfirst and moaning back into the moment.

He kissed her pussy with the moist, firm stroke of his lips and tongue, and brought her quaking to the edge of orgasm in twenty seconds flat. Fisting her bound hands, she arched up off the bed and ground against his mouth. And he sat back on his knees and returned the head of the vibrator to taunt the outer folds of her sex.

"A couple days," Treah answered before she could voice her thoughts of the achingly slow and wickedly torturous payback that awaited him. "Due to a scheduling mix-up, Mona, the manager down there, had to bring on a couple new healing coaches without their going through the full training. I want to make sure they're working out."

Dana smiled in spite of the urge to thrash him. "I love how much this place means to you."

"I love you—"

The breath snagged in her throat. Had he really just said that?

"—at my total mercy," he finished.

She let her breath out on a whoosh. No. Apparently, he hadn't said that. At least, not what she thought he'd said. What she realized she'd wanted him to say so badly that her rapidly beating heart felt like it might burst from disappointment.

Expectation in his eyes, he allowed the vibrator to finally penetrate her labia and take a direct, buzzing path to her clit. "You'll go to the Pacific branch with me?"

Her hips shot off the bed and she cried out with the breathtaking contact. She was liable to do anything with him so long as he didn't take the toy away again.

Exquisite tension mounted in her core with the vibrator's nonstop whir against the swollen bead. Her sex spasmed its plea for relief. Treah slipped a finger beneath the vibrator and impaled her pussy. He worked the digit and toy together in a press and release game that had her mind threatening to fragment from the intensity of the heat and pressure whipping through her body. Gasping, Dana tugged at her wrist bindings, thrashed in an attempt to get out of both them and the ankle ties.

And then she figured out what he'd meant when he'd referred to himself as an ass two nights ago. Because the rotten ass pulled back his finger and the vibrator.

She attempted to clamp her thighs together to impede the

loss. Then, accepting how futile it was, resorted to a glare. "You are *so* going to pay."

"Can't wait." Humor gleamed in his eyes. "*You* don't have to wait. Orgasm's just a press of your button and a word away."

So easy, he made it sound. But then, he didn't have to call Claude.

Damn, she didn't want thoughts of her fiancé in her head. Focusing her attention on Treah's gloriously naked body and the wanton heat sizzling through her own, she purred out an anxious reply. "Yes. I'll go with you. Now make me come. Please."

"There you go with the begging again." Tender affection warmed his eyes and cloaked the roughness of his voice. "I should have known I still love you the second you wrapped your legs around my back and begged for my cock Saturday night."

Dana's breath wheezed out as the vibrator drove deep, though she wasn't sure if it was because of his admission or finally having her throbbing pussy filled. Odds were good it was because of his admission, because she came with that first thrust.

Came with his name on her lips and a near certainty that she'd never stopped loving him, either, somersaulting through her mind.

Considering how badly she'd wanted to hear them, it was amazing how easy it was to ignore Treah's words of love, Dana mused as she packed a borrowed overnight bag for this morning's trip to Ecstasy's Pacific branch. Almost as easy as it was to ignore the fact that she'd yet to call Claude.

"Liar."

All right, so it wasn't that easy disregarding either of those things. At least, she was also no longer able to ignore the voice in her head.

That voice had been spot on with its observations from the start. It had been right in labeling her afraid to blurt her feelings for Treah yesterday, as well. He'd mercifully let her play the ignorant game. Even let her go off to her own bed last night. Where she'd proceeded to toss and turn and wish she was back in his bed, snuggled up against his warmth and the soothing comfort of his strong arms.

Tonight, she would share his bed. Tonight, she would own up to how she was feeling, even if it was only to admit that she wasn't 100 percent sure about anything yet. Right now, she would take advantage of Treah finishing up a few things down in his office before they left for the airport, and call Claude.

Dana was walking into the kitchen when someone knocked on the front door. She glanced at the door twenty feet away and then at the cordless phone resting on its wall mount within reaching distance. If she didn't call Claude now, she might not have another chance until the middle of the week. Of course, at this point, what were two more days?

The knocking came again, harder. Whoever was out there obviously wanted in. Who was she not to let that person enter?

Accepting the move as the poor excuse it was, she went to the door and pulled it open. She expected to find Claire or Chris. Or maybe Sonya, though Treah's assistant seemed too introverted to come up to his house. The woman who stood at the top of the stairs on the other side of the door wasn't Claire or Sonya. She wasn't a carbon copy of Dana, either, but she was close enough to one for Dana's pulse to race and her mouth to fall open.

Deanne gave a small smile and a little wave. "Good morning."

No, it was *not* a good morning. Not any longer. "What are you doing here?"

Deanne's smile vanished. "Claude called me. He couldn't reach you, and figured I knew where you were since I was apparently supposed to pick you up on Saturday."

Hell. But what did Dana expect when she hadn't called him for nearly a week? "I'm not ready to go home."

"I know, and I hated to bother you, but something's going on at the Galleria and he said it's too important for you to miss."

Dana frowned. "What do you mean, you know?"

Guilt came into Deanne's eyes. She hesitated a few seconds, looking down at the beach and then back at Dana, before admitting, "I've sort of been keeping tabs on you."

"You've been checking in with Treah?"

"No." Deanne looked away again and then nodded into the house. "Can I come in?"

Dana stepped back and let her enter the foyer. Crossing her arms, she eyed Deanne expectantly. Then she eyed her even harder as the color of her sister's skin and clothing registered. She was golden tan and dressed to attract. Deanne generally only spent enough time in the sun to get from place to place. She didn't wear clothes to downplay her figure, but she also didn't wear little black shorts, strappy black sandals, and a white sarong-style top that exposed the rise of her cleavage.

The change was for the positive, yet shocking all the same. "What happened to you?"

Deanne glanced down at her body. Pride entered her brown eyes and her smile returned. "Sexual healing. Or I guess it's supposed to be sensual, but the sexual part's been pretty incredible, too."

Sexual healing? Did she mean like the kind offered at this resort? "I don't understand."

"You were supposed to be swapped out for me. But you weren't. We were both brought here."

"You've been here the whole time? Where?" And how could Dana not have known? They usually did the twin vibe thing quite well, enough that she should have detected Deanne's presence.

"In a cabin on the other side of the island. I told my healer I was a semi-recluse. Actually, that was Claire's idea." She looked down at her body again. "She was also responsible for packing my suitcase. I have to admit at first I was a little upset—I don't think these clothes even came from my closet—but now I like the look. I love the person I've become."

Dana was thrilled to see the good that time at this resort had done for Deanne. Right now, though, she couldn't voice that happiness for the way her mind was spinning with the idea Claire had known about her sister's presence on the island all along. What about Chris? And Treah? And what exactly was the point of keeping Dana in the dark? "Why lie?"

Deanne's smile disappeared. She did another of those pause and look away things before confessing, "Because if either you or Treah knew I was here, you would have believed me the one responsible for forcing you guys together."

Treah didn't know. Dana felt a small measure of comfort in that. Then the meaning behind her sister's words sank in. "You're the one who vandalized the boats? The one who siphoned out the gas? Cut the radio wires?"

"Um, yeah, that would be me," she divulged sheepishly. "I just wanted to see you happy, Dana. Marrying Claude will never accomplish that."

Maybe not, but to push her at Treah? That had been a huge gamble. True, it had sort of paid off. She had been happy the last few days. Really and truly happy. And alive. She'd felt more alive with Treah this week than she had even once in the years they'd been apart.

And now Claude had to ruin it all. "What's going on at the Galleria?"

"I don't know. But he said it would affect your employment status."

Oh, God, her job was at risk? There was the reality that if she didn't have one, it wouldn't be able to come between her and Treah. But she loved her job, had spent the whole of her adult life working to obtain her assistant curator position. She was neither losing it nor giving it up. Not even for him.

"What are you doing here, Deanne?" Treah's question came from behind Dana.

Dana turned to find him standing in front of the open door that led to the first floor. He'd been smiling when he'd gone downstairs after making her breakfast, teasing and flirting with her in true Treah fashion. Now, he looked concerned.

"Sabotaging your boats," Dana offered. Deanne's narrowed eyes called her a traitor, and Dana sent her a wry smile. "Not very nice being sold out by your own twin, is it?"

"You did—" Treah started.

"She did," Dana cut him off. "But right now I have more to worry about." Tension coiled in her belly with the knowledge that he wasn't going to take her choosing her career over him in a good way. Or maybe this time he would understand.

Yeah, right. "I have to leave, Treah."

"We are leaving," he said succinctly. "For the airport in ten minutes."

"I can't go with you. Claude called—"

"I see." Disappointment weighed down his words.

"No, you don't. Something's happening at the Galleria. If I don't get home, I may not have a job to go back to."

"You really think they'd fire you when you were on vacation?"

"I'm sure it happens."

He smirked. "I'm sure fiancés get nervous when their better halves go missing for a week and would do or say anything to get their women home, too."

Dana had known he was going to take this badly, and still irritation funneled through her. "That has nothing to do with this."

"He probably doesn't even know that she's with you," Deanne offered.

Dana scowled at her sister. "*Probably?*"

"I might have kinda, sorta let his name slip out."

There was no "kinda, sorta" about it. Going by Deanne's anxious look, it was a big fat absolutely. "Jesus, Deanne! How could you?"

"Don't go, Dana," Treah pleaded, the disdain gone from his voice.

Her heart squeezed as she turned back to him, already knowing how he would look. Despairing, exactly the same as he had the first time she'd walked away. He'd spoken the same words and broken out rare pleading then, too. And he'd loved her then, too, enough for his feelings to last almost an entire decade.

She'd considered that their relationship had come full circle the other night. But did it really have to come so damned completely full circle? "I have to go, Treah."

"You don't. Not if you love me."

"I . . ." Damnit, she couldn't speak the words if there was even a chance this was truly good-bye. Not for her sake. And not for his, when she knew he'd already lost, either to death or futility, far too many people he loved. "I don't have a choice."

Treah's smirk returned, along with a cool glare. "Because he expects you to run to him the second he calls and knows you'll do precisely that."

No. But maybe. Or yes.

If it was yes, then it was only because Claude was more than the man she'd agreed to marry. "He's not just my fiancé. He's my boss."

"What am I?"

Something else. Something better. Something she was probably going to have to face the rest of her life without, even if the idea of doing so had her belly roiling. "I don't know."

He shook his head as sorrow moved into his eyes. "I was wrong. You aren't a snob and you also aren't afraid of happi-

ness. You're afraid of not living up to everyone else's expectations. Everyone's but mine." Stepping back toward the stairwell,
he grabbed the door handle. "I'll have the boat ready to take
you to the mainland in ten minutes. Don't expect to run out of
gas this time."

11

Past the rental coupe's windshield, Dana eyed the three-story glass and steel building that she'd loved from first sighting. Inside the museum was a man she'd also loved nearly from first sighting. At least, she'd thought she loved Claude. The last days with Treah and, more, his final words about her living up to everyone else's expectations had her reassessing her feelings for Claude yet again.

The tense-as-hell boat ride to the mainland and an equally edgy fifteen-minute trip in one of Ecstasy's onshore trucks followed by a brusque departure at the rental depot across from the airport's terminal had given her plenty of time to think. By the time she'd pulled into the museum's employee lot ten minutes ago, she'd accepted the truth.

She'd never loved Claude. Instead, she respected him. Loved his accomplishments in the art world and contributions to the Galleria. He'd been her idol for years. As such, she probably had tried to live up to the example he set for their colleagues.

And maybe she'd even tried to live up to the examples others had set. After all, she'd never liked feeling an outcast. With Treah she wouldn't have had to live up to expectations, because he'd always loved her as is. Even when it came to her career, he might never have understood it but he'd never shunned the work that she personally did.

He'd also never made her feel undesired or uncherished, the way she could admit now she'd often felt with Claude.

At least, Treah hadn't made her feel that way until this morning. Even then, she knew that he hadn't meant to. He'd been hurting and acting out on it.

Now, it was time to go hurt another man, by breaking their engagement.

"Right. As if he'll shed so much as a tear," Dana acknowledged dryly as she stepped from the coupe.

Of course, while Claude might not act all that upset over the end of their relationship, he also wouldn't be happy about it. Which was why she'd sat in the car so long, working up the courage to head inside the Galleria.

Nerves warred in her stomach as she pushed in the unadorned staff door, which opened into a hallway decked with paintings from all eras and styles. The managerial offices and break room were to the right. The main museum entrance to the left. Thankful no colleagues were around, she hurried down the corridor to Claude's closed door.

Through a narrow horizontal window, she peered inside. He sat at his desk, gaze fastened on a flat-screen computer monitor. He was attractive, with dark blond hair and a tall, lean body. His eyes an appealing shade of green. His bank account well fed. For some woman, he would make the perfect match.

The sooner she got out that she wasn't that woman, the better.

After taking a deep breath, Dana opened the door and stepped inside. "Hi, Claude."

He looked up as she closed the door, and a glowing smile formed on his mouth. "Dana, darling, it's so good to see you. Wait until you hear the news."

Really, this would have been much easier without his smile. He actually looked eager to see her. Like he'd truly missed her.

Focusing on the "news" that brought an early end to her time with Treah, she moved up to his desk and pulled up a chair from its position against the wall to sit down. "You're smiling. Whatever the news is it can't be bad."

"Bad?" He chuckled. "This is outstanding!"

Wow. Coming from Claude, that was really saying something. It also made it sound like her job had never been in jeopardy. "How does it involve my employment status?"

Beaming, he pushed back his chair and rounded the desk. She thought he was going to pull her into his arms—or, God forbid, kiss her like a man who'd gone a week with no contact from his soon-to-be bride—but he bypassed her to grab a brochure off a shelf behind her.

Returning to his seat, he handed the brochure across the desk. Dana took it and frowned. It was for the headquarters museum in Pennsylvania. "Why is this significant?"

"Because I've been asked to step up as director of the Philadelphia location."

"But how will that work, with me living here and you there?" And, more importantly, how did it involve her job?

"You'll move with me, of course." Excitement sounded in his voice as he added, "As my assistant."

Obviously, he thought she was going to be ecstatic at the opportunity for advancement. Even if she hadn't spent the last nine days with Treah, she wouldn't have liked the idea of taking the position. Not in Philadelphia. "You expect me to move hundreds of miles away from Deanne?"

Claude's smile lessened a fraction. "She's a full-grown woman, Dana. She'll be fine."

The Deanne who appeared on Treah's doorstep this morning probably would be fine without her. But Dana might not be so fine. They had never lived more than fifteen minutes apart and she wasn't about to see that happen today. "I won't leave her. Not when I haven't even been given a choice in the matter."

His smile disappeared completely. "I can't turn down this position. It's a once-in-a-lifetime deal."

Actually, it wasn't. He would be up for the director's position right here in New Hampshire when Jane retired in a couple years. Clearly, he didn't want to wait. And, clearly, he had no reason to do so. "You should take the job. But I won't be going with you. I also won't be marrying you."

Outrage flared on his face for a heartbeat. Then it tapered off to shock. "You're breaking our engagement because of this?"

"Yes. Or no." She was ending their relationship because between his anger and surprise there had been no sorrow.

"Which is it?"

"I'm breaking our engagement but not because of this." Feeling amazingly better for finally getting the words out, Dana stood. She reached across the desk to take his hand and give it a squeeze. No little jolts of awareness shot up her arm, which just made for another reason she had to end things. "I'm sorry. I truly am, but I don't love you enough to be happy together forever. I think in time you'll see that you feel the same way about me."

Releasing Claude's hand, she stepped back. It felt like there was more left to say, some assurance that they could still work well as colleagues. But since he wouldn't be around much longer, more words would probably be wasted breath.

With a warm parting smile, she went to the door. She turned back when she reached it. "I hope they realize what a genius they're getting in Philly."

"I hope this ex of yours realizes what an amazing woman he's getting."

Dana's smile froze on her lips. She'd forgotten Deanne had let slip about Treah. Or maybe she'd buried the knowledge in the hopes it would never become an issue. "I didn't call off our engagement because of him. I don't even know if I'll ever see him again. Frankly, I don't know if I'm meant to be with any man in the long run."

Dana felt a sense of déjà vu with the knock on her front door. It had been this same time of morning three days ago when Deanne had appeared on Treah's doorstep and started a chain reaction of devastating proportions. Or maybe not so devastating. Maybe just life in motion.

Setting the towel she'd been using to dry her breakfast dishes on the counter, she moved through the open kitchen and into the small living room that doubled as a receiving area. Then, like three days ago, she opened the door and felt her mouth fall open with the surprise of finding Deanne on the other side.

Her sister should still be on Ecstasy Island, enjoying some first-rate sensual healing for another week. Had Treah sent her home early to make sure Dana was okay? "You're home early."

"It's only a temporary leave. I had to know that you were all right."

Not here on Treah's bidding, but her sister's worry still felt incredibly good. "I'm . . . not all right," Dana admitted, moving inside the house and sitting down on one of two chairs in the small living room. "But I'll survive."

With unguarded concern in her eyes, Deanne sat in the other chair. "What happened with Claude?"

"He's moving to Philadelphia."

"That's unexpected. What about you?"

"I'm not."

Relief slid into Deanne's eyes and then quickly slid back out again. "Please don't tell me that you stayed because of me."

"That was part of it, but not the biggest part."

"Good. Because I'm moving, too."

Dana jerked to the edge of her seat. "*What?* Where?"

Deanne gave a soft smile that immediately became a huge, pleased one. "To Ecstasy Island."

With Treah?

How would she ever be able to handle visiting her sister, knowing he was so nearby? Dana wanted to believe they could still have a chance at a relationship, but even if they could get over the whole work thing, they lived hours apart. She hadn't been able to handle the thought of a long-distance arrangement with Claude, and she hadn't even loved him. Treah . . . Treah she couldn't be involved with only when it suited both of their schedules.

"It's a resort. Real people don't live there," Dana rationalized. "I mean some do, but only employees."

"I'm an employee now."

"Doing what?"

"Being a healing coach. When Treah got home last night, I mentioned to him what a great thing he had going on, but that the male half of the population was missing out. He agreed and hired me to be his first female healer. I still have to do the training and stuff, but I'm really excited about it."

Dana smiled while her belly roiled. "I'm happy for you," she said honestly. "You look happy. Confident." She nodded at the golden highlights mixed with Deanne's dark brown hair. They hadn't been there earlier in the week. "Love the hair."

Deanne ran a hand over her mid-back-length locks, which now looked identical to Dana's. "Thanks. Claire did it. Hey, did you know she's the one who wrote that article in the *Herald*?"

"She seems great. Really nice. Just watch out for her pink drinks." They were known to make a woman do unforgettable things, like grinding her overheated body against her ex-lover and asking him to take her upstairs for so much more.

* * *

Treah had acted an ass, just as he'd known he would after making love with Dana again. It was just too bad he'd acted like the wrong kind of ass.

Last time, it had taken him eight years to get her back in his life. This time, he wasn't going more than three days. Deanne's request to be taken to the mainland so she could check on her sister worked well in his favor. Going by Deanne's smile as she exited Dana's house now and started for his truck parked alongside the curb across the street, Dana was ready for him.

Deanne opened the passenger's side door and slid onto the bench seat. "She's all yours." She laughed softly. "I mean that both as in her time now and the rest of her forever."

"Hell, I hope so." He pushed open the driver's-side door. Dropping down onto the sidewalk, he tossed the keys onto the seat. "Go ahead and take the truck to your place. I know you're eager to get some stuff packed up before we head back."

Her smile waned. "You're sure you want me to take off?"

"I'm not leaving until we work this out."

"Well then, good luck."

His heart pounding with the fear he was going to need all the luck he could get, Treah crossed the road and moved up the short driveway to Dana's front door. The truck fired to life as he stepped onto a small porch with big red pots of yellow and white flowers on either side. He waved as Deanne took off down the road, and then sucked in a breath and knocked on the door.

Dana obviously hadn't gotten too far in the time that Deanne had left the house, as she opened the door after a handful of seconds. "Forget somethi—" Her eyes went wide and she gasped, "Treah? What are you doing here?"

He grabbed hold of her arms, lifted her off the floor a couple inches, and pushed his way inside. In case their conversation escalated into a fight, he didn't want the entire neighborhood overhearing. Better yet, and the only option he was settling for:

When their conversation escalated into mind-blowing makeup sex, he didn't want some elderly neighbor having a heart attack while playing voyeur.

"What are you doing here?" Dana repeated as he set her down.

He turned around to close the door, then turned back and allowed himself ten seconds just to look at her suntanned face with its uppity nose, her hair pulled back in a sexy ponytail, the matching pink short shorts and mini tee covering her dynamite curves. Another ten just to stare into those copper-laced brown eyes and say without words how much he loved her.

Just in case.

And then he stepped off into the deep end. "I'm not losing you for another eight years, Dana. I told myself that night we made love on the patio I was going to be a possessive ass and never let another guy touch you. I *was* an ass. But not in the way I was supposed to be."

Amusement touched in her eyes. "There's two different ways of being an ass?"

Treah offered a light smile. "More like a hundred." Her gaze lost its humor and he lost his smile, as well. "Remember when you asked how I could be so accepting of Blair's death?"

"Yes."

"It's because of you. Because less than a year before he died, I had to deal with losing you. You didn't die, but that didn't make it any less damned painful. Your leaving this time was painful, too. Too painful to accept it. I'm not letting you go. I love you. I've never quit loving you, and we *are* going to make this work." He was throwing out orders not options, asking her to rise to his expectations after he'd accused her of doing that same thing with everyone else but herself. This time, though, it seemed the only way.

Dana didn't get annoyed as he thought she might. Instead, the want to be with him shimmered in her eyes. "How can we?"

Treah took her reaction as the good sign he needed. Moving so close their bodies nearly touched, he reached for her hands and threaded his fingers through hers. That old familiar heat of intimacy coursed up his arms. He'd needed that, too. Needed it so much, his voice shook with his next words. "Compromise. The same way we should have done the first time, but obviously were too young and blind to know."

His fingertips rubbed against her bare ring finger. She hadn't worn an engagement ring while on the island, but then she'd always taken off her jewelry to sleep so she wouldn't have been wearing one when Ecstasy's pick-up guys had taken her from her house. Now, she should have been . . . if she had a ring to wear.

Feeling like his pounding heart would race into his throat, he asked, "Are you still engaged?"

"Why wouldn't I be?"

Ah, fuck. The schmuck was still in the picture. "You aren't wearing a ring. And I thought after—"

"I never had a ring. But no, I'm not. You were right. He didn't make me happy. And maybe you were right about my doing what's expected of me, too. That doesn't change that we have a serious issue between us." She tried to shake her hands from his, but he held firm. Seeming to accept she wasn't going anywhere, Dana continued, "I love my job, Treah. I won't leave it. I can't do that even for you."

"I know. I reacted badly the other day, but I do know what it means to you. I could never let you give it up and still believe you were completely happy."

"Then how could we ever work out? We live hours apart. Sometimes I have no choice but to work twelve-hour days, seven days a week. I can guess your job is the same way. I do love you, but I can't handle the thought of a relationship with a man I only get to see when it works with both of our schedules. Not when you're that man."

She loved him. Treah had believed as much, but like the

sound of her voice, knowing the effect it had over him and actually hearing it were two vastly different things.

He bent his head and slanted his mouth over hers, tasted her sweet flavor sugarcoated with a healthy dose of brazen. She kissed him back without reservation. Slipped her tongue into his mouth and rocked his world while hardening his cock by rubbing her pelvis needfully against his.

Dana pulled her mouth away breathing hard and smiling like a minx. "You've got the yummy part down," she said in that low, smoky tone he could never forget. "Now tell me how the rest of this is going to work and make it too good to refuse."

"It works because of the compromise. I don't have to live on Ecstasy Island. Chris knows the ropes there as well as I do. The Pacific location is set up so that the manager runs it and I drop in every other month or so, like I did this week. I can do 90 percent of the ownership work from wherever you are."

"You would leave your island paradise for me?"

"In a heartbeat." The island didn't have anything on Dana. Her presence alone soothed him as well as, if not better than, the most spectacular view of the ocean ever could.

"You'd still have your home on the island, too, right?"

"Of course, and Deanne's going to be living there, so we'll plan to visit whenever your schedule allows. I might have to do a solo trip for business now and again, as well, but after eight years apart something tells me we can last a few days without each other. We're going to accept our differences as the challenge for us both to grow and make this work."

"Yes." Happiness sparkled in her eyes. "I want to do that."

"Then do it."

The happiness in her eyes turned to another kind of pleasure, and she shook his fingers free to push her hand down the front of his shorts and beneath his briefs. "Will you do it, too?"

Treah laughed as his cock pulsed beneath the heat of her touch. "Something tells me the 'it' in question has changed."

"This 'it' is about the fact I still owe you for tying me to your bed and trying to kill me with ecstasy Sunday night." Dana eyed his groin as her hand pulled back out to jerk his short's zipper down. She shoved the shorts and his briefs down a couple inches, just far enough to have the head of his cock peeking out and her slipping her tongue out to dab anxiously at her lips. "This 'it' is about me and you and a long, wet night ahead."

A night they would be spending on Ecstasy, since she still had another week of vacation scheduled and Deanne had called the museum to make sure they knew Dana wouldn't be returning early. But Treah would fill her in on that detail later. Right now, he had much better things to do with both his mouth and his time.

Turn the page
for a tantalizing preview of
NIGHT OF THE HAWK,
by Vonna Harper!

On sale now!

1

Captured in flight, the hawk commanded most of the photograph. Its wings were spread as if it were embracing its world, talons stretched, haunting yellow eyes seemingly trained not on the world below but on whoever had taken the picture. The rest of the picture was a blur of greens and browns, undoubtedly an image of the forest it lived in, but the hawk's image was so sharply defined Smokey could make out the individual tailfeathers.

Stepping closer, Smokey continued her study of the 11-by-14-inch picture that had been placed at eye level on the wall of the art gallery. Except for the faint drum and flute notes from the Native American instrumental playing in the background, the gallery was silent. She could hear her heart beating, feel the pull and release in her lungs as she breathed.

What could be so incredible, mesmerizing, captivating, eerie? Eerie?

Yes, she acknowledged, there was something otherworldly about both the hawk and the way the photographer had frozen the predator in time and space. It wasn't that large a bird, certainly not as imposing as an eagle or osprey, and yet there was no doubt of its confidence and power. What would it be like to have such faith in one's physical ability, to be utterly at home in the wilderness?

"Pretty amazing, isn't it?"

Startled, Smokey turned around. Behind her stood the young woman who'd greeted her when she'd first come in the door. As they were the only two people in the building, she shouldn't have been surprised that the woman—whose name tag identified her as Halona—had joined her, but the hawk had captured Smokey's attention.

"*Amazing* is the right word, all right," Smokey acknowledged as she returned to her study of the photograph. Her fingers tingled, and she longed to be holding a paintbrush. "I wonder, do you know who took that shot? I'd love to paint the bird."

"That's one of Mato's creations. In fact, he's responsible for every wildlife and wilderness photograph in here."

"Mato?" The name seemed to settle on Smokey's tongue. "He's local?"

"As local as they get. I don't know how many generations his family goes back. Certainly long before white men arrived."

Halona was dark skinned with high cheekbones, most likely Native American herself. "No wonder he knew where to find this magnificent creature." Smokey indicated the hawk, who now seemed to be watching her. "But that doesn't account for the quality. What does he do, work for *National Geographic*?"

"Hardly, although I think he's good enough. He contracts some with BLM—the Bureau of Land Management—in addition to managing his own timber acreage."

Although Smokey wanted to say something, for some reason she couldn't concentrate enough to put the words together. In her mind's eye, she clearly saw Mato slipping silently through the forest, a shadow among shadows, camera at the ready, senses acutely tuned to his surroundings. He saw the forest not as a great unknown but as home, *his*. Maybe the creatures who lived in the forest sensed this about him and shared their wilderness knowledge with him.

A man like that would be physically hard, primal, alive, real. If he saw a woman he desired, there'd be no game playing, no dance of attraction, no slowly getting to know her. Like the animals who shared the forest with him, he'd claim his mate, take her down, and fuck with her.

Struggling to ignore the heat chasing up the sides of her neck at the decidedly uncivilized thought, Smokey concentrated on swallowing. "What do you think?" she tried. "Any chance he'd sell me that picture? I notice it's not for sale."

"None of his work is, because he wants visitors to see and appreciate what exists around here."

Around here meant the Oregon coast, specifically the vast forest that extended to the seashore and that was in danger of swallowing the little town of Storm Bay, where Smokey would be spending the next few days.

"I'll tell you what," Halona continued, "I can give you directions to where he lives. Hopefully your vehicle's made for off-road travel because the road into his place can get pretty hairy, depending on the weather."

"Mine's a four-wheel drive," Smokey supplied. Her gaze strayed to the one window and beyond it, the gray clouds and wind-whipped trees signaling an approaching storm. As though she didn't feel isolated enough. "He wouldn't be there this time of day, would he?"

"I doubt it. I don't know how pressed you are for time, but I'm sure of where he'll be tonight."

A small alarm went off in Smokey's mind, but she kept her expression neutral. "Oh?"

"The meeting." Halona made it sound as if nothing else mattered. "The whole town's going to be there. There're even reporters hanging around, although maybe they're still here because that man's been missing since a week ago."

Not breathing, Smokey waited to see if Halona would ask if she was one of those reporters. Instead, Halona shrugged as though dismissing the whole thing.

Lying could come back to haunt Smokey, and damnit, she wanted to be open and honest with this engaging young woman, but she had a job to do, one that wouldn't be easy and maybe would be impossible if she didn't keep certain things to herself, starting with her full name, Smokey Powers. Reconciling herself to deception—though she already knew the answer—she asked where the meeting was going to be held and when it would start.

"The school auditorium, seven o'clock. The school's the only place large enough to hold everyone."

"It sounds important."

"It is to us. What's at stake is whether the land our people have lived on in harmony for generations will remain unspoiled or if greed . . . I'm sorry, I'm sure you don't care. You're on vacation. You are, aren't you?"

Shrugging, Smokey divided her attention between Halona and the piercing yellow eyes that wouldn't leave her alone and that seemed to have seen beneath her deception and omission. "How will I know who Mato is?"

"He'll be speaking, I'm sure of that. And even if he doesn't—" pressing her hand to her chest, Halona sighed, "—he's the sexiest man alive. Early thirties and in his sexual prime. Unless you're dead from the neck down, you'll know."

"Oh."

"Okay." Halona grinned. "Maybe not the sexiest man alive but definitely the finest representative of his sex I've ever seen, not that I've observed that many in this one-horse town."

Smokey hadn't come here to lust after a man. She'd driven

south and west from Portland because what had happened in Storm Bay—not just recently but over a long period of time—had gotten her reporter's juices flowing—more than just flow: She'd been both fascinated and horrified by what her digging had turned up. When she'd told her editor at *Northwest News* about the story she wanted to do, his reaction had been exactly what she'd wanted.

"Hot damn, that's unbelievable. Fucking unbelievable! Go for it! Your instincts have yet to fail you, which is what makes you so damn good at what you do. Just be careful. There's something seriously weird going on there."

Well, *careful* didn't get the story researched and written. Probing, listening, watching, questioning, and sometimes taking chances did. And because Smokey was who and what she was, she was willing to take those chances.

"I don't know about trying to approach him," Smokey said, pretending a hesitation she didn't feel or at least wasn't willing to admit. "If he's all involved in this meeting, he's not going to want to talk about selling a picture or giving me permission to paint it." Taking a deep breath, she looked at the photograph again. Yes, no denying it, the hawk was staring at her. How could she not paint something that intense? "But if I go, I'll at least get some idea of how my request will be received, don't you think?"

"When it comes to Mato, I don't make predictions. You know that saying about what you see is what you get? Well, there's a lot more to him than what shows on the surface, not that I have any objections to the physical package."

"He sounds interesting."

"Interesting?" Halona winked. "Let's talk after you've laid eyes on him. See if you still say the same thing. If I was ten years older—"

"Is he married?"

"No. Not sure why. Maybe because he's so restless."

Like me. "Mato? Is that his first or last name?"

"First. Full name, Mato Hawk."

Against her better judgment, Smokey again glanced at the photograph. "Same as the bird."

"There's nothing woo-woo about the connection. At least I don't think so. After all, he's taken thousands of wildlife pictures; you just happen to have zeroed in on this one of the red tail."

Halona explained that the rich, russet red coloring of the predator's broad, rounded tail identified it as the largest hawk species, this one weighing close to four pounds. What fascinated Smokey was that the wing span could be as much at fifty-six inches, and its cry resembled a hoarse, rasping scream—two pieces of information Mato had told Halona.

"I'm sure he believes I'm nothing more than a curious kid." Halona sighed. "Little does he know that when I'm asking him about his photographs, it's so I can stand close to him. What is it about some men? They give off this electrical charge, this heat. Shit. Mato's heat is enough to set the woods on fire."

You have to be exaggerating. "Sounds fas—ah, about the meeting. Will there be fireworks? I'm thinking it must be about something important if so many people are going to be there."

The youthful eyes sobered. "Yes," she said slowly. "That's something everyone here feels passionately about. It might not matter to outsiders, but there's no reason for greed and money to jeopardize this precious land, none at all! Whatever it takes to protect it, we will do, and no one is more committed than Mato."

Committed enough to kill?

Before Smokey could come up with something to say, the gallery phone rang. Rolling her eyes, Halona headed toward the front counter. Alone again, Smokey deliberately avoided looking at the endlessly gliding hawk. Though the art gallery was small, the pieces on display were first class. Mato's photography was the star of the show, but among Storm Bay's residents were also a master

wood-carver, an oil painter specializing in ocean scenes, two spectacular free-form metal pieces reflecting the overhead lighting, and
excellent pottery in a subtle rainbow of colors.

This wasn't what Smokey had expected when she'd decided
to come to Storm Bay to dig into a number of mysterious
deaths going back more than a hundred years. Small and isolated, the town had apparently come into existence as a fishing
village, although Indians had lived here since before recorded
history.

She'd learned that with fishing in decline and timber harvest-
ing controlled by complex regulations, the town was losing its
economic base. It had lost some population but not as much as
she'd expected—proof maybe that something beyond econom-
ics kept people here. Whatever that something was, it obviously
fed some residents' creativity.

What fed Mato Hawk's creativity, his photographer's eye,
his patience, his ability to find and capture what lived among
the massive rain-fed trees? One picture was of a great bull elk
nearly hidden among dense ferns, a thin ray of sunlight high-
lighting its antlers. Another, obviously taken with a powerful
zoom lens, showed three young foxes—kits, she thought they
were called—wrestling while their exasperated-looking mother
watched. A third shot zeroed in on a white butterfly about to
land on dead pine needles sprinkled with either rain or dew. A
close look revealed a spider clinging to one of the pine needles.

A man of contrasts? One willing to stand up for what he believed in and speak passionately, one capable of becoming part
of his surroundings so he could identify and share its life force?

A sexy man.

She didn't know about the sexy part. After all, Halona might
not yet be twenty-one and could be filled with the romantic
notions that came with youth and ignorance. Once she'd put a
few more years behind her, Halona would learn there was more
to a man than what lay between his legs. Broad shoulders and

narrow hips might still get Smokey to occasionally, very occasionally, spread her legs, but it would take a hell of a lot more than that before she'd even consider hooking her life with some man.

And until or if she found the man with that nebulous something, she'd concentrate on a career she loved. And do a little painting on the side.

Glad she'd left her cell phone in her car, because she didn't want anyone guessing the real reason for her being here if a work-related call came in, she continued her aimless wandering. She'd come into the art studio because she had time to kill until the meeting started. Oh, she could have stayed in the cabin she'd rented, but doing nothing always made her a little crazy. She didn't want to go into the one bar in town at which she figured the other reporters would be killing time, because she didn't want anything they said to influence her—or for them to know she was here before absolutely necessary. All too soon word would get around that the driving force behind the *Northwest News'* award-winning column "Just the Facts" was hot on a story.

Some fifteen minutes later, Smokey pushed open the gallery door and stepped into a swirling wind. Lowering her head against flying pine needles and other debris, she made her way to her SUV and closed herself in. When she picked up her cell phone, she saw she had two messages, both from her editor. True to his nature, he had kept his messages brief: "Call me."

"You were supposed to check in," he snapped when she got through to him.

"I did. Called this morning to let you know I was almost there, remember?"

"What have you been doing since then? This assignment you gave yourself's making me uneasy. If you're right about a series of deaths passing as accidents when they're really murders, that's serious shit. It's bad enough that no one's seen hide nor hair of what's-his-name in over a week—now you're there alone in enemy territory."

"His name was . . . is Flann Castetter, and so far I don't have proof that this is enemy territory." *Feels a bit like it.*

"The official search for Flann's been called off. Did you know that?"

"Yes," she said without revealing that a state-police source had told her yesterday. "There's no sign of foul play, nothing to justify expending more man hours looking for someone who may have decided he'd taken enough heat for a while and was getting out of Dodge."

"He brought the heat on himself," he pointed out unnecessarily. "Him and the rest of that NewDirections bunch. I can't say I blame the locals for not taking kindly to that resort proposal of theirs."

She muttered something to the effect that she agreed, but she didn't bother adding that Castetter's disappearance might have been the latest in a number of strange things to have happened around Storm Bay. She'd already laid out what she'd uncovered and didn't need him to keep warning her to be careful. Hell, she wouldn't be the successful newshound she was if she'd taken the safe route, if she didn't question and probe. Let other reporters chase after celebrities. She thrived on real stories, gut-churning sagas about real people.

People like Mato Hawk?

Trying not to own up to the shiver down her back and a certain increase of heat on her breasts and in her crotch, she told her editor she'd call him after tonight's public hearing. Then she hung up before he could get another word in. However, instead of starting her vehicle and going to one of the five cabins that passed for a motel in Storm Bay, she stared out at the world around her. The art gallery was set back several hundred feet from coastal Highway 101 at the end of a narrow gravel road that snaked through the dense vegetation. Though there were signs that someone had recently cut growth back from the road, what remained made her think of a living green wall.

Isolation. In a word, isolation.

And that makes you vulnerable; never forget that.

Where had that thought come from, damnit! She thrived on her fast-paced life, the thrill of chasing down rumors and getting to the truth. Pouring the truth out through her fingers and onto the keyboard made her feel strong and in control, not vulnerable.

Mato Hawk.

Startled because she hadn't known the name had been about to burst free from her mind, she leaned forward and brushed condensation off the windshield with her sleeve. As her surroundings cleared, she looked up but could barely make out the clouds for the trees. That's why she was feeling a bit spooked. Who wouldn't when it felt as if everything were closing in on her?

Mato Hawk.

"Knock it off!" she snapped. Just the same, the heat and energy between her legs increased. Damnit, how long had it been since she'd gotten laid? That's all this was, a little pent-up sexual frustration on a miserable day in the middle of nowhere while trying to run down some information about a man who might have met with foul play but more likely was off getting some R & R.

She'd see this Hawk character tonight, put him in his place somewhere far from her mind.

Either that or learn he had something to do with Flann Castetter's disappearance.

A whoosh of movement killed the thought. Gripping the steering wheel, she shivered.

No, she hadn't just seen a hawk!

Or had she?